Peace & War
1999

HELP US
COMBAT
STRESS

The Ex-Services Mental Welfare Society

Published on 11 November 1999
by
Combat Stress (The Ex-Services Mental Welfare Society)
registered charity no. 206002

Editors: Clive Booth & Colin Crawford

ISBN 0953279111

Typeset by Elite Typesetting Techniques, Eastleigh
Printed by Antony Rowe Ltd, Chippenham

CONTENTS
Peace & War 1999

Foreword   7

JOYCE ANDERSON *The Mine Dance*   9
MARY ATKIN *Remembrance*   13
SUE ATKINSON *Tea*   15
STANLEY SIMM BALDWIN *Awkward Squaddy*   18
M J BARON *Shellshock - The Effects Of War*   21
K BLAKELEY *My War*   24
DAVID BLAXILL *Somebody Ought To Remember George*   26
VIVIENNE BOYES *Remembrance*   30
JANE BRACEWELL *Bernadette's Bereavement*   33
JULIA BURROWS *Headmaster*   36
FRANCES CARVILL *Counting Down*   39
GORDON COOPER *Sleep At Last*   42
JULIAN COX *Something Sharp*   44
JOHN CREE *The Effects Of War - On The Children*   47
DIANA DAVIES *The Children Of God*   50
K S DEARSLEY *On A Foreign Field*   53
OWEN DUFFY *Gulf War Memoirs*   56
GUS EGE *The Cycle*   59
JUNE ELFORD *How Love Fled*   62
JOHN ELLIOTT *Bodies In The River*   65
D ENTICOTT *Weep For Reggie*   67
MARY EVANS *The Hidden Cost*   70
SALLY FAWCETT *Walsh's War*   73
NORMAN FORD *Laugh? I nearly Died*   76
PAMELA FRASER *September Saturday*   79
GAZ GALLAGHER *The Queen's Shilling And Beyond*   82
BERNARD GALVIN *My War, 30 March 1943-22 September 1947*   85
MURRAY GARDNER *Birds And Birdmen*   88
KEVIN GAVIN *Why?*   91
PAUL GENNOE *Home Comforts*   94
H S GIBB *A Waste Of Good Life*   97
JAMES GOFF *A Return To Normality*   99
TOM HALLGARTH *Moonlight Sonata*   102

JUDITH HAMILTON *Dada*   105
IAN M HENDERSON *Their Eyes On The North Star*   108
J HINDE *Margin Of Error*   111
ROBERT HOGG *Tobruk Remembered*   114
BARBARA HUMAN *Expecting Me To Answer When
  I'm Dead*   117
EDWARD HUNTER *Yours Sincerely*   120
JOHN HYGATE *Conduct To The Prejudice*   123
D JANSEN *A Soldier's Song*   126
R E JEFFRIES *Not A Grand Finale*   129
JOHN ALAN JONES *The Hunt*   132
RON JONES *Lack Of Moral Fibre*   135
RORY KILALEA *Temba Went Penga*   138
HAROLD HENRY KING *The Time, The Place, The Action*   142
JEAN KING *Plenty Of Apple Pie*   145
B J KINSELLA *War's End*   148
STEVIE KNIGHT *Message Of Love*   150
GEORGE KNOX *The Day The Soldiers Came*   153
CLIFFORD LACKEY
  Blood From A Stone... An Effect Of War   155
WILLIAM LEWIS *The Siege Of Tobruk*   158
JACK LOVELAND *Time Is Not Always A Healer*   159
JOHN LUNN *Autumn In France*   162
LESLIE BRIAN LUX *Sandcastles*   165
T F MARLAND *From Pegasus A Poppy*   168
ELIZABETH McKAY *A Day To Remember*   171
ROSE McNAMARA *The Legend of Angels Of Mons, A
  Ghostly Tale Of World War 1*   174
C MEADE *Shadows Of The Evening*   178
T S MELDRUM *Johnny*   181
ARTHUR MOORE *My War*   183
MIKE MORGAN *Alamein Angel*   186
KEVIN W MUIR *Volunteer For Nothing*   189
WILLIAM R NEWRICK *Symbol Of Unity*   192
GWENDOLINE NYSS-SANFORD *Remembrance*   195
LEONARD GEORGE OLIPHANT
  It Was A Long Time For Some Dates   198
ROGER PAINE *Marks Of Respect*   200
COLIN J PEARCE *One April Day*   203
LES PEATE *Going Home*   206

KAREN PHILLIPS *Jack's War*   209

ANDY PHIPPS *Echoes*   212

JEAN PIMP *Sorrow Upon Sorrow*   215

DAVID PIPER *An Ordinary Gunner Under Combat Stress*   217

JOHN POARCH *Lest We Forget*   220

IVOR PETER POWELL *My War*   223

DAVID PRATT *Christmas 1914*   226

E J RAE *Remembrance*   229

JOHN RAVENSCROFT *A Long Shot*   232

RICHARD REEVE *Dismissed*   235

EDITH A SANDERS *The Time Machine*   238

JACK SHARP *The Effects Of War*   240

LOUISE SHAW *Final Liberation*   243

JOHN SHAWCROSS *Marcel's "Guest"*   246

DOUGLAS SMITHSON *A Flight To Captivity*   249

LES STEPHENSON *Help And Understanding*   252

P W STOCK *Smithy*   255

SAMEER KAK SUKHDEV *The Obsolescence Of War*   258

FREDERICK PHILIP SYLVESTER

 Able Four Has Casualties   261

RICHARD THATCHER *War Correspondents*   265

F THOMPSON *Ollie's Dad*   269

HAYLEY B C THOMPSON *Remembrance*   271

BRIAN C TOTHILL *The Pledge*   274

JOHN TRYTHALL *Not A Soldier*   277

T S TURNBULL *Border Control*   280

NICK WARDLE *Back Home*   283

JANE WENHAM-JONES *Coventry*   285

RICHARD WHITTLE *Tag Lady*   288

JOHN U WILHELMY *Saturday September 2nd. 1939*   291

ENTRY FORM 1999 COMPETITION   294

Complete list of entrants to 1998 Competition   299

FOREWORD
Peace & War 1999

For the second year running, Combat Stress ran its Short Story Competition in 1998 and as before many of the entries were of a very high standard. Once again they were whittled down, this year on a monthly basis, and a monthly prize-winner named. Subsequently all entries were judged for the main prizes.

John Cree won the first monthly prize, with his evocative memories of childhood during the First World War, and the day that his father, wounded at the Somme and subsequently medically discharged, nearly drowned on a day out at the beach. John Trythall, told a moving story about the death of a great school friend, wholly unsuitable for military life, but nevertheless called up with all his friends.

Mike Morgan recounted in sharp detail a well-known legend of the War in North Africa; and Tom Hallgarth again reverted to growing up in war time, on this occasion during the bombing raids in Coventry during 1940/41. Louise Shaw's haunting story of one survivor's memories of a concentration camp, brought the inhumanity of the Second World War to the fore. Finally Mr T S Meldrum, a young serving officer in the Gunners, wrote 'Johnny', a sharply defined story of disillusionment after service in the Northern Ireland Troubles. All these were keen candidates to win the main prizes.

However, the judges eventually chose John Shawcrosse's 'Marcel's "Guest"' a wryly amusing tale of the difficulties encountered by a farmer tilling the soil that had been fought over, back and forth, during the First World War. His uninvited guests, who caused more trouble than unexploded bombs, were quietly returned to the earth whence they came, in pursuance of a peaceful life, and the humorous twist in the tale was much enjoyed. 'Johnny' came second for Mr Meldrum, and third prize was shared between John Trythall, Mike Morgan and Tom Hallgarth.

Combat Stress would like to acknowledge its debt to all who entered, and apologise to those whose stories could not be published in this volume for lack of space.

Thanks are also owed to The Royal Armouries Museum,

Leeds, who have helped so much in publicising the competition.

The list of people involved in helping to produce this anthology and supporting the Competition to ensure its fund-raising success continues to grow. In particular Sylvia Williams, Blair Eames, Gwen Howgate, Lisa Dengate, Norman Hampson, Natasha Ramirez, Matthew Powls, Kieli Smith, Lesley Booth, our multiple entry writers and *everyone* who put pen to paper, deserve many thanks.

The number of prizes available for our 1999 Competition are much increased compared with those on offer in 1997 and 1998. This year poetry will also be considered.

We very much hope that you will continue to try your hand at writing; please urge others to do likewise and encourage a record entry. All the proceeds of each Competition entry fee go to help Combat Stress (The Ex-Services Mental Welfare Society) directly. Details of the work of the charity and the 1999 Short Story & Poetry Competition appear on page 294. Further details are available from the address below. A stamped addressed envelope accompanying all letters requiring a response would be much appreciated.

Thankyou for buying this book, and thankyou for your continued interest and support in the work of Combat Stress (The Ex-Services Mental Welfare Society).

Clive Booth, Colin Crawford, Editors
15 April 1999, London SW19

Please Note

Whilst every effort to avoid mistakes or inaccuracies has been taken by the editors we would be grateful if any errors could be highlighted in writing to the address below:

Combat Stress
(Ex-Services Mental Welfare Society)
Broadway House
The Broadway
Wimbledon SW19 1RL

JOYCE ANDERSON
The Mine Dance

Jacaranda trees had shed their purple leaves all the way down the avenue. They lay in faded rings of lilac, like wreaths around each tree. Gwen Williams turned left at the last one and pulled to a stop in front of the Government Miners' Training School.

The black heels of her court shoes sunk deep into the yellow gravel as she got out. The Library had obliged her with four tickets and she carried the heavy books on 'The Zulu War', 'King Ceteway' and 'The South Wales Borderers' up the path to their quarters.

A condensed book on Charles Dickens fell from her grasp as she reached for her key. Mr De Rouseau, the mine manager, bent down and retrieved it from the rain gutter.

"Ah!" he remarked approvingly. "Martin Chuzzlewit." He beamed, like he'd found an old friend. "You managed to get your reference for the mural then?" he smiled.

Gwen nodded and thanked him for picking it up. "I thought we could do something with page 612," she smiled. De Rouseau's fat fingers turned the pages until they reached an illustration by Fips. It was a beautiful sketch of a stage coach and horses. The carriage was full of Dickens' characters. "Excellent!" he beamed again. "We could use the scene on the far wall in the lounge. Do it in bright colours. You can start it as soon as you finish the drillers in the miners' bar."

He closed the book and placed it back on top of 'The Zulu War' which, fortunately, was obscured by her cardigan. "Remember not to outnumber the whites by blacks Mrs Williams!" She watched him stride off across the lawns in front of the Gold Mining Camp. His broad Afrikaner's figure silhouetted against a backdrop of pure blue sky. He reminded her of an overgrown schoolboy with his sweaty palms and safari shorts. Always the beige sock on the left leg untidily curled around his ankle.

The room smelt musty with the smell of the red wax polish. The cleaners had been and the single beds were pulled apart. The rope that bound them together in the night was rolled up neatly in a ball on the dressing table. Everything felt touched and explored except the books from the library. Dusty and old they gave her a strong feeling of security. A silent privacy of thoughts that were exposed only when someone who revered them opened the pages.

Matthew returned from the mine shaft at 2pm. They shared a late lunch in the canteen. He hardly spoke or ate and when they got back to their room he lay on the bed staring at the ceiling. Suddenly, he cleared his throat and announced. "There was a terrible accident down the mines today. A winch cable broke lose in the elevator cage. Six Zulu miners were killed. They died of appalling injuries. The swinging cable severed their limbs and heads." He sobbed in her arms for ages until he fell asleep.

"Missi!" hissed the Zulu chef the next day from the swing doors of the kitchens. Gwen turned carefully on the top rung of the ladder and eyed him curiously from behind the bar.

"You go to mine dance at Bloomfontein tomorrow?" he asked. "You and Mr Williams? You enjoy lots of colour Missi, noise and drums!"

Gwen smiled. 'Till then she'd only been thinking of going but now, in light of what had happened the day before, she considered it to be an excellent idea.

Carefully she dipped her paint brush in some bright canary yellow to highlight the helmet of a black driller in the stoppes. "I think we all need a mine dance to cheer us all up. After all, the show must go on." Black pupils stared back at her from their pools of white, their light shining merrily out at her. If peace never reigned in Africa then tolerance surely abounded.

Next day she finished the mineshaft mural and took her brushes out on the lawn to clean. A babble of angry voices came from behind the hedge in front of the trainees' quarters. Drying the hog hair bristles quickly with a rag she rounded the corner to see what all the commotion was about.

An armed guard was standing outside their room. A Bantu cleaner was throwing her arms up in the air and screaming. He marched her suddenly out onto the grass square in front of the billets and still holding his rifle in his hand, began to shake Gwen's pillow vigorously.

Clouds of feathers fell from a small hole in one of the corners. They caught the breeze before touching the ground and billowed freely about in the air. The heavier ones cascaded into the rain gutter and sailed along on a river of foam from the cleaner's bucket towards her.

"Your pillow!" roared the guard, spotting her look of horror. He dropped the pillow and beckoned her forward. Reaching for a clipboard, he had perched on their windowsill, he began to write figures on the inventory. Gwen tried feebly to explain the damaged pillow and how it was 100 miles to Johannesburg craft shops. It seemed so innocent at the time to borrow a few feathers to stuff the car cushion she'd so lovingly crocheted out of utter boredom.

Apologies and payment for a replacement pillow helped pacify the situation. Gwen sobbed with guilt and shame alone in the cool dark room and cuddled the library books for comfort. The cover of 'The Zulu War' was rich in colour and she found herself lost in its contents. 130 scarlet uniforms of the South Wales Borderers' Garrison at Rorkes Drift leapt out from the pages. 4,000 Ceteway warriors descended upon them despite the hail of bullets.

Matthew drove her to the mine dance at three o'clock. She took her seat high up on the wooden benches around the stadium. A cloud of dust rose from the centre as 20 Zulus appeared pawing the ground with their boots like animals. Coloured feathers and beads decorated their knees and they each wore a vibrant headband and carried a spear and shield.

In complete formation they jumped high in the air thrusting their shields towards the sky. White teeth flashed as their red tongues flayed their lips in a high pitched warble. Shuffling together in semicircles around the stadium they stomped their boots in the dust to the rhythm of their spears drumming on the ground.

When they finished everyone stood and cheered, Gwen more than most. Zulus were so evocative of Africa. They were all things to all people. They were the fear, the pride, the tall giants of strength and the defiance for freedom, for culture. They were the hunters and the hunted all rolled into one. Their bravery and noble retreat in respect for a garrison of soldiers who had fought on for twelve hours set them apart from many an opponent.

She and Matthew had a drink that night with some friends. He had made the decision to leave the mines. His heart was not in it and he hated apartheid. They raised their glasses to their friends in agreement. "Let's sell everything and go on Safari and see the real Africa! We know it's out there in the veld somewhere."

Gwen felt happier than she'd done in months. On the morning before they left she climbed the stepladder armed with paint.

"Missi! What are you doing?" inquired Johannes, the chef.

"I'm painting another two Zulus in the mineshaft."

"But that will be three drillers and one white man sitting on the floor!"

"I'm telling it like it is, Johannes," she smiled.

MARY ATKIN
Remembrance

I remember that Sunday morning in September 1942 so well. Although I was only seven years old the war had long been long enough for me to be very patriotic – and after all, we were the 'goodies' and in those days, to my innocent mind, the goodies always won – and lived happily ever after! It was a glorious day more in keeping with simple countryside pleasures than the fight to the death pursuits I witnessed. The clear blue sky looked very high and the two planes up there almost like birds.

I watched with my parents and neighbours in our back garden in Redcar. We urged our man on and cheered as he got his first hit and then as he moved in closer and burst again there was another hit. Smoke appeared and down the enemy intruder plummeted, straight at first and then tumbling over and over as it disappeared behind distant roof tops. We danced up and down and cheered and hugged each other. What a great day. Later that week I heard my mother quietly telling her sister, "He was only a young boy".

To the child I was then, that Sunday morning was more or less, luckily for me, the extent of my war, it was certainly the highlight. Then almost fifty years afterwards I was at a meeting and I suddenly realised that the speaker, an eminent local historian, was referring in his talk to my bit of war. Evidently there had been two German planes and they split their directions as the chase started. The unlucky victim who had crashed into that North Yorkshire field under the Cleveland hills was only a young boy.

I now had a name for him, Edward Czerny, and he had died on his 23rd birthday. I thought of my son who was only twenty three. How could we have laughed and cheered when a mother many miles away was soon to be heartbroken? I suddenly felt ashamed and couldn't wait to visit the local Garden of Remembrance to find his grave, pay my respects and ask forgiveness.

The day I visited the skies were overcast, not the beautiful blue I associated with the day of the crash, but strangely the same Cleveland hills in the distance overlooked his final resting place. As I reached the secluded little corner of the cemetery, peaceful and well cared for, it started to rain. It only matched my spirits. It was very moving to recall that wartime morning face to face so to speak. Perhaps to the gardener who politely acknowledged my presence the tears on my face were only raindrops. Sleep well, Edward.

SUE ATKINSON
Tea

The worst thing is the screaming at night. I've tried everything. Mostly I just hold him and whisper it's OK. But he trembles for hours and sweats something terrible. I feel so helpless that sometimes I shake him I get so angry. Not angry at him. Course not. Ain't his fault, is it? But all this rage is inside me and there's no-one there to help me to let it out. So I end up yelling at him.

I don't mean to do that.

They offered me counselling. I went for a bit. Nice chap. Very modern, you know. That's how I found out about the rage. He said it was there so I believed him. Now my mum, she said it was dreadful me talking about it all to some stranger, so in the end I stopped going.

I don't know how to make it any better. On the really bad nights I goes down and makes him a cup of tea. At least I feel I'm doing something for him.

Him. My husband. My gorgeous hunk of a man...that was. Was until the war started. Now it's all nightmares, panic attacks and no job because he can't cope.

I do my best. I got a little job cleaning early mornings, then I gets the bus straight into town. Been at the bank almost ten years. Ain't a great job. I don't get to sit at the counter or anything like that. It's just typing. I make the tea there too. One thing I will say about myself is that I can brew up a pretty good cuppa.

"How's Jeff coming along?" they say.

"Fine," I say. But I can see they think "stupid wimp".

I thought that for a while too. When he first came back the doctors said he'd be fine in a couple of weeks. Couple of centuries more like. But our GP is OK. He's kind every time I lose a baby. But I can still tell that he really thinks that Jeff should get off his backside and get out and do something.

I could tell that at first Jeff believed all them doctors. He'd smile and say "I'll get there my little squirrel, I'll get there" and he'd stroke my head the way he always did and pull me to himself.

Them were the days when we both had hope.

Tried everything we have, and don't get me wrong, up the

hospital they was great. I began to lose count of the different doctors. Anyway, none of it really helped so a few years ago we tried acupuncture. Then hypnosis, then something else with some name I can't remember. Expensive, you know, but we had to try.

One woman lit candles and put bits of rock on Jeff's belly and stroked him and said he'd get better except that I had a negative aura around me and that was pulling him down. Stupid bitch. I thought of all kinds of things I'd liked to have done with her bits of rock.

At least that let Jeff blame me for a bit.

He's not the only one like this of course. Him and his mates gets together. They wears their medals sometimes. You know who your real mates are when this kind of thing happens and people are so kind.

Depression one doctor said. Depression, so take these tablets and it will go away. But Jeff wouldn't take them at first. He reckons it was all them tablets they gave them that caused it all in the first place. Then he tried to top himself. Three times he done that. Weeping for hours he was clinging on to me. Mum said it was just a load of old rubbish and she had far more reason to be depressed that he ever had. He'd look at her. I didn't know what he was thinking.

I wrote to a depression charity. They was ever so kind. Made me cry...you know, just that someone is there listening to us. They said it was best if Jeff did take the tablets. Wrote him letters and all that kind of stuff. But he still says he's a useless, hopeless person so he would be better off if he was dead.

I try to make him promise not to do it. I tell him I need him. I hold him. I tell him our love will bring us through it but that just makes him cry more.

So I make another cup of tea.

His hands shake as he holds it to his lips.

I suppose we won't have any babies now. I know it is all much worse for him. I know that. Not being able to put one foot in front of the other some days and the memories burning through his head.

Thunderstorms freak him out. When I hold him I can feel it trembling inside. His whole body lives in a world of tanks and bombs and gunfire and the threat of slow death by burning. Stupid thing is he says he hardly saw any real action. That don't seem to stop him living in it now though. Some days it's so bad I see why he'd like to be dead.

But it is bad for me too. I feel so lonely. So helpless. I walk home some days through the park just to get a bit of space. I know there is all this rage inside me but it wouldn't do any good, would it, to let it out? That won't get Jeff better. That won't bring us a baby or a job. That won't make the doctors help us. That won't make the next ten years any easier.

I just don't know what I can do to make it any better. So I just go and make another cup of tea.

STANLEY SIMM BALDWIN
Awkward Squaddy

Scruffy Roberts and I shared at least one distinction: we joined up on the same day, almost at the same moment. As a consequence our service numbers were consecutive. The last three digits of his were 987 and I was 988.

When we walked into Brancepeth Castle camp I looked back; he didn't. Perhaps that summed up the difference between us. We reported to the guardroom and as conscripts we were directed to the initial training centre orderly room. I was about to walk into it when I was stopped by a scream. It came from an impossibly smart man who pointed a large cane at Roberts. "Get that cigarette out! Wheredoyouthinkyouare!" (This was not a question. It was a long expletive.)

Roberts was a big lad but the sergeant-major, although smaller, frightened us both. Roberts cupped the cigarette in a huge hand, squashed it and palmed it to the floor in a skilful movement learned by thousands of workmen adept at making a cigarette vanish the moment someone in authority appears. This make the sergeant-major even more angry. Fortunately Roberts was getting all the attention. I was quietly fading into the walls of the castle in case the man redirected his wrath to me. And that's how it came about that Roberts was processed before I was: received his number, yielded details of his next of kin, religion and birthplace.

He was an awkward lad, and later when we had been steered through the wonders of the quartermaster's store and had been issued with our kit, he looked like a huge clothes-horse as we made our way to the hut that would be our home for the next six weeks. The first item with which I had been issued was a pint mug. Roberts managed to drop his mug as we crossed a road.

During that six weeks we had frequent kit inspections and had to hold up articles as they were called out by a plump soldier mysteriously titled colour sergeant. "Drawers cellular, two pairs...drawers long woollen, two pairs...shirts men's khaki, three...plimsolls brown, one pair..." Roberts never acquired the system of presenting these items folded and neat. His drawers, socks, shirts and towels all flopped and dangled. To see him grasping knife and fork as he ate was worthy of a stage act.

He had an enormous appetite: three meals a day in the mess hall then supper in the Naafi was routine.

Our intake passed out of initial training then the 30 of us destined for the infantry were posted to various regiments. Roberts and I went to the same battalion. Somewhere between the three-tonner and two crowded trains he lost his bag containing the unexpired portion of his day's rations. You can imagine his gratitude when I offered to share.

Eventually we went to North Africa, after that we invaded Sicily, the Italian mainland then another beach landing at Anzio. After that we slogged up the mountains. Although a taciturn man, Roberts soon acquired the words for food and its varieties in whatever country we served. His skill at making himself understood wherever grub was concerned placed a lot of us in his debt. He had long since been nicknamed Scruffy and was often in trouble, probably because his height made him stand out in a group of misbehaving soldiery. He showed massive unconcern about military life. He went his way unchanged from the 18-year-old I met at Brancepeth Castle. The rest of us found ways of adapting to the world of numbers, signs, forms and procedures that enabled us to avoid its pitfalls. Out of the front line Roberts somehow forged local contacts who could produce food and wine. In the line his efforts were complemented by George, a rifleman but also an efficient cook who had a special way with hard rations. During one day's fighting we made such good progress that we weren't as careful as we should have been.

There was an explosion and George was sprawled on the snowy ground crying in agony. I could see, even though keeping my head down during bursts of heavy fire, that he had caught his packet from an anti-personnel mine. The correct drill was for one or two of us to crawl to him probing the ground ahead by bayonet to clear a safe path, marking it with tape. Two of us, Arthur and I started the crawl to George. We were slow but speed was vital: I had never seen so much blood as was pouring out of George. Suddenly a voice hissed: "Get back". It was Scruffy.

He started over the sinister ground, broke into a run, got to George and boomed: "Sorry, bonnie lad, it's going to hurt. Bite on this". He pulled from his pocket a bar of hard, dark, bitter, Army issue chocolate. Scruffy scooped George up and staggered to the path that Arthur and I were clearing. We rushed George to the regimental aid post.

A few weeks later battalion Part 2 Orders announced Private Roberts 987 had been awarded the Distinguished Conduct Medal. It was one of the few good announcements ever made about Scruffy.

When the battalion was put in reserve one of those posh BBC correspondents got permission to interview him. Scruffy put his foot in it again. "What thoughts were in your mind as you crossed that terrible minefield?" the reporter asked. Scruffy replied: "George cooks for us. He's a bloody magician with the stuff they give us. I wasn't going to let the platoon lose the best cook it ever had. I'm not stupid".

Next year the war ended. Scruffy Roberts, DCM, was among those listed "missing believed killed". George survived, though the mine cost him a leg and an eye. However, the effect of war for him was good. He set up a low-cost cafe with his gratuity. It prospered and now he owns a chain of restaurants. His most celebrated pudding (you've probably had one yourself) is an outsize, floppy confection of cream with pieces of dark, bitter chocolate set off with an Italian liqueur. George named it a Scruffy Special after the special man who saved his life on a snowy hillside in Italy.

I can't help thinking that Scruffy would be prouder of this than of the silver medal pinned on his chest by the King.

M J BARON
Shellshock – The Effects Of War

The hot morning sun shone brightly through the cabin window, lighting up the whole interior. For a while life seemed better. Gazing out, John Boyd could see the array of beauty in the well kept garden, which was now a mass of colourful bloom. The fresh scent of flowers and blossom was like an aphrodisiac, teasing his sensitive nostrils which had become used to another more acrid and pungent smell. These little moments of beauty and relaxation were few and far between and he would savour them as best he could. This was how life should be. But how long would it last?

John had lived in the cabin for six months following his discharge from the Army on the grounds of ill health. Physically, he was still quite a fit man but mentally he was a shadow of his former self after suffering a complete mental breakdown. When he was released from the Army Rehabilitation Centre he was transferred to the house, which was owned by his aunt and uncle, who were his nearest living relatives, taking on the huge responsibility of being his carers. They were not young themselves but, luckily, active and healthy. Not having any children of their own they treated John like he was their own son.

The cabin had been carefully constructed at the foot of the garden and was specifically designed so that he could have as much independence as possible. It catered for most of his needs and even had a push button bell located by his bed. This was linked to the house in case of emergencies. However, his doting aunt and uncle always seemed to be on hand when he most needed them.

Although John had only just passed his twenty first birthday, he felt he had aged a lifetime after being called up as a young soldier following the outbreak of war.

Lying there in his secure home he recalled those first glamorous days when he and his mates swaggered proudly down to the recruitment office to sign on.

"We'll sort them out," he bragged, "Let's get at 'em."

It was like a big game to all the young men and a chance to show off in their smart uniforms.

"What a way to impress the girls!" They all agreed.

Little did they realise what they were really letting themselves in for. They all regarded the war as a great adventure and egged each other on with their camaraderie.

The crunch came in 1916 with the introduction of conscription. Britain already had thirty-six Divisions on the Western Front. The total strength of the British Army was now five million men. In July that year, the Battle of the Somme began and raged on until November. Never had there been such a long battle, in such a brief time, with the suffering of so many casualties. It was called the "Big Push", but failed to break the German lines. Many regular soldiers and civilian volunteers were killed. The thrill of danger in a foreign land had changed to a feeling of desperation.

Many obstacles stood in the way of the attacking troops as they tried to break through. The rain soaked land became like a muddy swamp and quagmire as the battle raged on. Barbed wire entanglements and minefields were littered everywhere. Things were getting very serious and the effects of war were sinking in. Long marches between water filled shell-holes gave an impression of sodden craters dotted on a muddy moonscape. Trees once green were stripped bare of bark and branches. The dank, grey air, like a thick London smog, was mixture of gas and smoke making it difficult to breath. There was a stench of death all around as numerous young bodies cluttered the trenches. The harrowing screams of the wounded tormented his senses, as large flashes lit the skies when the bombs exploded. Sporadic "Tap Tap" of machine gun fire and that terrible droning sound as the German planes flew over. Fear had crept in, of losing one's life, or seeing friends blown to pieces, or mortally wounded. It all became too much for this once happy-go-lucky individual who, in the pitch of battle, had turned into a hysterical shaking wreck.

John had suffered a total nervous breakdown and was transported by the Red Cross back to England with many of his compatriots. He was to spend several months in one of the Army's nursing homes. During those last exchanges on the battlefield he had become a zombie on the verge of insanity. It was going to be a long haul back to reality.

As his thoughts wandered to those traumatic times, all in the garden was peaceful on this sunny day. All, that is, except for a bee which was busily buzzing around the flowers picking up nectar. It was a familiar sound and seemed to get louder, almost as if a swarm was gathering. Irritatingly it seemed to turn into a droning sound.

"That infernal droning," thought John.

In his mind the German planes were on the way. He clasped his hands over his ears as the sound grew louder.

"Oh no! Not again!" he cursed disparagingly.

The momentum began to build up like a giant humming top rising to an unbearable pitch. He was now in a cold sweat and in sheer panic, trying to hide his head under the pillow on his bed. Loud crashes thundered out and bright flashes filled the room like a mighty firework display. He felt the ceiling was going to cave in and his body shook from head to toe. Nothing was real anymore.

In his mind's eye he was on the battlefield again, crawling through the mud and barbed wire. Haunting cries of lost colleagues echoed in his ears and all he could see was blood. He was back in the trenches with nowhere to go.

K BLAKELEY
My War

It was the fourth year of war. We had become used to sirens and bombs along with separations and loss. We lived in a small village about three miles out of York. The railway sidings ran along the side of the village, it was the direct, main line out of York so we were used to being out of bed most nights as the station and goods wagons were targets for the bombers. We had an underground air raid shelter but I hated the creepy crawlies inside so I used to take my two girls, both aged four, suitably dressed in siren suits and we would sit in the field at the back of the village pub my mother and I ran. My father was a railway signalman working twenty days out of twenty-one. In the war effort husbands and brothers were in the forces abroad so we had to be self-sufficient.

One particular night, which I always remember, was a Thursday and we had had a busy night in the pub; the customers were mostly servicemen and a few pensioners. We cleared up, washed glasses and ashtrays and put the stools and tables up ready for the cleaner next day, then went to bed. My father was on night duty so my mother, sister, my two girls and me were left in the house. After making sure the girls were all right I peeped through the blackout blinds and saw the moon; we used to call it a bomber's moon. It was still like daylight outside. As I climbed into bed I thought to myself "I hope they don't come tonight, I'm tired out". I must have been tired because the next thing I knew my mother was shaking me saying, "Wake up Kathleen, the siren's gone". I quickly found my torch, hustled the girls into their suits and wellies, grabbed my slacks, jumper and coat and we rushed downstairs. We had the usual argument about why I would not use the shelter but as usual I took the girls into the field, put a rug down under a hedge and we sat and watched the sky. The moon was full and we could see the German planes quite clearly, their target was York station and we could see the flashes as the bombs struck and also fires breaking out and getting higher. The bombers then found the goods wagons along the sidings; the searchlights were on and the Ack Ack guns fired full blast, the ground shuddered under us, the noise, the fires, the bombs and guns. With the moon and fires it was light enough to read a book. We knew this night they would not miss. Then the guns fired at a plane and it veered off course trailing smoke behind it, we knew it was doomed.

In the meantime all along the sidings about half a mile from us bombs were exploding and wagons full of war essentials were bursting into flames and shattering into pieces. One of my daughters sat up and screamed "The hedge is on fire", there were flames roaring towards us. I grabbed the girls and we dashed into the middle of the field. I watched in dismay as the flames roared across the hedge, it was in direct line of one of the houses in the village. I knew if this caught fire the pub would be next and then perhaps half of the village. We were covered in smoke and bits of soot but suddenly out of the smoke emerged four figures tottering towards us. They were what we laughingly called "our firefighters" when they were first formed they consisted of about half a dozen pensioners. We used to say they had put paraffin on their first fire to keep it going. They got the hoses on the burning hedge and soon half the village had come out of the shelters, mostly women and children, and were busy giving unwanted advice and uncertain help. In the end our fire brigade put the fire out.

My mother then said "I'll open the bar and get you lads a drink". The lads gladly came in for a drink and so did a few of the women and their children. We made them tea and praised our heroes. I put the girls both with blackened faces and smelling of smoke back to bed. I stood outside looking at the wreckage still smoking and the wagons on the siding and I suddenly felt a rush of joy, I could have screamed with delight. "We are still alive," I shouted at the top of my voice just at that moment about 7am my father turned into the pub yard on his motorbike. As he took his helmet off I could see his tired face after a 12-hour shift. He smiled at me and said "Rough night, eh lass". I said "Come on Pa I'll get you a cuppa" and then the thought came to me "We also serve who stand and wait".

The next day we found out about the damage to the station and that our ancient clock on the church in Coney Street was gone.

DAVID BLAXILL
Somebody Ought To Remember George

"Do you want to talk about it?" enquired Molly Fletcher of her pensive looking daughter that afternoon. "After all, that's what mums are for."

"You wouldn't understand," came the reply. "Oh, I'm so miserable; it's all my fault."

"Look, Hilary, you mustn't go blaming yourself; these things happen. And I do understand, I lost my first love, you know."

Hilary was immediately curious. She had always found it hard to believe that her mother was once young, although she knew it must be true.

"Were you really in love with someone else before you met Dad?"

"Oh yes. Don't ever say anything though; I've never told him. It was during the war; he was the wireless operator on a Lancaster bomber. He was stationed at the same aerodrome as me. Stan Robertson his name was; he was a sergeant – ever so handsome."

A roar came from the front room where Hilary's dad was watching television. "The bloody Germans have equalised," he cried disbelievingly. "Two all! Now it'll go to extra time!"

Hilary ignored the interruption and pressed her mother further about Stan. This was far more interesting than football; she wanted details.

"What happened then? Why did you break up?"

Molly smiled forgivingly at her daughter's naiveté.

"We didn't break up. He was killed, love. His plane didn't return from a bombing mission. It was sad, really. He was only twenty."

"Oh, Mum, that's terrible! I never realised..... I'm sorry, I'm so stupid and insensitive sometimes."

"Oh, you weren't to know. It happened all the time in those dark days. Too many young men lost their lives on the bombers; it was a dangerous job. They all used to joke about "getting the chop" but I never thought it would happen to Stan. Other blokes maybe but not him. But there's no sense getting maudlin, no sense dwelling on the past."

Hilary held her mum's hand and smiled; now it was her turn to comfort.

"Perhaps not," she sympathised. "But there's no harm remembering him sometimes, is there? Somebody ought to. It must be awful, to die so young in a war and nobody remembers you. Did he have any family?"

"I don't rightly know. But he was brought up by his grandmother, I think."

"Then you're possibly the only person alive that knew him. That's spooky. Do you think about him very often?"

"No love, I don't. I suppose I ought to but it wouldn't be terribly loyal to your dad. But we're supposed to be talking about your problems, not something which happened over twenty years ago."

"There's nothing disloyal about remembering someone you loved, Mum. You shouldn't feel guilty. Oh, I wish I knew where I went wrong with Pete!"

"Well, for what it's worth, I think you slept with him too soon. You've got to keep men interested even if that means crossing your legs when Nature tells you to open 'em!"

For the first time in her life Hilary was shocked by her mum; not because of the incorrect assumption, but by her simple, earthy logic.

"But Mum........we didn't! Well, we never went all the way."

"Well you surprise me, Hilary, what with this permissive society you hear about nowadays......I thought everybody under the age of twenty was at it."

Molly went into the kitchen, leaving her open-mouthed daughter in a state of disbelief. The time was getting on and she had to get tea ready.

As she made the sandwiches she couldn't stop her thoughts straying back to 1943 when she received the dreadful news about Stan's plane going down over Berlin. She had shut it out of her mind for so many years but now it all came flooding back. She sighed. Nobody got out, they said. The plane took a direct hit on the bomb run. Stan would probably have been blown to pieces: all of them would. Seven young lives cut off in their prime; snuffed out in an instant. Young men she had laughed and fooled around with, some of them barely old enough to shave.

Even now she could picture them all playing darts in the White Horse. They were a happy crowd, especially the baby faced

Australian; what was he called? George? No; Len. Len Oldfield, that's right – he was the pilot. 'Skipper', they called him even though he looked so young he'd have had difficulty getting served in the pub were it not for the DFC ribbon on his tunic. Twenty years old, like Stan. Didn't even have a driving licence, yet he was in charge of a four engined heavy bomber. It didn't seem possible. There was a New Zealander too – what was his name? Hungerford? Yes, Jack Hungerford. Or was it George? There was a George, she was certain. Stan mentioned him frequently. It was such a long time ago.

With the back of her hand she wiped a tear aside, almost poking herself in the eye with the knife she was holding. In vain she attempted to blank out the thought of the exploding Lancaster; it would not go away.

A jubilant "Yes!" from the front room brought her abruptly back to the present. England must have scored another goal.

It was surprising she had never felt remorse. Unwittingly Hilary had shamed her into remembering, and it was right that she should, however painful it was. Then suddenly it struck her. Perhaps she should try to remember the good times, to remember him, not what had happened to him. She did love him, at least, that was how she felt at the time, despite knowing him barely two months. She recalled when the fog was so bad the squadron had been grounded for a week. Stan was upset. His crew had almost finished their tour and he wanted to get it over with. She had let him make love to her in one of the dispersal huts; it was his first time. At least she had given him that. She smiled at her hypocrisy. Who was she to lecture her daughter about sleeping with boyfriends too soon! Mind you, things were different then, there was a war on.

"I wonder if I've still got that photo?" she thought.

Blowing her nose she took out the old shoe box and started to rummage. After several minutes she found the one she wanted. Five of the faces she couldn't put names to any more but there was Stan on the far left, wearing that heavy fleece lined flying jacket he would put round her shoulders sometimes.

A shivering sensation came over her as she studied it. Seven lifetimes condensed into a dog-eared photograph! It was the only material link left. Not even a grave to visit. Oh, if only she could remember all their names! She turned it over and the shiver returned. In Stan's handwriting was scrawled 'Crew of Lancaster G – George. RAF Ashington, October 1943'.

Of course. George was the aircraft. Hungerford G – George was its call sign.

But like thousands of others, George would call no more. Such a terrible waste of life. Such pointless sacrifice. What on earth had it all been for?

Once again her thoughts were disturbed by the rejoicing from the front room. Geoff Hurst had just found the net again she was informed.

"Has he, dear?" she replied. "That's nice for him......" Geoff Hurst? Wasn't he the navigator?

VIVIENNE BOYES
Remembrance

Remembrance Service, they mean 'Forget'. Anyone who lived it and survived has to forget. Forget to survive. Become numb. Remembrance means to remember – to release everything, accept and feel all the pain. There is no release. It's impossible to feel all the pain. So we pretend to remember, just as we pretended to be soldiers, when really deep inside we were just humans in uniform. Forget is better.

I put on the ordinary, grey suit. My wife attaches the red poppy. I remember red, lots of it, I remember a blood-red sea, rivulets of red from the beach draining into the sea, red on the beach, in my friends, on men who were all men – the same as me. "Hurry up dear, it's raining – you'll need your hat," shouts Doris – she is old now but still beautiful to me. "One minute, I'm nearly ready," I reply. "Just need to slick down my hair, where is my hat? It's cold." I remember the cold, the wet, the hunger, the lack of sleep. When I reach for my hat I remember the hats we had in the war and the way the bullets left jagged holes. Like the jagged hole in my life, in my heart. Remember, they call it. What do they remember? Who dares to remember? Go through the motions. I remember that well. The numbness of survival. Simple motions. Fight, shoot, eat, sometimes sleep, urinate, run, walk, get cold, wet, tired and hungry. Forget. Remember home, remember my Doris and little Alice and George.

Tears mingle with the rain and sea- spray. The salt water stings my mouth and lips. "30 seconds." The ramp slowly lowers. In front of me men fall. I run over the top of them into the cold numbing water. All I can hear is men screaming, officers shouting orders, machine-gun fire, the ramps, explosions from grenades and eventually the calm of the lapping red water, nothing else. The noise slows. I slow down. I see coldness and the darkness of the dragons teeth – a temporary refuge, a safe haven, I run towards it. I throw myself down and hide. I want to dig a hole and stay there. Never, ever move again. I want to sleep. But I don't. I look around. My Commanding Officer orders us to advance to the hole before the pill-box. Another hole. He tells us where to run. We run.

The pain in my chest makes me check to see if I'm wounded. I am wounded but amazingly not in my chest and heart. The pain is in my leg – half of it is blown away. Like Doris and little Alice and George. I forget they exist, I'll never get out of this hole. You see. My friends are lying around me, I roll over and nudge them, I speak to them, Gordon, Arthur, Thomas, but they don't reply.

"It's OK," I tell them, "it will be over soon and help is coming I promise you." They get colder. I get colder. I drift – it's safer. But the feelings drift through my head and frighten me. I try to hold on to Doris and Alice and George but they won't stay. I let them go because I know I won't see them again. I'm dying.

Physically I don't die. The medics are busy, busy and shout at me. I look at them from a numb, blank space. My heart hurts. My leg doesn't yet, I can see my leg bandaged at the knee. I put my hand on my leg, I feel it even though it's not there. I don't laugh. I put my hand on my aching heart. I feel it, even though it's not there. I don't laugh. I try and remember something, my name, or Doris, or little Alice and George. I can't see them anymore. I remember their names but not their essence, I can't picture them either.

When I return home I see them again, I even touch them, hold them to me but like my leg they're just not there, so I stop. I prefer to push them away. I look at them with blank eyes. I am afraid for them. I am afraid they will pick up the way I can't feel anymore, I am afraid I will taint them, harm them in some way and they will grow up feeling as I do. I try and remember what it used to be like. When we were a family. When we knew each other, really knew each other openly and honestly and loved. I can't get it. I can't remember. I know I should be able to get there but my heart deceives me, I never knew a heart could let you down, I thought it helped you. It tells me the pain has gone, I want to believe it, so I do.

Tears mingle with the rain. The pain in my chest makes me check to see if I am wounded, I feel pain in my chest, down my arm, in my heart and mind. I recognise the service, it happens every year. It usually rains.

But I, me, yes me, you remember, I remember, that person I see every day in the mirror, I touch my heart to remember but feel nothing. Remembrance means forget. There can only be forget and the motions. The motions that tell me I'm alive. So that's it, the motions are the remembrance. It's a significant shift, I understand now. I can live with that. The real pain is in forget. I joke to Doris "We should call it the service of forget, not the remembrance service". She smiles back at me with sadness in her soul and says "Yes Harry, we should call it the service of forget, I really like that, it means something to me". As always Doris fully understands. The service of forget – that would be nearer the truth.

JANE BRACEWELL
Bernadette's Bereavement

The large, oak table was the focal point in our little cottage. Tonight the aroma of Mum's famous lamb stew floated through the air. A huge earthenware pot adorned the centre of the table tempting our taste buds but we all sat waiting to eat, listening attentively to Dad. Only six of my brothers and sisters were there tonight, my two eldest brothers were 'out'. But I had pride of place as I sat on Dad's knee peering into his pale blue eyes, playing with his ginger, tousled locks and hanging on to his every word (even though I had heard the story many times before).

A number of our relations lived in our village and our house was the meeting point for unannounced arrivals, usually at mealtimes when the food and beer flowed. Tonight was no exception and Dad once more recounted that night in May 1972 in Kelly's Bar when so many of his friends were injured. He recalled in harrowing detail, and a hint of heroism, his part in that dreadful tragedy. He said "I put my pint to my lips. There was a 'whoosh' sound and the world went up around me. 'Twas the strongest drink of my life.".

Whilst I listened to him I reminisced on that short time in my own life before 'The Troubles' and had a vivid recollection of those subtle but very significant changes. Before 1969 I remembered that all my friends were the same; we all had arms and legs; we all spoke the same language, we seemed all happily mixed up then, even my best friend, Lorraine; I didn't enquire (or was interested) in her religion! I often wondered why however, our parents kept their distance. But now adults' policies seemed to have ruined our childhood world and as I sat on Dad's knee that night I was soon to realise the stark, painful reality of that fact.

The next morning, February 18th 1973, was cold and frosty. As usual I watched my father walk briskly to his car. I waved him goodbye, turned back toward the school bus-stop, when the foundations were rocked with the force of an explosion. I didn't want to (I had lived with 'The Troubles' too long) but instinctively I looked back. I sunk to my knees cowering with fear and trying to 'shut out' the inevitable sight in front of me. But the smell permeated my senses, lingering in the air, not letting me rest: smouldering tar, burning tyres, melting metal. Shaking and rigid with head still bowed there came quite suddenly, for just a few seconds, an eerie silence over the scene. So I lifted my head and opened my eyes hoping that for one moment Dad and I would be sharing just another of his 'stories'. But as the dust and the clouds settled the dreadful carnage started to reveal its ugly head. There sprawled in the middle of the road lay a crumpled mesh of blue-grey metal and pinning it down (almost asking for submission) lay a concrete lamppost. This was Dad's much beloved Rover car... but more importantly below that lay the much beloved Light of my Life. Our brief moment of togetherness was suddenly shattered by pandemonium and the lane became full of people feverishly trying to extract Dad from below the tangled rubble. Eventually the emergency services arrived but they worked with such caution and deliberation. "You're working too slowly!" I heard myself splutter out uncontrollably. One of them turned and explained the importance of proceeding carefully to ensure Dad was extracted from the carnage successfully. Three long hours passed when, with the dust and smoke filling the air, Dad was eventually freed from the wreckage. His body was quickly covered in a red blanket starkly inconsistent against his ashen face. His eyes were open although I felt disconcerted because his gaze remained steadfast and he appeared not to recognise me. He had to live, I willed him to live.

Mum was there at the hospital when we arrived. With relief and amid tears we embraced. I now felt that much needed gush of support. We were led directly into the visitors' room. A young doctor walked in, his head appropriately bowed, and informed us clinically and concisely that had Dad lived they would have amputated his legs. I didn't listen, I just stared blankly at the eye test above his left shoulder.

We returned home empty-handed and in silence. I went to my shared bedroom (suddenly I despised that). I lay on the bed shaken by sobs. At last, however, that deceptive peace of exhaustion drained my tears and I drifted into a mindless state of non-feeling, no thoughts and eventual sleep.

Without Dad, the cornerstone of our family unit, that bomb splintered my family. Mum's health gradually deteriorated. She developed fainting fits when she heard a car back-fire and almost became agoraphobic. So, like many other of our neighbours, my eldest brother, Joseph, decided we should move further away from 'The Troubles'. Now not only were we all struggling (individually interestingly) with our grief and loss but we had to adjust to our new environment. I had a new home, new friends to make, new school, new social life and suddenly we had little money. Two of my brothers were unemployed and lazing around the house all day. In the evenings they would 'go out' and Mum would naturally worry for their safety. My eldest sister had now married and, with a young baby, lived in Belfast, which caused Mum further anxiety.

My Mother continued with bizarre behaviour. She still set Dad's place setting at our now meagre table and we were forbidden to sit in His chair. As a result I felt isolated, adrift and neglected. The organs of our family body now lacked their linchpin, the heart... gone was our routine, warmth, love and support.

JULIA BURROWS
Headmaster

Mentally he rehearsed the phrases. "Come to say goodbye, Strether?" Or Barnes, or Motson, or Liveredge – whoever it might happen to be. "Quite right. As you go forth into the world, I need hardly say..."

The morning's ritual, an annual duty for Dr Broome on the last day of the summer term, was nearly upon him. All the members of the upper sixth, the leavers, would one by one knock upon his study door and present themselves to make their farewells. Adults now. Young men whose gaze would meet the headmaster's at or near his own eye-level. In the case of Bowley, rhubarbing up eight inches in the last two years, well above his own eye-level.

Each time he would rise, pace around the desk and meet the outstretched hand on equal terms, or almost equal, given that they would still defer to his years and status.

"As you go forth into the world, I need hardly say..."

He cleared his throat uneasily. Out beyond the window the creaking old school landau, generally known as The Cart, was transporting younger fry in batches towards Everton Halt. 'Top Schoolers' asserted their independence by arranging to go by cab. And one or two lads would be fetched by their people in that modern phenomenon, the family motor car.

Dr Broome turned to the reassuring order of his study. Walnut bookcases, snug along the walls, supported cups and trophies, some from his own rowing days, the rest marking various school triumphs. Roses in a silver bowl on the side table asserted their fragrance. The housekeeper saw to these and had today chosen 'Peace'. Alongside them lay this morning's 'Times'. Its bad tidings could wait.

As you go forth into the world, I need hardly say...

How could he face it? The manly handclasp, frank and honest gaze, the upright posture. The example. How could he force himself through this hypocrisy again? Must he admit, after all, failure?

And yet, no, surely not. He was still comfortable with the boys up to about the fourth form. And Griffins was a happy school. It was by no means hubris to count himself the equal, at least, of the heads of other such establishments, certainly along the south coast here.

Only now, as the boys passed the age of about sixteen, did this terrible unease set in...

It had been a singularly successful upper sixth this time, in the classroom as on the sportsfield. Medals, scholarships, exhibitions, the inter-school cricket trophy – the games master, Mr Appleby, had been cock-a-hoop.

Fatuous Appelby!

The clock uttered its single half-hour chime and a rap of knuckle on wood announced his first caller.

"Enter!"

They sorted out their own order of precedence. Which one would it be?

Around the door appeared Mainwaring. Ah, what a charming and comical child Mainwaring had been! Tufty hair, cheeky grin, batwing ears – 'Jumbo' Mainwaring before he had hardly set foot in the place. Now, grown to full stature he had acquired dignity.

Dr Broome steeled himself.

"Well, Mainwaring. Come to say goodbye?"

"Yes sir."

"Quite right. As you go forth into the world..."

Exerting maximum control he responded in kind to the quick, firm handshake, sustained the pitch and rhythms of his voice.

And so it went. Strether; the gangling Bowley; Gregg; wicket-keeper Wilson; Robin Sterne, the poet. These ordeals punctuated the morning until he lost count.

Was that everyone? It must be.

No. One more tattoo, surely the last.

"Enter!"

Oh, and the relief, the blessed relief. Hugh Johnson. Dr Broome had quite forgotten him. Pale, sardonic Hugh Johnson, no different today from another day. The slow beat of dread that had throbbed through this room all morning slowed to a halt. The air cleared. Dr Broome made his way slowly round the desk to give crippled Hugh Johnson time to make his way across the carpet.

"Johnson!" he cried, thankfully. "Come to say goodbye?"

"Not goodbye sir," Johnson cut in. "More like au-revoir in my case. I shan't be going where the others are going."

Dr Broome opened his mouth and closed it. The generation we've betrayed, he thought.

"I'm same as you sir; I'll still be about," Johnson was saying lightly. "And I'm the last one in. We thought it would be easier for you this morning."

He was speechless. That they should have understood! That they should have taken time out from their own imminent concerns and done this for him! Just to spare his feelings. The strain of the morning had tried Dr Broome sorely. This was unbearable! Regardless of the lad's presence he pressed a hand to his eyes to still the hot, shameful tears.

God forgive us, thought Dr Broome, whose only comfort now was that his universal disaster must be the final lesson; that it must never, never happen again.

When he came to himself Johnson had gone.

He turned to the window and cast his gaze beyond the school gates and up to the downs. Up there, walking with Appelby one morning – some time ago. Three years was it? Three? Yes. Three generations of sixth form boys.

That had been his first intimation – the remote boom of the guns.

"Pity we're too old," Appelby had said. "Shouldn't have minded a go myself. We've just missed our chance, I'm afraid. Anyhow, it'll all be over by Christmas. Everyone knows that".

FRANCES CARVILL
Counting Down

The two men faced each other across the street. Guns at their sides and berets pulled down tight.

"Looks quiet this morning, Ash."

"Yep, only two weeks to go and we're home."

A door slammed behind them. A woman was taking her children to school early on the other side of the city. The ground was glassy as the girls slid to the car, their shiny shoes bright against the dull ice. They clambered inside and the soldiers split up covering opposite sides of the street. Two soldiers had been killed by a car bomb the week before. Ash had known them and their wives from mess dinners. The feeling in the barracks now was low, claustrophobic.

The sky above them was grey and cold. They patrolled a length of waste ground, their breath racing ahead of them in big white clouds. Winter had stripped the trees of their warm, green camouflage. The men stood like insects, vulnerable below skeletal giants.

They moved back to the rows of red brick houses which ran like a warren connecting every part of the city and broken only by barricades. Around them people were leaving for work. The pavements were filled with chatter as neighbours walked each other to work. Some called abuse at the two men from a distance. Others averted their gaze.

Sam and Ash turned off the main road. Up ahead they could hear kids shouting. As they got closer they could see two boys dragging each other around sumo-style, flailing punches at any soft spot. Their audience screamed support, punching the air around them.

Doors began to open as the noise filtered down. Ash and Sam saw a woman appear on the edge of the battle. She screamed instructions at one of the boys, spitting at the other. Just as the soldiers reached the fight she began delivering kicks to the boy who lay curled up and crying in the road. She yelled abuse at Ash as he grabbed and restrained her. Those who had been watching from their doors cheered the woman who raised her fist in a jubilant salute as she was taken away. The boy was hoisted into an ambulance as his friends ran all the way back to their side of the barricades.

"Got anything special planned for going back home?"

"It's my little one's birthday the day we get back."

"Yeh? Can't wait to see the missus myself."

"You thought about having kids?"

"Give us a chance, it's only been a year since we tied the knot and I've been away for six months of that. Anyway, why d'you think I can't wait to see her?" he said, laughing.

"Tell me about it."

Ash and Sam patrolled the shopping precinct. Grandmothers and fathers sat sharing news and watching grandchildren with one eye. They were silent as Ash and Sam passed, staring proudly, speaking only with the hate in their eyes.

Ash ducked quickly into a baker's buying them both bacon rolls. He bit into the juicy meat, cold, rich ketchup oozing all over the inside of his mouth.

Almost out of the dingy precinct and into the near sunshine they were on the ground before they knew there had been an explosion.

The ground shook as they lay catching their breath. Simultaneously every shop window the length of the precinct shattered, spraying them with glass. Screams filled the air as Ash and Sam ran back to the scene. To his left Ash saw the supermarket manager trying to restore calm. He could see people lying motionless in the aisles, checkout girls cowering in their booths.

To his right he saw Sam carrying one of the toddlers who had been playing minutes before. The child had borne the brunt of the blast. His face was gone, bloody, unrecognisable and he had one leg missing from the knee down.

The glass crunched under his boots as Ash went to help. The sirens were still far away. He broke out in a cold clammy sweat as he knelt down over the pile of bodies. He sifted through the limbs listening for life. As he separated the bodies a woman whimpered grabbing his hand. Behind them ambulances arrived, their blue light bouncing off glass, blood and bodies.

Back at the barracks Ash lay on his bunk the explosion still ringing in his ears. In the bunk below he could hear Sam crying. The child had died in his arms as the ambulance arrived and they had spent their evening drinking in the mess. Ash wanted to say something to comfort his friend but his head was filled with the smell of burning flesh and torn bodies.

They never talked about it the next morning. Counting down the patrols they had to do before they could go home they chatted about Christmas and families instead.

Retracing the steps of the previous day they fell silent as they walked through the precinct. Only blood stains and shattered glass signalled what had gone before. The shops would start trading again in a couple of weeks and life would carry on as before.

The men carried on deeper into the warren. Ash bent to tie his lace at the traffic lights and Sam's body was falling before Ash had heard the shots being fired. He dropped flat to the ground, his knees trapped underneath him as he was smothered by his friend's body. He lay rigid as footsteps circled them. But no more shots were fired.

He searched for a pulse groaning in disbelief. He pinched Sam's cheeks contorting his blank features. He couldn't see the entry wound but as he stroked Sam, whispering comforting words in his ear, his hand slipped into the invisible wound in his chest. Ash gagged, holding down his vomit, gulping the fresh air. He started to shake as a warm trail of urine ran down his thigh. He clutched his friend's body as he waited for help to arrive.

GORDON COOPER
Sleep At Last

Steve was smiling, I wanted to say how overjoyed I was to see him but I couldn't speak. I wanted to shake him by the hand and hug him but my arms and legs wouldn't move. How smart he looked in his uniform, his hair slightly too long. He was always getting into trouble for that from Sarge, but he didn't mind.

His teeth were perfect, with looks a film star would envy. Steve was always popular with the girls but he was also a man's man, would do anything for anybody. I've missed you Steve. We were true friends, we hit it off straight away, remember Steve, when you came to the village school? The terrible twins they called us, always getting up to mischief.

It was a wonderful time, long hot summers, pretty girls and sandy beaches. We would stay up late into the night and you would tell me how you would become rich and buy a yacht to sail the seas. I would tell you how I would lead an army and conquer the enemy and be a hero.

What a fool I was. How I wish I could turn the clock back. I'm so sorry Steve. Wish I could say so but my throat is very sore. We were 17 years old when we put those uniforms on. Did I feel proud! How we managed to get that far without being caught, I'll never know.

You didn't want to join but you were my friend and friends stick together. I'm dreadfully sorry Steve. It was an adventure. Village life was becoming boring. I desperately wanted to be the hero. I begged you to come with me and you did.

Training was a doddle. I got to shoot a real gun. I was a man. Do you remember crossing the Channel? I was sea sick. You looked so calm and confident, you gave me courage. When we landed I had this tightness in my stomach. Must have been the sea sickness. Did you know that was my first time out of England? I wish I could talk to you Steve but my throat is really hurting.

Do you remember that first night abroad sleeping under the stars? It was a magical night. Why did it have to end? I didn't tell you at the time Steve but next day when we were travelling in the truck towards the sound of the battle, I was scared, very, very scared but I didn't say anything to you.

I didn't want to let you down. You were laughing and joking, trying to put everyone at their ease. You were a tower of strength. I wanted to go home. At the beginning I thought it was all a game but not now. This was for real and I was frightened.

Pat was the first to get shot. He was in a lot of pain, I can still hear his screams. Then Len, Harry, Ted and so many others that I cannot remember their names. Why can't I remember Steve? I tried to make myself as small as I could, tried to bury myself in the mud. I didn't want to be a hero anymore.

I couldn't sleep, Steve, the screams kept me awake at night. They never went away. Why did you walk off Steve? The Sergeant told you to stay, you should have stayed Steve. I tried to tell them you were no coward, not you Steve, but they wouldn't listen. Have to make an example, they said.

I was very afraid, sorry Steve, I'm sorry. I should have been there when they brought you out, I should have tried to stop them. The firing squad hesitated, Steve, just a little. I didn't think they would do it. It wasn't a game was it Steve?

The war was over two weeks later but my nightmares have never left. I can't sleep anymore, Steve. It's been really good to see you Steve but I must go now. The rope is cutting into my neck, I can't stop it. I hope someone will find me.

I'm going to sleep at last Steve.

JULIAN COX
Something Sharp

My grandparents' shed was not one of those fragile clinker-built boxes but a solid outhouse complete with concrete floor and tiled roof. However, it was not its architecture that fascinated me but the fact that it housed an extensive collection of items irresistible to an eight year old boy who had an obsession with gadgets. Cupboards, boxes and shelves all held a variety of functional objects whose precise purpose was often a mystery that had to be pondered, guessed at and finally confirmed or revealed by my grandfather. On a top shelf were two small cases and my grandfather would regularly lift down the top one and lay it on the work-bench so that I could pore over its contents in the light of the window. He said that the second case was not suitable as it contained something sharp but he would not elaborate. The sharp something was a splinter in my curiosity.

My grandfather was one of the gentlest men that I have ever met. He spent most of his time tending his garden, about a third of which was put over to growing vegetables and fruit. He always put out food for birds and squirrels and accepted that a proportion of his crops would be eaten by badgers or rabbits that did night time forays from an adjoining wood. He never raised his voice in anger. His peaceful nature must have made it all the more unbearable when, in 1914, his country sent him to witness and presumably carry out acts of brutality, condoned and applauded in the name of war. He had fought at the Somme and Ypres, been buried under mud and shot through the leg.

Like most children I believed war to be a case of the righteous and willing fighting, and naturally defeating, the evil aggressor. My knowledge of war was based largely on the image portrayed by the film industry and my own naive miscomprehension about human nature. My grandfather had been on the side of the 'goodies' so I had invented an appropriate hero who killed easily and with panache.

It was a particularly bright day and I had gulped down my lunch and hurried to the shed. I sat on a stool at the bench and my grandfather reached me down the case and then went to pull some rhubarb. I pressed the two sliding catches outwards and the locks clunked open simultaneously. I lifted the scratched leather lid releasing dust into rays of sunlight. Amongst the string and wire the case was full of the most extraordinary objects such as locks that could be dismantled and understood and brass glass cutters with turned handles as exquisite as chess pieces. Despite the many times that I explored the case I always seemed to find something novel but on this occasion, after rapidly dismantling a brown bakelite plug, my thoughts wandered to the other case. It had become irresistible.

I suppose that I had reached that age when I had discovered that adults too were fallible; an unfortunate, if necessary, step towards independence. I dragged a large wooden chest into position below the shelf and then placed the stool on top. I carefully climbed up and slid the case over the shelf's edge showering myself with dry, dead woodlice. I placed it on the floor, hesitated for a moment and then opened it. Inside there was an old, grey cloth rolled up and a small, plump, red book which had no pictures and appeared to be a dictionary of some sort. I replaced the book and carefully lifted out the cloth which contained a rigid object slightly longer than a twelve inch ruler. I closed the case and slowly unrolled the cloth on the lid breathing deeply with anticipation. Suddenly there it was, the sharpest dagger I'd ever seen. It consisted of the incongruous mixture of a warm soft handle make from the foot of a deer, an oval fingerguard and a long, thin, treacherous, steel blade as pointed as an icicle. Next to the guard was a small piece of red felt which could be slid up and down the blade to clean it.

A shadow fell across the case.

"So, you had to know what was in there, did you?" The disappointment in my grandfather's voice and eyes shamed me more effectively than any anger.

"I'm sorry," I handed him the knife. "Where did you get it?"

"It was during the war." He leant against the door frame. "It's German." My mind raced ahead to a scene of a young soldier killing and claiming spoils.

"I found this young chap about the same age as myself. He was in a pretty bad state and, to be honest, didn't look like he'd last much longer. I helped him back to our medical fellows who managed to patch him up. He was very grateful and gave me the dagger and the little German/English dictionary. He too had a wife and children waiting for him."

My grandfather rolled up the knife, put the case back onto the shelf and the war back into its past.

"How about a cup of tea and a slice of Gran's cake?"

"Yes please." I held his hand.

I had some adjustments to make about my definition of a war hero but it was with respect and happiness that I realised that my softly spoken grandfather had managed to retain his humanity even in a world where all around were losing theirs. This was a real man I could be proud of.

JOHN CREE
The Effects Of War – On The Children

So many children lost their fathers during the turmoil of battle in two World Wars. Others, born in time of peace, learnt to live with the effects of war. I was one of these children.

I was born into a street where every father was disabled during the Great War of 1914-18. These man had lost a leg, an arm, their sight or were otherwise affected by shell blasts and poisonous gas.

As children, we grew up with the limitations war had imposed on our fathers. Their individual problems were part of daily life with our activities revolving round their ability to cope. However, we were a very happy community and our many pleasures stemmed from the manner in which all our parents conducted their own lives.

My own memories will be comparable with so many others in our street. Only my sisters and myself can relate to our own father; the damage inflicted at the Somme on 28th July 1916. A German shell took out one eye, severely damaged the other and embedded many small pieces of shrapnel in his head. Like most casualties of war, those who survived tried to put it behind them and go on with their lives.

Dad was an easy man to live with, although quite strict and no doubt I deserved punishment when it came. There was many an evening when I was put to bed without supper because of some trivial indiscretion. I never recall him lifting a hand to me but there were situations when my mother had said, "This hurts me more than it hurts you".

Without sufficient sight to read newspapers, a magazine or a book, Dad put great store in the wireless. With a tall aerial mast in the garden and the best receiver he could afford to buy, he would get most of the news and topical information through the air waves. However, I do recall many occasions when Mum would spend an hour or so in the evening reading a novel to him. That was long before stories were recorded for the blind.

As a little boy it was marvellous to watch Dad take his glass eye out of its socket. Some evenings I would go up to him and ask if he would show me how to do this. Dad would oblige and I would try to take my own out; but I could never get the hang of it. What a very clever Dad I had!

There were many evenings when Dad would just sit in his armchair in silence, with his eyes closed creating the outward signs of tranquillity. He would be trying to shut out the world around him. Being a typical noisy child Mum would say to me, "Play quietly, your Dad has a headache". These were not ordinary headaches and Mum knew the signs. The little pieces of shrapnel in his head would be on the move again. Dad would just sit and quietly bear it. Whether this brought back memories of an intensive artillery bombardment or the single shell that changed his life completely, I do not know. He did not complain – just suffered in silence.

The day that sticks very much in my mind was the first Sunday in September 1933. I was seven years of age and it was the day I almost lost my father.

We spent much of our lives down at the beach. At the most it was a fifteen minute walk from home. Dad enjoyed a swim and, on many a nice Sunday, I was happy to go with him. It was many years later before I learnt to swim but in those days most of my time was spent playing in and out of the water. Dad normally stayed within his depth and would swim back and forward parallel with the shore. He had sufficient sight to know where he was – or so we all thought.

On this particular Sunday, Dad asked if I was going to the beach with him or with my elder sister to our cousin's new home. This house had a large sloping garden full of trees. It was more like a jungle to us. As it was new and exciting I went with my sister.

Dad went for his swim but did not realise, that with the ebb tide, he was being carried out of his depth and into strong undercurrents. He was being dragged down and shouted for help. Some of his bathing friends thought, "That's Dave Cree playing the fool again". They ignored his cries.

Eventually three others, who were coming in to bathe, took greater notice. They swam out and brought Dad back to dry land.

As he was unconscious somebody applied artificial respiration. They tried and kept on trying to revive him. Dad told me many years later that he heard a distant voice saying, "It's hopeless, we've lost him". He thought, "If only I can move. They will know

I am still alive". A voice said, "Look, his fingers moved". They got back to work and eventually brought him round.

We got home from our cousin's early that evening to find the house in silence. Dad was very ill and we were told, "He almost drowned".

As the years rolled by, I realised if I had gone to the beach that day I could have taken up Dad's cry for help. That thought has now been with me for a great many years. Like the rest of the men in our community he was very special.

DIANA DAVIES
The Children Of God

Deidre had been posted to Cornwall as a Projectionist showing films for the Initial training of Air Crew.

The other W.A.A.F. on the course had not wanted to be far away from London and it seemed to them as if Cornwall was at the end of the world. But Deidre was delighted to be near the sea and the wildness of the Cornish coast. She worked with Education Officers and the R.A.F. Cadets who came and went were a good crowd.

Now Deidre was completely in command of her job. So much so that when the projectionist in the town's local cinema was called up she was asked by the commanding officer if she would like to run the cinema possibly three times a week in her spare time. She would be paid of course and she happily accepted.

She had started working there with the civilian projectionist before he finally left.

Soon after this the C.O. asked to see her. He had rooms in the town with his family and Deidre had often done some baby-sitting for him so she knew him quite well and found him a kind and easy person.

She stood before him in his office while he looked at her thoughtfully. She wondered what on earth she could have done, or why he wanted to see her.

"You are doing very well in the local cinema," he began, "but you will now be on your own there. I think you will need some help."

She stared in surprise. Was he going to suggest one of the Cadets? But they all had so much work to do.

"I am sending an officer – a grounded pilot to assist you. He will do whatever you suggest as regards the cinema." He paused as if he were a little uncertain how to proceed – then he said, looking at her carefully. "You are a sensible young woman and I am sure would not be influenced by looks..."

Looks! What on earth did he mean?

"This pilot has been severely burned," he went on, "and also I have been told has suffered from stress – he was on ops for some considerable time – he may not be easy but I am quite certain you will be able to manage the situation. Your next film is in a couple of days time. He will report to you at the cinema. Do you understand?"

He tried to hide a certain uneasiness that in spite of his faith in her he could not altogether dismiss. Deidre smiled. She was quite sure she could manage even if it was a somewhat unusual situation.

"I shall be happy to have the help sir and I do understand!"

He smiled at her as she saluted and departed.

She stood at the door of the cinema, waiting.

He was walking rapidly. An R.A.F. Officer with pilots' wings. She saluted as he approached.

His face was indeed badly scarred, but his eyes were untouched.

"I believe I am to give you a hand in the cinema," he said. His eyes were bright and unsmiling and his voice was tinged with bitterness. But Deidre found she was quite able to accept the fact of his scarred appearance and was determined to make their odd partnership work.

"I'm not a real projectionist, sir," she began.

"You needn't bother with all that 'sir'," he said abruptly. " Call me Hugh but I was not told your first name?"

"Deidre, sir – I mean Hugh," she replied quietly.

She led him into the Projection Room and showed him the projector, the reels of film and the repairing tapes.

"I've had a bit of experience with projectors," he told her. "We had one at home and I'll soon get the hang of this one."

He avoided looking at her and was so obviously tense and withdrawn that Deidre wondered if she would ever get through to him. She decided the best approach was to ignore his obvious reluctance to be there and treat him as if he were one of the Cadets.

A week went by. The films were shown. They had one or two breakdowns and the audience, mostly Cadets, shouted and whistled and stamped. Hugh was annoyed at first and then when Deidre laughed and told him to ignore it, it was "part of the show", a slight smile lit up his eyes for the first time, and she returned the smile, and they repaired the broken film together – a new feeling of comradeship suddenly shared.

After the second week they were getting along tolerably well and she knew that he was much more relaxed since his first arrival. One evening after they had finished he suddenly turned to her and said slowly, "I had a very strange experience once, walking by the sea....."

She waited, saying nothing. He was aware of her complete attention and he went on quickly

"Some time ago I was wandering along the shore, the waves were rough and very high. I stopped to watch, the sea always has some odd fascination about it, and while I stood there an old fisherman came along and started talking to me about the days when he was young, when there was no war and he took a good catch of fish most days.

"Suddenly this odd moment happened...

"Some children were dancing in long flowing dresses near the sea but they were some way off. It was uncanny, they looked as if they were dancing on the waves and their faces, even at that distance seemed to be shining...

"They will not stay long,' the old man said to me, 'but you have been privileged to see "The Children of God"'. Then they disappeared, melted in a sort of sea mist. 'They will bring peace,' said the fisherman and walked away. Queer wasn't it?" He hesitated "Then not so long after this episode I crashed..." He looked at Deidre unsmiling.

Deidre had listened to his story in wonder and now she said quickly

"Surely this vision, those children, it was a good omen, they must have been sent to help you."

"Help me?" he stared at her.

"It's not the crash," she said almost breathlessly, "it's now."

She took the thin scarred hand and held it. He did not stop her. He was very still.

"You know that. Don't you?"

K S DEARSLEY
On A Foreign Field

Private Leonard Henry Stanton stared across the field trying to blot out the sound of whistling, the rattle of arms and helmets being picked up, the clamour of memories – everything. The ground they were about to walk across was a summer meadow much like the ones he had taken for granted back home. Between the tall bleached grasses waved poppies and buttercups. High overhead he heard the heartachingly joyous song of the lark. All seemed still and at peace. Private Stanton, Lennie, and his comrades did not belong there any more than the soldiers awaiting them behind their dug-outs on the other side of the field, yet some would be staying forever.

The jaunty whistling competing with the birdsong became too much to bear.

"Shut up for a minute, can't you George?" he snapped. His comrade, in his late teens but with old eyes much the same as Lennie's, grinned.

"No one appreciates my musical talent. Ciggie?" He offered Lennie the pack. Lennie took one. Neither needed to say what was really on their minds. Both were so scared it would be a miracle if they could force their legs to move when the signal came. They just had different ways of dealing with it.

George had always been a joker. When they had been schoolboys together it had been George who mimicked the resulting lecture from the headmaster, despite his caned knuckles. That was always his way; clown around and pretend nothing is wrong. He had been the same when they had joined up. There had been no question that they should both go.

"It's our duty to stop these bullies," Lennie had urged. "They've got to learn they can't trample over other people just because they're stronger."

"You can save the world if you want to, Lennie, old dear. Me? I want to find out what the foreign girls are like after dark." George had winked and his mischievous, mocking grin had lit up his face. Over the following months it had come to hold more and more mockery and less pure fun.

How innocent they had been then! It had seemed a simple

thing, no more than justice, to go and kill the enemy. The campaign posters and news report painted them as brutes, barely human, who were capable of virtually anything. They all heard tales of babies snatched from their mothers' arms and dashed against walls; of prisoners of war who had been run through with bayonets despite the fact they had surrendered. Right was on their side.

The opening shots of the bombardment made Lennie flinch and he fought the desire to clamp his hands over his ears. Right now those shells would be tearing into human flesh as well as enemy weaponry. They would be ripping into the body of the earth and laying it bare, a wound that would last for years whatever the outcome of today's action. It was not the noise and smoke that made his bowels cramp these days, nor the thought that with each action he survived unscathed the odds of him being scattered over the field next time shortened – it was the doubt.

The first tendrils of it had gone unrecognised until the day his company had liberated an occupied village. They had rested at a farmhouse afterwards; he, George and a couple of their mates. It belonged to a woman, her baby and an old man – her father. Instead of the rapturous welcome they had expected they had been met with wary hospitality. While the old man had chattered on about the old days and the bestiality of the enemy, the woman had prepared a meal. Lennie had watched her. She stooped, round-shouldered, keeping her eyes averted and her lank hair curtaining her face. If she had stood upright and filled out a bit she would have been a stunner.

As she had brought the plates to the table, Lennie caught her eyes. What he saw in them turned the sweet taste of victory sour in his mouth. Her hatred was only held in check by her fear. It was a look that made Lennie want to cry out in protest. The baby had begun to whimper and her eyes had filled with panic. She had surged over to the cradle, but not before George had reached over and picked the little one up. The woman froze as he rocked it.

"Don't know what you're crying for, Spud. You've got a cushy number here."

"Let his mum have him, George," Lennie had struggled to keep his voice calm. Babykillers! To these people they were all babykillers, whatever the uniform.

George had looked up startled at his tone. "Okay, old son." As

George had passed the baby to its mother she looked about to sink with relief.

George took a place at the table and the soldiers had set about demolishing the food. Lennie's appetite had gone – for food and for fighting. Perhaps they were all the same. Both sides fighting for what they believed was right, both longing to return to the simple pleasures of home and family; both committing unthinkable acts when pushed beyond endurance.

The enemy artillery was returning fire, spraying earth high into the air. Then suddenly, silence. The reverberation of shells pounding was replaced by a stillness so absolute it seemed even time was pausing for breath. Not long now before the signal would send Lennie and his comrades forward. In that bruised hush a bird began to sing – of summers past, of summers yet to come when the grass and poppies would once more bow and curtsy in the breeze and those who died here would be forgotten. And what would they have achieved? Perhaps only the recognition that whatever uniforms they wore, underneath they were all the same.

OWEN DUFFY
Gulf War Memoirs

The Gulf War broke out in the TV lounge of MacDonald Hall while we were drinking Newcastle Brown and watching a dull football match. An announcer said they would get back to the game as soon as possible then they cut to a room of talking heads and The Gulf War rolled onto our screens.

"Jesus," groaned Sean. "You lucky bastard."

I smiled. "Only losers call it luck." I was forty pounds richer having just won our pool on when the war should start.

"Look at the clock, it's twenty to twelve. Twenty bloody minutes, it's not even as if they're going to have time to kill anyone today."

Rhys shrugged. "A bet's a bet. There was never any mention of a body count, just the war's starting is enough. Face it, we lost."

"I know, it just seems so unfair."

That was our first experience of the war. We were drunk and happy and the prospect of a war being fought on live TV still seemed a novel idea. We had the conflict to ourselves for about ten minutes before a young, pretty looking hippy wandered into the room and asked us what was going on.

"The end of the world's just broken out," offered Sean, cheerily.

The girl looked stunned. "They haven't really started it have they?"

"I'm afraid so." I tried to sound concerned, she really was very attractive.

"But this is terrible."

"You're not kidding, we were trying to watch the football." The girl looked at Sean with genuine loathing.

"You heartless bastard." She shook her head and left.

Rhys tutted. "I'm not convinced she appreciates your sense of humour."

"Well she would do if she was as drunk as me."

I shook my head. "Sean, no-one's as drunk as you."

The hippy was soon back but she was no longer alone. The news rippled through the building and the students came in twos and threes with tired, worried-looking faces. Some of them looked so scared it was almost as if they expected the war to stretch out and touch their own lives. They spoke, if at all, in hushed whispers. We didn't. We drank our beer and enjoyed the show. The picture of a reporter on a roof-top describing a scud attack fizzled out and we laughed at his prospects.

"I'm confused," said Sean, pointing at an imaginary horseman. "Is that Pestilence or Famine that just rode past."

People were muttering and staring at us as we cracked drunken joke after joke. Eventually a giant of a man sitting by the hippy girl stood up.

"Can you three shut up, this isn't funny you know?"

Sean blinked. "Why not?"

"People are getting killed and all you can do is laugh."

"And what am I supposed to do? Yes, people are going to die and that's a tragedy but I can't stop it. Once you accept your helplessness you might as well admit it, death and destruction make for great television."

"You're sick."

Sean stood up, a dangerous rage in his eyes. "Well how come I aren't sat here watching this on my own? Look at you all: isn't this dreadful, isn't this terrible, oh don't turn over, they're just getting to an exciting bit. I may be sick but at least I'm honest. You lot, you're just sick."

The giant took two steps towards Sean and the hippy caught his arm. "Leave it, Lionel, don't you know violence is never the answer?"

Rhys rolled his eyes and I got up and put my hand on Sean's shoulder. "Come on, Sean, it's time we were leaving."

For an uncomfortably long moment he didn't move and I thought it was going to happen. It wasn't Lionel I was worried about, he was huge but looked fat and slow, I'd seen Sean fight and even drunk he could take him. It was everyone else that scared me, if trouble started there were three of us and a lot of them.

"Time to go, Sean."

Sean shrugged. "Sure." With my hand still on his shoulder I guided him to the exit. We stepped out into the cold night air and Rhys lit up a cigarette.

"For a moment there I thought it was really going to kick off."

Sean shook his head. "No way."

"There were twenty lads in there all itching to kick the shit out of us."

"Pacifists the lot of them. What were they going to do? Form a committee and pass a resolution that unless we behaved they'd be very, very disappointed? Fuck them."

Rhys sighed.

"I told you he was crazy."

"Anyway," continued Sean, "they never did get back to the football. I think I'll write in and complain."

GUS EGE
The Cycle

Ukata, if left to evolve, would eventually become a township but was currently an expanding refugee camp, a safe haven. Like communities the world over, Ukata had its upmarket area where the dwellings were constructed of corrugated iron, its middle income dwellings made from wood and plastic sheet and finally its slum area where cardboard and sticks were the only protection from the elements. The rainy season had finished and the mushy ground added to the general hardship. The torrential rains had swept through the camp carrying away its waste along with some of the makeshift properties. The inhabitants had a few months before their construction methods would again be tested by Nature with the onset of the windy season. Yet the people never complained for they were the lucky ones. Lucky to have survived a civil war that was now consuming its second generation. A generation that was ignorant of the original cause of the conflict but bore the same depth of hatred and bitterness as the original combatants. Ukata, like many refugee camps, was devoid of young men. Households consisted of grandparents, mothers and young children. The difference between Ukata and the many other settlements was Ukata had for some time been under the watchful gaze of the Movement Against Sectarian Killings, or MASK, as they called themselves.

Nelson had led MASK for almost a year, assuming control when the previous incumbent had stumbled across a landmine. Whilst other members of the group had turned away and some cried Nelson coolly and calmly collected the pieces and prepared them for burial. Leadership of the group naturally fell to Nelson as he was the eldest and with his five younger brothers made up almost a fifth of the troupe.

Meals were sparse in between raids and typically consisted of starch with palm nut soup and wild berries. Afterwards the group would assemble for parade. Their weapons consisted of AK47 assault rifles for the oldest and longest serving members. Machetes or knives for all and sticks for the non-rifle holders. Nelson summoned his eldest brother, Samson, to act as the enemy. Using his rifle he pointed out all the areas where a single bullet would render a body lifeless. Ammunition was even harder to come by than weapons so it had to be used carefully. Picking up a machete Nelson demonstrated the strokes and angles at which it was most effective. After the demonstration the troupe returned to its usual round of afternoon games and singsongs whilst Nelson went to his vantage point. Looking down on Ukata he smiled, for tonight it would belong to him and his boys.

Long after dusk MASK began their march towards Ukata. While Nelson led the main group a number of scouts forged ahead with a dual purpose: to initiate the attack and to act as human mine detectors. Nelson had learnt an important lesson from his predecessor. When the scouts reached the settlement, being illiterate and carrying no time pieces, they sang the MASK anthem four times to give the remainder of the troupe time to take up their positions. Each of the scouts began pouring kerosene onto the makeshift shacks and then setting light to them, after doing this for five MASK anthems they retreated to a safe distance. Smoke began to engulf the properties and the occupants poured out. The blazes soon lit up the night and acted as flares for the MASK bullets that rained down on the elderly men and women, mothers and children. The inhabitants called out for their menfolk long since slain by the civil war and prayed to the ancestors to protect them, but neither answered. Gradually the screams subsided and so did the bullets.

MASK descended upon the camp to claim their spoils; weapons and food were retrieved from the smouldering ruins. Machete-wielding members of MASK dragged a young girl from one of the hovels and pushed her to the floor at Nelson's feet. She begged and pleaded for her life to be spared whilst weeping hysterically at the devastation and destruction that lay all around her. Given the loss of her home and family, death was probably her best option. Nelson stared long and hard at the girl but could only see the dismembered bodies of his father, mother and only sister – the five-mile walk to school had saved him and his brothers. This girl before him came from a tribe of murderers and if allowed would breed more murderers. MASK had been formed to stop these sectarian killings; he raised his hand and turned his back, oblivious to the screams and the sound of metal against flesh.

Nelson returned from one of his solitary walks to rejoin his troupe having their morning meal, after which they assembled for parade. Everyone was happy, they were still enjoying the previous day's rout and the riches it had brought them; spontaneously they sang the MASK anthem. When the noise died down Nelson spoke.

"From now on we will only train in the afternoon." Samson, Nelson's eldest brother and self-appointed group spokesman, asked why.

""Because I have somewhere I want you all to go in the mornings."

"Are we not good soldiers?" Nelson smiled."You are very good soldiers but this morning I discovered that a missionary school will be started in Igari Township. If we are to form a government it is important that you all learn to read and write."

"We are happy to do as you say but are we old enough to study?" Nelson nodded.

"It's a primary school, five to eleven, I don't know all your ages but you should all be in that age group."

"Will you be coming with us?" Nelson shook his head.

"No, school cannot teach me the lessons I need know, I can only learn from the army."

Nelson looked at the smouldering remains of Ukata that now belonged to him. Looking further he could see the more established townships, he smiled. In years to come they also would be his.

JUNE ELFORD
How Love Fled

The constable had a firm grip on Robert's arm. "Evening, ma'am," he said, touching his helmet. "You're Mrs Thornton?"

Helen nodded, fear turning to panic. Robert's coat was torn, his face bruised. "What's happened?"

"Don't come near me," Robert snarled, raising his hand.

"Now, Sir, you've no cause to behave like that," the constable said.

"Is he drunk?"

"No, ma'am. He's been going on about the war, shouting we shouldn't have fought the Boche. That's how he got into a fight."

"You'd better come in."

Raving, a jumble of words and numbers she didn't recognise. "If you'll go for the doctor, I'll get him upstairs and into bed," said the constable. Helen ran down the dark street.

Doctor Banks checked Robert's eyes. "His pupils are dilated and his pulse is a bit rapid. I'll give him a sleeping draught." Helen fetched a glass of water from the washstand. "Has he ever talked about the fighting in France?"

She shook her head. "But he still has terrible nightmares."

The doctor helped Robert to lie down. "I've seen men behave like this when I worked in an army hospital. Robert could be suffering from delayed shellshock. Your baby died a month ago?" Helen nodded. Her eyes filled with tears at the memory of Robert holding the dead child in his arms... "If Robert bottled up the horrors he saw in the war," continued the doctor, "and buried them in his subconscious mind, a traumatic experience like the child dying could trigger off this breakdown."

"He doesn't know me," she sobbed.

"Helen, Robert may have to be committed to an asylum."

Helen looked up. "Why? Why can't he go to a military hospital?"

Doctor Banks sighed. "Because by 1919 most of them were closed and any ex-servicemen were transferred to local asylums as in-patients."

When Helen met the superintendent of the asylum in the lobby he pointed to a plaque on the wall to the memory of staff who'd died in the Great War. "A fitting tribute, don't you think?" He led the way into his office. "I'm sorry you felt it necessary to make the journey."

Helen sat down. "I'm worried about my husband. How is he?"

"We couldn't assess him while he was under restraint."

Fear, that new emotion, but not for herself, for Robert. "What do you mean?"

"We have to use restraint to protect some patients from hurting themselves. He had periods when he hallucinated."

"From shell-shock?"

"I prefer not to use expressions which are euphemisms for the truth; expressions like 'the buried-alive neurosis' or 'soldier's heart'." He picked up a pen and balanced it between his fingers. "Your husband's symptoms are identical to those in most common hysterical disorders – symptoms often found in women patients." His pale eyes were devoid of sympathy. "Does that answer your question?"

"Yes, but why is my husband dressed like the other patients? I was told he was entitled to wear his own clothes."

He raised his eyebrows. "The Ministry of Pensions and the General Board of Control haven't classified your husband as a Service Patient."

"But you've applied?"

He got up. "There are over 500 patients in this institution. These matters take time."

Helen was told Robert was in the day room of the men's ward. She found him sitting by the long windows overlooking the exercise yard. He had no idea who she was.

He was dressed in a grey worsted suit and black boots. The other men sat round the room, moaning, smiling at some private joke, hugging or rocking themselves. Would it always be like this with Robert, a ghost of himself, imprisoned by the past? He wasn't dead but she'd lost him; she was a widow and wife.

Could she let go? Gerald said she should leave him. After he and Robert returned from the war they spent their gratuities buying two ex-army vehicles from the Ministry of Munitions and set up a haulage contractors. She couldn't have managed without Gerald's help.

A promise – in sickness or in health but with only a memory to love? The charge nurse rang the bell. Robert looked at her blankly as she bent to kiss him. "Goodbye," she whispered.

Helen hurried along the red and black tiled corridor and out of the main door. "How was Robert today?" Gerald asked.

"He still doesn't know me."

"Helen..."

"No, Gerald." Her eyes were bright. "I'm going to take Robert away from here."

"He's insane. Where can he go?"

"To the Crichton Royal Hospital. I went there with Doctor Banks last week." She looked at the redbrick building in front of them. "It's not like this: it doesn't even look like an institution. The patients at the Crichton are treated individually. They get open-air rest – the rooms open on to a veranda – and special medication and dieting. The physician I met said he wished Robert had come to them earlier."

"But did he say Robert would get better?"

"No," Helen said, quietly. "He didn't make any promises."

She remembered seeing the portrait of Emily Godshell, the hospital's benefactress, in the hall. A small determined-looking woman, Emily Godshell had recognised the way society treated the insane. At Crichton Royal the mentally ill were treated humanely.

Gerald reached for her hand. "Robert's a shell of the man you married? Do you want him for the rest of your life?"

Helen took a deep breath. "Yes, for the rest of my life."

JOHN ELLIOTT
Bodies In The River

Harry saw the bodies again, tugging and twisting against the little currents of the river before bobbing, mercifully, out of sight. His daughter called, asking him for the second or third time to open the wine, and when he looked back the Torque was running by as it always did, clean and shallow, familiar home to moorhen, water rat, eel and trout.

He had come to Normandy, back to it, ten years previously and bought the cottage close to the river, with its views of the hills of Calvados and the sounds and smells of the farm all around. No nightmare then; they had started soon after the summer of 1995, conjured out of deeply-submerged memories by the seductive catharsis of a nation celebrating the 50th anniversary of Victory in Europe. Harry had loved it. Half a million people in Hyde Park, his family around him, and Dame Vera singing on a warm, unforgettable night.

There, making use of his privileged entry to the veterans' centre, he had taken the chance to meet comrades he had not seen for thirty, forty, fifty years. Not long afterwards he had seen the bodies again, had woken in desperation as they spun, lifelike in death, through his dreams.

The first time was soon after D-Day, on the river Dives somewhere between Ouistreham and Dozule. He and the rest of his company were dug in, anticipating a counter-attack. They had heard, away to their front, the cough of British tank guns and knew the battle might ebb back towards them. But only the bodies came back: Wehrmacht soldiers, caught upstream, probably fording the river in small boats when the shells found them.

Harry and the others in his company counted 25 bodies over the next day and night, some floating on their backs, some on their fronts, one upright, trapped air turning his tunic into a passable lifejacket. Harry could see the dead soldier's eyes, then the river-washed hole in the back of his skull as the current spun him round. Lifeless eyes, splintered skull, eyes, splintered skull, until the stream carried the corpse out of his vision.

Harry's war ended three days later, over before it had really started. He was helping to push a Bren gun carrier out of a ditch when it jolted itself free, a track skewing across his foot, trapping and shredding an ankle. He had spent months in a hospital in Brighton before he could walk again. Several more operations over the next few years had repaired much of the damage, so that Harry's limp was now hardly noticeable.

Perhaps it was his own agony that had driven away the memory of the river of bodies, or a helpful subconscious sparing him the trauma of sights which, at 18, he had been too young to comprehend. That had changed at the VE Day commemoration in the veterans' centre, when he had met not one but five members of his old company. They had fought with the battalion most of the way to Berlin.

Taken by injury from his unit so soon after the invasion, Harry thought of his too-short period of active service only as a source of shame. He knew that many others had died in those short weeks before his left ankle was crushed, but it still seemed to him an easy way out. Damaged, not by enemy action, but by a stupid, avoidable accident. In his own eyes his war wound was fraudulent, a mean thing that had robbed him of his chance to "do his bit". A ticket home without honour.

His daughter looked at him, concern in her eyes. "What's wrong, Dad? Something's bothering you." "It's nothing, my love," he replied, smiling gently as he reached for the corkscrew. She knew he had been here, briefly, during the war, but only because her late mother had told her. She guessed that some distant memory was causing him pain but knew she would never know the cause of his anguish. And nor would anyone else. Not for a moment did Harry consider his nightmares were anything but his own private hell. In common with tens of thousands of his generation, now all in their seventies, combat stress was something which afflicted today's soldiers. He would no more seek treatment for bad dreams than he would for a stubbed toe.

The bodies in the river were his legacy... and they always would be.

D ENTICOTT
Weep For Reggie

"Can I help?" There was a sob in the woman's voice.

The old man's eyes flicked open.

"No. No, please...send her away."

His voice so low that Len had to lean right over him, ear to bloodied lips. She couldn't have heard.

"It's all right, love." Len looked up at her. "I'll take care of him, there's a young lad hurt over there if you..."

She was gone before he finished.

The old man shuddered trying to raise his head. Len leant down over him again. His words came between breaths. "Couldn't...bear it...if she..." he screwed his eyes tight-shut on the word "...cried.".

"That's all right, old mate, lie still, don't try to talk, help'll be here any minute now."

Len did his best to sound calm and confident.

"You'll be fine."

The old man didn't seem to be in pain but Len felt a sticky wetness under his knee. His wished he knew what to do. God, make them hurry.

The old man twitched, muttering, "Poor old Billy," his voice strengthened. "It's me this time, Billy. Same as you, except I deserve it."

Ears tuned for ambulance sirens, it was a second before Len registered the half-heard words. He stared down at the old man. It must be a coincidence. His question came out sharply. "Was Billy with you when the bomb exploded?"

There was no answer.

"Billy, who's Billy? A friend of yours?"

The response was irritable, impatient.

"Billy? OLD Billy was a bull, killed in the war...German bomb."

The clock turned back. Len was picking his way through debris in the farmyard toward the end stall which had taken the brunt of the bomb. It was 1941, Old Billy the bull had been killed outright. Len was eleven years old, the same as his best pal, Reggie. Reggie crying like a baby at the yard gate, too upset to say

"Goodbye" to their old friend.

"Reggie, Reggie! It's Len, remember..."

The old man's head jerked up and fell back with a deep-drawn wailing cry. He looked even more deathly than before. No word came from him . He was absolutely still. As Len fumbled for a neck pulse he felt the old man's chest rise and fall. Thank God. He shouldn't have snapped at him. But why had he cried out like that?

Pure chance had brought Len to the top of the street as the pub windows blew out in a booming flash of red, way down at the far end. Gas? Or IRA bomb? More likely a bomb. He tried to run but had to slow to a walk as his chest tightened. The bar had been crowded and by the time he got there casualties were already being helped and carried out. A man stood where the door had been.

"Don't go in there's enough in there," he said. "You look after that one, he's badly hurt." He pointed to one of the forms lying on the pavement away from the building.

As he tried to rub warmth into the flaccid hands images flooded through Len's mind of the excitements he had shared with Reggie. Barrage balloons like floating elephants climbing slowly into the sky. Anti-aircraft gun barrels swinging, their shells exploding amongst high-flying raiders. And the ultimate thrill one clear blue day, of Spitfires screaming down upon "Bandits", guns chattering.

He remembered summer holidays on the farm. The shock of "Old Billy's" death. The intensity of Reggie's grief and the whispered concern of their mothers.

Len brushed a wisp of white hair aside and peered again at the old man's face. Somehow he couldn't think of him as Reggie.

A fire engine swung into the street, followed by a solitary ambulance. There was an overturned coach on the motorway, the paramedic explained. He glanced up from the old man with a small shake of his head.

Tucking the blanket back around him, Len recalled the Christmas holiday when they had worked as temporary postmen. The war had spread to many fronts. Wives and mothers waited on their doorsteps desperate for the comfort of a letter. "Anything for me?" so often a despairing, tearful plea to which they could only say "Sorry".

None older than fifteen, all the delivery boys felt guilty at the distress that dogged their footsteps. The effect on Reggie after just a week was frightening. Taken off deliveries his recovery from weeping withdrawal was still long drawn out.

Then came the terrible day when a lone hedge-hopping Messerschmidt reached the town without warning. Len's mother was killed in a back street by the pilot's random strafing. She had always had a soft spot for Reggie and her sympathy had helped him in his recovery from the breakdown. Her death tipped him back into depths beyond the reach of kindness.

Alongside the blackness of his own grief Len never forgot the sound of Reggie weeping and screaming as he was taken away in an ambulance strapped to a stretcher.

That was the last Len saw of him and after his mother moved to be near the hospital all contact was lost.

The old man moved.

"Len." His eyes were wide open, blinking rapidly.

"Take it easy, Reggie, you must be next for the hospital."

"There's something I must tell you... I mustn't..."

Len's own chest tightened at the old man's agitation.

"Tell me later, after they've had a proper look at you."

The old man spaced the words out.

"I – killed – your – mother."

Len gasped, he was out of his mind again. "Sssh, Reggie. That plane..."

The old man cut in:

"No-one ever knew. I've never told anyone – ever, even in that hospital. I found her lying on that street. I was running for the shelter. She was lying there twisted...blue bone..." He shuddered, eyes screwed tight, "...crying.

"I wanted to help her...but I couldn't...I didn't. I ran away."

The paramedic pulled the blanket up over the old man's face. Len wept. For his mother and for the old man who once was Reggie.

MARY EVANS
The Hidden Cost

"Preston, James. I have an appointment to see Dr Rawlinson at 10 am," said the tall, gaunt man, his voice clipped, abrupt, specific.

The receptionist looked up momentarily from the hypnotic lights of the computer screen. "Take a seat, I'll call you when doctor is ready for you," she replied, like an automaton, returning to her work before she had even finished speaking to him.

James Preston, Sergeant, Royal Engineers (retired) looked around the crowded waiting room and chose a chair nearest to the door, a sort of inbred survival instinct.

In the corner a wooden enclosure, engulfed by half broken toys, caged in fretful children who ignored the fluorescent cartoon characters that gyrated across a nearby television screen, while their mothers gossiped, inured to the cacophony around them.

The utilitarian clock that adorned the far wall showed that it lacked but two minutes to the hour. His fists clenched tightly and involuntarily in the hidden security of his pocket and he squared his shoulders against the hard unyielding wood of the chair.

Like most servicemen he drank. He had drunk to erase the boredom, the almost religious seclusion from ordinary life. Drunk to ignore the brutality of his fellow men. And drunk to expunge the fear of fear.

But in the last six months since he had been demobbed he had drunk to expel the flashbacks. The Falklands war, the Gulf war, the screaming nightmare that his confused brain could no longer disentangle, reality and unreality intermingled, the sweat that drenched him in terror, the nameless dread that paralysed him. He had drunk to blot out his total incomprehension of civilian life, his inability to either be or not be anything but the trained soldier he was. The half bottle of Scotch had become a full bottle and then he had stopped counting.

The hands of the clock pointed to ten minutes past the hour and he tried to calm his rising impatience. His turbulent thoughts were interrupted by the old man who sat next to him and coughed into a scrappy, stained handkerchief, his lungs rasping like a sponge saturated with engine oil as he vainly fought for breath, for life.

Ex-Sergeant Preston wondered if he should do anything and hoped to God that he would never be that old, that ill, that helpless. No-one else seemed to have noticed the old man and he tried to close his mind to the unequal, painful struggle.

The sonorous ticking of the clock in the stuffy room showed that it was now twenty five minutes past the hour and he began to wonder whether he had somehow failed to hear his name in the confusion that surrounded him.

Eyes, suspicious and wary of queue jumpers, alert to such tactics of subterfuge, followed him as he approached the reception desk once more. "Excuse me," he said, his voice sounding overloud in the hushed stillness. "But I think there may have been a mistake. My appointment was for 10 o' clock and it's nearly half past," he informed the receptionist, who looked past him with unseeing eyes.

"I'll call you when doctor's ready for you," she repeated, an edge to her voice. She was used to dealing with the difficult, the recalcitrant, the bloody minded. The hostility in the room was palpable as he regained his seat and fought back the angry bile that flooded his body.

A small child that had somehow escaped the enclosure and the unwatchful eyes of his mother was crawling unsteadily towards him, the stench of his soiled nappy magnified by the excessive heat and the suffocating proximity of the waiting sick.

He tried to ignore the boy who stretched up grubby hands towards him slobbering onto his boots and he watched as the spittle oozed over the polished toe cap and onto the floor.

Someone called out a name, the wheezing old man dragged his unwilling body to the nurse's room and a fat woman quickly sank into the abandoned chair like a grave robber. He looked up at the clock, it was ten to eleven.

There was standing room only now as he jostled his way back to the reception, not caring, unaware of who he pushed aside. He had spent over twenty years regulating his every move, his every thought to discipline, order, precision. Like a finely tuned instrument he had been set aside, abandoned in this world where chaos ruled. Where nothing that he had been taught to respect had meaning.

"Excuse me," he said to the receptionist for a third time, his voice booming across the hushed waiting room. "I had a bloody appointment at 10 o' clock and it's now nearly 11 o'clock," and he slammed his fist down on the sterile surface of the desk, the blood drumming in his ears.

The receptionist eyed him measuringly. "I've already told you," she replied, coldly. "Doctor will see you when he's ready."

"Lady," he said, his voice dangerously calm. "You just get up off your arse and tell your precious bloody doctor that I don't wait an hour for God, never mind a bloody medic," and with a single movement he upended the desk, the splintering sound of the computer's glass screen echoing the receptionist's scream and shattering the silence as it crashed inertly to the floor.

"Call the doctor and the social worker out, lad," said the duty sergeant. "Looks like we've got another one from that place up the road. Bloody post-traumatic stress," he sneered. "Put 'em in the police force for a bloody year, that'd sort the buggers out."

The cell was cool, silent. He lay on the bunk and stared up at the ceiling, there was an atmosphere of order and control. There were men in uniforms, men who understood and responded to discipline. He was a soldier, he could handle this, this made sense.

SALLY FAWCETT
Walsh's War

Morning had come. Announced by a cockerel whose echoing sound had perched on the encroaching mist. Its utterance ricocheted along the turgid mud. Guns rested muckily by the heavy eyed soldiers' bodies. Wearily, Walsh looked down at the mangled limb. Was it his? Ahead of him, in the death-filled day, was the agony of living. As those around him stirred he felt a first drop of rain fall from the sky above his head to the trench beneath his soul. He remembered a time, so long ago, when he had been glad to open his eyes. With delight he would lie on his back, staring at the four cornered ceiling and plot the stages of his day along the lines where wall and inner roof met. The first line was predictable. At its beginning he would arise, execute the necessary domestic chores, explore the words in his newspaper, storing them selectively in his mind to feed on as the day progressed. After this he would order and tidy his rooms. From here life was less certain. At the end of the line, where walls met, he would make a sharp 'left turn' and step onto the second phase of his day. This, and the two other remaining lines could be travelled variously. Some days he would act impulsively and quite by chance find meaning through his work. Often the lines would wrinkle or thread and he could hide impishly in their cavities. Around the corners, where others eagerly awaited him, he would disseminate knowledge, personality and leadership. On reaching day's end his heart, soul and body would almost run along the division which returned him to his haven. Here he would ponder his actions. Assessing his achievements and calculating how he had empowered others. Through him they would be able to accomplish tasks, serve their king with dignity and be meritorious in all aspects of their lives. It was with satisfaction and a feeling of self-worth that he would pour a small Scotch and light his evening cigarette. Years ago in training he'd been given an hour to list, in order of priority, the three most important things in his life. After thirty minutes he had unscrewed his pen lid, adjusted the angle of the paper and taken sixty seconds to set down, under each other, the numbers 1, 2, 3. Without hesitation, next to the number one, he had written in bold letters, MYSELF. This small six letter word had singled him out. Separated him from others in the room. This connection to his ego had set him in his own camp. This apparently simple word had indicated that he had leadership qualities. He wasn't arrogant, conceited or pompous – merely excellent quality, leadership material. They had said so. He had proved it. He proved it every day during training and on the parade ground. He proved it on the Military Exercises and in the Officers' Mess. He had proved it to his mother, his father and his entire paternal line. He would prove it to his regiment, each one, his men. He'd looked up 'Prove' in a dictionary once:- 'To test, experience or suffer'. Words in a book. Comfortably sitting on a page. Black print standing out, sharply defined on the white paper. Smart, neat words. Aligned to each other. Marching across the page. Halting abruptly at the end of a line, obediently beginning again below. Each word giving meaning to its neighbour. Knowing its place in the ranks. Only the capitals rising above the lowly stationed lower case letters. Mendacious words. What did they prove.

He had been a young, clean-shaven, optimistic man. His hair, cut regulation army fashion, neatly parted on the left.

He looked down at the mangled limb. Was it his? Ahead of him in the death-filled day was the agony of living. He tried to picture the paper on which he had written a simple word. In that other life of his. Did it begin with the letter 'M'?

The mist had been burned away and that which had been shrouded was now revealed with stark lucidity. He thought perhaps the sun was shining but lifting his head to look up at the open sky was not an option. He could not raise his eyes from the scene of carnage so far, surreptitiously hidden by the haze. Ahead of him in this death-filled day was the agony of the living.

To test, experience or suffer.

Test, experience or suffer.

Experience or suffer.

Or suffer.

Suffer.

Suffer his eyes (both functioning) to look along the trench at what lay before him. Knowing himself to have died and descended to Hell, he opened his mouth (teeth all present and correct) and began to release a sound. A foul, disembodied sound which came from deep within his soul. He knew where the sound emanated. If he could just remember the word...... The sound changed nothing in him. Nothing before him. Nothing around him. Nothing could alter this harrowing vista. Heavily he raised the right arm (four fingers, one thumb intact) in an attempt to cover the eyes, rid himself of the vision. But the hand would not obey. Having found the mouth the fingers had reached inside trying to deaden the noise, to quieten the shocking sound of unmitigated fear. Teeth began chomping down upon fingers, they knew the sound must not be halted. It was alive. It had more life than anything else on the field and should not be suppressed. Higher and higher it rose, maniacally calling to all who lay beneath. It resonated and was absorbed by mortals with shattered senses. Now they began. Almost inaudible, imperceptibly building, gradually impelled to take on the same refrain. A gut wrenching primeval ululation.

The ears on his head (whole and attached) heard the echoing noise. He knew, as the eyelids slowly lowered that he had found the word. The word that separated him.

That connected him to his ego and his men to him.

It had begun with 'M'.

Mea culpa.

NORMAN FORD
Laugh? I Nearly Died

Max Miller. Tommy Trinder. George Formby. They still raise a chuckle even after fifty years. I was beginning to wallow in nostalgia as the radio poured out its story of "75 Years of Radio Comedy". How lucky we were to have this unique sense of humour that foreigners (especially Germans and Japanese) were too stupid to understand. Sandy Powell (Can you hear me, Mother?) Rob Wilton (The day war broke out...). "Big-hearted Arthur" Askey.

I loved them all. Well, nearly all! Till they played that dreadful tune, that satanic signature tune that suddenly made my blood freeze and boil at the same time, as it had done on that awful winter night in Holland over 50 years ago. It was that man again, curse him. No, not that man, but "that man again", the one that the announcer was calling "the greatest of them all", who flooded the world with catch phrases like "Can I do you now, Sir?", "This is Funf speaking" and "Large gin? I don't mind if I do". ITMA! Mr Tommy Handley!

Not many laughs in Holland in the winter of 1994/45. The winter offensive had slithered to a halt in conditions more akin to Siberia that western Europe. We were not sorry to be ordered to dig in, indicating that there would be no further attacks for the time being. Things could be worse....

They soon were. "C" Company had been selected to provide a patrol to sit the night out somewhere in the frozen wastes ahead of us, sending back any information about enemy movement, gun-sites etc. The Sergeant Major was calling for six volunteers. No volunteering for me. I was duty wireless operator. Constant communication was vital.

The wireless set...Infantry...Number 18 was a remarkable piece of World War 2 equipment. Difficult to tune, impossible to adjust on the march, heavy and clumsy to carry, it rendered its operator incapable of using a weapon, lying flat on his face or running very fast, the last two at least being considered highly desirable skills for an infantryman in a battle zone.

The aerial, which had to be tuned separately, consisted of a number of foot-long copper rods which slotted together. Any change in length necessitated retuning.

Nowadays, when a pocket size telephone can connect us to a subscriber in the Amazon jungle, it seems incredible that then the lives of a thousand men could depend on this monster which, at best, had a range of only a few miles and could, in the wrong terrain, fail at 200 yards.

The 18-set had, however, one virtue. It could sometimes pick up short-wave transmissions of standard BBC broadcasts, enabling us to inform sceptical comrades that the war was being won and the Germans were fleeing in terror from our advance.

The set was behaving well as we trudged out in the face of an icy wind, past those now comfortable looking trenches whose occupants had, by donating their rum ration, indicated clearly how they viewed our bleak task. I was receiving BHQ's signals loud and clear, though I was forbidden to reply until we reached our destination and it was considered safe to do so.

Our luck did not hold for long. We had scarcely cleared our lines when a burst of enemy gun-fire sent us scrambling for what cover we could find. There were no casualties – except for the radio. In my haste to reach ground level I had lost some lengths of aerial. I had lost HQ!

With no chance to re-net, we plodded on what seemed like miles to our allotted observation post, a ruined farm too close to the German lines for comfort.

Crouched, freezing under a broken farm cart, still forbidden to transmit, I frantically searched the airwaves for Battalion's signal. Nothing!

Then, it came, so loud that it blasted the headphones and made me seize the volume control in panic. That awful tune. "It's that man again. Mr Tommy Handley is here!"

He was there all right. At every spot on the dial!

It seemed to go on forever.

"Can I do you now, Sir?" I could have cheerfully done the whole moronic crew that night.

We were out for something like ten long wind-swept hours, gathering all kinds of important information, I never did re-establish contact. Our dangerous night vigil became, and remained, a nightmare.

We crept back at dawn, snow-covered and stiff with cold and fatigue, facing new perils from trigger-happy sentries who had given us up for lost. Our control, also fearing the worst after failing to raise us, had long ago switched off.

Along with the rest of the battalion, they were packing up to move to a new location. No-one was interested in our intelligence report.

"No harm done," said the Signals Sergeant. "You're all back safe. By the way, we picked up a marvellous comedy show on BBC. That Tommy Handley...he's a killer!

PAMELA FRASER
September Saturday

We tried to pretend that it was just another Saturday. At lunch-time we sat as usual at the large, scrubbed kitchen table with its snowy cloth and sparkling crockery and cutlery. We made the usual conversation, laughed at familiar jokes and made no mention of what might happen the next day.

After lunch the younger children gathered velvet violets and butter-coloured primroses from meadow and hedges as they always did in Spring. Their chatter and laughter, arcing across the flower-scented fields, were deludingly reassuring to the adults. How could anything possibly happen to destroy that annual idyllic ritual?

But the news did break the next day and though the distant drums of war would always remain distant to our South African ears, our hearts, in the years to come, would throb and mourn with other families all over the world.

We never experienced the air-raids, the actual noise of battle or the deprivation and upturned turmoil of a daily life. We did share with others, though, a change in inner beliefs beyond recognition, the loss of innocence which would never be recaptured. As time marched on to echoes of war we gazed aghast at the wounded from other countries coming to us for treatment and recuperation, friendship and temporary forgetfulness. It was some time before our own young men – and old – began stumbling back, or never came home at all.

But on that Saturday, the day before war broke out, we tried to do all the Saturday things we normally did, hoping that the feared announcement would turn out to be only an imagined nightmare.

As the youngest of six children I was unable to comprehend fully the horror of what might follow. My sister, ten years older than I, very susceptible to atmosphere, easily moved to tears, sat almost silent with large expressive eyes glistening.

My two youngest brothers had recently joined the Scouts and Cubs movement and tried to look suitably serious while methodically packing away our favourite Saturday lunch: grilled lamb chops, fresh home-grown vegetables, home-made tomato sauce.

My father made an attempt at humour.

"The gannets are at it again." He laughed, but with sadness in the depths of his eyes as he looked at the two young and healthy, totally absorbed, boys. We laughed at a nostalgic family memory. All eight of us had perched on some cliffside rocks to watch a flock of gannets diving opportunely to gorge on a shoal of small fish which had misguidedly strayed too close to their feeding territory.

My father's eyes strayed frequently to my two oldest brothers. They were well within the soldiering age and were finding it difficult to suppress the universal excitement of uniforms and war songs and heroism. My father, the youngest originally of eight boys and one girl, had been the only son too young to enlist in World War I. On that Saturday he was trying to hold at bay the haunting remembrances of his sharp-tongued mother and gentle, deeply-loving father, which had dispelled all visions of glory and heroic pageant.

Of his seven brothers, three died in those unspeakable places I was to read of much later in Sassoon's tortured writing. Two were ruined forever by the nightmares of gassing. One carried to his death a metal plate in his skull, at times unnoticeable, at times turning him into a haunted and violent demon. One returned unscathed, never able to talk about his experiences, never able to sleep again without the return of spectres, taunting and shouting at him to ensure that he would always feel guilt at being the unscathed one.

My mother's only beloved brother had returned irreversibly damaged by shells exploding around him, though his mother never lost her secret feeling of devoted gratitude that at least he had come home alive.

We children noticed, without comment, that my father touched my mother's arm more often than usual and that they had altered our table positions slightly. My mother sat on his right instead of at the foot of the table as usual. We children noticed, and talked of it later, that my mother ate her meal using mainly her right hand, my father used his left and they held hands as much as possible. For dessert there were all our favourites: freshly-churned ice cream, sweet smelling fruits straight from our bountiful trees, small luxurious biscuits and, my favourite, almond-flavoured petit-fours with the coffee.

There was no "finish your vegetables before pudding". My father suddenly remembered that he had overstocked the supplies for the coming Christmas and hauled out festive crackers for all of us.

My mother, near to tears, looked up at him as he squeezed her shoulder while smiling at us – their six children. My two older brothers tried to look wise and understanding in their too fast approaching adulthood. The gannets continued their rewarding diving with disbelieving delight. I was uneasily confused. And my sensitive sister burst into tears.

The technicalities of war seemed to have little to do with that South African Saturday afternoon, to the younger members of the family at any rate. By evening the windowsills and tables were filled with vases of violets and primroses and the wafting fragrance of those delicate flowers spoke to us only of peace and beauty and nostalgia – no hint of violence and hatred and wanton destruction.

As it happened we were all together for that Christmas – complete with adequate crackers and a larger than usual supply of the festive fare and seasonal accompaniments. But it was the last one on which the family remained intact. We would always remember the ripples following that day which would ensure that two brothers would miss Saturday lunches – and family Christmases – one for many years and one forever.

And all over the world life would never again be the same as it was on that Saturday, the day before World War II broke out.

GAZ GALLAGHER
The Queen's Shilling And Beyond

In April 1988 I left the Grenadier Guards, after 23 years 185 days exemplary colour service, and marched into the great, big, unfriendly world beyond the Barrack gates. "Change Step" would bring me into line I thought but it was more like, "Break Into Slow Time" with long bouts of "Mark Time" thrown in.

"Roll on death, demob's too far" the Old Soldiers had told us many times in NAAFIs and Messes across the world, but here it was now, happening to me. "How could they do this to me?" I asked. I tried back pedalling at the end but it only made things worse. I shouted at the wife, kicked the cat and the kids steered clear of me.

But it didn't stop it happening to me. Here I was, nearly 40 years of age, no confirmed job prospects despite having written to scores of employers telling them that I was the man for them. It all seemed so very wrong that life went on, the old job had not ground to a halt, while here I was having a real mid-life crisis.

It just wasn't right. I tried adopting a casual laid back approach by telling myself, "Life begins at 40, start taking Philosan, enjoy a drop of Wincarnis, go to Steradent parties and workout on my Sony Walkman frame!" To be positive I had a roof over my head plus a good retirement lump sum and pension to look forward to.

When the big day arrived I woke early and depression set in as I lay there waiting. Nothing happened, it was just another very ordinary day, no bells rang, nobody from the "firm" phoned because I was now a civilian. Me, of all people – a civilian! The gloom quickly dispersed as my daughters came into the bedroom with my presents and cards.

It was my birthday and the front of the house had a large banner wishing me "Happy 40th Birthday Dad". I put on a brave face but the 14th of April was the longest, most miserable day of my entire life. It is now some 8 years further on and miraculously I have survived it all.

I have a paid job, been promoted twice, moved to a bigger house and have had time to compare what I have now to what I had previously. I miss the discipline and organisation which we all tended to take for granted. In a battalion everything was within easy reach. After discharge the first thing I needed was a national insurance card.

To get it I had to phone around, catch a bus, walk a fair distance, join a smoking, coughing queue, speak to some very rude indifferent people, fill in forms and wait five weeks for it to arrive. Did people really have to endure this? In the Army you were someone: Sir, Sergeant, Corporal or Guardsman. Part of an elite team but now I was just plain mister!

On the employment front I found to my surprise that Army life had prepared me quite well for Civvy Street. I had learned how to assess problems, draw up solutions, do the job with a minimum of fuss and cope under stress, while enjoying the challenge. On the few occasions things did go wrong I accepted the criticism but never let it get the better of me.

My ability to shoulder responsibility and my sense of humour made me popular with both my peers and my bosses. While serving I was regularly contributing for someone's farewell party, now it seems that a week does not go by that I don't donate to a wreath or at best a wedding present.

Civvy Street is the real world where jeans, T shirt and trainers is the normal everyday attire for everything from going for a pint to attending a wedding. Where you have to protect yourself against burglars, joy riders, football hooligans, muggers and vandals. Survival of only the fittest.

Although often while walking home through the deserted streets, carrying my rolled umbrella, I find myself stepping out, bringing the umbrella into the horizontal position and I slip quickly into fantasia. I am the Sergeant Major pacing the minutes, on the battalion form-up, flanked by my trusty Drill Sergeants.

Improvising my battered brolly for a highly polished pace stick, I give an immaculate salute to the right as the Commanding Officer comes on to the parade. Followed by a quick glance over my shoulder to see if I have been observed, as I slip back to reality. I miss Army life with all its drawbacks but looking back I can only remember the good times.

Life goes on and so should I. At work I often listen to people telling their stories but I don't get drawn in or involved. Instead I have a quiet chuckle to myself and go on my way. Often when I have time to reflect I think, did I really do 23 years? Did I really go to all those places and do all those things?

Horsemeat steaks in Larzac, camel burgers in Sudan, zebra sandwiches in Kenya, octopus in Cyprus and iguana in British Honduras. Washed down with world famous brews like Swampi, Arrac, Cachasso, Amstel, Dortmund Pils, Double Diamond, Watney's Red Barrel, White Cap, Tusker and Tiger.

Paid for in Deutschmarks, Dollars, Francs, Dutch Guilders, Cyprus Pounds, Kenyan Shillings and Baths. Taken to my banquet by Rover, Humber, Daimler and Rolls Royce engines. It didn't detract from the occasion that the engine was in a Land Rover, Humber Pig, Daimler Scout Car, Saracen Armoured Personnel Carrier and one occasion a 62 ton Chieftain tank!

Being back in barracks by 23.59 hours and on parade next morning "gassed but gleaming". Dinner at the Ritz or breakfast at Tiffany's were not in the same league somehow. Again back to reality and the present. Time to go down to the local Royal British Legion for a few gills, after all I am their Standard Bearer!

BERNARD GALVIN
My War – 30 March 1943-22 September 1947

Brussels – September 1944

We had slept on the floor in a large school in a Brussels suburb, snug, warm and under cover for the first time in three months, after being feted by the liberated local populace until midnight. The early reveille at 04:30 was unexpected since we had arrived the day before to be told that we were going to be a garrison for at least three days.

Extract from diary, Friday 8th September:-

"Arose 04:45. Moved off at 08:00. Went to eastern end of Albert Canal and attacked across it at night. We had a hell of a night with Jerries all round us."

Hitler Youth Battalions were mounting a rear guard and holding up the Allied advance and the Guards Armoured Division near Beringen. I was No. 2 on the P.I.A.T. (Projection Infantry Anti-Tank) in C Company, 8th Battalion D.L.I., 151 Brigade, 50th Tyne Tees Division. Private Cutts from Sheffield, and a veteran of North Africa, Sicily and D Day, was my No.1. I was aged 19 and had been a regimental signaller in HQ Company, 10th Battalion D.L.I. 49th Division which landed in Normandy 12 June (D plus 6) until 23 August. After decimation of the battalion attacking across the river at Mezidon, 10 miles southeast of Caen, 18 August, the remnants were split into four groups to reinforce 151 Brigade. We were just sundry infantry. Our C.O. had the bright idea of sending us over the wide exposed canal at night in collapsible boats, pulling ourselves across on ropes fixed by engineers. We were met by intense machine gun fire from Spandau L.M.G's firing on fixed lines. The surprise element never materialised. Casualties were heavy and the opposition badly underestimated. Our company managed to advance under cover of farm buildings across two fields with desultory fire all night and all next day while Cutts and I dug well in.

Extract from diary, Saturday 9 September:-

"No grub until late that night. Moved back into D Company position and D Company took ours."

There was little movement but still lots of small arms fire, if anything a short lull – chance to sleep and dig in again.

Extract from diary, Sunday 10 September:-

"Moved forward and got surrounded but 6th battalion got a lot of P.O.W's and we knocked a Tiger out."

It was attack and counter-attack with German Infantry all round us and two or three tanks. They were just the other side of the hedge and some of our company were killed, wounded or taken prisoner but we stayed doggo and well dug in. As the 6th D.L.I. moved up on our flank the Germans were in retreat. An ex Duke of Cornwall Light Infantry Sergeant organised a bayonet charge with negative effect and more casualties, including himself. A Tiger tank on its way back passed close. Cutts and I shot off with the P.I.A.T. from our position and immobilised it. Another tank crossed our front followed by a group of German infantry in retreat and several of us blasted with rifle fire from some 150 to 200 yards away. They dropped in their tracks only to get up and run away a few minutes later. Only two or three were hit.

Extract from diary, Monday 11 September:-

"Moved further up and linked with Green Howards. We are reserve company but we had a bit of shelling. Got relieved by 15th Division and went back across canal."

Support, proportionate to the opposition, had arrived. The bridgehead over the canal had been deepened and widened and overwhelming available fire power had been brought to bear.

We left behind many dead and wounded and some were taken prisoner. My overriding memory was of a young rifleman, as recently arrived in the battalion as I, and whose name I did not know, lying under a hedge with a bullethole in the middle of his forehead. I never saw the Sergeant, who had led the bayonet charge, again.

As Cutts and I marched away from the canal to a safer area he cast the P.I.A.T. into a ditch, saying "I don't mind carrying the bloody thing in, but I'm not carrying it out!" The four remaining bombs were no use without it, so they followed.

Extract from diary, Tuesday 12 September:-

"Moved further back to a marshalling area on R.A.S.C. trucks. Bit of an air raid that night but had a good sleep."

Extract from diary, Wednesday 13 September:-

"Got transferred to Signal Platoon. A civvy woman did our washing for us! Had a very good sleep."

Extract from diary, Thursday 14 September:-

"Went to R.A. Battery for training on a 19 Set across the canal. Had a good day out. Lovely weather."

Just another week in the life of an infantry private soldier June 1944 to May 1945. More young lives lost. I never knew the great majority of them as they had arrived as reinforcements only a week or two before. What we had tried to take with two depleted infantry battalions, took Divisional Artillery and the whole of the 15th Infantry Divisions to achieve. 50th TT Infantry Division had been to the fore again in North Africa, Sicily and D Day with new young fresh faces who came and went.

More casualties in a week than the whole of the Falklands War. Hardly an officer in sight, so no factual reports or recommendations, so no medals. Counselling was not invented. Post War Reunions seemed irrelevant for such a limited association with young men from scattered backgrounds who just wanted to resume normal life and forget. Just imagine putting a Tiger tank out of action from a hole in the ground now!

On Saturday 16 September we were down in the town of Lommel for a drink and a night out. By the end of the month we had charged up from Lommel Cross Roads to Nijmegen and Elst over the River Waal in a vain attempt to reach the Airborne landings at Arnhem, but that's another story.

MURRAY GARDNER
Birds And Birdmen

On 12th December 1941, while a Flight Commander in No.451 (RAAF) Squadron RAF, I flew in my SAAF Hurricane I on a tactical reconnaissance out of Tobruk. During this I shot down one fighter type enemy aircraft, and, when making out my sortie report, I duly claimed one enemy aircraft destroyed.

Imagine my amazement, a few days later, when, instead of the expected mild pat on the back, I received from the Air Officer Commanding a rather backhanded message. "It was not the job of Tac R aircraft to shoot down enemy aircraft."

It reminded me of an occasion in East Africa a year before, very early in the morning on 17th December 1940, when nobody had complained about Tac R aircraft shooting down an enemy aircraft. After the successful land battle of El Wak there was a large concentration of South African, Gold Coast and East African troops and their transport vehicles in that bushy area and Brigadier "Piggy" Richards of the Gold Coast Brigade felt that their evening and early morning cooking fires were bound to attract the attention of the Italian bomber aircraft from Mogadishu. A short, fat man, with a ruddy complexion and a large moustache, he accordingly donned his red, flanneled cap and went to talk to our C.O., Major Jimmy Durrant.

As a result, at the end of the day, during which our B Flight 40 Squadron SAAF had done all the reconnaissance and close support work, three of us, in our Hawker Hartbees fighter bombers climbed out of the British El Wak strip in loose formation, and cruised around with lights on to advertise our presence and discourage any Italian bomber aircraft. The sun set and down came the darkness with tropical speed.

Nothing to do now except formate on the Major, check our instruments from time to time, and wait for our bush strip, Ndege's Nest, to appear, straight ahead and dead on time! Not quite as simple as that. Rather like looking for a Foreign Legion fort located in the middle of a bushy Sahara Desert.

Ah! There's the magic lookout tree, on the edge of the Habaswein to Wajir road, showing a bright white light. Now it's my turn to land. All set for me to fly down the flarepath, turn across wind, and on downwind, just as my port wing passes abeam the lookout tree, switch on the wingtip landing flares, bright as daylight. Turn on to finals and make a nicely judged touchdown with the wingtip flares going out just as I came to the end of my landing run. Thank heavens for that! I should hate to get incinerated at the end of such a long and busy day!

"I enjoyed that," I told the Major. "But I will be quite happy to let the Hurricanes do their stuff early tomorrow morning." "No such luck," said the Major. There are very few Hurricanes and they are only allowed to fly in full daylight. So we will have to do that one too. Take off at 04:30!"

It was cool and dark as the Major briefed us next morning. "No lights, complete radio silence, keep formation. Our main chance of an interception is surprise." I did my checks and stifled a yawn as I lined up for take off in turn. We came off easily and I turned almost at once to join up with the Major. That was nearly a mistake. The aircraft's trim was rather nose down and I had to pluck up the nose rapidly as a tree below seemed a little close.

As we neared British El Wak I noticed a signal lamp blinking at us out of the bush. It said "Aircraft North East!" and it got me scanning the horizon very carefully. Eventually I did see a dark shadow under the lightening sky. And it was growing and becoming more distinguishable. I looked at the Major and willed him to look at me. But he didn't. Now we were almost at Italian El Wak. Desperately I willed the Major again to look. But he didn't. Was he in a time warp of his own?

It was unmistakably a large three engined aircraft, probably a Caproni bomber. It was closing fast. I could wait no longer. So, stick back, full throttle and up I shot like a rocket! Over and down on the big bird's tail as he dived for home, scattering his bombs as he went. Down like a lift! 240 miles an hour on the airspeed indicator. Not bad for an open cockpit bi-plane! Down through the yellow flashes, down through the rattle of guns. Suddenly there he was dead ahead and levelling out. Close in behind that big tail and give the rear gunners a squirt. One for the upper, one for the lower and one down the middle of the fuselage for the cockpit crew.

Closing too fast now. So break out to starboard and watch for reactions. Nothing. Just one Hartbees diving on his tail and away again. Another racing ahead to give his rear gunner a shot. Slide in again and aim carefully for the wing racks. First for the port engine then for the starboard. Watch it! He's down! But, heavens, how close to the ground I got! Hadn't the Major said only a few days ago, "Birds and Birdmen fly by day. Only fools by night!"

I circled the downed aircraft and noted that it was beginning to burn. As I flew back to El Wak, feeling thoroughly chuffed with myself, I gave a friendly "Thumbs Up" to a Hurricane that came snuffling along the frontier "Wire" looking a little irritated.

I was amused to hear, on landing, that "Piggy" had been an enthusiastic spectator and had danced for joy on the roof of his caravan!

KEVIN GAVIN
Why?

The sun was setting over the hills behind my position. Turf Lodge Estate lay in the shadows, shrouded in a golden grey hue which hid its deprivation. I lay huddled against the wall of sandbags, an uneasy feeling crept over me. The quiet of the observation post added to my apprehension...

The electricity sub-station had long been used by the security forces because of its unique location high on the outskirts of Belfast. The winding road, which entered the estate from the rich countryside, ran only a few yards from the main gate and was a favourite entry and exit point for terrorists.

A section of infantry had set up a vehicle check point around the first bend, out of sight of the estate's prying eyes. The quiet was disturbed as I heard them pack up and start their vehicles. Within minutes the sound of the engines faded. The haunting quiet returned.

Instinctively I searched the sky as my ears picked up the bop, bop, bop as the home made mortars left their drainpipe launchers. Mesmerised, I watched three mortars tumble out of control towards us. The first hit the sub-station perimeter wire and fell to the ground harmlessly. The other two cleared the fence, hit an area of loose pebbles and exploded. The orange flashes sucked the oxygen from my lungs. I threw myself flat on the floor. The bombs, packed with six inch nails, sent steel and pebbles flying over my body. Jeff hadn't moved quick enough, the blast forced him into me. His blood and torn flesh oozed through my fingers as I pushed him off and placed him into the recovery position. Nails were embedded in his back and legs, some had been forced under his skin, stretching it into grotesque shapes.

Seconds later the quiet returned, only the dust and smell of spent explosives remained to tell the tale. Jeff lay conscious but without sound or movement. His eyes said it all, the shock showing deep in them.

The medics had been quick to respond. Jeff had been stabilised and waved to the rest of us as the doors of the armoured ambulance slammed shut.

I held that scene in my mind as his replacement arrived. Jock

McCann was a tall, lean man whose dark bushy eyebrows met in the middle. In our elite unit we worked in small groups of four. Jeff gone, Jock's presence put us back to strength.

I briefed the new arrival and made my way back to the observation position. Dave Bryant took up his position at the main gates. Jock stayed with the radio and I lay watching the estate with Andy Hall close to hand. The night took hold. Once again the quiet set in and the uneasy feeling returned. My senses heightened and I peered into the dimly lit streets, expecting something, but not knowing what. In the background I could hear raised voices. I strained to listen, it seemed that Jock and Dave were arguing. Before I could clarify my thoughts, instinct, once again, forced me to the ground in response to a sudden, sharp crack as a weapon discharged. A second shot rang out. The noise stopped as suddenly as it started. I heard the screams of someone in pain. My thoughts and gaze turned to the main gates and the road leading into the estate. I half expected to see another lorry, mounted with smoking weaponry, but there was nothing to be seen. Puzzled, I moved towards the injured. Two more shots rang out, the bullets passing above my head. The thud as they hit the sandbags confirmed their high velocity. I ran and dived for cover, hiding between the massive electricity machinery. By the time the third shot rang out I'd realised that I was being targeted. I moved quickly, dodging in and out of the machinery until I came to rest at the foot of a concrete pillar. I had a clear view of the gates which lay fifty foot in front of me. One of them was open, the body of the injured man preventing it from swinging shut. He stopped screaming and lay motionless. The sound of his sobbing filled the gap between us. I couldn't make out who was lying there. I wanted to shout at him but feared giving my position away. I scanned the area. There was no cover for me if I ran to his aid. My fear wrestled with my conscience. "Why? Why me?" I thought, "I shouldn't be here, I should be back at home with my family, I'm only twenty. Don't go, stay where you are, it's safe here," thought after thought ran through my mind. Suddenly my training took over, I leapt from my cover and hurled myself towards the gate. Nothing moved, no shots rang out. I pulled the semi-conscious figure towards the gate. Dave's face was distorted with pain. I pulled his smock open. A trickle of blood ran down from a small hole in the side of his stomach. The smell of his involuntary bowel movement made me heave. I ripped his field dressing from his belt and forced the pad against the wound. I ran to the radio. Jock had gone. I called for assistance and took up a defensive position overlooking the estate. Peering into the dimly lit streets I could clearly make out the figure of Jock as he ran towards a known IRA 'safe house'. Moments later a black taxi arrived and carried him away. Realising that he had defected I rang off a volley of shots, but to no avail. I watched in disbelief as the taxi headed towards Belfast, slipping through the searchlight of the advancing helicopter, which, minutes later carried Dave as he passed over Belfast and out of this life.

The quiet of the night crept back, the feelings of unrest abated and I cried.

Twenty six years later I still cry...

PAUL GENNOE
Home Comforts

I was certain I'd got him this time. Dead centre.

I'd been sniping away for long enough, patiently waiting for the small mistake, the moment of weakness which would finally open him up. He'd always managed to slip away before, neatly side-stepping everything I could throw at him. Now I had all the angles covered, pinning him spread-eagled against the target so that he had no option but to face the ultimate truth.

He was one of my heroes. Churchill and Montgomery were the others but they were long gone. Dad would talk but he only told me as much as he wanted to. If I touched a nerve he'd slide out of reach, dropping into the slit-trench of silence or ducking behind the bastions of humour for protection.

His memory was infallible and I'd learned to read between the lines of his matter-of-fact description to understand the atmosphere of unreality in which people performed terrible acts in the name of their country. I wanted more than that though. I wanted to feel the emotions of the young man at war, grieve at the grotesque horrors of action and sample passions of brief sojourns in temporary respite. He knew what I was up to and so far he'd been too clever for me.

I'd planned the sortie well. The heavy artillery of roast beef and Yorkshire pudding had softened him up and subtle sappers of Famous Grouse had worked insidiously to clear the approach throughout the familiar minefield. I advanced with caution knowing the strength of his waiting armour.

At first it didn't seem any different. He tapped unerringly on the Morse keys of his memory, deciphering my code easily and enciphering at will. We followed the usual route, into the Signals, around the Cape in the red-leaded rust bucket with Aldis flickering across wind-whipped crests to unseen destroyers in the darkness, reunited with the beloved wireless truck and its British 9 kit in the itching, fly-plagued, blinding, dust-stormed heat of North Africa.

The first thrust had taken us too far. I knew about Tobruk and the shambles of Knightsbridge when the useless two-pounders had finally been replaced by six pound tank killers too late to make any difference. What I really wanted to hear about was shore leave at Cape Town, invitations to family dinners in the sunshine and what Penny had looked like – Penny, who wrote letters to him in the scented South African air while he scrabbled desperately in the baking sand to escape the screaming Stukas which bombed and strafed the convoys on the coast road to nowhere.

Too late. We were already south of Benghazi, bucking and bouncing in the wireless truck only just ahead of the Axis push heralded on the horizon by rolling rising clouds of dust and trumpeted over the echoing landscape by the driving, drumming roar of armoured divisions on the move. When the sucking sand swallowed us a passing Stuart blew the heart out of the truck and we clung like flotsam to its back while it careered precariously to safety.

I changed the mood without luck. The transparent detour to revisit the fleshpots of Alexandria, where women were all too plentiful for troops with no obvious incentive to consider the consequences, provoked nothing more than a brief and unrewarding encounter with heat-seared hotels and boot-black bars.

As we moved forward through the Alamein battlefield after the victory I probed fruitlessly for the innermost recesses where minds scream impotently at shattered fly-blown bodies bespattering torn and twisted wreckage under the merciless eye of the morning sun, baking and blackening bloody wedding-ringed fingers and sightless searching eyes.

The silence was broken on the millpond to Sicily. Last on meant first off at the other end and then north across the straits to grab a toehold on the barren foot of Italy. This would be my last chance. I watched while he sweated over the American 19 set, supplying Shermans to the front line units. We fought our way north with the New Zealanders, passing casually over the Oak Leaf for maintaining communication under fire on the long road to Milan. Then, suddenly, it was all over.

This was the opportunity I needed. I took him by surprise as he climbed into the belly of the Lancaster to sit with his feet down the rear turret all the way home. How did he feel when he read Penny's letter saying that she was getting married and wouldn't be writing again? There must have been other girls? Surely there were moments amidst this unbelievable carnage when home comforts were the only way to stay sane?

Bullseye. At last I'd broken through. I saw the pain cross his face as the eyes filled. Perhaps it had been the girl in Italy, the one he'd had to abandon on the street when the transport to the transit camp arrived without warning, knowing that he'd never be back. I waited while he prepared himself.He constructed the phrases slowly and carefully. Of course unpleasant things had happened. It hadn't been a normal situation but if he had thought about it too much he would have ended up like Hewitt, running wildly through the dunes calling his wife. He shifted uncomfortably in the chair. Yes, some relationships were special and he'd never forgotten this one.

She had been with him from the beginning – they had learned together, him and her. She meant everything to him. He took her all the way from Swansea to Hell and she never complained once. When they had to part company he buried her in the sand and watched the shell burst her apart and blow her all over the desert. He drove other trucks afterwards but they were never the same.

Neither of us spoke while the years passed.

I looked deep into the wise, old eyes and acknowledged my defeat. We smiled at one another. He closed the notebook for me and reached for the whisky.

H S GIBB
A Waste Of Good Life

I can remember as a child the hurting remarks made by friends when I refused to "play soldiers" and shoot the enemy with pretend guns made from sticks. Never did I visualise that one day this pretend game would become reality.

When war was first started back in 1914 there was no conscription in Britain as the feeling had been that with such a great sea power the need for a large standing army was unnecessary. There was a great rush of young men eagerly waiting to go off to the front and fight for their country. I'm quite sure the majority of them didn't know what they were really fighting for.

Much to my horror the reality arrived a few short years later. Due to heavy casualties at the Somme Battle it became quite clear that more and more men were needed to fight. All young men were called up with the exception of some who were doing industrial work.

Being a Quaker it was against my religion to take life. Personally I feel that killing is murder under any circumstances. I never wanted to fight. So, feeling as strongly as I did about this, I had refused to help the war effort in any way. I suppose I was what is known as an absolutist.

To deal with people like me tribunals were set up by the military people and they decided what was to become of us. Waiting for my case to be heard was a very trying time as few of my friends, or even my family for that matter, understood my feelings towards senseless killings. I always liked and enjoyed female company but many women whom I had known all my life just refused to speak to me as they felt that a man refusing to fight for his country deserved to be degraded and ignored.

I didn't receive a white feather but I know men who did. They were sent to prison where they were maltreated by fellow prisoners. Under stresses of war unkindness is always shown to the objector. In fact, we were hated and ridiculed by most people and treated as cowards. My fate was decided in due course and, like quite a few others before me, it was decided at the tribunal that I should be sent to France where there was much heavy firing in the front line.

The trenches were a frightening spectacle with young men killing their enemy on the command of some "brave" officer. At night the maintenance work was carried out and I can still hear the "click, click" of the spades and picks. The spade was a very important part of our gear at this time.

When morning came we could see the sunrises but the bitter, black night seemed more fitting to land such as this.

In the miles of trenches I used to think of the thousands of men planning against one another. Some new device of death being introduced. During this time I became more convinced that all killing is wrong.

The agonies and miseries the men had to go through in the trenches cannot be fully appreciated unless you were there. Paddling about during the day, sometimes with water above the knees or standing on sentry duty, as I was made to do at night, with drenched boots and breeches which became stiff like cardboard with freezing cold air. We were never warm, never dry, very tired and weary in mind and body. Soldiers were white-faced and many had a look of fear from the constant strain. They were nervous and tense.

Each of us dreaded the day when we had to go over the top. This experience is hard to describe. Most of us felt the same. On our first go especially. When I first went over the top my pulse was racing and I was aware of myself fidgeting with equipment. Short ladders were placed against the parapet. Up we went. Straight into action. Burdened like pack-horses we were expected to fight for our lives. With bayonet if the need arose.

The sight that met our eyes when going over the top is one which will remain with me always. Bodies hung grotesquely on the barbed wire. Or some poor man who could take no more just wandered off into the enemy line of fire. We certainly lived side by side with death all the time.

All those years I was forced to fight against my will.

The sufferings and heartbreak that all the killings brought made me feel even more strongly what I still believe to be a waste of good life.

JAMES GOFF
A Return To Normality

Jackson woke from deep sleep in an instant. Lying still, keeping his eyes tightly closed, he enjoyed the last remnants of his first full night's sleep in many days. The sounds of men's rough voices, of weapons being stripped and cleaned and the hiss and crackle of the radios drifted in to him along with the smell of breakfast all mixed with the acrid odour of sweat and unwashed bodies, of clothes too long without being aired and the sour smell of old brickwork from the Victorian wash-house, part of the derelict gasworks, where he, and the 30 men he commanded, lived.

The clatter of metal serving trays on the steel hot plates in what had once been a changing room for the workers in the gasworks told him that breakfast was being served. This, and his full bladder, forced him out of bed at last. He dressed quickly in multi-pattern combat trousers and khaki wool shirt, slipping on socks and boots which he didn't bother lacing up. The room where he slept had once been a small storeroom for the cleaners. Now it was home. Just enough room for a bed with his clothes, kit and rifle hanging from nails driven into the ancient brickwork. But he could shut the door and this privacy was something to enjoy in a world where men lived closer to each other than they did with their own families.

He left the room and walked down the corridor and out into the early morning sunlight. Tall and lean he moved easily like a trained athlete. The night's sleep had left him refreshed and some of the strain had gone from his face. Outside the early morning sunshine was welcoming after the fuggy smell of the accommodation.

"Good Morning, Sir," the sentry greeted him from the sand-bagged sanger at the entrance to the building as he passed.

"Morning, Anderson," he returned the greeting. "All quiet?"

He didn't stop for the reply but kept going to the latrine, his need now becoming urgent. He noticed that the sentry was washed and shaved and correctly dressed and armed. The forecourt had been cleaned and swept and he was in no doubt that when he got back to the building it would be in the process of being cleaned.

The latrines had been cleaned and the fumes from the cleansing fluid stung his eyes as he emptied his bladder. From where he stood he could look out over the area of the gasworks. It made a depressing sight, even in the fresh June sunshine, full of rusting machinery and potholed roads. Surrounded by a high red brick wall, built when man-power had been cheap, the only entrance to the works was through a wide gate under the former office building. Jackson had nightmares of driving through the gates to find a terrorist stood across the street with an RPG 7 aimed at him. Next to the old wash-house was an enormous gasometer allegedly containing thousands of gallons of naphtha. It was some comfort, Jackson thought, to know if that gets hit we won't know much about it.

He checked into the tiny cell that he laughingly called the operations room. His troop sergeant, a dark, squat Welshman, sat yawning at the desk watching the early morning news on television. He looked tired like everyone in the troop. Not the tiredness that comes from a sleepless night but a deep-seated tiredness from the weeks of tension and danger. They had had more than their share of shootings and bomb attacks in the past three months. The thought of losing a man in the last few days of the tour was a fear that occupied Jackson day and night.

"Right, Taff, let me get cleaned up, properly dressed and some breakfast and I'll relieve you. Do we have anyone out?"

"Bdr Thomas, 11A, went out at five, he should be back soon," answered Taff, unsuccessfully trying to stifle a yawn.

"Good, in that case he can check that everything here is okay when he gets back and I'll take my driver and a couple of escorts and take a drive round the patch."

He finished his breakfast and took a mug of coffee out into the sunshine. He lit the first cigarette of the day and stood enjoying the unusual moment of quietness. The traffic in the street outside the red brick wall seemed muted. The air was still and he could hear a bird singing somewhere in the rusting machinery. For one illusionary moment the world seemed at peace.

He felt the explosion first – a trembling feeling under his feet, before he heard the dull thump followed by the sound of shattering glass and shouts of fear and pain. Behind him in the tiny ops room the radios burst into a chorus of shouted orders, questions and orders.

Amongst the confusion, and before he could turn and enter the building, he heard the stressed and excited voice of 11A on the radio and the shouting and screaming in the background. "Hello, 11A. Contact, contact, contact. There has been a bomb go off outside the Elbow Room. The pub's gone and there's a lot of civilian casualties. And I think at least two dead. We need back up and quickly."

The one brief moment of peace was gone. The normality of Belfast had returned.

TOM HALLGARTH
Moonlight Sonata

"When I was a child... I spoke as a child,
  I understood as a child... I thought as a child:
  but when I became a man I put away childish things."
  Manhood came to me at an early age. War does that to you.

By 1941 I had lived the nightmare of the sound of sirens, the whistle of incendiaries, the scream, the thud of bombs, and that awful silence which follows... then the realisation that there is a tomorrow.

As a sixteen year old growing up in Coventry amid the ruins of a once fine city was a constant reminder of one's vulnerability – no counselling to overcome the trauma, no soft touch to chase away the bogies but a determination to survive – "nil illigitami carborundum" – (don't let the bastards grind you down).

The night of November 14/15, 1940 became that moment... "I put away childish things..."

The Germans called it, 'Moonlight Sonata'.

In 11 hours over 500 Heinkels dropped 30,000 incendiaries, 1,400 high explosives and countless parachute mines.

The irony was the Prime Minister knew forty-eight hours earlier that the raid was planned! To warn the city would compromise their intelligence source – a cryptic cipher machine called 'Ultra' which broke the Germans' codes. Churchill referred to it as "my most secret source". They even knew the pathfinder and bomber groups to be deployed.

By a strange coincidence Neville Chamberlain was buried on the 14th November. It seems he found his bit of peace!

A few spasmodic raids during the weeks that followed brought an uneasy calm to the city and as each day passed a normality founded on hope.

Someone once said "he who sows the wind reaps the whirlwind". I was a flight Engineer in bomber command at the time of that harvesting (having lied about my age to join the RAF) but that's another story.

Early 1941 found me at a volunteer First Aid Post. Each night we reported to what had been the local Junior School, now serving as an emergency field hospital. Friendships prospered and it became more of a social club where, after first-aid lectures, we indulged in table-tennis, cards and whatever took our fancy. We slept in one of the classrooms on camp beds the fellows at one end of the school and the girls at the other. Seems we weren't to be trusted in those days... they were right too!

*

April 8th 1941, I called for my mate Geoff, who hailed from Burnley and had an accent that defied all understanding.

The long tree lined avenue seemed forbidding, the darkness, accentuated by the blackout, clung like an invisible cloak. An occasional chink of light showed from shuttered windows and the sound of a radio broke the ominous silence. Geoff was prattling on about Burnley football club and how he knew every blade of grass at Turf Moor. At the top of the avenue across the main road was a garage on whose roof stood 'Moaning Minnie', the air-raid siren.

Please Min not tonight was the silent prayer.

Inside the school the dormitory was warm and light, the beds were pushed back against the walls and someone had organised a table-tennis tournament. The girls sat around on the beds and the non-participants vied for their favours but as half of them were married it was like a dress rehearsal for a non-performance. Geoff and I were quickly eliminated from the competition as the exponents of back-spin and crashing volleys knocked out all the scrubbers. Not too difficult to tell who the organiser was, he pocketed all the tanners.

We decided to get some fresh air, the stuffiness and pungent odour of wartime scent was proving too much. We sat on the back step of an ambulance in the playground. The building, surrounded in sandbags, sombre and dark added to the strange quiescence which enveloped us. No wind, a bright star-filled sky with the moon occasionally breaking through wispy clouds. Even Geoff was silent!

Suddenly Minnie moaned her mournful cry the peace shattered. We stayed put, eyes searching, ears straining... soon the vroom, vroom of distant aircraft, that awful unsynchronised throb of Heinkel engines. Somewhere to the right a solitary searchlight swept the sky but only picked out the barrage balloons – you could almost hear the bomber crews.

'Vielen dank Englander!'

A battery of rockets discharged in the local park and just after a brilliant light descended from the sky.

'Look!' said Geoff, 'they've shot down the bloody moon!'

'It's a parachute flare... you wassak!' I exclaimed.

Alongside was another parachute silent and sinister!

They disappeared from sight and then... whoosh... a noise like an express train leaving a tunnel, a blast of hot air that threw us yards across the playground, a huge mountain of flame rose high into the air and then came the sound, a crescendo of noise that almost burst our eardrums, all hell was let loose as we disappeared under a pile of rubble.

It had been a para-mine which detonated half a mile away but still devastated half the school – miraculously no-one was killed.

Scrambling from the wreckage breathless, bloodied, covered in muck and broken glass, shocked, but delighted to be in one piece, we stared at each other. It was at that moment, Geoff grinning from ear to ear, a trickle of blood coursing down his cheek uttered those immortal words that will remain with me for ever.

In his broad Lancastrian accent he said quietly

'Eeee, that were a grand-un weren't it!!'

JUDITH HAMILTON
Dada

"Boom" calls the child from its cot,
Dark London lights up.
The young mother reaches out
To comfort baby
And hears her own mother tap
On the bedroom door
To gather them to safety.

Generations of women wait
For men to return.
"See this is Granddad's portrait,
He died to end wars."
"Dada" says the infant girl.
All men are Dada,
A stranger in uniform.

He'd come in the front door as quietly as his boots would allow, putting his kit bag down with the smallest of sighs before opening the kitchen door. "Surprise, I got leave." Robert's arms, which had been open to embrace Stella and the baby, dropped to his side when he saw they were not on their own. Norman, four-eyes Norman, who had been at school with him, sat at the table opposite his wife.

His mother-in-law was the first to greet him. "Hello son, you must be hungry, I'll get you something to eat."

"Thanks, Ma." He gave her shoulder a squeeze as she got up. He loved Stella's mother, more than his own really, and it was best for the moment to live in her house. He turned his attention to Stella who sat with Babs on her knee.

"How are my two favourite girls?"

Before she could answer Norman chipped in. "They're just fine, Bob, I've been keeping an eye on them for you, giving a hand with the vegetables and that. I only live a couple of doors down now since we got bombed out at the old place.

Stella spoke at last. "Hello Robby, this is a surprise. I wish I'd known, I must look a right mess." She brushed her hand nervously through her brown, wavy hair and smiled at her husband. They'd been married well over two years now but she didn't suppose they had spent more than a couple of months together in that time. Every leave she felt as if they were meeting for the first time. Her stomach knotted with excitement.

"Let me help you, Mrs Comrie." Norman snatched the tray from her awkwardly as Dora came back in, dribbling tea on to the tray cloth while making a grab for the bread and jam that was sliding to the edge. "I could do with another cuppa. We've been talking so much I'm quite dry."

"Don't you have to be getting home, Norman, your mother will be wondering where you've got to?" Dora Comrie looked at him, jerking her head almost imperceptibly towards the door.

"Mum knows where I am. Quite at home I am here lately, Bob."

"I can see that but if you don't mind Stella and I have got a lot of catching up to do and not much time to do it in." He lit himself a cigarette without offering Norman one and waited, eyebrows slightly raised.

"Oh, right I see, better be off then. See you before you go back?" Getting no response he turned his attention to Babs. "Bye, pea pod, be good."

"Dada," Babs waved a chubby fist in Norman's direction and beamed as he reluctantly let himself out by the kitchen door.'

"He seems to have got his feet well under the table here, 'Dada' indeed. Always was a toady even at school, blimmen teacher's pet. Hope you're not encouraging him, he was always after what belonged to someone else."

"Don't be cross, Robbie love, he's all right. Been quite a help to Mum and me with the heavy stuff. It's not his fault he's got bad eyes. Come on, forget him, it's just us now. How long have you got home?"

"Only twenty-four hours."

"We'd better make the most of it then, hadn't we?" She twined herself close to him as Dora closed the door gently behind her saying, "I'll say good night now, see you both in the morning. There's a vegetable stew in the larder, just needs heating, if you want some."

They looked at each other, ill at ease now they were alone.

"Hasn't she grown?" he said, picking up the child.

"Unkie," Babs said and poked her finger in his eye.

"No, it's Daddy, say Dada, Babs."

"Unkie," she repeated and started to scream.

"Give her to me, she's tired and that uniform's probably rough on her skin the way you're holding her. I'll heat up the stew, shall I?"

Neither of them was hungry but it was something to do. Robert wouldn't speak of the war to her, not now, not yet. She felt her own hardships at home too trivial to bother him with. It didn't seem decent to go straight up to bed though that's what they both wanted.

Babs screamed in anger when she was put in her cot. "She's used to being with me now, it's easier if we have to go to the shelter," Stella apologised, trying to soothe the screaming child.

"Well she'll have to get unused. Give her to me."

She poked her finger into his eye again as he took her and Robert swore. Stella had never heard him use language like that before but she didn't say anything. "That does it." Robert put Babs in her cot, rubbed his painful eye and then dragged the cot out on to the landing. "She can sleep out here tonight and I don't want you going to her, she's got to learn."

Stella lay silently under him, her heart torn between the anguished wails of the child calling "Dada, Dada," and the needs of the tense and angry man with the callused hands; so far removed from the gentle boy she'd met at the Palais too tired even to ask her to dance till the evening was almost over. After a little while she heard her mother come out and take the frantic baby into her own room. She relaxed as the house fell silent and concentrated on rediscovering the stranger who was her husband.

IAN M HENDERSON
Their Eyes On The North Star

The flickering light momentarily startled him. For an instant his mind had drifted. The flame's pulses had become bright stabs of rifle fire. Every resting moment his mind returned to that awful day.

He was a captain now, few enough officers survived that fight. Pittsburg Landing they called the place. Others mentioned a small, plain church at a crossroads called Shiloh. He didn't much care what they called it. Hell was the best name he could think of, for that day was surely the nearest he'd ever get to the infernal regions while still alive.

The captain looked down at the sheet of paper in front of him. Writing to his wife had been a joy at first. Almost every day he put pen to paper. After Shiloh the letters diminished.

That day he had run. When the ragamuffins in butternut and grey came screaming from the woods with their devilish yell his Illinois regiment broke, running all the way back to the river. A seedy-looking bearded man, looking for all the world like a hard drinking teamster, ordered him back. At that moment the rebels seemed a safer bet than tangling with General Ulysses Grant. He rejoined the fight and now he was a captain.

Looking down at the single sheet of paper he knew that he must write however difficult the process might be. Committing his thoughts on paper might help drive out the demons that beset him. Facing death no longer troubled him making sense of all the death he encountered did. It was the first week of September, he had not written for almost three weeks.

His thoughts drifted back to that last patrol. They set off two mornings ago, the mist hiding the desolate, worn-out land in its grey embrace. The morning sun burnt away the gloom revealing the ill kept fields and scattered ramshackle dwellings. It was a poor land made worse by the ravages of war.

"My dearest Emm." He wrote in the manner he commenced all his correspondence to her. "I know it is some while since I last wrote and that you fret so much as to my welfare."

It was not that his love for Emmeline had diminished, far from it. Too much had happened these last months creating a resolute barrier in his own mind. How could he express his love as eloquently as before when pain and suffering were the only valid emotions.

"I am as well as conditions allow, as are all our friends here who are still with us. I cannot express my gratitude enough for your own letters which are glowing beacons of sanity in a swell of madness."

The captain paused for a while allowing his thoughts to crystallise then recommenced writing.

"It is a dreary country hereabouts and a wonder how the people scrape a living from such poor soil. The few white folks we come across are as impoverished as the Negro they take such pains to lord it over.

"Yesterday while on patrol we came across a broken-down shack in front of which stood a white woman with her six children. I don't suppose she could have been much older than the both of us but the look of her betrayed a life of unending struggle. Yet there was a fierce defiance, almost hatred. Not a word came from any of them as we passed by, just hard defiant stares. They are truly a 'stiff necked people' down here. I never knew what hatred could be instilled in others until this war."

As they marched on the land improved. He wrote of Negro field hands lining the road standing still as the white woman had but with looks of silent hopefulness.

Before the war the captain had no love of slavery but neither did he care much for its victims. Now in their own land the sad uncomplicated faces deeply affected him. What depth of suffering did these expressions mask, he pondered, then continued the letter.

"We saw the plantation house from a good distance. As grand a place as I have ever seen. Red brick built with a broad white porch and four columns, in the Grecian style, flanking the entrance. Of its owners there was no sign nor of any field hands or even the house slaves."

"The reason became clear enough. In the barn we found what I took to be the house slaves hanging dead from a crossbeam. We found the others, twenty or so, hiding in the fields.

One of the field hands told us the owner fled south when our army came, leaving the house slaves to look after the place. He even gave them a letter of authority. Two days before we arrived a detachment of rebel cavalry came by, took them for looters and hung them all. We found the owner's letter crumpled in the mud."

Like his men he came to see slavery as the root cause of the war. The old notion of simply restoring the Union had changed. All they had seen and witnessed brought on the realisation that until slavery was utterly destroyed there would be no peace in their land.

"We gave those poor wretches a decent burial and said a few words over them. The surviving Negroes sang a strange, mournful song the words of which we knew not. We returned to camp the way we came, the Negroes following behind, a sad, helpless throng but looking resolutely ahead, their eyes on the north star."

The captain had finished his letter expressing his love and hopes for the future. He promised he would write again soon and briefly mentioned that another advance was rumoured.

Those hopes were never fulfilled. On September 19th 1862 the Union army clashed with a rebel force near the small village of Luka, Mississippi. Soon after four in the afternoon the captain was killed as his regiment took part in an attack on General Little's rebel division. That letter proved to be his last.

J HINDE
Margin Of Error

From the chapel the path wound through beach and chestnut trees opening into a wide, white cross filled glade. Each cross was clean and weatherworn, and bore the names and details of long dead sons of France.

The WW1 cemetery lay quiet beneath a summer sun; its silence interrupted by occasional exclamations when a visitor found something of interest, or a soldier that they knew or sought. Nearby, the sudden sound of anger drew my thoughts from the grave of my old comrade Emile Loubart.

"SHAME! This one is only 19! What a shame... and for what!" I carefully turned to see the owner, slowly moving along the flower decked graves, not 3 metres away. She had the pretty face, and a rose complexion of her race. "Excuse, Mademoiselle," I bowed and said in English, "Please forgive an old man a moment's indiscretion, but I heard your remark, which asked the question: 'For what?'"

Her cheeks became two crimson flowers. "Oh!" she said more to her female companion, who merely shrugged and walked on past. "I didn't mean." Her eyes were green and bright.

"Of course you didn't." I shrugged in turn as the eyes took in my medals and the empty sleeve.

"But, so many," she continued with such sadness in so young a face.

I was on my annual visit from my home in Paris and, in the hot sun, felt a need to rest. I beckoned to a seat nearby. "Please, Mademoiselle, if you will kindly permit.... Perhaps I can explain. You see, these men," and my good arm slowly swept across the sea of stone, "are my comrades, my regiment and they died for France...and horses."

We were now seated below green branches in which small birds would chirp and dart inside their cooling shade.. "Horses?" My new found companion said aloud. "I don't understand, or were they cavalry?" She smoothed her dress and settled back expectantly.

"Not so," I replied. "Infantry...proverbial cannon fodder!" Her puzzled expression fuelled my story…

The Germans had over-run our Portuguese allies, turning our Front onto a full retreat. The British were compelled to stop the columns, fleeing in their desperate thousands before the onslaught of the massive offensive. Their objective was Paris and a French capitulation.

Enemy planes were strafing the columns along the roads; machine gunning the troops; the horse-drawn guns and supply wagons. Fright and pain, along the overcrowded roads which were littered with the dead and dying shattered carcasses of animals and wagons. Occasionally an army, a human tide, hoped to find safety somewhere for its damaged load. Panic filled the air, like fire and far off shellbursts helped to feed the flames!

In a large, ornate, Rococo styled ballroom of a chateau 60 miles behind the lines, the general entered and enquired: "What is the news?" and yawned.

Regimental dinners were a bore, and went on far too long! An officer; red tabs fixed to his collars and one of many, pointed to a large pin flagged dotted cover that hid a long oak dining table placed there for the purpose.

A lighted crystal chandelier reflected off the General's map of France. "Still falling back, sir," he said scathingly, "at this rate the blighters will have us in the sea!" The general coughed.

"No one made a stand?" he barked.

The shrill sound of a telephone accompanied the entrance of a mudspattered despatch rider who saluted, then handed a message to a major...who read it then stabbing at the map, called out: "Here...and here and here!" at which another 'Red Tab' drew a thick red zig-zag line between the points.

"Etaires! sir," exclaimed he who held the phone. "The message!" snapped the General, and, monocle adjusted, read through the desperate words:

10-4-1918. Secret/Immediate.

TAKING EXCESSIVE CASUALTIES. EIGHT HORSE TEAMS AND SUPPORT AFFECTED. ALL UNITS ENSURE HORSES SAVED... REPEAT... DISREGARD HUMAN CASUALTIES, SAVE THE HORSES AT ALL COSTS.

The sun had fallen below the tress. It was cold now and my young companion looked puzzled. "I still don't understand," she said with irritation.

"It was the historians," I explained, "who, after the War, found out that despite the heroic efforts of my comrades, lying here today, the German Army had to halt their offensive and retire in any case!"

She suddenly surprised me and blurted out, "Napoleon?"...

"Yes," I agreed, "the enemy had outrun it's own supply lines. Without fresh ammunition and other essentials, the advance could not continue. The rest is history!"

I still receive a postcard from her... Mon dieux! If only I was young again!

ROBERT HOGG
Tobruk Remembered

World War Two, The Western Desert, 1941

My unit, 1st Battalion Northumberland Fusiliers, a motorised machine gun unit was part of the garrison in Tobruk along with the 9th Australian Division and various other units. It was quite a large defensive perimeter and some sectors were much quieter than others. During the nine months siege the only relief a company got was to be moved to a quieter sector for a spell.

Each gun section had three gun positions. One was the normal day time position, the second was a night firing position nearer to the enemy lines and the third was an alternative day position to which the section could be moved if it came under intensive shelling if it had been spotted by the enemy.

There was a saying, a machine gun found is a machine gun lost. This meant that if the enemy found a position he never let up until it was destroyed. That meant it was lost to us.

On one occasion when we were being shelled, the Platoon Commander, who had recently joined us asked me if one ever got used to it. I could only speak for myself, of course, but I said no, each attack was as terrifying as the last.

Our camouflage must have been pretty effective, as we rarely had to use the alternative positions. During the day we lay doggo. Even when an enemy spotter plane came within rifle range, we chose to leave him alone rather than make our presence known.

Talking of shooting down planes, on St George's Day 1941 we counted twenty one enemy planes shot down over and around Tobruk. One of the pilots who had baled out landed a short distance in front of one of our gun positions. He did not move and was left until dark. He was alive and had a pistol in his hand under his jacket but made no attempt to use it. He had a broken leg and kept repeating schwein-hund as he was carried away.

When we moved forward for a night shoot, the Australians would send out a patrol to observe the effect of it. On one occasion they came back jubilant as we had caught Jerry in the act of changing over units and both were in the open totally unprepared for attack. There was nearly always an argument when a patrol was going out, as all the Ozzies wanted to go, and were annoyed if not chosen. Even in Tobruk they could find the time and place for a game of pitch and toss.

Half an hour before dawn we always 'stood to' prepared for a dawn attack. I remember one occasion, when we stood down, I went forward to the Australian positions in front of us to find everyone asleep. There was not even a sentry to challenge me. They said they were not worried because we 'Pommies' never slept.

Early one morning, before stand to, we heard tanks move into our vicinity. A sergeant went to have a chat with them but came racing back to say they were Jerries. Soon we heard our own tanks approaching and we witnessed a tank battle over our heads. One armour-piercing shell went into our underground cookhouse. Luckily, no one was astir and it passed over them and buried itself in the wall of the dugout. Fortunately the Jerries were driven back.

We surfaced only at night and as Platoon Sergeant, I visited each of the sections. One night a shell fell quite close to me which made me jump right into a tangle of barbed wire. Then a flare went up and I felt the enemy would see me. Then a Spandau opened fire but its tracer bullets showed it was not me he was after.

Another night as I reached a section, a lad called Scott was holding forth as they sat on the side of the gun pit. As I listened to him, his voice seemed to ring a bell from the past. I asked him if he had a brother who used to work on a farm in East Heddon. He said yes his brother Billy. I knew him very well. He used to come to our farm to play quoits and he entertained us with his mouth organ. Scott said he was then a fighter pilot.

There were no facilities for training in Tobruk, and the Commanding Officer was not satisfied with the standard of replacements we were getting. He got permission to set up a machine gun training wing at No 6 Infantry Base Depot at Genefa on the Suez Canal. To this end, Captain Bonham – Carter, Company Sergeant Major Jim Harris and myself were detailed to go and set it up.

We could only leave by destroyer at night, which did a quick turn round as the harbour was shelled most nights. Once clear of it, we travelled at full speed to get as far away as possible before daylight and possible air attack.

Many of us were seasick and lay on the deck rolling in our own vomit. A Petty Officer asked Jim and me if we would like to go down to their mess for breakfast. We said yes but when we smelt the hot bacon and the hot fumes coming from below decks, we decided to give it a miss.

We arrived at Genefa without incident and started from scratch. The Captain was in command, CSM Harris was in charge of stores, administration and training programmes. I was the chief instructor assisted by NCOs passing through when necessary. All reinforcements for machine gun units were assessed and if necessary given further training before joining their units.

It was a welcome break for me, but after some ten or twelve weeks, I was recalled to the battalion on promotion to Company Quartermaster Sergeant.

BARBARA HUMAN
Expecting Me To Answer When I'm Dead

We returned to London in good time for Hitler's first secret weapon, as did thousands of others in the summer of 1943. After four years of war, evacuees were tired of living out of suitcases in other people's homes. The LCC school in which my mother taught returned to its London premises. King's College moved back from Bristol to The Strand; I was eighteen and had been accepted there.

The stored contents of our pre-war home had been destroyed in the blitz, so our suitcases held all our possessions. Thanks to National Government grants and utility furniture, we made our new flat quite comfortable, on the top floor of a mansion block in Maida Vale.

During bombing raids that winter, most of us in the building discovered an instinct which was later to save our lives: a fear of being buried if we sheltered downstairs.

In 1944 we were alarmed by the arrival of V1s, or 'flying bombs'. In a world long accustomed to guided missiles, it is hard to imagine the shock of our first encounter with aircraft flying all by themselves, directed from hundreds of miles away.

On a light night in June, I removed my bedroom blackouts before lying down. Then I found myself gazing round the room, convinced that I would never see it again. "Don't be silly," I told myself, and went to sleep.

At half-past one, I awoke suddenly. As I discovered later, nobody else was startled, but at that same moment our neighbour's cat howled in terror and hid under the bed. I felt a powerful urge to run out to the passage, since my bed stood beneath a large window; but again I told myself not to be silly.

After half an hour, the air raid warning sounded, and simultaneously I heard a flying bomb. Almost immediately, the sound changed as it began to lose height. I rushed to the passage deciding not to wake my mother because her bed was in a safe corner of her room and time had run out. The engine cut, the bomb descended with a screech, and my last conscious thought was, "I am to die now".

In the blackness, my mother's voice called my name. Dazed

with concussion, I thought, "She's daft, expecting me to answer when I'm dead". Deciding to view the next world, I opened my eyes and peered through a gap in the portion of roof which had fallen on me. Rearing up before me was a huge sheet of flame.

Disconcerted, I changed my mind about answering my mother. Then I found that my mouth was packed full of dirt; I was not dead, after all. Slowly, with Mother's help, I crawled out from the wreckage. Neither of us had broken bones, and we were not yet feeling our multiple cuts and bruises; so we thought we were perfectly all right, apart from my dizzy head. The great flame died down. The bomb had fractured and ignited a gas main behind the building, and it burned itself out harmlessly; a miracle.

More miracles followed. Leaving the flat, we found the staircase intact, but covered thickly with broken glass. Our clothing was cut to ribbons and we were barefoot; yet we walked downstairs without cutting our feet. Since all doors had been torn off, we could look into each kitchen on our way down. The doors had gone from all the coalite stoves, leaving piles of glowing coals exposed; yet not one coal had fallen out. We were saved from fire again.

We stepped out of the building to cheers from the crowd of survivors in the road; they had been worrying about us. Then we were collectively caught up in a burst of joy. We were alive, with all our arms and legs; we had been wonderfully delivered.

Our elation vanished when we suddenly realised that six people were missing. ARP men and ambulances arrived, and the bodies were found, all together. They had been sheltering on the ground floor.

We stood silent while the dead were carried out. Then Mother and I gratefully accepted shelter with neighbours who had merely lost their windows. Once there it was, as always, a little thing which brought home a great loss: I was plunged into desolation because I did not have even a toothbrush.

Our kind neighbours gave us clothes; they were much too big and looked terrible, but to us they felt wonderful. In the morning, walking to the bank to report the loss of our cheque books, I could not understand the gasps and horrified cries of all the people I passed. I was still physically numb and until I eventually looked into a mirror I had no idea that my face was a swollen mass of cuts and multicoloured bruises.

Mother and I went back to our flat to see if we could retrieve anything. It was open to the sky and ankle-deep in rubble. My bedroom had disappeared, sliced off the building. I had lost all my books and all my first-year lecture notes.

The furniture was ruined except for Mother's wardrobe. The clothes inside seemed undamaged. Happily I took hold of two dresses; then my hands, when I opened them, were covered in blood. The clothes were full of powdered glass. We could not salvage anything.

We were departing when I noticed the telephone, poking out of the rubble, and remembered that I had not explained my absence from college. I lifted the receiver – and heard the dialling tone! There in the ruins I talked with my tutor.

After tea we left London, thankfully, to spend a few days with friends far away from the bombing. That night we both started to relax, and became aware of our aches and pains but we were fortunate compared with others.

Five months later, in another London flat, we started all over again...

EDWARD HUNTER
Yours Sincerely

France, in the Autumn of 1916. A dirty old town in Picardy that lacks compassion and seems devoid of all reason. All buildings are bomb-ravaged and bare. Desperation mixes easily with the smell of cordite that hangs in the air. Screams rattle through empty houses, echoing off blood spattered walls. Death has left its calling card delivered to every street corner.

"Oyez, oyez, read all about it. Murder and mayhem set up home in northern France."

The Grim Reaper's ominous message is conveyed with unrestrained glee. Misery is at epidemic proportions and nobody can find the wherewithal to prevent this catastrophe from continuing. Man-made craters shape the landscape where birds refuse to sing anymore. What was once plush, rolling, verdant countryside is now a pitiful, barren, black and desolate land. All trees and greenery laid to waste. Young men, boys really, their hollow eyes haunted by hopeless despair, retreat hastily in the forlorn hope they might make it back to a trench or a foxhole and relative safety.

"Over you go, get out and fight."

They hear the orders bellowing at them repeatedly. Orders that must be obeyed, must be adhered to. No-man's land is there for the taking. Hear the bugle, dance to the tune. Sarn't Major's right, he's always right.

A brain-splitting shell lands inches away. Another moon-like crater instantly appears. The smell of rotting flesh and decay hang in the mist. As the nostrils fill up on it, the stomach turns over once more. But you learn not to part with your breakfast such as it was. Even in this hell some things are precious. The sight of limbs or heads ripped from their sockets becomes all too commonplace. Blood and mud gel inexorably making the latter softer and the former unrecognisable, but you still keep your breakfast.

Smudger and Tommy, Tommy and Smudger. That's how it was. That's how it would always be. Whether it was the playground or the battlefield nothing would separate them. Infantrymen both, they would take up their arms, with every brother, father and son. Kitchener needed them to fight for their country. They would do it with pride and with honour. No matter that millions might die, this was their chance to be men.

Politicians asked questions in the "House", ordinary people wrote letters to "Sir" in "The Times". The public wanted answers. Who was responsible for the death of their loved ones? Young boys had signed up for fun and adventure, with the promise to free France and the low countries from tyranny. Not one of those young men was aware of the horrendous fate waiting them. They were promised "a land fit for heroes" at the recruiting office and on railway platforms. A global challenge and their chance to be a part of it.

Smudger and Tommy, Hans and Fritz. The names didn't matter, nor the uniforms. They were all casualties of war. Cannon fodder for the powers that be. No quarter was given, no prisoners were taken. The fittest survive and every man for himself "stretcher bearer, stretcher bearer" booms out across no-man's land interspersing the sound of whistling shells.

"On your toes, lads, or this man will die," barked the Sergeant. If there's a bullet with your name on it it's to be avoided at all costs. 5% common-sense and 95% luck might see you through the day. One false move would see you in Hell.

Smudger and Tommy had little option back home. The dole or the army awaited them. The "King's shilling" seemed more appealing at the time. Six months on and sharing the same foxhole they reminisced in their minds of warm summer days, singing and dancing, garden fetes and picnics. Now in mid-winter they're in France and the reality that is war. Enemy voices float on the mist. It's as if you can reach out and touch them. Your mind can drift to warm parlour fires and Sunday morning strolls. Church choirs harmonising while fish play in the stream. Green rolling countryside – smell the clean air.

All replaced by blackness and carnage. Rifles, bayonets, bombs and grenades. Everyone a killing machine. There'll be none of this when we're back in Blighty. Ma and Pa will cheer loudly "There's our boy", they'll beam with pride. Smudger and Tommy will march side by side grinning at each other like Cheshire cats, gleaming rows of medals pinned to their chests. Two home town boys filled with honour and pride. No more tin pot generals telling them what to do.

Tommy is hit, he slumps to the floor. Smudger can't reach him as hard as he tries. He's trapped by snipers. He must get to him, at whatever cost, his best friend depends on him. They're comrades, brothers-in-arms. He can't desert him now. Slowly, finally, he's got him. He pulls him over his shoulders slumped, dead weight. He stumbles through this thick mud – every footstep seems an eternity. Tommy's skin feels colder. He is colder now than he deserves to be. A sniper's bullet rips through Smudger's midriff, both bodies crash to the floor. Smudger can't move, Tommy is too heavy. Damn this war. His mind is drifting back to the hills. To Annie and her golden curls. To a time of innocence and romance. Tommy is too heavy, his breath is shorter. Smudger knows they are both close to their maker. Time to make peace, to remember Mum and Dad, brothers, sisters. To remember they were heroes whether they stood or fell.

Smudger and Tommy lay dead, entwined forever. All on the orders of the great and the good. Let them be remembered in despatches, on a headstone or cross. It is not to be ignored that they still died alone.

"Dad, Dad, there's a letter from the Ministry. Could it be about our Smudger and Tommy?"

Smudger's dad opened the letter apprehensively. It read, "We're sorry to inform you of the loss of your son. He was lost in action at the battle of Paschendaele. Your son died a hero. You should be very proud."

Yours sincerely.

JOHN HYGATE
Conduct To The Prejudice

It was a moonlit summer night, a lot of years ago, on the coast of what had then been Palestine. From all over Europe those who had survived Hitler's attempt to exterminate the Jews were trying to reach their promised land. Of the many thousands clamouring to get in only a few were admitted. It was a situation made for exploiters and they weren't slow to profit by it. The technique was to charter anything that would float, cram it with this walking freight, keep them alive for the short trip from Marseilles to Haifa, then land them from boats on to the beaches along from the port.

On this particular night I had been in command of a patrol whose job it was to seek out these poor devils as they landed and turn them over to the Navy who put them back, if they could, on the ships they had come in. It was one of the worst things I had ever had to do and, as a rule, I took good care to avoid picking anyone up. This time, though, there was no avoiding it.

God knows what lies they'd been told on the ship but they came straight up to us, chattering away like a works outing just off the coast. Then they saw our guns. The chattering died away and you could hear the lap of the waves and a truck engine fading away on the coast road behind us. I suppose where they'd come from, soldiers with guns were bad news whatever the colour of their uniform.

The silence stretched out for quite a while, then there was some subdued muttering that I couldn't understand and one of them detached himself from the group and came up to me. I lowered the Sten so that it pointed at his feet instead of his stomach and there was a general letting out of breath.

"English soldiers?" he asked.

"Yes," I said, "we're English soldiers and our orders are to take you to the port and put you back on the ship."

He turned round and repeated this to his party, speaking in German. The commotion that broke out was even worse than before. Some women among them started wailing and the whole thing was getting out of hand. I took a couple of paces forward and raised the Sten again. Again there was silence except for some choked off sobs from one of the women.

"Listen," I said to the spokesman. "You must keep your people quiet or we shall all be in trouble." Until that moment I hadn't decided what to do but as soon as the words were out I knew the decision had been made. It was obvious, too, that the other chap had realised there was some hope for them. He stood up a bit straighter; I think he thought he was standing to attention and I could tell he was searching inwardly for the right words.

I felt we couldn't wait all night while he made up a speech so I took hold of him by an arm and walked him a few paces up the beach away from his group. As I walked him off I saw, out of the corner of my eye, Corporal Harris step forward, Sten in hand, and take over; that was the sort of unit we were, you didn't have to give many orders. We stopped.

"Look," I said. "Have you enough English to understand me properly?"

"Yes," he said, straightaway. "I have lived in England for five years before the war, in..."

"Never mind where," I said. "We haven't got time for a chat. Understand this. I haven't seen you and you haven't seen us. If you walk your people along the beach for about half a mile you'll see a signal box on the railway. Go on past it for a hundred yards or so, cross the railway and then the road and keep walking inland. With luck you should come up with some of your own people, they look out for you, but get as far away from the coast as you can while it's dark. And remember, no-one saw you, you came straight off the boat, no matter who asks."

I could feel the relief he felt. To have got so near and then been turned back would have broken him. I had some idea of what he had come from, though not much about the camps had been released. The names Belsen, Auschwitz, Treblinka weren't yet part of the language but enough had filtered through for us to have an inkling of what had happened.

"Come on," I said. "Get moving and if you want to live keep your people quiet." Quite a bit of good old English reticence must have rubbed off on him during those five years before the war because all he said was "Thank you".

"Good luck," I said, and put my hand out. Probably not all that many people had offered to shake hands with him during his last few years and what with that and the relief it was much as he could do to keep up the stiff upper lip performance. To his great credit, though, he managed it, though he did enclose my hand in both of his.

I hoped they made it and after all these years I still do.

D JANSEN
A Soldier's Song

The elderly soldier, seated on the bus, had scarcely glanced at the newspaper headlines, when his gaze was arrested by "In Memorium, Pt Denis Collins of the Middlesex Regiment, 11 November 1916, the Somme, beloved father and brother".

The dreary, dark clouds, which had threatened since dawn, were unburdening themselves. The rain outside was splashing up the earth as it fell so harshly on the ground and mud spatters now covered the new passengers climbing aboard the bus. Not as muddy as them, not as wet and as chilling as the trenches. He shuddered and buried his head in the newspaper.

The instructions had been simple, for the Bombardier had to take a three day duty with his patrol at the Listening Post in No Man's Land. The boot black night they left, provided ideal cover for the journey across the barbed wire to 'Home Sweet Home', as the wearily drunken notice said at the shell hole, which now served the listening living. The dismal days in the stench and squalor passed with little to do. The usual exchange of shelling with sporadic flares relieved the monotony, but it was a quiet patrol.

The Bombardier became concerned when the expected relief patrol was some hours overdue. The dry rations were nearly finished, the water too and they only had the bare essentials of ammunition. Their eyes showed the ache to be back in the comparative safety of the Front Line, somebody would come soon, wouldn't they? There was little they could do except their duty and eke out the meagre remnants of supplies with the last cigarette carefully shared among them.

Time stretched endlessly. Forgotten, after all that, they had been forgotten! Feeling the responsibility of his rank, the Bombardier reviewed the impossible situation and decided to return the patrol for fresh orders. They reached the trenches with little problem for the enemy was too busy regrouping to notice them.

The Sergeant faced them and, like a wailing banshee, realising his own error, verbally lacerated them. "Return to your post or I'll have you all shot!" Their protests froze mid-sentence. The devastated men crawled back from whence they came. When the Front Line moved forward only the Bombardier had survived the swift gas attack which had seen to the disposal of the Listening Post and its occupants.

The driver consulted his watch and the bus juddered to a sudden halt. Over the radio, the message came, "Prepare to observe the two minutes silence," followed rapidly by the distinctive chimes of Big Ben, at their most sombre on this eleventh hour of Remembrance Day.

Earlier that morning he had been to East Street Market to pass the time. Isn't that what old soldiers did, just filled the time between glory for King and country and death? Gassed and wounded, he had returned to civilian life and a hero's welcome. What good is that when you've left your friends behind dead in No-Man's Land? He accepted his own survival as destiny for one day he would avenge Collins and the others.

Unexpectedly the opportunity he had waited for was there. The Bombardier saw him near the fish stall, or was it? So many times before there had been false starts, look-alikes, or just imagination playing tricks. His chest tightened with the anxiety and he began to stalk his prey, keeping close to the market stalls to conceal his hunting tactics. Somehow it wasn't like he'd envisaged. The spectre of his nightmares had aged and withered, with hair now white and the tattered rags that covered his ravaged, wasted body hung on him like a scarecrow. He was shuffling along the gutters, picking up the rotting fruit and vegetables.

The soldier fingered the needle-sharp blade of the bayonet in his raincoat pocket, kept so ever since that fateful day on the Somme, waiting for such a moment. The ragbag halted, trapped, caught by the plastic tie around his feet and ankles, carelessly thrown by the stallholder from a box of fruit. As fast as he struggled, the plastic grew tighter and panic was evident on his skeleton-like face. He began to talk to himself now visibly frightened and gibbering.

The Bombardier in civvies stopped sharply and wheeled at speed across the uneven street, bayonet now visible in his hand and at the ready. He paused by the defenceless man and there was a glint of steel as he slashed with the blade. With one swift gesture it was over, all those years of waiting.

The body slumped to the curb, bowed over, winded by the sudden and unexpected freedom from the coils that had bound him. "Thanks, mate!" said the sergeant, just another casualty of war. The hapless victim groped for a cigarette butt in the gutter, dribbling as he did so. The Bombardier turned abruptly, not looking back, only the sounds of the market ringing in his ears, mocking the whine and crump of shells.

The windscreen wipers brought him from his reverie with a sickening, scratching sound. As he peered through the rain, he thought he could see the red of poppies descending, but as he wiped the bus window mist away, he saw that it was only the red of the request stop. He was startled by the booming of the guns rapidly followed by the haunting notes of the Last Post from the Cenotaph and then the sudden jarring of the bus engine.

He could not bring Collins and the others back by revenge, but had he betrayed them by showing mercy? Somehow, he knew that they would have understood, for he had not dishonoured them by adding yet another death to the carnage that had claimed their young lives.

His destination reached, he unsteadily stepped from the bus onto the slippery grey pavement. As he moved away with his head up, shoulders back, and arms swinging, he appeared to march along and he was whistling a soldier's song.

R E JEFFRIES
Not A Grand Finale

One of the side effects of the second world war in which I was involved, was the exodus of the Jews from the horrors of Europe.

It all started on a lovely June, on a grassy bank overlooking Portland Bill. I was lying on my back holding hands with a dark-haired young lady, who claimed to be the current Weymouth beauty queen. It was probably true, because time passed, and when I eventually sat up and looked down to the bay, I was dismayed to see a flurry of activity around the warship at anchor there – HMS Sheffield.

This was the ship that was to take me out to the Mediterranean to take command of three motor fishing vessels, that had been converted to patrol vessels!

I gave the lady a hurried kiss and stumbled down the hill to the jetty, commandeered a launch and sped across the bay, waving my arms to the crew on the quarter-deck as they began to weigh anchor.

The officer in command waved back frantically, and I gathered it was too late! I only found out later that in fact he was waving me on.

Finally, I sailed from Portsmouth on HMS Maidstone, and joined MFV 101 and the two other MFVs in Valetta harbour, Malta. These converted fishing vessels had a huge hold which used to contain the fish and were now the crews living quarters. A huge cast-iron stove burned away continuously providing heat and a means of cooking our meals. The crew consisted of a Petty Officer, an engine room artificer and eight seaman, and a dog called 'Sippers'.

After a couple of months of overwhelming fun with the hospitable Maltese families, and their very chaperoned daughters, we sailed in convoy to the East, via Crete and Cyprus, to our destination – Haifa, Palestine.

Our three ships were berthed in a compound, guarded by the Palestine Police. On the first morning after our arrival I was woken by a horrific smell wafting through the porthole of my cabin. I peered out and saw in the bay a huge ship, battered and rusty, sprouting hundreds of men, women and children from its decks and port holes, some waving, others draped listlessly over the rails. These were the illegal immigrants desperately seeking a lasting haven.

The British White Paper of 1939 had limited the intake of immigrants to 70,000 and when we arrived this allocation had been used up, and under pressure, the British Government substituted a new policy of 1,500 a month. This was unacceptable to the Haganah (the Jewish resistance force) and when an Anglo-American recommendation of 100,00 certificates was rejected by the British, all hell was let loose. Bridges and railways wrecked, curfews were imposed and British troops were forbidden to associate with the Jews.

Warships were strung out along the coast to block the entry of the leaky, rusty cockleshells – but still many got through. From 1945 to 1947, 70,000 in defiance of the law, secretly wormed their way through, and disappeared into the safety of the local established families.

Later that morning we were instructed by the Commander of the base on our duties. We were to arrange a roster to patrol outside Haifa, day and night, reporting signs of immigrants making for the shore, and on the look-out, especially at night for members of the Haganah stealing out to the anchored destroyers, trying to attach limpet mines to the sides of the vessels. In this we were helped by the famous Lieutenant, Commander 'Buster' Crabbe adorned with his fiery red cheek whiskers, who dived to recover the mines.

One very dark night, I was on patrol around the bay. The lights of Haifa were twinkling in the distance, and Terry, one of the seaman was in the bow, sweeping the sea with a hand searchlight. A quarter of a mile away we could see (and smell) the hulk of a newly arrived ship, waiting to be dealt with by the authorities in the morning.

Suddenly there was a loud scream from the ship, and a phosphorescent dent appeared in the calm waters. We turned towards it. The searchlight picked up a struggling figure, who did not seem to able to swim. We pulled alongside and dragged out a whimpering little boy.

He stared jabbering and crying. Joe, the Petty Officer bundled him down into the hold, stripped off his soaking clothes, wrapped him in a blanket and sat him in front of the roaring stove. The next day we were able to re-unite him with his family who by now had been herded into a camp along the coast.

When I was off duty, I often changed into civvy clothes (it was dangerous to be in uniform) and sat at the nearest bar for a beer. I became friendly with a young Jewish girl called Ruth who served behind the bar. Her mother was French and she liked to be called Rutienne.

I had only a few weeks to go before my spell in Haifa was over, and I would go home to be demobbed, so I asked her if she would like to go to the pictures one night. She was a little doubtful, because Jewish girls were not supposed to be friendly with British boys. However we arranged to meet outside the cinema and quickly slunk into our seats in the dark.

After the show, we peered out of the foyer. Rutienne went first and I followed a little behind. Suddenly there was a shout and a scuffle and I just saw her being whisked into a waiting car by two burly men.

She was not behind the bar the next evening when I went in. Nobody would venture to tell me where she was, or what had happened. I never saw her again.

JOHN ALAN JONES
The Hunt

The black uniform shoes paced up and down the bridge of the anti-submarine trawler. Six feet above them the face of Lieutenant Commander Briant, R.N.R. wore a concerned expression. He looked at his watch, it was twelve noon. They had been at sea for five hours. Time was running out.

Briant stopped pacing and entered the small radio room. He looked at Lockheart whose face was keen with concentration as he listened through his head phones for any sound from the quarry below them.

"Any contact yet, Lockheart," asked Briant.

"No, not yet, Sir," answered Lockheart.

"Carry on."

"Yes, Sir."

Briant resumed his pacing of the bridge.

He had been in charge of the seven hundred ton anti-submarine trawler for three years. During that time they had seen a lot of action: seven convoys; three in the Mediterranean and four in the murderous North Atlantic.

When they were not fighting the enemy they were fighting the elements on those convoys to Murmansk and Archangel. Each convoy seemed an eternity with death so close at hand. If they were torpedoed they would either burn to death or freeze in the icy sea. No man's thoughts dwelt on the possible fate that awaited him.

The ship had a good record; six aeroplanes shot down and two submarines sunk. Although she was an old and slow deep sea trawler, Briant was proud of his ship and crew. They both served him well.

Briant's thoughts turned to his new number one officer. He glanced over his shoulder to the port bridge wing where Thompson was surveying the horizon through a pair of binoculars.

When war had broken out Thompson had volunteered for the Royal Navy. He had a Commission and after five weeks training at "King Alfred", he was posted to Plymouth where he spent the next ten months laying buoys and mine fields. He had become disillusioned with the quiet life and had wanted to feel more a part of the war effort. He had applied for an anti-submarine course and after training had been posted to Briant's command. Thompson had joined the ship at the crack of dawn that morning and the orders had come from the Admiralty to put to sea.

Briant was thinking about Thompson's lack of experience when the steward came onto the bridge with mugs of tea and corned beef sandwiches. Briant received the tea with enthusiasm but looked upon the corned beef with contempt. Every man in Scapa Flow had eaten the stuff until it was coming out of their ears. Briant felt sick looking at them.

Thompson picked up his tea and clasped the mug lovingly. "Do you think that there are any enemy subs around here, Sir," he asked.

Briant looked him in the eye and said, "I don't know, son."

Thompson resented being called "son". He felt out of place with such a war hardened crew and why hadn't Briant shown the orders from the Admiralty to him? he wondered. He turned away and resumed his post on the port bridge wing.

As the little ship rolled and pushed its way through the unrelenting sea, every man was aware that the hunt was on. They waited nervously at their posts for something to happen. The lull before the storm, some thought.

Suddenly, Lockheart shouted. "I have contact, Sir." The storm appeared to be imminent. Briant ran into the radio room.

"Good man. How far off?"

"Five hundred yards. Five degrees to port, Sir."

"Five degrees to port, cockswain," ordered Lockheart.

"Aye, aye, Sir," answered the cockswain, turning the wheel.

"Four hundred yards," shouted Lockheart. The tension was building up. Thompson could feel the hairs on the back of his head standing up.

"Two hundred yards," continued Lockheart.

"One hundred yards."

"Simultaneous echo, Sir," said Lockheart. The quarry was directly below them.

Briant pressed the "Fire" button and a wail sounded from the stern of the vessel. A trigger was pulled and a single depth charge rose slowly into the air and fell into the sea with a splash. Thompson held his breath as he waited for more depth charges to be fired off but he waited in vain. Only one depth charge was fired. He could not understand it. Only one? They will be lucky to hit a submarine with only one depth charge, he thought.

All available eyes stared hypnotically at the ever increasing circle that was left by the depth charge on the surface of the sea. No-one spoke.

There was a dull thud and then a great roar as a cloud of water reached for the sky and, as if in a desperate attempt to become part of the ether, it transformed into a mist but fell back into the sea. The stern of the ship was lifted half way out of the water with the force of the explosion and it shook from stern to stern as if in acknowledgement of a good try.

Briant and Thompson looked over the side of the ship in silence. Suddenly, floating on the surface was proof of their kill. Thousands of them. Thompson's eyes grew larger and his jaw dropped as he realised the truth.

"Suffering catfish!" he exclaimed in disbelief.

Briant put his hand on Thompson's shoulder and said.

"No, son, Cod. There will be fish and chips in Scapa tonight."

RON JONES
Lack Of Moral Fibre

N. Africa

Bridie, I can't say where I am exactly – even though I'm not sending this. If Jerry got hold of my biscuit tin – CARELESS TALK COSTS LIVES.

Yesterday we had a Hurricane go down in no-man's land. They sent out a jeep for the pilot but someone had to guard the plane. Corporal Hill picked me and they took me into the desert and left me with a 303 and five spare rounds. Me and six bullets looking after a shot up Hurricane! It was very hot in the afternoon – bloody cold in the night. First I thought I'd get fried – then I thought I was going to freeze.

I'm all mixed up, Bridie. First time we got strafed I run out in front of the Hurri and started popping off but Corporal Hill grabbed me. He said stop trying to be a hero Jonesy you can't hit a flaming Fock-Wolf 190 with a Lee Enfield! Then I dived under the Hurri but he made me run AWAY from the planes. He said Jerry wasn't after us he was after the planes – leave shooting the planes to the RAF Regiment ack-ack boys.

Then once we got into a scrape in a little Arab town on a 12 hour pass and Jockey Harris fell out with some huge squaddy who started giving him a pasting. I said come on mate, pick on someone your own size. This squaddy was like a tree compared to me and Reg Davis whacked him with a bottle and we legged it. Reg said I had a screw loose if I really wanted to fight a goliath. I said I didn't want to fight no goliaths but someone had to help Jockey.

Bridie, I'm a farmer not a fighting man and like it says we can make swords into ploughs. That's what I want to do – plough. A man can avoid scraps. It's not big to scrap – though when I was younger I got into the odd one. I think a man has to keep himself to himself and look after his family.

The desert was cold but I could've managed – but it was so dark, Bridie. Real darkness moves – did you know that? Then the Hurri started to cool down and make noises. By midnight I was jumping out of my skin.

At night the Ghurkas go out in no-man's land. They have these cookris in their mouths and you can't hear them or see them. If you're standing up they feel your bootlaces. Jerry ties his differently. The wrong way and clop – your head's off. If you're lying down they can tell if you're Jerry from your uniform shoulders. If they're wrong – clop again.

Well, I kept thinking what if they feel my boots and the laces are wrong – clop. Or what if they feel my shoulders and they're wrong. Clop. And there's a snake called the shoelace snake here, Bridie. It eats your laces and in the morning you go to do up your boots and zip – that's it, you're dead.

And anyway I couldn't do anything to save this Hurri if I wanted to. I only had six bullets. If Jerry wanted the plane he'd need a low-loader and eight men at least. If one or two Jerries turned up they couldn't pinch a whole plane and if about eight came – well, I wouldn't have enough bullets even if I shot like Davy Crockett.

So I walked back to camp. But, Bridie, I kept thinking about you and the baby and that maybe this was lack of moral fibre – that I wasn't the man you'd hoped I'd be and that maybe if we had a son you wouldn't want to call him Ron, after me. I nearly went back then. You know, sometimes when a chap does something that looks brave it's because not doing it is more scary that doing it and getting hurt or worse.

But I couldn't look after the Hurri. If one wog came along I could shout WHO GOES THERE and frighten him off but what would an ayrab on a camel want with a bloody big plane anyway?

Well I got back and I went to Corporal Hill. I said, Corp I walked in. Well Corporal Hill his face was a picture. He said walked in from where and I said walked in from where the shot up Hurri is and he looked a bit off and then he seemed to realise something and he said oh shit (pardon my French).

Jest buzz off to your tent Jonesy he said – come see me about eleven. It's that time already, Bridie – that's why I'm writing this letter and putting it in the biscuit tin. I think I'm up on an LMF charge. They can put you away for quite a while for LMF – even shoot you if they want to.

They keep telling us that all this fighting – traipsing across North Africa and I s'pose all the way up Italy some day – getting machine gunned by 190's and standing in the desert guarding shot up Hurris is the same as looking after our loved ones. They keep telling us it's about freedom and not standing for Jerry's shenanigans – give an inch he'll take a mile.

Well, I don' t know, Bridie. I know that I shot at the Fock Wolf 190's but I couldn't help it. And I know I stood up to that squaddy but that was only because he was too big for Jockey Harris. But standing in the cold and dark in the middle of the night next to a shot up Hurri with snakes and Ghurkas after your laces and you can't do anything if Jerry comes after the plane anyway – that doesn't make any sense – and if that's lack of moral fibre then it's lack of moral fibre.

RORY KILALEA
Temba Went Penga

Maybe I just imagined it all... That can happen sometimes. You glance at a person and your eyes lock, caught by something.

As if you've been vacuumed into a fold of time, or memory..

Or it might have been the heat...

I was a black soldier, fighting on the white side. White Africa against black Africa.

The side of right and wrong.

Walking in others' tracks.

The white Commanding Officer smiled as I parked the vehicle in the sun.

The black prisoner sat in the back of our Army Land Rover, wrists chained to his ankles.

There was a grey, fine powder of dust on his dark head, his eyelashes, his boots. His whole shape was shrunken. It wasn't just the manacles. He had always been a prisoner.

"Temba Ndhlovu, top tracker from the anti-terrorist unit," the Special Branch policeman said, flicking off facts as if he was dispensing food rations.

"He was one of us..."

"Had to be arrested by his own men..."

"Men he had fought a war with..."

"They say he went 'penga'...totally out of his tree..."

His own men now examined him like a piece of dead meat.

The white C.O. smiled. "Thirsty work, this war."

"Care for a beer before you leave, Sir?"

The C.O. glanced at the sun. "Why not – we're not pressed for time?"

I wasn't invited.

"Keep an eye on the prisoner."

The white policeman strolled off. Yellow haze wafted up from the dirt. A cold beer would have been good in the heat.

"Shade?" I asked. "You want shade?"

Temba Ndhlovu did not look at me.

So we stayed in the sun. He did not move – even when droplets of sweat trickled into his eyes. He did not move an inch.

I imagined him, proud, strong, loping though the bush.

The gun, not the spear; a warrior tracking animals, not men.

Temba stared at the hot metal floor of the Land Rover as if he was looking for something.

Maybe it was the wild animals of his past.

I stamped my feet to try and keep awake. My boots left deep corrugations on the African dust.

Through the heat Temba saw the tracks.

Guerrilla footstep tracks. Tracks into a village which looked just like home. The village he had left for the Rhodesian war.

Temba clutched his rifle, tried to stop the dull ache of his mind.

He prayed to his ancestors to make it all safe. A place for him to rest.

From the pain of fighting white wars with a black heart. Of fighting with his mind, of silent battles no-one must know, otherwise they would call him mad, penga.

Alcohol helped, until tomorrow.

Then everyday despair sucked sense from his mind, ate at every thought, forgave nothing.

Not even suffering.

Through the mirage of heat he saw a shape.

An old man sat in the shade like his father. He was sharpening a knife with a stone.

He welcomed Temba – Temba nearly cried with relief. It was safe. The enemy had gone.

But then a dark eyed girl slipped from behind a tree, ran ahead of him. He raised his weapon.

She stopped suddenly. Almost brazen. She was young and soft.

And he knew, more than anything, he needed her, it would help the pain.

But then she laughed again. A different sound. Mocking.

"You are not even a black man!" she taunted him.

He looked at his skin – it was black, like hers.

His heat rose quickly, angry dust from the soil.

She gave herself to the Comrades, to those fighting for Zimbabwe, not Rhodesia. He pushed her to the dirt.

"I don't want you!" she spat.

The old father of the village watched the game, battered by the morals of this war.

"You will have me," Temba gestured with his rifle.

The Comrades at night. The Rhodesians by day.

She didn't resist him but she didn't give to him either.

Like dead meat.

So the peace did not come to Temba.

He tried again.

"Black men lose their strength when they pretend to be white men..."

Her soft body mocked him.

The old man stared at Temba's Rhodesian boot prints in the dust.

"You're not a white man, you're a black traitor," he said. But the father did not look at his daughter. Or Temba. He sharpened his knife on the stone.

Temba felt he was following tracks with no end. Even this young girl had refused to share his nakedness.

His last refuge.

When the white soldiers came they found Temba sitting beside the body of a black girl. Under the tree a lifeless old man slumped over a bloody knife.

Temba's rifle lay on the dirt.

It was a clear cut case, they said.

Temba went penga.

The shot had ricocheted through him, killed his mind, sounded in her groin.

As the old man watched the last of his family die.

The heat waves rose around me. Everything looked distorted, unreal. Temba raised his eyes and looked at me.

I felt accused.

I fingered my rifle, uselessly. I wanted to go into the shade. My rifle was too hot to touch. I wondered about letting him escape our tracks, our Rhodesian tracks. Let him go back to the bush.

The C.O. swaggered down the veranda steps, breathing beer.

Like a malaria shiver in the heat.

I put the rifle on safe.

"Once a black man has killed his conscience dies with the victim..." The C.O. observed.

"Yes, Sir..."

Maybe I just imagined it all. That can happen sometimes. From the heat... I drove fast out of the gate, swirling up the dust, trying to hide Temba's shape from me.

But he didn't go away. I stared at the C.O.

He wouldn't go away.
I flicked the rifle off safe.

HAROLD HENRY KING
The Time, The Place, The Action

8th April 1941, the Italians surrendered Massawa on the Red Sea, freeing Eritrea, 14 Squadron, to move from the high humidity and heat of Sudan to other theatres of the war.

The ground crews celebrated in the NAAFI with song and beer before embarking on the SS Khedive Ismael on the 9th April 1941.

"Oh we are leaving Sudan.

In a Cattle Saloon.

We are sailing, by night and by day.

The Skipper, looked over with pride.

He would have blue fit.

If he saw any sick

on the side of the SS Khedive Ismal."

14 Squadron, equipped with Blenheim bombers, arrived at Heliopolis via Port Tewfik on the 13th April 1941. They found Heliopolis with all the comforts that the ground crews could wish for. 14 Squadron was transformed into a fully mobile unit, with new transport, with drivers for each three ton lorry, two lorries for each flight, A, B and C together with wireless and photographic covered lorries, chance light and breakdown lorries, carrying spares, all that was necessary to keep the Squadron flying.

14 Squadron, arrived at Landing Ground number 21 with their 16 Blenheims and 20 newly recruited air crews, were due to leave the Squadron at a critical time with newly promoted senior N.C.O.s in charge of ground crews in the Western desert on the 1st May 1941.

On the first month of operations in the desert, providing a double shock during attacks on German armour, the Blenheim proved to be more vulnerable to the German aircraft machine guns, with heavy losses. With the German airborne invasion of Crete the Squadron attacked Maleme Airfield on the 25th May. More aircrews were lost. Again on the 27 May bombed enemy troop concentrations with the loss of three more aircrews. With 98 sorties in a month, 12 aircraft lost and 27 brave young aircrews killed or missing, ground crews serviced aircraft in the most awful conditions. Sand storms, rain and heat, meals of Bully Beef or MacConachies (mutton and veal stewed) fried, hashed or cold. Water was at a premium, one pint to drink, to wash and shave, airmen in battle-dress looked a sorry sight.

4th July 1941, orders came to move to Palestine, aircraft and their crews flew directly from LC21 to Petah Tiqva near Tel Aviv. The ground crews by lorries to Ismaila, through Gaza strip to Petal Tiqva. The main camp was in part of an Arab orange grove where the ground crews pitched their tents. This made life a little more comfortable, water rations were increased and meals got a little better.

2nd August 1941, orders came to move to Persia, the ground crews and their lorries took six days from Petah Tiqva, via Haifa, Mafrag, on to RAF Station Habbaniya, Iraq, some 800 miles of mostly desert. It was really a hell of a journey, the heat, sand carried by the lorries, no-one wanted to travel behind the lorry in front, they were almost line abreast, travelling at first light to escape the heat, resting at midday, onwards at first light next day.

8th August 1941, the ground crews arrived at Habbaniya. At the entrance to the RAF Habbaniya was a road sign. Pointing east it read, Baghdad 55 miles and pointing west it read, London 3,287 miles. Ground crews were in tents, all the comforts of an overseas RAF camp, showers, swimming pool and a NAAFI, which had over the door a sign which read "Abandon hope all ye that enter here".

21st August 1941, 14 Squadron was the only fully equipped mobile unit, moved to Gaiyarah about 15 miles south of Mosul. Gaiyarah had a runway 1,800 yards long, it was hot and smelly. The Squadron had changed into K.D. from the desert battle-dress, M.T. and aviation fuel was still being supplied in four gallon tins making refuelling difficult.

25th August brought the invasion of Persia by Britain and Russia to safeguard the oil supplies. Persian Authorities complied with the Allied demands. At Gaiyarah on 9th October a photograph of all 14 Squadron's all Ranks was taken, as there were rumours of a move back to the Western desert.

12th October 1941, 14 Squadron left Habbaniya for the return journey of some 800 miles in road convoy. Arrived at Berg El Arab on the 21st October and arrived at L.G. 116 near Fuua. Setting up their tentage camp at Maatern Bagush in late evening, the ground crews lined up for a meal of MacConachies with mess tins at the ready, a mug of hot tea with knife, fork and spoon.

In from the sea came what looked like a very fast Blenheim expecting to see a flare of the colour of the day. Instead they saw four black objects dropping from the aircraft. With cries of "it's not one of ours" the meal queue dived for the ground.

"I've been hit," said one airman, only to find that his mate's mug of hot tea had hit him in the back. Two airmen in the photographic lorry, sat eating their meal, had a direct hit. Both were killed – the enemy aircraft bombs had hit the transport compound.

The Squadron's 27 Blenheims arrived on the 22nd October 1941. Immediately went into action in support of the Eighth Army who were now attacking and advancing into Libya. The Squadron moved to Gambut and Agelebia, where one airman composed a song in December 1941, airmen back in battle-dress as the desert comes cold at this time of year, the song went like this:-

"There is a little place called Agelebia.

Situated just behind the firing line.

Where the Airmen have no song or women.

All they have to drink is Italian wine."

25th December, Christmas Day, Rommel's army in retreat, we were winning the war in the desert. The Squadron had something to celebrate.

JEAN KING
Plenty Of Apple Pie

The end of the war and the beginning of the peace was not proving as happy in our family as was anticipated. My mother finished her job at the munitions factory and was finding lonely days at home rather tame. I had left school and had a long journey to work and my father had reluctantly taken his stirrup pump, bucket and tin helmet back to ARP headquarters. Even worse, my sister's American Captain had been killed flying gliders and she was very sad. We all missed past companionships, united goals and even the danger, and my father, particularly, was very downhearted. His men's outfitting shop was not packed out with customers at the best of times and as clothing was still on coupons, this did not help matters. Everyone struggled to save these for something special, begging and borrowing from other members of the family. Being the youngest, mine were freely distributed and I blame my deep voice on the fact that for the whole of the war I slept in boy's pyjamas and wore their shirts to school.

Dad came home one day with the news that he had, on the spur of the moment, purchased twelve acres of farmland and was going to transform it into an apple orchard. It was Mum's turn to go quiet on us but after a while we all began to get interested. Dad took us to see the plot about ten miles away and it looked like any other field, only worse.

The first job tackled was the erection of a large, corrugated iron shed. This was furnished with the bunks from our underground shelter at home and various other items such as oil lamps and primus stoves. It worked and it was warm but that was about all. The land was prepared with the kind help of the farmer and in due course we planted 1,000 young, selected apple trees. Most of them seemed happy to be there and Dad was pleased with our efforts. He was returning to his old self so our extra work was worthwhile. Most light evenings and definitely weekends would see us all doing our allocated jobs to get it shipshape.

Mum was seconded to be in charge of six beehives, fully occupied. After all, she was heavy-handed and sharp with the rest of us so she was obviously the right choice. The bees responded to her magnificently and worked their little bodies relentlessly to please her. She never once got stung, which is more than can be said for the rest of us!

Planning permission for a bungalow was applied for and granted and things really started to move. The orchard took care of itself for a few months and loads of friends with varied skills performed incredible tasks to help us construct a suitable dwelling. It was small but light and well-built and we happily moved in.

About this time Mum found a young jay with a broken wing and, after a few repairs with sticky tape and cotton, "Peter" took up residence in an empty birdcage we had and seemed quite happy to be there. His wing mended nicely and the day soon came to release him. Mum shed a few tears and Dad opened the cage. After lots of fluttering and a few hesitant tries, Peter took off, circled the house and then disappeared. All that week Mum grieved and constantly checked to see if he was in the vicinity, but no sign. The cage had been left in the outhouse, the door of which was always open, and about a couple of weeks later Mum found Peter fast asleep there. He lodged with us for a year, getting his fair share of titbits and following Mum round on her daily walks through the orchard, flying from tree to tree and dive-bombing her every so often. I think he loved our Mum more than we did. One day some flighty female came calling and he was smitten. Without a goodbye they flew off together, never to be seen again.

To keep herself busy my mother bought 100 day-old Rhode Island chicks and these were reared in our old empty shed. With the aid of heat lamps and lots of cuddles most of them made it to adulthood and made excellent layers. They seemed to have a calming effect on my volatile mother and she became more at ease with herself and with us too.

My dear sister had fallen in love again and was really quite decent towards me. There had always been sisterly arguments and scenes because of the difference in our ages but she had "switched off" since the bereavement and did not rise to any irritable teasing on my part. Now I could do nothing wrong (well, hardly) and was even sometimes included in quite personal conversations with our mother. I was indeed walking tall.

I remember seeing my father, a successful year later, sitting under a tree full of blossom, in an orchard alive with colour and plump chickens and it was obvious that happiness and fulfilment had caught up with him at last. I was aware then that family life, as we knew and loved it during the war, would never be the same in peace. In spite of everything, however, my young life had had its share of sweet happenings and I, too, was content.

B J KINSELLA
War's End

Robert Kenyon walked slowly towards the flight lines where his Sopwith Camel was being prepared for the morning patrol. The briefing had been somehow different today – almost going through the motions he thought and what did the C.O. mean when he specifically requested them to be back at the aerodrome by 11 am at the latest? For two or three weeks now rumours had been rife but always on the same topic, the war might end soon. Putting aside the thought how marvellous it would be!

Robert greeted his mechanic, Jim Leafe, a dour but talented Scot with an almost uncanny knack at tracing mechanical faults that no-one else could find. "All ready, sir," said Jim, as he assisted him into the cockpit to be acknowledged by a wave of a gloved hand as Robert went through the starting up procedures.

Soon he was winging his way towards the enemy lines with Captain Meckiff leading the loose "V" of five planes. The earth stretched below a seemingly endless terrain of churned up brown mud and shattered trees relieved only by the silver gleam of rivers and streams.

Soon they were over the front, taking note of signs of enemy activity, although there did not seem much of it at the moment and what there was seemed to consist of columns of enemy troops marching away from the front. Suddenly, Captain Meckiff waggled the wings of his plane, an agreed signal that enemy planes had been sighted. Robert quickly looked all round and there over his left shoulder and coming out of the sun were at least eight Fokker D7 fighters, newly launched at the front and reputed to be equal or superior to the Sopwith Camel. In a matter of seconds both flights broke up into a climbing, diving, turning melee of planes, each trying to gain ascendancy over the other. Robert saw a Fokker and a Camel race towards each other, guns firing, but neither plane would give way and they collided in a burst of flames and a shattering of wings and fuselages which, slowly at first, but ever faster, whirled towards the ground several thousands of feet below. Robert tore his gaze from the locked planes and just managed to avoid the fire from a silver coloured Fokker that was behind. Just below another Fokker twisted and turned in an effort to avoid his guns but Robert held on grimly pouring little bursts of fire into his panic-stricken opponent, suddenly a tiny flame appeared towards the end of the fuselage which quickly became a deep red fire which consumed the wooden plane at speed, it fell away and Robert was just able to see a dark object detach itself and fall quickly earthward – the pilot preferring a quick death to one of being burnt alive.

Suddenly the sky seemed almost empty in that strange way that often happens in dog fights. All that Robert could see was one solitary enemy plane that was climbing back to his level. Quickly he turned and gave chase to use his height advantage, he could see his bullets stitching their way through the Fokker's right wing towards the helpless pilot who suddenly fell forward in his seat as his plane nosed over towards the ground below. Robert quickly followed to make sure the pilot wasn't feigning death, firing as he went, but there was no mistake, the dive got steeper and the plane crashed into a wood. Robert looked at his watch. Gosh! Ten minutes to eleven already, he would get a rocket from his C.O. for being late. He had lost a lot of height in the pursuit of the fallen German fighter and he was fast approaching a small town with a prominent church steeple. As he circled it to get his bearing there was the slow distinctive chatter of an enemy machine gun, it was sited in the church steeple. Cursing himself for running into unnecessary danger Robert kicked the rudder of his plane hard over, in seconds he would be out of range and on his way home. Suddenly there was a searing pain in his chest and he felt his vision clouding over, he realised dimly that he had received a mortal wound as his strength ebbed and he could no longer keep the plane level. Slowly the nose dipped and he dived towards the ground. His last thoughts were of his family whom he would never see again before the plane smashed into a slight rise in the ground.

At the same time the church with the concealed machine gun nest broke into loud chimes heralding eleven o'clock on the eleventh day of the eleventh month.

STEVIE KNIGHT
Peace At Last

Message Of Love

Private James Crane looked to the sky and the rain hammered down onto his face. "What a place to spend a birthday, standing knee high in mud in a filthy stinking trench," he quietly thought to himself. "I wish I was back with Mary, how I miss her."

At that moment his train of thought was interrupted. Private George Long tapped him on his shoulder and he nearly jumped out of his skin. "Hey, Jim, we'll be off over again soon, that bastard sergeant's on his way down the line and I bet yer anything yer like he scratches his ear, real fierce like."

Jim's heart was beating like thunder. "Bloody 'ell, George, if the Boche don't get me I'll die of fright instead."

"Sorry, Jim, didn't mean to scare yer, the lads 'ave 'eard a whisper."

"What about?"

"We're going over the top again, Captain Carter's seeing to us now that bloody Captain Mercer's dead."

"Yeah well, it can't be any worse."

"I wouldn't bet on it, you know who he is don't yer?"

"Am I supposed to – what is he, bloody royalty or something?"

"Nothing quite so grand, Jim, he's the one they call the butcher, nasty piece of work by all accounts, no regards for us expendables – his words not mine."

A wave of realisation swept over Jim. "You mean the one who sent Tommy Jeffries' lot over the top?" he asked.

"Yeah, while he never so much as stuck his 'ead up, the bastard."

Jim's face dropped as he remembered his dead friend. "They knew the Boche guns were strong there, they didn't stand a chance, slaughtered, and for what, couldn't see the mud for the bodies that day?"

"You two, what do you think this is, a church meeting? Look sharp, get that rifle out the mud, lad, or you'll be sorry," Sergeant Lawson's voice boomed out.

Both privates watched intently as he walked by, scratching his left ear. "There yer go, whenever we get ready to go the Sarge gets nervous and rubs his ear 'til it's red raw, always the left one at that."

"Shit, look George, if I don't make it, I mean I want you to..." Jim reached into his pocket and pulled out a dirty crumpled envelope. "I only wrote this last night – it's for Mary."

George stared at the letter then he replied, "Yeah, I had the same idea, great minds think alike, hey Jim?" He then produced a letter of his own, "Let's hope one of us makes it or we'll have written them for nothing."

They exchanged the letters and placed them in their pockets.

"How is Jenny?" Jim asked.

"Lonely – even though she's got the young uns for company, it can't be much fun."

"Look around, George, we're not laughing either, not exactly a fairground, is it?"

"No, more like a bloody circus and we're the poor fools jumping through circles of fire."

"The problem is, George, somebody left the clowns in charge."

At that moment Captain Carter appeared, immaculately dressed in a uniform amazingly devoid of dirt.

"There you go, George, all he needs is a red rose."

Then the silence was shattered. A hellish scream pierced the air as the artillery started up again. The heavens were on fire once more.

Pandemonium set in as men scrambled for the nearest cover. There they trembled, crushed into the sides of the mud ridden trench.

Dirt and flying metal cascaded through the night air and whizzed around the two privates, closer then closer still until a fearful explosion of blinding light came between them.

In the aftermath and out of the smoke came pitiful cries of pain.

George pulled himself off the ground and shouted at the top of his voice, "Jim, Jim, for God's sake man, where are you?"

A weak sound emanated from the darkness and through the haze. Then a hand grabbed George's leg. It was Jim.

"Here, I'm here, oh Jesus, I've been hit, hurts like 'ell it does."

George could see the blood and as he cradled Jim he felt the sticky wetness seeping through the shrapnel torn uniform.

"That's me done, George, I've had it mate."

"No listen, Jim! Hang on, hang on man you'll be going home."

Jim coughed and spluttered as blood dripped from his mouth.

"George, the letter, promise me you'll send it to Mary."

"I promise but you'll be all right, you can give it to her yourself, I'm sure of it."

Then Jim slumped down motionless and George stared helplessly into his open eyes. "Jim, Jim," he shook him violently but it was no use. Jim was dead.

George closed the eyes of his fallen friend and gently retrieved the letter. The envelope had been ripped open by a sliver of shrapnel which left the final page exposed to the world. It read,

"... every now and then the guns fall silent but it doesn't make any difference, there is still a pounding in my head that never leaves me.

"I fear the scars of this war, this nightmare, will haunt me for the rest of my days.

"As I look around this wasteland I cannot in my mind's eye conjure up those once beautiful sights. Instead all I see is a grave to the many fallen souls who have sacrificed their lives.

"My thoughts return to England's green fields and the places we loved to go together, indeed, the only thing that keeps me going is the hope that you and I, my sweet Mary, will see them together once more.

"I will hold you in my arms under the tree where we first met. Do you remember how we carved our names and declared our love for each other, its seems so far away now?

"I hope we can be reunited again soon and together we will go there and listen to the symphony of rustling leaves and singing birds.

"Until we meet again Mary, you will be forever in my thoughts.

"Always yours,

"Love, Jim."

GEORGE KNOX
The Day The Soldiers Came

They came in the morning. There must have been nearly a hundred of them in the village that day, outnumbering the villagers by two to one. Mostly they just sat in the sunshine, cleaning weapons, eating, smoking. Hard to believe they were in the middle of a combat zone.

The villagers eyed them warily. There had been many days like this, many soldiers like this, one side or the other. Sometimes they were just passing through either on foot or in the heavy, armoured vehicles. Usually they stopped. They might want food, they might want to interrogate the villagers. Either way it was never very good for the inhabitants. This was their home and country. The soldiers were strangers in their land, thousands of miles from home, not wanting to be there or even understanding why they were there.

More than an hour after they had first arrived the soldiers stirred into some sort of action. Their movements were slow and lethargic as if they couldn't really be bothered but were just going through the motions. They sought out the head man and the interrogation began. The interpreter was a shifty-looking, weasel-faced small man whose status had elevated him to delusions of grandeur. The questions were always the same, just put into different languages. They wanted to know who had passed through the village, who had stopped there, where all the young men were, where food was stored. On and on relentlessly. The head man answered as best he could but as nearly always it was unsatisfactory. Then the beatings started. Other villagers were dragged up to face the "weasel".

There had been no young men in the village for many months. They were either dead or had gone off voluntarily or otherwise to join the various factions fighting over this war-ravaged land. The soldiers knew this – everyone knew this. It made no odds. The beatings continued. Old men, women and the older children, none escaped. The violence escalated as if on a given signal. A young girl, her baby still at her breast, was dragged into a hut by four soldiers not much older than herself. A teenage boy was rifle-butted to the ground. The head man was once again receiving attention from the "weasel" who, by now, had worked himself into a frenzy and was virtually frothing at the mouth.

Then, as quickly as it had started, the vicious onslaught stopped. Whether the soldiers grew bored or if someone in command realised things were getting seriously out of hand no-one knew. But stop it did. The soldiers did not leave however, but went back to sitting around in their little groups.

Then it became clear what was happening. An armoured command vehicle arrived with its escort. The Commanding Officer was on the ground. A stocky, dapper man, he strode around snapping orders, taking control. He would probably never know what went on in the village that day, it was no concern of his. He was only interested in results. How he got those results did not really matter to him as long as his hands were not dirtied or his reputation tarnished in the process.

Several "prisoners" were loaded into the escort vehicles. These were only villagers who might or might not know something useful.. They might be returned to the village in a few days, weeks, months. Sometimes they never returned.

The Commanding Officer and his convoy left in a cloud of dust and diesel fumes. The soldiers still in the village prepared to move out. They got their equipment together, checked their weapons and ammunition and left for their next assignment on the patrol.

There was no sense of shock in the village. This had become a way of life for these people. The war had been going on for several years now and if it wasn't this group of soldiers it would have been another lot. That's the way it was. The villagers stoically carried on with their life, accepting it for what it was.

So who was to blame? The villagers for taking it? But then what choice did they have? If there were any innocents in this war it was certainly them. In any war the innocents always make their share of sacrifices. Were the soldiers to blame? At face value certainly. A breakdown of discipline, not enough control exerted over them or indeed self-control. But then again spare a thought for those soldiers. A long way from home, frightened, ignorant of the cause they were fighting for, seeing their comrades killed or maimed on a daily basis. Bound to have effects on people. The effects of war. Maybe we should look elsewhere for someone to blame. But where?

CLIFFORD LACKEY
Blood From A Stone… An effect of war

They call it Britain's finest hour. Her fate lay in the courage of The Few who rode the skies over the south of England while the country held its breath and waited.

Over the Channel it was a beautiful August day; sunlight made diamonds on the wave tops, the turquoise sky was dappled with a pearly cloud here and there.

At 12.50 the watch on the wrist of Flight Lieutenant Bill Knight stopped ticking. Flames licked round his hands, still clasped tightly on the controls of his Hurricane. The heat was so intense it had melted the watch glass; the instrument panel was dripping like treacle and Knight's flying suit had begun to burn. Fragments of shells from a German fighter had wounded him in his face and back.

A calmness which surprised him took control of his thoughts: If I'm going down I'm going in a blaze of glory.

He pointed the Hurricane directly towards a Messerschmitt and, with his guns firing, pursued it like a flaming comet. The Messerschmitt spiralled down into the sea.

The magic boost of combat passed. Bill Knight realised his hold on consciousness was slipping. Must concentrate, concentrate. He looked all round – the skies were clear. His had been the last dog-fight of the air battle.

He had a chance, but pain told him it was a slim one, a very slim one. He must hold on...think positive. Yes, positive – he had a wife and a baby due to be born in weeks...he thought about them.

The Hurricane was still flying evenly, still obeying all his instructions. Yes, he had a chance, a chance, a chance... He kept repeating the two words like a mantra. The plane's main controls appeared to be undamaged but how long before the flames stopped its heart? He knew he and it could not hold on until they reached an airfield.

He pointed the plane towards England and he almost bit through his lip in an effort to remain conscious.

The green of the coast appeared beneath him. He turned the plane back towards the sea to avoid any houses, muttered, "Thanks, lass" and baled out.

He floated down in a silence which was more startling than the crackle of machine guns and cannon.

Weeks struggled past at the speed of pain.

Then Bill Knight's son was born and Bill reached the point where he now had the strength to argue with the doctors that he could make the journey to his home in the North to see his wife and his son.

"How can you do it with both your arms and hands still in bandages? You can't hold even a teacup properly..."

"I'll do it. People will help me."

The doctor looked into Bill Knight's eyes, saw the determination there and decided. "I agree... Go!"

In the queue at the railway station snack bar, a man in a dark business suit was standing behind Flight Lieutenant Knight. Bill turned and a twinge of horror passed over the man as he saw the scarred face.

Bill asked him: "Would you be kind enough to take a £1 note out of my left tunic pocket and pay for a coffee?"

The man looked down at Bill's heavily bandaged hands: "Of course".

They got the coffee and made their way to the pay desk. The man put his hand in Bill's pocket, took out a £1 note, paid, got the change and put it back in the pocket. But he kept his eyes away from Bill's face.

"Thank you." Bill turned but the man had gone without buying anything for himself.

Perhaps he couldn't stand the sight of my face, was Bill's first thought. Ah well, I suppose I'll just have to get used to this.

Sam Stone did not look round as he left the station snack bar. He was a thief...and a good one. Few pickpockets had more dexterity in slipping a wallet from an inside pocket, a purse from a handbag or even, when he felt he should put his talents to the test, a watch from a wrist.

His defensive armour was his looks; his face spoke of kindness, honesty and understanding.

Sam had a precept – steal from anyone except the blind. This exception however, was not out of compassion but because the blind, with all their senses concentrated on sound and touch, were the most likely people to catch him in the act and scream blue murder.

Sam Stone opened the palm of his hand and, with long, slim fingers, checked that he had taken three £1 notes from the uniform pocket for himself.

He asked for it, he thought. Put your hand in my pocket and take out a pound note, indeed. The dope.

But the thought of the torn face, the bandaged hands, the wings and the medal ribbons would not be forced from Sam's mind.

To hell with him and his wings.

But the picture held on, refused to be suppressed, refused to be argued away.

At the station entrance a young girl in a school uniform rattled a collecting can in front of his face: "Help save your home, sir. Help to buy a Spitfire."

Sam Stone stopped. He wanted to walk on but he didn't. Now all he could think of was a house in ruins and a shattered face. Then he did something which puzzled him for the rest of his life. He took the three £1 notes from his pocket, folded each one carefully into a thin slip and pushed it through the narrow slit of the collecting box.

He walked away, stopped suddenly as if someone had ordered him to halt. He turned back, took five £1 notes from his wallet, again carefully folded them into slips and pushed them into the collecting box.

The girl was so surprised she could not even say "Thank you".

Eight pounds!

More than her father's weekly salary...and he was in a well paid job.

Why?

WILLIAM LEWIS
The Siege Of Tobruk

The year was 1941, I was twenty years of age and had never left the shores of England, most of us were leaving BLIGHTY for the first time, all feeling very apprehensive as to what was to come.

We were sent to Tobruk, I was a Private soldier with the 2nd Black Watch. Early morning on the 18th November 1941, we broke out under heavy shelling, men were dropping dead and wounded all around me.

My luck held out until we were held up, we rested for what seemed like hours, until we heard music, it was our Pipe Major, Rob Roy, on his feet, playing his pipes and marching forward.

The men got up from their rest and started to fire their guns, after a short time the enemy began to surrender, they came in their hundreds, we then marched towards Tobruk.

We were all gathered for a roll call to find out how many of us were killed or wounded, as we gathered around we were heavily shelled, killing and wounding many more, I myself was hit in the right arm and ear, I thought I had lost my arm as I was in terrible pain, it was unbearable, blood was all over me, I crawled along the sand, it seemed I was lying there for hours until a patrol found me.

I was taken to Tobruk Hospital for the rebuilding of my arm, which lucky enough was saved, after a week I was transferred to the 64th General Hospital Alexandria, Egypt.

Mr William Lewis
Army Number: 3133684

JACK LOVELAND
Time Is Not Always A Healer

When the Suez farce took centre stage for a few days, Richard was one of the actors. His tour of duty ended swiftly when an ammunition dump went up whilst he was on guard, he was injured quite severely. In a nearby hospital Margo nursed his wound and helped to still the images that raced through his brain.

They subsequently married, I am now their neighbour. The full story of their wartime ordeal has not been fully revealed to me but the mental stress that holds them both in its grip is plain to see. I look out of the window for a sight of their car. A visit to a hospital to find out the result of tests is something nobody enjoys.

At the end of their garden stands a small chalet. Richard worked like a beaver to level the site, we all worked to get it in place with the help of the instruction sheet. "I'll be able to get on with my writing now," said Margo. Richard gives a wry smile as he checks the closure of the door, I pipe up, "I'll believe that when I see it.". I never learn. Margo shot into high gear and verbally trounced me. I am a male person and Margo despises the male, Richard included. How she would cope without him I cannot think.

When Margo is on a "high" she is a dazzling firework and everyone stands clear. Her moods go wild, she will write, she will become a counsellor, she joins "groups" but they seldom, if ever, see her. She declares she is not fulfilled, she intends to move forward – until the next "low" arrives. Nothing ever develops; except, she did give a charity shop a whirl but she whirled so fast that helpers were dispersed and they disappeared, much to the sorrow of the charity concerned. She enjoyed counselling the customers with their many problems when she was on a "high". Unfortunately when the pendulum swung she would relive that night in the Mediterranean when all hell let loose, later she was hauled from the sea semi-conscious with fourteen other nurses. Something in the brain absorbs that moment where it remains to remind and inflict damage in the years to come.

Margo promoted a coffee morning at the shop. I produced small posters to advertise the event. A selection of music was chosen to be played on a radiogram which was waiting to be sold.

Unfortunately the "high" vanished a day before the event –
Margo found the effort of changing a record was too much. For
the next month Richard walked on eggshells but over the years he
had learnt to live with his partner's mental yo-yo.

Slowly the string twitches then the yo-yo fairly jigs up and
down for a few more weeks. Then my neighbours are
transformed, doors swing open, car doors slam, various packages
arrive by post or courier but so far the chalet has produced no
masterpiece.

Richard shows stress in a totally different way. On moonlit
nights I've often watched from my bedroom window as he paces
their lawn, often dropping to huddle in the shadow of the shed.
The first time I hastened to his side – apprehensive, but soon
realised my help was not wanted at that time, but over time his
life in the RAF and those hectic days of Suez filtered through to
me. I realise now that in some way he attempts to drive out those
memories walking under the stars. On another occasion I was
able to help when a distraught Richard arrived at my door.

"What have I done? What have I done?"

I sat him down wondering if he had finally snapped.

"I'm redundant, I've signed to say I'll take early retirement,
how am I going to keep Margo in the style she expects? Oh, what
have I done?"

For a couple of weeks, head in hands, Richard was often at my
table. Flung into the role of counsellor I believe I helped to bring
him back on an even keel. Thankfully Margo at that time was on
a "high". At a later stage when Richard had finished work she
decided a rerun of the coffee morning could be staged but this
time in her own home, naturally everything had to be perfect.
Neither Richard nor I could escape. All our instructions being
delivered with machine gun speed and the spray of a Sten gun.
Richard over the years had managed to "switch off". He now
found his defences overwhelmed as Margo swept all before her.

It went well, browsers from the shop left the sorting of the
"goodies" to another day as they rolled up to Margo's coffee
morning. Richard was already well known as he helps at times in
the shop and drives out to pick up donated goods. It was good to
see it going well for both of them. Richard was now at home full
time and he was finding it very hard to adjust. He must have
wished that Margo's instability would also go into retirement. It

certainly hasn't, he revealed to me that at the end of a "high" her sleep pattern changed, she frequently awoke gasping, sometimes a stifled cry for help, her dreams of the sea were lurid. However her "high" days were a great help to Richard as he was given no time to regret or dwell on his past working life, Margo made sure they both had plenty to do.

I can see the car turning into the street. I wonder, I wonder. A while ago Margo had found a small lump. The tests are completed. Thankfully Margo is smiling. Richard closes the car door, comes towards me, crosses the path.

"Not good I'm afraid they want to operate Friday."

Her smile? I had forgotten Margo was on a "high".

JOHN LUNN
Autumn In France

"Autumn, season of mists and mellow fruitfulness," muttered Corporal Jenkins, as they peered into the fog. "Well, we've got the ruddy mists all right today, boyo. How we're ever going to find Jerry in this lot God only knows. If this breeze lifts suddenly let's make sure we've got some cover or we'll be sitting ducks out here. I just wish we'd gone round by the hedge now. Keep your eyes peeled, Joe lad."

Wallace didn't need urging. He and the tubby Welshman had been sent out on reconnaissance before dawn. They knew Jerry was up ahead somewhere but with all these miles of fields and hedges it was like looking for the proverbial needle. Oddly enough they'd passed a haystack by the gate into the field and the musty smell of the hay had make him feel homesick. Now, inevitably, the wind suddenly strengthened. The mist rose like a lifted veil and all at once they were standing tall in a wide meadow, bounded by thick, high hedges. A few yards away was a fresh crater; instinctively they scuttled forward and slid down into it.

"Well, that's another fine mess you've got me into," Jenkins grinned. He was a great Laurel and Hardy fan. He grew serious. "We can't stay here, anyway. I think we'll go back to that gate then work round by the hedge, like we should have done in the first place. My fault, Joe. Sorry. I'll go first while you cover me then you follow and I'll cover. Seems quiet enough but you never know. Here we go then. Cymru am byth." He clambered over the lip and crouched on one knee.

From somewhere came a sound like tearing calico and as Wallace watched in horror Jenkin's shoulder exploded into scarlet fragments. He screamed and in a tangle of limbs and webbing and Sten gun tumbled back to the bottom. But a bloody arm still lay in the long grass. There was nothing Wallace could do but hold him as he died. "Try and get back, boyo," Jenkins whispered, "I'm done for. When you get home give my love..." And he was gone. Wallace closed the anxious eyes and laid him gently back. So much for four years of training and waiting and more training then these last weeks of fighting. Taff Jenkins had seemed almost indestructible. But no longer. Now Wallace had to consider his options. If he made a break for it he was dead, that was certain. All he could do was wait, either for dark or for something to turn up. Long hours dragged past and the sun climbed higher in the blue, blue sky. Doves cooed and a skylark was singing.

He took out the letter he'd received from his wife yesterday and read it yet again. "The baby's due any day now," she wrote, "Don't forget, if it's a boy we'll call him Christopher after your dad and if it's a girl she'll be Margaret after Mum. I wish you were here with me now but never mind, when it's all over we'll have all the time in the world and lots more babies..." Yes, Chris Wallace sounded pretty good, he thought. Margaret sounded nice too, if it was a girl, but he'd like Chris first, really, then Maggie later. A grasshopper landed on the page. Brushing it off he peered cautiously over the edge.

Something was happening. A middle-aged couple were pushing bikes through the gate. They leaned them against the haystack and sat down chatting. Wallace studied the bikes with interest; touring models like the one he'd left in the shed at home. Then reality flooded back. The idiots, he thought. Didn't they know there was a war on here? The man was facing away from Wallace but even so he seemed in some way vaguely familiar.

Now something else – a distant noise – a deep diesel roar and the squeal of tracks coming slowly closer. Probably a Churchill and about time too. Wallace thought. He could point them towards that machine gun then watch while they dealt with it. Here it came, crashing through the hedge, no messing about. Now in the field it stopped and the turret started turning, searching. As it tracked round the black and white cross slowly came into view. Panzer. He had only seconds to act before the turret came back to bear on him. He scrambled up out of the crater and ran desperately for the gate. There came the sound of ripping cloth and then the hammer blows in his back, hurling him forward. He felt no fear. No pain. Just a deep sadness that now he would never see his son. As he sprawled beside the chatting couple the man turned his head. Suddenly everything fell into place. In a last moment of understanding, Wallace knew – he positively knew – who this man was. Then as it all went dark, he closed his eyes, contented.

The man was saying, "Isn't it nice and quiet here, Jenny? You can't hear any traffic or anything, just pigeons and that skylark. Thanks for coming to visit Dad's grave this morning. I'm sorry I sniffled a bit though." "Don't be silly," she said, smiling, "You've been meaning to do this all your life and I had to be with you on this day of all days. And I was really proud that you were man enough to cry for him. That Corporal Jenkins in the next grave was in the same regiment, killed on the same day. I wonder if they were friends." "I wouldn't be at all surprised," Chris Wallace said. "Look, I know this sounds daft, but although I never knew my dad, I've got the strangest feeling that here in this field, we've just met."

LESLIE BRIAN LUX
Sandcastles

The old man shuffles along the sand, troubled with a bad cough. Limbs, once fit and strong, were now riddled with arthritis making progress slow, and painful.

It was a beautiful morning on the idyllic island in the English Channel. The sun shone down on a blue sea that twinkled as though festooned with a myriad of diamonds. A screaming seagull made him look upwards, wistfully, and watch it soar majestically into the sky.

"You are free, my friend," wheezed the old man. "But will I ever gain my freedom? Will I be able to live my life, free of bad dreams?"

He knew this island well, having lived on it for over twenty years on his own in a small cottage overlooking the harbour. The old man, his previous ramrod-straight back now bent, had settled happily. Although a foreigner, he had been accepted by his neighbours. The only visitors, these days, were tourists happy to exchange the frenetic lifestyles on mainland Britain for the precious treasures of that island: peace and tranquillity.

As he bent down to pick up a smooth round stone, his face grimaced with pain from his aching back. He looked at the Mediterranean-blue sea, took careful aim, and hurled the stone seawards. It flew in the air, spinning, hit the water and began to bounce several times. Briefly a smile lit the creased features of the old man: seven bounces before sinking meant he had beaten his previous record.

Continuing his walk across the sand, he passed two small boys engaged in making a sandcastle. He nodded appreciatively at their efforts, then looked out to sea and thought he could see specks on the horizon that could have been ships.

Today, he knew, was a celebration, and French Navy ships were visiting his island bringing people back...back to frightening memories of a time when only terror and suffering reigned supreme, until the British liberation thirty years ago.

The old man gave a wry smile: today also happened to be his birthday. He stared at the sea; the specks were now clearly recognisable as two sleek grey frigates moving swiftly towards the island.

Reaching the end of the beach, the old man turned up a road that meandered along until it reached a small outcrop of rock that gave a good view of the harbour. The frigates were now tied up and disgorging their passengers, some in wheelchairs.

As they were helped down the gangplank onto the harbour wall, some of the visitors burst into tears as bad memories returned. The old man watched as a fleet of cars took the visitors to a simple memorial nearby and a service of remembrance for all those who had perished during the dark days of the island's history.

His head bowed and tears coursed down his face as he heard the wailing voice of a rabbi recite the Kaddish, the traditional Jewish prayers for the dead.

The old man waited until the gathering had been taken away for a lunch at the town hall, then walked down to the memorial and stared at the plaques.

"It was a bad time, mon ami," said a voice, and the old man turned to see someone of similar age by his side. He had a deeply lined face and was wearing a faded brown suit and a black beret on his head.

"Were you here – during the war?" asked the old man.

"Oui," came the reply. "I was the mayor of my town in France; my crime being a Communist."

"What happened?"

"Les Allemands, the Germans, came to my office and took me away for a...chat." The man gave a ghost of a smile. "From there I was taken to the docks, and here."

"Some holiday," said the old man.

"At least I survived. So many of my friends are buried here."

"Tell me," said the old man, hesitantly. "What do you think of the Germans now?"

The eyes of the Frenchman blazed with anger. "Les Allemands? I won't drink German wine, will not ride in a German car. I hate them all."

"So they were all bad?"

The Frenchman thought for a moment, then shook his head. "I was forgetting. There was one officer, from University I think and a professional. Not like those scum from the SS." He smiled as he remembered. "He hated the Nazis and if he caught a soldier ill-treating a prisoner, shouted at them."

The old man looked closely at his companion. "Do you know what happened to him – the officer, I mean?"

"No, mon ami. I know he was sent away from here because of his humanity. Did hear he was sent to the Russian front." The Frenchman chuckled as another memory returned: "Do you know how he liked to relax?" The old man shook his head.

"He used to go down to the beach and spend hours on his own making beautiful sandcastles. I hope he survived; probably the only German on this island that deserved to."

The two men parted and a smile crossed the face of the old man as he remembered the words of the Frenchman. Walter Hartman, now called Harrison, former Major in the Wehrmacht, survivor of the Russian front, felt an immense sense of guilt lifted.

Almost a spring came into his step as he retraced his path. He walked past the bullet-pitted sea wall, where so many prisoners had faced the firing squad, and reached the beach.

The two boys were still trying to build their sandcastles as Walter walked over to them.

"Hello, boys," he said, and knelt down. "I'm going to make the largest and most beautiful sandcastle you've ever seen."

Author's Note.

I was present for the 30th anniversary celebration on Alderney and the story of the Frenchman is true: I spoke to him.

There were many other terrible stories told me and I have many photos of the remembrance service.

Special to me is the pack – given to all the former Alderney prisoners – commemorating the event. Inside is a special medal struck for the 30th anniversary. It was given to me by a lady who had been in the French resistance. Needless to say it is a priceless piece of memorabilia for me.

Walter Hartman is – of course – fictitious, though rumour does persist that a former German guard on that island came to love it so much he did settle there after the war...

T F MARLAND
From Pegasus A Poppy

Vroom, crump, crack, the sound of the mortar rounds dropping all around him, made the soldier dig deeper. His hands were torn and bleeding with the strain he had put on them. The trench tool which began the operation lay to one side, broken.

The rounds were coming closer and closer. He dug harder, breaking fingernails on the unyielding rocky ground.

His whole body was black with the mud slime. The steel helmet he wore was weighing heavy on his forehead. Perspiration soaked his body. Every breath drew in the smoke and the cordite fumes that were all around. The smell of death was lying heavily in the atmosphere.

The boy didn't know what had happened to his section. He had only one aim, survival. Thoughts of team-work and regimental spirit had long been cast aside.

From a brief flash magnified by the bleak landscape, he noticed the luminous hands on his watch. The time 04:00 hours, had it only been an hour since they moved up from the forming-up spot?

The forward move, just after first light, had gone smoothly enough. Following the luminous band painted on the back of the soldier in front's helmet, their progress up the steep slopes had been quite fast. Their objective had been the high ground above "Goose Green", a small area through which the main attack had to move. They only expected slight opposition because the enemy only had young conscripts manning their positions, they were no match for the tough young professionals of the "Parachute Regiment".

The mortar fire moved closer. Whoever did the observing was doing a very skilful job.

The young paratrooper was face down, his fists beating the ground with frustration and fear. He was crying. The tears doing nothing to ease the awful stomach cramps he was suffering.

Gripping his rifle firmly he pulled it beneath him. His weapon training, so well rehearsed, imprinted on his mind. "Keep your weapon clean," had been drummed into him from the square at Aldershot to the decks of the ship which had brought them from England.

The steel ricochet that had struck him felt only like a hard thump. Seconds later he felt the agony and realised it had cleanly removed his calf. The sounds of explosions drowned the screams from his dry lips. Puddles around his feet took on a new colouring, as his life's blood was pumping furiously from his severed veins. "Must stop the bleeding." He remembered instructions given by the Medical Officer. His hand moved to a dressing tucked into his helmet. His hands shaking, he rammed the sterile dressing into the wound. Within minutes the dressing had become as filthy as he was.

Through the gloom he tried to find assistance but to no avail. The ground wasn't prepared to release any living thing. He realised it would be only minutes before the shock would attack his pain-wrecked body. Lying back in the mud-filled hole he resigned himself to the roll of the dice that fate had decreed. He knew his chance to enjoy a nineteenth year was not to be.

He hoped his parents wouldn't take it too hard. His elder brother, Mark, a Corporal in the RECCE section, had moved out two hours earlier. They were attacking the slope approximately ten miles east. There had only been brief sounds of gunfire. To the observers it had only been random contact.

"God, what a way to go, on a small island thousands of miles from home. Still, that's the chance I took!" Sliding into unconsciousness, Private Paul Bradley resigned himself to death. As he lay back in the muddy water he hoped the end would be quick.

The bangs and flashes grew fainter.

The time was 04:30 hours.

As the young paratrooper peered through his pain-filled eyes he suddenly saw a paratrooper standing before him, completely oblivious to all the death and destruction around him. Hands reached down and pulled the soldier to his feet, the pain almost causing him to stumble. Something seemed very familiar about him, "Mark, is that you? But how?"

Struggling and using his rifle as a crutch the badly wounded soldier kept his eyes fixed on the red shape before him, with the pain it looked more like a red poppy. With the same determination that had got him his coveted beret, he fixed his mind on following the poppy.

The figure beckoned and started to move downhill.

The ground became easier. For the last hours he had followed the paratrooper, being urged and pushed. Still the poppy guided him like a magnet. "Rest now, you'll be all right."

The young paratrooper collapsed, his back rested against a rock.

Looking back and upwards, he peered through the early dawn light. Had he really emerged from the hail of fire still sounding further up the hillside? How had he missed the small craters, pitting the ground like some false moon landscape?

"I must leave now. Rest," said the soldier, as he turned and made his way back up the hill. It was only then the paratrooper realised the poppy shape had been the red beret worn on his head.

"Mark? How?" The question was lost on the wind.

The time was 07:00 hours.

The converted liner, now a hospital ship, moved gently in the wave swell. In a cabin once used by the rich stood two men, both looking at the heavily bandaged figure lying before them. "He's young, he'll make it. It's a miracle, he was the only one of his section to survive," said the man in the white smock to the Padre. "I'll come back later. I'll leave this here," said the Padre, as he placed a folder on the locker top.

A single streak of light fell across the heavy black print. The letters fell into shape and read –

FATALITIES – GOOSE GREEN.

BRADLEY, MARK. CORPORAL – RECCE SECTION, PARACHUTE REGIMENT.

KILLED IN ACTION – APPROXIMATELY 02:30 HOURS.

ELIZABETH McKAY
A Day To Remember

Danny's picture sits on the mantelpiece in the place our mother put it over fifty years ago. The photograph is in black and white for that's the way the world was then. It occurs to me that Danny was favoured with the secret of eternal youth.

I stoop to tie my shoe-laces and the pain in my left leg ricochets through my whole body, winding me. Sometimes that's all it ever is, a pain. At other times it becomes my persecutor, stabbing and burning me. Especially at night when I'm lying alone in my bed. But I don't yell or scream or cry, for I know I'm lucky.

Dr McLeod told me I was lucky the day I went to see him, wearing my new suit.

"It's my leg, Doctor," I said, giving him only a very brief description of the blast that claimed my two best friends.

He examined me with quick , rough hands. While I was pulling on my trousers he lit a cigarette, inhaled and shrugged, before telling me I'd just have to learn to live with it.

"Lots of men never made it back at all, you know," he said, through swirls of grey smoke spewing from his mouth. "And many others have come back minus arms and legs."

He told me that. As if I didn't know. As if I didn't lie beside them, shivering in the mud. As if I didn't help drag them to the ambulances, wading through the stench of terror and bits of human debris that had once been whole people. As if I didn't know how lucky I was.

I look outside and see rain falling from the sky like huge teardrops and I'm not surprised. There are only so many memories one day can bear.

Limping through the hall to fetch my coat I glance at the clock. It tells me it's after ten. There's a brass plaque at the bottom which says it was presented to me by the GPO for twenty five years of faithful service. You might think a postman was a strange job for someone with a crushed up leg but at the time I was glad enough to get it.

I remember my mother giving me a few shillings from my first pay before snapping the rest inside her purse. Later she went into town and bought a silver frame for Danny.

Many's the time I came home to find her rocking gently in the chair, nursing the photograph at her breast. I often wondered then, and sometimes I still do, if my mother was disappointed that it was me who came back instead of Danny. I felt guilty.

Sometimes I went into the Railway Hotel after work, for company. One night I came home late and very drunk. My mother was disgusted.

"How could you?" she screamed at me. "How could you do this to me on your brother's birthday?" As if I didn't know. As if I didn't know it was his birthday. It was mine too.

The clock is ticking louder now, trying to catch my attention, telling me to hurry up, the way Jean used to.

"Come on, we'll be late," Jean used to say to me. "You know you can't walk fast with that leg of yours. The first picture will have started by the time we get there."

Jean was pretty then. A lot of people were surprised when she agreed to marry me. She'd been engaged to Larry Carter who worked in the bank and who was killed exactly two weeks and a day before the end. I told her it didn't matter about the baby, that I would treat it like it was my own. But she died three weeks after she was born and Jean never wanted any more.

Two women in one house is a situation best avoided if at all possible. I know that now but it was only supposed to be until the council could rehouse us.

They ganged up, my mother and Jean, going to the pictures together, and later on, the bingo. When Mother died Jean took to dusting Danny's photograph, carefully lifting it from the mantelpiece, rubbing it gently with a yellow duster and smiling at him before setting it back in exactly the right place. When Jean died I thought about moving the picture into the hall but somehow I just couldn't bring myself to do it.

Walking down the main street towards the square I'm aware of how empty the town is. No different from any other Sunday I don't suppose but somehow I thought it might be busier today.

There are children of course. Lots of children dressed in blue and green and black. Children in uniform. I wonder what Danny would think if he knew they send the children out with tributes too heavy for them to carry, while the adults stay in bed, or rush to get the best parking space at the DIY. Or compete for medals on the golf course.

It's cold. The cold makes my leg go numb. I stumble. A hand reaches out to steady me. A child's face looks up into mine. He stares and stares at my face with screwed up eyes and I think he must be reading between the lines. Then he smiles with eyes that are young and bright and have never seen the things that mine have seen and I hope they never will.

"Are you all right, Mister?" he asks me. "Do you want me to get the first-aid man?"

"No thanks, son," I say. "I'm fine."

He runs to join the others in his group. When his turn comes I watch him march solemnly towards the monument and lay down his circle of red flowers. His face is serious and his eyes go deep into his self. Now I remember why we did it. Now I know I'd do it all again.

ROSE McNAMARA

The Legend Of The Angels Of Mons, A Ghostly Tale Of World War 1

The legend of the Angels of Mons is:- An army of angels saved the tired, but heroic British Expeditionary Force from certain death at the Belgian/French Border town of Mons.

Did a phantom army save the British Expeditionary Force (BEF)?

If anything supernatural did happen it was in the last days of August 1914, as the superior German forces pushed back the BEF, which was greatly out-numbered by three to one.

The British Expeditionary Force were hopelessly pinned down at the Belgian/French border town of Mons. There was not a hope for our lads on that mossy awful day. The Germans had surrounded them, and they were now preparing for their final thrust.

As dusk fell, the British were just waiting for the final attack to come, and knew it would mean complete annihilation for them. Simply prayed to God for help in their hour of need.

As they stood waiting and peering at the enemy lines. They saw a shimmering mirage appear above the enemy camp. Then slowly, one, by one, figures began to materialise out of the haze. Figures tall and winged, like angels.

From the German side came an account that their men refused to charge a point where the British line was broken because of the presence of a large number of troops. According to Allied records, there was not a single British soldier in the area.

Did soldiers see angels? Or was it brought on by fatigue, loneliness, despair and fear. It could have been, but was it? Did their tired brains play tricks on them? Was it mass hysteria or imagination? Was it a mirage? Or was it true? Who can say for sure?

The First World War dubbed, 'The Great War,' was the first of its kind. There was nothing to measure it by, therefore no one could say for certain what would, or could happen.

It was easier to believe in angels in 1914, as until then, people had led a somewhat more orderly life, and they still had their faith.

Did a phantom of angels save the British Expeditionary Force from certain death, who knows? I don't know what these soldiers saw, but I do believe they saw something. I would love to think that angels came to our rescue on the battlefields of Mons, but cannot see why they didn't make their purpose known.

Understandably the enemy fell back in confusion. In the unearthly lull that followed, the British soldiers gained precious time and marched through the night to safety.

The battle took place on August 26th 1914. When the report appeared in September most of the survivors were still in France. In May of the following year a clergyman's daughter, Miss Marrable from All Saints Clifton, wrote in the parish magazine what she had been told by two officers. Both of them had seen the angels. They said that they expected annihilation as they stood there almost helpless. Then to their amazement the German army just stood there like dazed men and never so much as touched their guns, or stirred until we had turned around and escaped.

One of Miss Marrable's friends, who was not a religious man, told her that he had seen a troop of angels between our soldiers and the enemy. He has been a changed man ever since.

An Army Chaplain, the Rev CM Chavasse, brother of Noel Chavasse, holder of the Victoria Cross, who later became the Bishop of Rochester, recorded that he had heard similar accounts from a Brigadier-General and two of his officers. Also a Lieutenant-Colonel described how during the retreat, his Battalion was escorted for 20 minutes by a squadron of phantom cavalry.

What made soldiers see angels? Why did soldiers see angels? Were they mad or mistaken?

The Bible has a view on this.
Why would a platoon of angels save only British soldiers? Did the German soldiers believe the angels saved only the British? If so why would they think that? Both sides are supposed to be Christians. Why would they keep on fighting if angels were present?

What did the soldiers see? Can angels still been seen in the 20th century? Are angels real? Have they ever intervened in man's affairs? And can angels affect our life now?

Were they good angels ? Or bad angels? Were they the rebellious angels that were cast out of heaven and thrown down to the earth. As told to us in the Holy Bible in Revelations chapter 12 verses 7 to 9 King James and the New World Translations of the Holy Scriptures. It reads like this:

(7) And war broke out in Heaven: Michael and his angels battled with the dragon, and the dragon and his angels battled (8) but did not prevail, neither was a place found for them any longer in heaven. (9) So down the great dragon was hurled, the original serpent, the one called Devil and Satan, who is misleading the entire earth: he was hurled down to the earth, and his angels were hurled down to him.

Could these angels be the ones that had just been hurled out of heaven? Had the devil and his angels just landed after being cast down? Were they just standing there confused? Not fighting anyone?

After all, no one mentions the angels were fighting, the soldiers said they saw a troop of angels standing between them and the enemy. Both sides saw that.

A British Lieutenant-Colonel said they were escorted for 20 minutes by a squadron of phantom cavalry.

Or, were the angels just going that way? Not even bothering about what was going on in the battlefield? Did the fighting stop from that point? It seems it didn't. Where did that angels go after saving the soldiers?

Obviously a strange event did take place at Mons. Whether it is true or false we shall never know for sure. But, as long as people believe the myth, and as long as people believe that God is on their side, victory is certain. Because, if God be for us, who can stand against us.

Some religious leaders and historians had hinted that 1914 was possibly a year marked in Bible prophecy.

A soldier in the 1914 War, who thought he saw angels, wrote the following poem:

I know they'll say the shining shapes
were but a soldier's dream,
Or borne of Autumn's lovely cloud
Beneath the moonlight beam,
But the English, Scots and Irish Guards
And Munster Fusiliers-

All the flower of Britain's chivalry,
The Lancashire's that stood the fires
Of Mons and Le Cateau,
And the brave Scots Greys that thrice that day charged through
the bloody foe
They saw and heard the angels pass
And misty squadrons glide,
They know that holy angels
Were fighting on their side.
Written by Dugald MacEchern.
Now nearly a century has gone by. What have we learned?
Nothing. This has been the least peaceful century in history.

History Assignment, Rose McNamara, mature student. Cassio College, Watford 1996.

C MEADE
Shadows Of The Evening

Each afternoon while those around me doze in their chairs or retire to their rooms, Memory beckons me out, my steps faltering, my stick gouging wounds in the damp soil, and accompanies me across the road and to this seat. These are the things she wants me to absorb: the heather-clad headland tumbling down to the beach, the sun turning the water into molten gold, the waves washing gently over the sand, the gulls weaving and wheeling, their plaintive calls dancing around me in the breeze; children playing, their voices clambering joyously up to me. She wants to imprint this scene of beauty and tranquility indelibly upon me, to replace the detritus that is gathered, festering there.

I was still a boy, only eighteen, when I visited my parents for a last holiday before taking my place at Oxford, too young to recognise the uncertainty, to share the undercurrent of doubt and concern. Life then was for enjoying to its fullest and I determinedly did so.

There is always a moment of wholeness, recollected when the world is ravaged and in tumult, a moment when innocence and a vague foreboding allows you to predict the madness to come. It was in that flawless summer that I determinedly pushed aside this prescience and concentrated on my youth. A sense of heightened animation pervaded everywhere, people laughed loud and played hard.

How can I describe that Colonial world? Union Jacks flew proudly everywhere. King, Queen, Prince, Princess and Regent Streets intersected the town. The Albert Hall, the Majestic Cinema and the King George, Queen Victoria and Royal British Hotels stood proud and imposing in the centre, the United Empire Bank looked down its prosperous nose. Just out of town was the British Army Garrison, so we were safe. It was something to be proud of, being British in those days and the British did not turn tail and run. The British never ran.

That was why, when the shit hit the fan, so to speak, there was chaos. Those who could, escaped; those who stopped to consider what they should do were trapped, and those, like me, who didn't know what to do, were drawn into something we didn't understand. We were taken to the hills and trained for jungle warfare by experts who themselves were trained for just such an eventuality. We learned to understand and identify the sounds and activities of the jungle, to eat the unthinkable and to booby-trap roads and railways; to make a swift, ferocious strike then slip silently back into the relative safety of the dank, smelling, dripping, perpetual dusk of the jungle. To kill silently and with precision and to dispose of a man with no more thought than swatting a fly.

We learned about attack and counterattack, to lay trip-wires to protect ourselves against enemy patrols, to hack our way through the undergrowth with a parang, to cope with prickly heat, malaria, bacterial infections, dysentry, vicious thorns, poisonous snakes and insects and gorging leeches. We learned which kampongs were friendly and to avoid those where the people melted into invisibility when we arrived; that one moment's loss of concentration could be fatal. I did what I had to do, calmly, and with merciless accuracy. And I grew up.

I saw bodies blown into a hundred pieces, throats cut while men slept, traitors shot out of hand, helplessly watched slow and painful deaths, heard the screams of the tortured or injured, the anguished cry of the mortally wounded and had to harden myself to the grotesque attitudes of violent death. There were times when I, too, was so near to death, my feet at the very threshold of heaven that I felt I had only to bequeath that last breath to the wind and the gate would open for me. But something held me back, the job was not completed yet.

This is what has remained locked in my head for all these years. These are the febrile thoughts which have eaten into my sleep, persecuted every waking hour. This is the detritus Memory wants to clear.

Sometimes, too, she brings me out at night, in those black hours when the blackest thoughts gnaw, when I am too tired to sleep, when the grief and remorse are so close that I can reach out and touch them, then it is almost more than I can bear. "See," she says, "Look at that moon, how beautiful it is, how it reflects upon the sea, the waves shredding it into a million pieces and spreading it wide. And that star, so low you could pluck it from the sky. Fill your heart with these visions." And I snatch greedily at them, forcing them into every available cranny.

I turn my head to take in the drifts of daffodils on the roadside, the cairn of stones built centuries ago, the banks of cumulous clouds, the flowering cistus, the soft colour of the foliage barely showing yet, and I store it all. You see, the more space I can fill with beauty, the less space there will be for the other.

I am an old man now and it is the way with old age that it draws you into the past, even when the past is the last place you want to be. Shards of late sunlight slice through the leafless tree and sprinkle me, piercing me with sudden chill. "Come," Memory says, "It is late, you must go back," but all my energies have gone into exorcising ghosts, obliterating conscience.

"Leave me," I say, and she creeps away. I concentrate all my powers upon a boy on the beach throwing a stick for a dog. He looks familiar. I lean forward to see better. The dog races ahead. "Scamp!" I call, and a surge of happiness swamps me as I race after him, my heart pumping savagely, "Wait for me!"

T S MELDRUM
Johnny

Lance Corporal Johnny Grant sat down in the mud. His knees drawn up to his chest, his hands wrapped around his shins, head bowed, rocking back and forth. It was cold. It was very cold. He wasn't sure of the date but he knew that winter was definitely on the way and that things were going to get a lot harder before they got better. His trench coat was covered with a collage of unidentifiable stains. It was ripped in several places. This provided ventilation in the summer but now it let in the cruel winter wind. Johnny no longer cared for the state of his uniform but he did take great pride in the stripe on his arm. It was the one thing left that gave him a sense of self-worth; that made him proud.

"It may not be much but it's 'ome," he proclaimed, smiling. He had spent several days in this bunker now. Things had started to get too dangerous in the previous one; even for a soldier of Johnny's experience. It was now a very long time since he had last seen his friends, his loved ones and he spent almost every waking moment in anguished thought, trying to remember, trying to recall what had happened to him. He knew that the others would recognise him if they could see him, despite his bedraggled appearance, the burst veins in his face, his matted hair and skeletal appearance. If only they would come looking for him. If only they would only remember him.

Somewhere overhead a deafening rumbling made him cower and hide his head between his painfully sore knees. "Leave me alone!" he roared above the din. The rumblings had been coming regularly now and he knew that it was only a matter of time before one of them led to the inevitable and his life would at last come to an end. He knew that he could just climb out of his bunker, walk into the path of one of the rumbling, hurtling dealers of death and end it. No more pain. No more hunger. No more wondering.

The worst thing for Johnny was not the agonising threat of those blasted rumblings, not the constant cold, not the biting wind or even the incredible pain caused by trying to hobble on feet that had suffered trench foot for as long as he could remember. The pain was no problem. "'S all in the mind!" he would say. The echoing words of his dead Sergeant would return to comfort him; "Pain? It's only a sensation lad...and sensations are there to be enjoyed." He could manage the pain. His childhood beatings at the hands of the older boys had taught him plenty about pain and how much the body could stand if the mind would let it. No. No, the worst thing for Johnny was the humiliation of having to scavenge for scraps to eat. Some of the things that he had forced down his throat were enough to make him vomit. He knew to control his retching and keep the valuable nutrition within his frail body. His Mother had always worked so damn hard to provide food for him and little Rose. She had been proud of the fact that, if nothing else, they had always had food on the table. She had even taught them to cook for themselves. Now look at him. It brought him to tears more surely that anything else in his miserable existence. He wanted to be found. Wanted to be remembered, but never wanted anyone to know that he had lived like this. Not Johnny Grant. Never. Not a Lance Corporal. Not with his pride.

The only benefit of the advent of winter would be the death of the pestilent flies. Johnny hated the flies that buzzed around his body. He guessed that they found him very appealing in this state. Smelling like he does. Rotting appendages. He just could not stop thinking about what the flies had been feeding on. He had often found himself surrounded by faecal matter and had seen, from time to time, corpses only recently deceased but writhing with maggots.

The wind started to get up again and a newspaper floated past, hitching a lift on the icy current. Johnny stuck out a filthy hand to grab it. He could not read very well but it would help to keep him warm in the weeks to come, he thought. Then he saw the date and then he saw the red flowers on the front page.

As he sat underneath the railway bridge in the middle of London he knew that even today he would not be remembered by his long lost family. He hauled himself out of his "bunker" and trudged painfully up to the railway track and towards the next rumbling, hurtling dealer of death. Lance Corporal Johnny Grant died underneath the Intercity 125 bound for Marylebone on the 11th of November 1999 at 12:00 hours. Nobody went to his funeral but the next year millions of people wore poppies in his memory.

ARTHUR MOORE
My War

I couldn't understand why everyone was laughing. At intervals there was a sudden outburst of laughter from those around me. Something to do, it seemed, with the changing shapes on the white screen in front of the hall; yet why should these continually changing shapes provoke laughter, or indeed, any response at all?

I was in the Garrison Theatre, sitting amid hundreds of my army colleagues, yet I felt isolated and withdrawn. Even the voices coming from the screen didn't seem to make sense, just strange meaningless sounds. I felt scared and left, back to my room at the end of the barrack block. Even reading, I found, was a disheartening exercise; why should different black and white shapes on a printed page convey any meaning? My mind had become hyper-analytical of everything.

There were physical symptoms too; a violent trembling of the hands and an uncontrollable trembling at the back of my neck. I took to dining in a far corner of the mess, alone.

I reported sick and was diagnosed by the M.O. as having 'anxiety neurosis' and recommended for hospital treatment.

There were, I suppose, a number of emotional shocks contributing to this condition. Having joined the Territorial Army in May 1939 and been called up on September 1st I was jolted when my regiment, in which I was a signaller, was sent abroad and I was forced to stay in England due to faulty eyesight. I was posted to a training unit where I had to carry out the duties of a batman to three officers. My frustration was increased, knowing that my two married brothers were serving abroad.

Two years in to the war I lost my girlfriend, largely due to my own neglect in writing to her. She found and married someone else.

Meanwhile, I had progressed from batman to sergeant drill and gunnery instructor. After further courses, I became a specialist instructor in mines and booby traps, aircraft and tank recognition. Exposed to explosions on our training area, I suffered a certain degree of deafness, but did nothing about it as I was thoroughly enjoying my job.

My officers seemed satisfied with my work and they

recommended me for officer training. The preliminary to this was an interview with the Colonel, a typical 'Colonel Blimp' type. From the questions he asked me there were three I particularly remember.

What school did I attend?

I think Eton or Harrow would have done nicely, but it had to be elementary school which I left at the age of fourteen to start work as an engineering apprentice.

Had I a private income?

No!

Did I ride? Did I ride!

No!

I failed the interview, a great blow to my pride and aspirations. All of these emotional jolts must have undermined my confidence and culminated in my present condition. Not exactly battle-scarred but perhaps the effects were similar.

I do not recall any specific treatment in the hospital apart from quiet chats with doctors and the ministrations of a very fat, jolly and lascivious Matron who dished out Benzedrine tablets like sweets and frequently invited me to relieve my tensions in her bed, if I so wished. I didn't wish.

One major form of therapy for me was establishing a hospital newspaper along with another patient who was a regular columnist for a popular paper magazine of the time.

Eventually declared fit and well, I was returned to my unit. It was at this time that preparation for civilian life loomed large in the military curriculum. I was seconded to the Army Education Corps as 'schooly', or education sergeant to my own garrison of troops and ATS, to whom I initially gave lectures on ABCA (Army Bureau of Current Affairs) and 'Boops', (British Way and Purpose), based on notes supplied by the War Office, assisted by a highly intelligent lance-bombardier. It soon became obvious that the large contingent of ATS needed its own facilities, particularly as we now had to provide classes to cater for many who wished to take Civil Service entrance examinations.

Volunteers were soon found among officers and NCOs to take classes in Maths, French and a leisure class in Art. I undertook classes in English grammar and literature, my innate love of words and wordcraft having been well nurtured at elementary school.

An ATS sergeant was assigned as their education officer and she and I shared an office. She was twenty, very attractive and had a nature and personality to match. On her first day I took her to the mess for lunch. She stood at the table with her head bowed in prayer. I remained standing, feeling embarrassed knowing that all eyes were on us.

She crossed herself and we sat down. I soon got used to this routine and prepared to defend her against any ribaldry but in fact there never was any and everyone respected her. It was her avowed intention to become a nun after the war, joining a sisterhood confining themselves to the convent and spending their lives in prayer.

I spent long, fruitless times trying to dissuade her. She was entirely dedicated and answered my arguments with her disarming smile and assured me her life of devotion would be as valid a contribution to society as getting married and having a family.

On my demobilisation in December 1945 her last words to me were:

"When I become a nun I will send you a postcard."

I can't remember how long after the war it was but a postcard duly arrived. No address, but the message was:

"The postcard as promised. I will always remember you in my prayers." It was signed, 'Sister Aloysius'.

It is ironic that over the years, married and with a fine family, I travelled the world on business, particularly the Far East.

I often think of my erstwhile colleague. Is she still genuflecting in her cell and remembering me? And is my post-war success and well-being a legacy of wartime medical ministrations or her continuing spiritual support?

Intriguing thoughts and poignant memories from the chequered pattern of my war.

MIKE MORGAN
Alamein Angel

A shimmering heat haze hung like a pall over the desert battlefield. The merciless sun beat down on the Eighth Army sappers, slaving feverishly to complete the deadly minefield in a last-gasp attempt to stop Rommel's savage offensive to smash through the British and Commonwealth lines.

This was make or break time for both armies. They had been slugging it out up and down the arid coastal strip of North Africa for months, like two brutal, bludgeoning prize fighters, first one gaining the upper hand, then the other in a fanatical, bloody no-holds-barred contest of sudden advance and crushing retreat.

Now, the British and their allies had their backs against the wall at this God-forsaken place called El Alamein. There would be no more running. It was death or glory and the day of reckoning was almost upon them.

If the Desert Fox broke through here there was nothing to stop the Nazis snatching the vital Middle Eastern oilfields, followed by a war-winning link up with their comrades storming towards that other place no-one had yet heard of – Stalingrad, in the heart of Communist Russia.

John Dean, the young sapper captain, pulled off his crumpled officer's cap and surveyed his men's devilishly cunning work. The unwary crunching of a track or tyre over one of the lurking mines would incinerate a tank or obliterate a truck full of men in the blink of an eye.

Sweat trickled down his craggy young face, meandering through the granules of sand which clogged his teak brown, sunburned features. "The boys have done a good job, we're as ready as we'll ever be," he noted quietly, with professional satisfaction.

Suddenly his steel grey eyes narrowed and his hands flew automatically to the binoculars which hung round his neck. As he focused, a growing puff of dust on the sunbaked horizon brought his well-honed senses to razor sharpness. "Jock, over here quick," he barked, motioning the lean Scots sergeant to man the heavy machine gun in the sand-bagged dug out.

"Jesus, sir what the hell is it!"

"It's a truck, heading straight for our minefield. And whoever's driving it is wearing a British helmet! They must be stragglers from up north. Bloody hell. Cover me, I'm going forward."

The men lost sight of the captain as he hared off and dropped into one of the many tank traps which had been dug in the coarse, roasting sand. Moments later, a muffled bang was heard, as though the rapidly approaching vehicle had backfired.

Corporal Jack Osmond, the driver of the truck, braked violently as the sprinting officer flung himself before the vehicle, arms waving frantically, with chest heaving, lungs bursting. "Minefield....dead ahead...stop...do exactly as I say," he blurted out to the startled soldiers through the truck's open window.

The driver needed no further bidding. "Inch forward a yard at a time and follow my directions to the letter," snapped the officer.

Back at the sappers' dugout, the captain's men watched in fascinated awe as the truck turned first this way, then that. Sweat trickled into the eyes of Corporal Osmond as he slowly, laboriously, picked a safe passage through the lethal, sandy maze.

"It looks like they're going to make it," hissed Jock, his hands relaxing their tension on the searingly hot Vickers machine gun. "The lucky bastards, it's a bleeding miracle!"

After an eternity of razor-edged tension, the truck was through. The courageous Captain Dean felt waves of relief flow over him and he slumped exhausted against a large rock. His chin fell onto his chest as tiredness took hold and his eyes closed in a silent, thankful prayer.

Corporal Osmond leapt from the truck and was mobbed by the cheering sappers. "That was some driving mate," said Jock. "How did you do it?"

"The officer of course, where is he? You must have seen him, he walked alongside us and told us not to panic. He said he'd supervised the laying of the mines and knew exactly where they were. He's a bloody hero. Where is he, I want to shake his hand?"

The CO, Major Brownlee, a grizzled sapper veteran of World War One, approached the jubilant driver and gently guided him to one side.

"This officer, did he have sandy hair and a crumpled cap?"

"Yes sir, that's him."

"Come with me son." The major took the puzzled driver 200 yards away towards a large rock, behind which a young officer lay slumped, his head on his chest, strangely still.

"That's him sir, but why's he sleeping? Must have nerves of steel after that lot. What a bloke."

"He's not sleeping son. He's caught a packet from a mortar. Happened a few minutes before you got through to safety. A splinter killed him instantly. He was my best officer, brave as a lion."

The blood drained from the driver's face as if he'd seen a ghost.

The kind major put his arm around the soldier: "You know son, something similar happened to me in the last war, at Mons. We saw angels in the sky, willing us to beat the Huns back, but when we told the brass hats about it after we'd won the battle they said it wasn't supernatural, or the hand of God on our side.

"They said it was the stress of combat. We were out of our minds because of all we'd been through. Nothing special happened, even though hundreds swore they saw it.

"They'll say exactly the same about this – the whole thing was a mirage, just hot, thirsty men under terrible stress on the battlefield somehow having a joint hallucination.

"You and I know different, but take my advice and tell the backroom wallahs what they want to hear. The nearest they ever get to action is reading about it in reports.

"Our boys at the sharp end will ensure this story never dies."

Over fifty years later, the legend of Alamein's angel is still very much alive.

KEVIN W MUIR
Volunteer For Nothing

As my faith solicits, this is my final confession, not to God on this occasion, but to society for my malignant iniquities. Although it is not my intention to seek absolution through excuse, there is however, one last burden which I feel as though I had to off-load before embarking upon my final vocation, which of all my sins, has to be cardinal.

I was born in Ireland, West Belfast to be precise, just off the Falls Road, a highway full of cracks and potholes that the workmen of British politics have turned their backs on. Not the magical, mystical, mythical and enchanting island garden, or eugenic fairy-tale kingdom that must have been God's intention and illusion, but instead, a land engulfed in the tragedy of religious hatred and bigotry.

An ill country where the only remedy to bring everlasting peace is death. Growing up in the deprived environment of the Republican enclave, where black flags draped unceremoniously from the lamposts and the constant threatening presence of armed personnel manoeuvring outside your doorstep, served as a constant reminder of the generations of persecution and torture, you soon learned to hate the opposition. In reality it's born in the womb, then you spend the remainder of your life kicking for survival.

Your initial education is in the home, it's not 'mind the traffic' it's 'watch out for the Protestants'. You wet the bed as you dream of them as axe wielding ogres coming to murder you in your sleep and that's reinforced when the Security Forces using their jurisdiction, ransack your home in the early hours of the morning, but find nothing. It then evolves to the playground, you hear the stories and read the graffiti and then you take your beloved terrain into your hands and throw it with verve and venom at the invaders from Britain. As a boy turns to an adolescent, the bricks are replaced by glass and petrol bombs, when some become men, then it's lead.

I guess it was my inheritance that sucked me into the vacuum of hypocrisy made by the propaganda demagogues, who prey on the people's intelligence with ancient history and failing economical statistics, for Belfast's main industry is two-sided terrorism, where the end product is hatred, measured by the grief of the death toll in square inches of cemetery. Following in my father and brother's footsteps, I volunteered my services to the 'Cause', but that was never the real motive, for that was the romance of the dream they'd indoctrinated into me. The exuberance of adopting the role of pest controller to rid my country from the foreign vermin gnawing at my roots, far outweighed the consequence of a long-term jail sentence, or in my case, the deploring guilt.

With the gift of hindsight it might have been different, but then again I should have seen it coming, especially after that dark winter's night in the clandestine room of my local pub, when my Intelligence Officer, an old cripple, informed me of my first real task of initiation. Having run their errands, surveyed the enemy and acted in scenes of stark anarchy, the time had come to prove my trust beyond fanaticism. Expecting a crack at the security forces or an influential loyalist, I was dismayed to learn my target was to be a man from own community who was dealing in drugs. My objection was quashed when informed that this individual was embezzling the source to fund our war. I don't know who was more terrified that night when I blew out his kneecaps, yet at this moment I think I know how he must have felt.

Now I had tasted blood, I thirsted for more, determined to make amends for maiming one of my own persuasion. The more I killed, the more I understood I was but an expendable pawn in their game. I wasn't fighting for the recrimination of the past atrocities the Catholic denomination had been subjected to, no, I'd been belligerent for the future, to line the pockets of astute, entrepreneurial political minds who saw the enterprise of making a 'fast buck' through the exploitation of history. I know this because of my penultimate target, which was designed to kill two birds with one stone. The man was a Catholic businessman who refused to pay his debts to our society. In executing the sentence of his punishment, not only would he be taught the ultimate lesson, but our unethical organisation would deny any link to his murder.

In effect it would keep the revulsion towards the Orange landlords simmering in our ghetto and strengthen our backing, as in the furore, the public would demand protection. Dumbfounded by the truth, the romantic illusion had been ripped from my heart, the love affair was over and I'd been duped.

In No Man's land it was Shakespearean irony which magnetised me to the only true love of my life, though I worshipped her just the same and lived the lie that my life had become. And God I loved her, yet knew the day would come when I had to betray my predicament and so it dawned. It was like the sun soaring above Belfast in the jealous cloud-free sky, for still it appeared overcast below. Perhaps if her love had been stronger then we could've survived , but I'll never blame her.

I was blind, now I see. No man is infallible, unfortunately, neither is any irreplaceable. I should have listened to my mother when in one of her lectures of wisdom, she'd said, "Volunteer for nothing son". But she hadn't always been right, for she told me "life's about learning from your mistakes," that was wrong, it's about taking responsibility for them. She also said "it's hard to be a man when there's a gun in your hand," well I know people have labelled me a coward for what I've been a part of, but what I do now makes me one of the bravest. Click....................Bang!

WILLIAM R NEWRICK
Symbol Of Unity

Hans Smit did not feel alone until he stood on the cliff top and saw the vague shape of the U-boat disappear beneath the waves of the North Sea. Now it all depended on him. He was prepared. No detail of his training or appearance had been overlooked. His English was accentless. He had spent two years in England perfecting it.

His documentation was the best Admiral Canaris's department could produce. If his failure to be in uniform raised any curious eyebrows he had "calling up" papers to show that in two weeks' time he would be reporting to Aldershot to perform that which the English curiously called National Service.

Smit remained hidden until dawn when he picked up his suitcase and started to walk into town. He had been told that no-one would think it unusual for a man to be walking to the railway station carrying a suitcase.

*

PC Law had just come on duty when he saw Smit walk into the railway station. He thought there was something odd about him. Something that didn't quite fit the scene. However he hesitated half a minute before following Smit into the station.

PC Law found Smit at the end of a short queue at the ticket window. "Excuse me, Sir." He asked politely, "May I see your Identity Card?"

Smit produced the forged card with a smile. His trainer had told him to smile at moments like this.

"Your name, Sir?" The constable asked.

"William Smith," he replied.

"You and a couple of million others," Law muttered, under his breath. "Your address, Sir?" he asked.

"45, The Broadway, Wapping," Smit recited.

"Thank you, Sir," Law replied. Unable to see any reason to detain him, Law handed him his forged identity card back.

The ticket queue had disappeared so that Smit now moved straight up to the window. He laid his identity card down for the clerk's inspection and asked for a single to Liverpool Street.

These actions puzzled PC Law. A civilian didn't need to show his identity card to get a ticket. Or had he simply laid his identity card there after taking it back from him? Asking for a single to London? Surely if he lived there he would have had a return ticket? And his accent. It seemed pure BBC. Nothing Cockney about it.

Law's thoughts were interrupted by the wail of the Warning siren. He took off his helmet and replaced it with his "tin hat" that had been hanging on his gas mask and brought the gas mask case round to the "ready for use" position.

He then moved into the main concourse of the station to help PC Jones of the railway police to shepherd passengers into the nearest air raid shelter.

Smit did not move towards the shelter but stood by the closed platform gates. "Please go to the shelter, Sir," PC Law requested.

"I've a train to catch, Constable," Smit replied.

"The train will not leave until the All Clear sounds, Sir."

Smit thought he had better conform and walked off to the air raid shelter.

PC's Law and Jones took up positions beside the doorway of the shelter. They were not there to stop people coming out before the All Clear sounded as there was no law compelling civilians to go into or stay in an air raid shelter. They were there to duck inside in the event of bombs falling in their vicinity or to render assistance should their services be needed.

"See that last chap to get in?" PC Law asked Jones.

"Tall chap. Sports jacket. Grey flannels and trilby?"

"Yes. That's him. Notice anything odd about him?"

"No, can't say I did."

"Well, I was wondering if he was a Jerry."

"Why don't you take him in?"

"I did that last week with a bloke. Turned out to be the Bishop of Norwich. My Inspector was not very pleased."

Jones laughed. "Same thing happened to me, only my chap was a Dutch naval officer. Anyway, what do you reckon is odd about this bloke?"

"I don't know. It's just when I first saw him I knew there was something wrong with him."

Further conversation was aborted by the All Clear sounding, ending what had probably been a false alarm.

The first to emerge from the air raid shelter was a WRVS

woman with four young children. All five carried their civilian gas masks, in their rectangular boxes, over their shoulders like badges of office or symbols of unity against Adolf Hitler.

Suddenly PC Law knew what was odd about the so-called William Smith.

Asking PC Jones to delay things in the railway station by looking at a few identity cards as the passengers passed through the ticket barrier, he nipped into the police call box and called the police station. Five minutes later Sergeant Feather CID, arrived on his bicycle.

"Where is he?" Feather demanded.

PC Law told him that the suspect was now inside the railway station under the watchful eye of PC Jones.

"And you want me to take him in because he hasn't got a return ticket nor a Cockney accent?"

"It's more than that, Sarge. Instructions say that if you think the suspect may be armed, call reinforcements. So I called you."

"Covering your own back more likely. What's wrong with PC Jones as reinforcement?"

"He's not one of us, Sarge. He's Railway."

Sergeant Feather looked up to heaven for inspiration. "All right. Let's go and get him."

Smit was armed, but surrounded by Law, Jones and Feather he realised he stood no chance of using his gun and escaping. He simply surrendered.

*

"Tell me, PC Law," Sergeant Feather demanded. "What made you suspect him in the first place?"

"No gas mask, Sarge."

"But it's not compulsory for civilians to carry their gas masks."

"Do you ever see anyone without their gas mask? It's as much a part of getting dressed as putting your trousers on."

GWENDOLINE NYSS-SANFORD
Remembrance

I was only three when the Second World War broke out but my recollections of those years back in India remain pretty strong and clear.

I first had an inkling – in a childish sort of sense – that something was wrong, when my mother's youngest brother, who was barely out of his teens, came to spend a few days with us prior to "joining up", as my uncle put it. He brought with him his beloved bicycle on which he took us children for many an enjoyable ride. I still have a photo of him with my brother and myself perched on the bike; all of us wearing solar topees which were de rigueur in those days.

Uncle finally said his goodbyes amid all sorts of questioning and promises extracted by his sister from her "baby brother". As I listened to them talking about going to war, I realised, even at that young age, that this meant something was up – something "big and sad", as Mum struggled to explain afterwards. Talk began to centre largely around the enemy: spies, concentration camps, etcetera. We were already aware that our parental grandfather was a German who had once served in the German Merchant Navy. Having arrived many years before on the shores of India he had then decided to buy land and property and settle down. "For God's sake," Dad had said, "Don't mention this to anyone or we'll all be for the concentration camp." Looking back it's really amazing how, as young as we were, we so solemnly took this all in. Never a word ever left our lips regarding this family situation. Meanwhile, we often saw our parents sitting in front of the radio listening to the BBC and relying on them for up to date developments.

By and by rationing was introduced, though I can't really remember us ever having to go without. My father was in the fortunate position of being a well-paid employee of the East Indian Railways and practically everything was available on the black market.

At the start of the war, and in order to boost morale, the staff in the railway shed designed and painted red, white and blue V's and fixed them to the front of our houses. Every day I climbed atop the large iron gate which led to our drive and sat gazing up in awe at this giant-sized V. I can say it made a very big impression on a very small girl and I was very proud of it.

Come 1942, my father received promotion, and as was the custom we moved lock, stock and barrel out of the province of Berar and into restless Bihar. There the "Quit India" movement created a great deal of anxiety among the railway people. There was one serious instant never to be forgotten. Word was passed that a mob was due to descend upon us. The running-shed foreman just managed to relay a message to a detachment of British soldiers up the line before the wires were cut. They arrived just in time. Barely had they set up their machine guns – using the ditches for cover – when the mob began marching towards us with burning torches. In the end no blood was shed on either side and thanks to those lads I am here now to tell this tale.

*

Time went on. The Japanese had entered the scene and a more sinister situation was developing. Drivers volunteered to do their bit. Dad would come home, after many days away, and tell us about the troops and ammunition specials being rushed to the Burma front. We got to meet some of these boys as they broke journey and set up camp in our area. A lot of the lads were billeted in our homes. One in particular we children got to know rather well. Titch was just a big kid at heart. He played all the board games with great enthusiasm – Ludo, Snakes and Ladders, Draughts and cards – and squabbled with us every bit as much as we did with him. On moonlight nights we all played shadow-tag. It always ended with the lady of the house sending her servant out with a jug of lemon juice and some glasses – a tactful way of telling us it was time to say goodnight. Our much beloved Titch moved on up to the front and in time we learned he had been killed in action.

Saturday socials were always popular with the soldiers. Everyone was welcome to contribute with a song, dance or anything else that took their fancy: and was there a wealth of talent! Inevitably there were a few romances and even a couple of weddings. Tragedy too, was to strike again. Another Titch, who had become engaged to one of our girls, was also lost at the Burma front.

With the fall of Burma into Japanese hands, the railway

community banded together to provide food and accommodation for the starving and exhausted refugees pouring into the country. The situation was now dire. Calcutta had been subjected to bombing and Pearl Harbour was attacked. As we sat with our suitcase packed in readiness our parents were to be found permanently by the radio listening in to all the news bulletins issued by both Radio Dacca and Radio SEAC. Gradually, the situation improved as the Japanese were beaten back. Our parents heaved a sigh of relief and things began getting back to normal.

Meanwhile, we learned that my uncle had fought in the 8th Army – THE DESERT RATS – at the battle of EL ALAMEIN. Thankfully, he came through and survived the war along with two other uncles. We continued to be linked inextricably with those who had passed our way and I have never, ever forgotten our brave soldier friends. It was all so long ago but somehow it feels like yesterday.

LEONARD GEORGE OLIPHANT
It Was A Long Time For Some Dates

My mam said the government had made my dad join the Air Force. I was eight and my sister was eleven months. One day we all went to the station and my dad kissed us all and got on the train and went away. He said he would come back soon but he didn't. It's funny when your dad isn't there any more. We didn't know where he was for ages because the government used to cut bits out of his letters if they said where he was. My mam said he was abroad and they didn't want the Germans to know where my dad was. This was a bit daft because they should have known I wouldn't ever have told the Germans where my dad was. One day my mam got a letter from him that puzzled her for a bit. In it he said, say hello to Ian, Ron, Ann & Quentin for him – but we didn't know anybody with those names. Then my mam laughed and said he had used a code that told her he was in IRAQ. The government didn't spot the code so they didn't cut that bit out. He was clever, my dad. My mam didn't laugh very much any more – in fact she cried quite a lot when she didn't think I was there. She cried once in a furniture shop when she was talking to a man in a funny black coat and striped trousers. I didn't like him. I remember the day when my Dad came back from being in Iraq when I was eleven. The doorbell rang and I was in on my own so I had to answer it this time. On the front doorstep there was a kit bag! Then a man jumped out from behind the door. He didn't look much like my dad – his face wasn't white anymore like it was when he went away – it was dark brown and wrinkly and his eyebrows were white, but it was my dad. It's great when your dad is back home again. He'd brought me some dates. The war wasn't over so my dad had to stay in the Air Force for a bit longer. This time the government sent him to an aerodrome near Carlisle so he could come home a bit more often. One time when he was home on leave he said I could go back with him and stay on a farm near the aerodrome for a week – and I could take my bike! We put my bike in the guard's van and got off the train at a place called Brampton where my dad had left his bike. The farm was nice and I had lots to eat – bacon and eggs every day. The farmer's wife said I needed fattening up. The farmer could make horse shoes and used to let me work the old bellows that made the fire very hot. When the shoes were still hot he put them against the horse's hoof and this made a lot of smoke and made me cough. I used to watch the planes fly over the farm and knew they must be going to where my dad was. When I went on my bike I could see the planes going lower and lower when they were going to land and if the wind was blowing in the right direction I could sometimes hear the roar of their engines as they took off. I followed the noise and rode along the country lanes trying to get nearer and see them land and take off. There was a big high fence along the side of the road and on the other side there were the Dakotas on the runway. I knew they were Dakotas because I'd seen them in my book of planes. There was a sentry at a big gate in the fence and I asked if I could see his gun but he wouldn't let me have hold of it. I watched the planes for a long time and then began to feel a bit cold so I set off back to the farm. I rode for a long time but the roads seemed different and I got lost. I was in the Scouts and I wished I'd remembered my compass. There was no-one about to ask the way from so I thought I'd go back to the aerodrome and find my dad. The sentry said, "Oh! It's you again, is it?" I asked him to please tell my dad that I'm lost and wanted to see him. He told me to go away or else. When I wouldn't go away he asked who my dad was. I said he was no. 12040459, Corporal Oliphant. I knew from the war films that you weren't supposed to give any more information than that, even to Germans. He gave me a funny look and went into a little hut and picked up a phone. After a few minutes a Hillman pick-up truck came and a nice man in Air Force uniform put my bike in the back and told me to get in beside him. We drove a long way inside the aerodrome and stopped at a big building. He took me inside and gave me a cup of tea and a sticky bun and said my dad would be along shortly. When my dad came he said he was surprised to see me but if I liked he could show me some of the aeroplanes. How big they were when you stood beside them on the ground. He took me in to a Dakota and let me sit in the pilot's seat and play with the joystick. He called it a control column but I knew Biggles called it a joystick. When I'd done a mission to Germany and looped the loop a few times he said it was time to go back to the farm. Next morning the farmer was very interested in my adventure and then he sold me his penknife.

ROGER PAINE
Marks Of Respect

The Royal Navy has many traditions. One that endures is that of stopping a warship at sea in the position where sea battles were fought or ships were sunk as a mark of respect for the sailors who were killed or drowned there.

Position 36.32N 6.16W

In 1958 when HMS Victorious sailed for the Mediterranean after ten years of modernisation, she was the most advanced aircraft carrier in the Royal Navy. As a young sailor in my first ship I was thrilled to be serving in this huge vessel and excited by the prospect of going ashore in Gibraltar. It was early October and the warmth of the sun was in a stark contrast to the chill Autumn days left behind.

The coastline of Spain was clearly visible but now we sailed to within three miles where the bright sunshine reflecting off the sea made the lighthouse on the cliffs seem unnaturally close. It was Cape Trafalgar. One hundred and fifty three years previously these same seas had witnessed the defeat of the combined fleets of France and Spain by the British fleet under Admiral Lord Nelson.

It was late afternoon and on the quarter-deck I was close to the sea which splashed over the immaculately scrubbed decks. The ship's engines had been stopped and for a warship with fifteen hundred men on board it was eerily silent. The ship rolled in the Atlantic swell and the chaplain conducted a brief service in memory of the 429 British and 2,800 French and Spanish sailors killed in the Battle of Trafalgar on 21st October 1805. We sang "Eternal Father Strong To Save" and our Captain read aloud Nelson's prayer, which he composed on the eve of the battle. The chaplain threw into the sea a wreath of laurel leaves. Slowly it floated away and we observed a minute's silence.

Suddenly I was able to visualise the wooden ships with their canvas sails billowing and signal flags streaming, sailing towards each other, and to imagine the fear the sailors must have experienced as their vessels fired broadside after broadsie at point blank range. I watched as the wreath began to sink down to where the hulks of the ships lay, entombing the remains of those brave nineteenth century sailors destined to never again see the ports from which they had sailed.

Position 3.33N 104.28E

After guardship duty in Hong Kong and leave in Subic Bay, amongst the United States Navy on "R&R" from the Vietnam War in 1972, it was good to be back at sea. I was now an officer in the frigate HMS Lincoln on passage to Singapore through the South China Sea. Just over the horizon lay the coast of Malaysia and the surrounding sea was busy with ocean freighters and tankers. At noon we slowed almost to a stop but remained in the shipping lane.

Thirty one years previously on a similarly clear, sunny day, Vice Admiral Phillips in the battleship HMS Prince of Wales, accompanied by the battle cruiser HMS Repulse, was returning to Singapore having failed to find the expected invasion by Japanese forces on the Malaysian coast. At 11 o'clock in the morning of 10th December 1941 both ships were suddenly attacked by bombs and torpedoes dropped from enemy aircraft launched from shore bases already held by the Japanese. Both ships were sunk within an hour of each other with the combined loss of 840 men.

The breeze created by our movement through the translucent sea had ceased and we stood in stifling heat on the open quarterdeck. The propellers continued to turn idly to create a soapsudlike wash. The heat from the deck came up through our sandals and perspiration soaked our white uniforms. The Captain read the naval prayer "O Eternal Lord God who alone spreadest out the Heavens..." and the Master at Arms threw a Chinese-made wreath of artificial flowers over the stern. As it churned away in our wake and we continued on our voyage to Singapore I remembered the two ships and their sailors, lying in their eternal grave two hundred feet below, but who were never able to complete the same journey.

Position 31.8S 45.26W

On Remembrance Day at sea a traditional church service is held. In 1982, I was serving on an Admiral's staff taking the first group of ships to the South Atlantic after the Falklands conflict earlier that year. HMS Antrim, our flagship, had been involved in the campaign. At 11 am on Sunday 14th November we gathered on the flight deck for our service. We were 600 miles from the coast of Brazil and over 1,000 miles from the Falkland Islands.

The ship was stopped and although it was nearly midsummer, there were heavy grey clouds and the ship rolled clumsily in the swell which, with its deep blue black troughs and breaking white crests, rolls incessantly between the sub-continents.

Remembrance services can sometimes seem remote from the wars which they commemorate. Not on this occasion. The recent conflict and the loss of 252 British servicemen was uppermost in our minds and everyone felt a sense of personal loss. When the words "They gave Their Tomorrow for Our Today" were said, followed by the traditional two minutes silence, the poignancy of the occasion raised the hairs on the back of my neck and probably moistened many eyes.

Wreaths of poppies were thrown into the sea. As they drifted away in the ship's wake an albatross, a frequent follower of ships in the Southern oceans, glided and floated above on its graceful wings as the ship rose and dipped with the waves. I looked up and watched its almost motionless flight and wondered whether it was too fanciful to imagine that this majestic bird, which legend says retains the souls of drowned mariners, was visiting to pay its own traditional mark of respect.

COLIN J PEARCE
One April Day

It was the smell I noticed first.

We'd beaten the Germans good and proper, it was just a matter of time before the whole bloody lot of them just threw in the towel for good and then we'd all be able to go home. But then we smelled that smell.

I pulled the Sherman off the road, its great drab bulk resting with one track on the verge and the other in the mud and the five of us scrambled out and began to stretch our legs a bit. There was Archie Bates, the gunner and my particular mate, Big Ron Appleyard, he was the radio operator, Chris Clarke, the loader; he had a stammer that got worse when he was under pressure but the funny thing was that he lost it whenever he sang, which thankfully wasn't often, because he had a voice like a bull with a sore throat that's about to lose his tackle. Then there was Bill Simmonds, our commander, and me, I was the driver.

We'd been together a long time, since before Normandy, and we'd seen lots of our mates come and go, mostly go, since D-Day and we'd come a long way together, all the way into Germany itself.

We'd seen a lot of fighting, more than I particularly cared for, and now that the end was in sight we'd learned to be a bit more careful, especially since the Jerries had been setting booby traps and little ambushes and other surprises. But this place seemed safe enough.

It was just a large village like any other we'd seen, knocked about by shells and bombs and that, but the locals seemed just a bit more eager to wave white flags at us. And there was that smell.

Well, our CO shot past in his jeep with his little escort group and the troop leaders stood about looking worried, but no-one seemed to know what was going on, so we just stood around our tanks, waiting. Archie and Ron got the stove out and we brewed up some tea and Bill went off to try and find out why we'd stopped, but then the CO came back looking like he'd seen a ghost and we got orders to round up every German we could find and stand them in line.

We was all a bit shaken by this but orders is orders and Bill told me and Archie to get our guns and go and look for Germans. Pretty soon we'd herded a largish group of them together, about a hundred or so, all looking very sheepish and the CO said that we should march them out of the village and up the road about a mile. Well, we still didn't know what was going on but the Germans started to make a bit of a fuss, crying and pleading away, trying to hang back, but we had guns and they didn't, so they went along without too much trouble. And all the while that smell got stronger and stronger.

And then we knew where it was coming from.

Up ahead we could see a fence and a lot of low buildings, like long sheds. And there were these people, hundreds of them, just standing there.

And the closer we got, the worse the smell got. Well, I felt pretty sick and as we got to a gate I could see that there wasn't just hundreds but thousands of them, all thin. They were the thinnest people I'd ever seen, like skeletons, dressed in rags and scraps and there were hundreds of people lying down on the ground. I thought they were sleeping, or sick or something but as we went in I saw they were dead and had been for days, and these other people were just standing there, looking at us with these bid, sad eyes.

Then the Germans we'd rounded up began moaning and groaning and crying and some of them tried to get away, but we made sure they stayed where they were.

And then we saw the children, stick thin and dressed like the others in striped jackets that hung from them like sacks, all just standing there watching us as we watched them. And they all stood there in silence, just looking at us. And the smell was awful, sort of sweet and sickly and sour at the same time.

Then the CO and his escort found some Germans in SS uniforms, mostly oldish types, not much use for fighting and he made them start digging trenches for the bodies. Then we got the civilians we'd rounded up to start collecting the dead, but they didn't want to do it, saying it was nothing to do with them, they didn't even know this place existed and even if they did, what could they have done?, but we made them do it anyway. And all the time these people just looked at us like we was from another world.

Well, we'd seen death. But nothing could have prepared us for this place with its corpses and its smell and all the people still living, but dead at the same time if you know what I mean, and most of us were sick to our stomachs with the sight of it and the smell of it and it was a mercy when some other unit, with bulldozers, took over a bit later on. But it's stayed with me all these years, and when it's quiet at the end of the day I can still see them standing there, watching.

I've been back there once and it's a quiet place, all heathland. There's no trees there and the birds don't sing. It's just filled with this immense sadness. There's these mounds, each marked with the number buried there and they're buried in their thousands. I remember when we got back to our tanks and moved on we saw a sign outside the village.

Belsen.

LES PEATE
Going Home

Norman knew that he was going home. Soon he would be back in his sleepy village and the nightmare would go away. No more nights spent huddled in knee-deep water in rat-infested trenches, no more lice and scanty rations, and most of all, no longer would he live under incessant bombardment and see his friends blown into fragments.

Everything that had happened over the last few days was a confused blur but he knew that now he would be going home – perhaps for good.

It was the second time in his eighteen years that he had been buried alive but now he was safe and wouldn't have to go back into the line again.

He remembered how he had crept out of his mother's cottage last year – it seemed a lifetime ago – to run away with his village mates to go for a soldier. Although the rigours of training camp were difficult for his simple mind, his chums helped him through until at last they all went on a ship, then on a long march, into the barren front line area.

He remembered the first time that he felt the terror of being buried alive. A big "Jack Johnson" landed on his dugout and he was crushed under tons of muck, timber and the bodies of his mates. When they dug him out, an hour later, he was the only one of his section alive. The Medical Officer sent him to the hospital and then to England and home for a seven day rest. Now he was going home again.

This time he was the only soldier left when a heavy artillery shell had destroyed the section of his trench where his platoon was waiting to go over the top. He was half-blinded, deafened and completely dazed. He wandered about the area trying to find his rifle (Sergeant Clifton had told him NEVER to be without his weapon, but Sergeant Clifton was dead with all the others).

The next thing he remembered was that an officer, whom he didn't know, asked him where he was going. Norman mumbled some sort of reply; his muddled mind couldn't remember what he said except that he was looking for his rifle. He didn't know how long it had been since the shelling – it must have been quite a while as he was tired and hungry. Soon afterwards a medical orderly from the "Rob All My Comrades" (as his friends call the RAMC) appeared to take his arm and lead him to an abandoned ruin, where he checked Norman for injuries, bandaged his cuts and scratches and gave him a mug of hot tea with (Norman was sure) a tot of rum in it.

Some time later, Norman recalled, he was led into a room where there were more officers. He didn't know any of them well, although he recognised one of them as his unit's new medical officer. They asked him a lot of questions that his befuddled mind couldn't understand and then a soldier conducted him to a room where he enjoyed the luxury of his own cot with two clean blankets. After the soldier had brought him a mug of tea and a bacon sandwich, he lay on the cot and, for the first time in weeks, slept soundly.

After the luxury of a wash and breakfast (his teenage fuzz didn't call for a shave) he returned to an exhausted sleep, although his dreams were plagued by nightmares of trench raids, rats and bombardments. Later in the day another strange officer came in to see him and read him something from a paper, but it was full of long words and he couldn't understand it. Anxiously he asked. "Will I have to go back to the trenches again?". The officer smiled sympathetically and replied that, "No, he would not".

Now he was going home. The friendly soldier who had been looking after him brought him another rum-laced mug of strong sweet front-line tea, shook his hand and said "goodbye". The medical officer, with Captain Marston, the chaplain from his own unit whom he didn't know very well, came to see him and walked with him into what was once the kitchen garden of the ruined farm. He noticed a group of members of his own regiment by the door – their clean uniforms and equipment a stark contrast to his own mud and blood-soiled khaki rags – the poor buggers were probably a new draft on their way to the trenches. He said "hello" to them but they didn't answer. He felt sorry for them and a little guilty; he was going home!

He sat in an old kitchen chair that they had offered him, enjoying the early morning sunshine. There was a nip in the air but that added to his feeling of well-being because today he was going home.

The MO pinned a label over his breast pocket. He remembered that last time he was sent home they had placed what they called a "casualty tag" on his uniform to describe his injuries; this must mean that he was on his way. Now the doctor was going to bandage his head – why was he doing this – it wasn't bleeding. Now the bandage is covering his eyes – something is very, very wrong – what is going on?

*

During the First World War, 265 Commonwealth soldiers were executed by firing squad for the alleged offences of desertion or cowardice in the face of the enemy. Many of these were of limited intellect. Some were still in their teens; others had previously been severely wounded. Several were suffering from shell-shock, a condition which court-martial boards frequently refused to recognise. "Justice" was usually dispensed without delay.

KAREN PHILLIPS
Jack's War

"Oh no, Jack's at it again!" exclaimed Claire, the overworked care assistant.

"What's that?" whispered Gareth, apprehensive of the reply.

"Jack's taken all the sugar off the tables and is refusing to let anyone have any," answered Claire.

"Why would he do that?" asked Gareth timidly, not sure whether he should be asking those questions.

"Well," said Claire, whom Gareth was shadowing during his work experience from school. "Jack lived through the last war and there was rationing of food. He thinks he's back during the war and he's hiding the sugar to stop people using it. He'll be singing next."

Sure enough Jack began singing war songs... "Pack up your troubles in your old kit bag ..."

Claire went over to Jack and, after some persuasion, Jack told her where he had hidden the sugar. Claire told Jack that rationing had finished and she put the sugar back on the tables before continuing with her duties.

Jack sat meekly back in his chair staring at the sugar bowls, not convinced that rationing had finished.

Gareth was curious about what had happened. Claire seemed to take it as commonplace but as it was his first day at the residential home he felt that he should not ask any more questions, besides, Claire didn't seem to have much time to talk to the residents let alone him.

*

The next day, however, Gareth plucked up courage to talk to Jack. He was singing, "It's a long way to Tipperary...It's a long way to go..."

"That's a nice song, Jack," said Gareth.

"I like it," said Jack.

"What's that flower in your lapel?"

"It's a poppy...for remembrance," he answered, surprised at such an obvious question.

"Remembrance?" queried Gareth.

"Yes, to remember those who lost their lives in the war."

"Were you in the war, Jack?"

He stared at Gareth. "Yes, all my friends and my brother too. For King and country," said Jack, proudly.

Jack was more alert now. Gareth wondered when was the last time anyone had had time to talk to him. Jack's eyes were bright now. "We weren't much older that you when we signed up. Cyril was older than me. We were together until I got wounded. That was the end of the war for me."

"What was the war like, Jack?" asked Gareth getting interested. He had never spoken to an old soldier before and Jack was pleased to have someone to talk to.

"Not very nice, lad, not very nice. But I met some good and loyal friends. It's amazing how close you get when you face death together. I've never known friendship like it." Jack was sad now as he recalled those days long ago.

"Do you ever see your friends now, Jack?" asked Gareth.

Jack looked out of the window with tears in his eyes and said, "No lad, most of them were killed. My best friend Jimmy, he caught a shell." Jack continued with a break in his voice. "He died in my arms." There was a long pause before he continued. "Only a few of us came back, lad. We weren't the same carefree young lads who had volunteered. The horrors we'd seen and lived through made us older than our years."

Jack was silent, deep in his own thoughts. Gareth too had lots to think about. He had never met anyone who had actually lived and fought through the war. He hated History at school. He found it boring and dates difficult to remember but listening to Jack made Gareth realise that history was about real people. Not just words and pictures in books, but real people. Gareth realised now that people had lived through an horrendous time. He understood that those memories had never left them. From this day on History would have a different meaning for him.

He was brought rudely out of his thoughts when Jack jumped up suddenly from his seat and was heading for the tables. He picked up the sugar bowls and put them behind the cupboard in the corner of the room. Gareth watched in amazement as Claire hurried after Jack and brought him back to his chair. She then patiently placed the sugar bowls neatly back on the tables.

Gareth, looking puzzled, asked, "Why do you hide the sugar bowls, Jack?"

"There's rationing on, lad. Mustn't waste it," Jack answered with a frown.

"But why do you hide the sugar?" asked Gareth again.

"Jack looked puzzled at, to him, such an obvious question. "There's rationing on, lad. We must keep some for Cyril."

"Cyril?" asked Gareth.

"My brother...Cyril. He hasn't come back from the war yet and we must keep some sugar for him."

Gareth and Claire, who had joined them, were stunned. All traces of exasperation had left Claire now and she suggested to Jack that they keep some sugar for when Cyril came home. She put some sugar into a plastic bag and gave it to Jack who, face beaming, put it into his inside breast pocket.

"Cyril takes sugar in his tea." he said.

ANDY PHIPPS
Echoes

There was no particular reason why David Levi always sat on his own in class. He was popular enough. He joined in his fair share of playground fun. But in the scramble for seats next to "best friends, never never break friends" he was always the odd one out.

It was Thursday morning, the last lesson before lunch. David sat, pencil poised over '32/4 =', staring directly into the sun that blazed through the classroom window. David's thoughts floated high above the anxious whispers of twenty eight seven year olds trapped in mathematical torment. Instant silence accompanied the entrance of the headmistress, a tall woman with half-moon glasses clamped on an arched nose. Her hand clasped the rigid fingers of a thin boy whose crew-cut hair stood to attention next to her bony shoulder.

"This is Christoph," she announced. "He is joining your class. Do make him welcome."

Christoph's hand was passed over to the moist plumpness of Mrs Bradshaw, the class teacher.

"Hello, Christoph," she said. "Welcome to Red Class." Her eyes perfunctorily scanned the rows of nudging children. "You can sit next to David over there. That will be nice won't it David?"

David did not reply. He stared straight ahead, uncomfortable with such abrupt attention. He noticed that Christoph's neck was red and getting redder as he hesitantly made his way to his new desk and sat down.

"Okay class, calm down," said Mrs Bradshaw with a clap.

David quickly polished off the sums as Mrs Bradshaw talked quietly to Christoph. He then reverted to staring out of the window, idly twisting his curly hair with the chewed end of his pencil.

When the bell unleashed the class, David and Christoph remained seated until the room was empty. Finally, David turned to Christoph, smiled and said, "Hello, my name's David. Do you want to go and play?"

Typically the good weather collapsed the week before the summer holidays, much to Mrs Levi's annoyance. It was hard enough to get David out from under her feet at the best of times, if the weather wasn't good she'd have no chance. Just what she needed, especially with Gran taking a turn for the worse: so this holiday, David wouldn't be able to spend hours and hours listening to her talk about the past, hanging on her every word. Though that might just be for the best, he was getting a bit obsessed. She involuntarily glanced at the newspaper cutting given pride of place amidst a jumble of memorabilia on the table under the stairs. Did he really have to keep it? It had been so long. A young woman, dressed in a coarse, striped dress, with a shaven head that made her look like a featherless sparrow, stared out through barbed wire in silent reproach.

Mrs Levi needn't have worried. First day of the holiday, as grey clouds scudded against the nearby hills. David was up, dressed and ready for breakfast: bright and early, raring to go.

"I'm going to play with Christoph today," he declared, spraying toast crumbs down his shirt.

And that was how it went throughout the long days of the summer holiday.

Christoph and David were inseparable, a fledgling Laurel and Hardy: tall, fair and thin forever playing with short, dark and stocky. Catch me if you can. Cowboys and Indians. David Ginola slamming in a goal. Soldiers grubbing in the undergrowth. Olympic athletes. Run, run, run just for fun, fun, fun.

Then they'd flop on the grass in delicious exhaustion and chatter non-stop, in half sentences, about how one day, soon, let it be soon, they'd go together to Christoph's real home, with its "hundreds and hundreds and hundreds" of different sausages and stretch-forever forests on reach-to-heaven mountains.

Every evening, Mrs Levi would chide her son for being so dirty but her temper was lulled by the warmth of seeing her David ruddy cheeked and worn out from doing "what seven year olds are supposed to do".

And that was how it went throughout the long days of the summer holiday...

...until the very last day, when the grumbling weather finally unleashed an angry storm that dared all comers to give it a try.

"Mum, Mum," moaned David. "Can Christoph come here to

play? Please. Please. Pleeeeeeease."

"Okay. But you'll have to be extra quiet. You know Granny's not feeling too well."

It was arranged in an instant, by David himself, keener than ever before to use the telephone. Christoph's mother drove him over and he dashed the ten yards up the path, discarded sodden wellies and cagoule and clattered after David up the stairs.

They sat on the floor of David's bedroom with a map spread out in front of them. They were giggling. David said, "Okay. In German, then. And it's a really big fire. Really big. Ready?" and together they leapt up, shouted "Feuer! Feuer!" and dashed out of the room.

"Raus! Raus! Schnell!... Raus! Raus! Schnell!... Raus! Raus! Schnell!..."

Then silence.

In a darkened doorway stood a trembling woman with a face like a creased sparrow. She was wearing a plain white nightdress. In a voice more powerful than David had ever heard her use, she cried out "Gotteniu! Shut up. Shut up. Not that. Please God. That language. Not that. Leave me alone. Biteh! Loz mich tzu ru!"

She crumpled to the floor.

"Granny," shouted David, running over to her.

Christoph stared, then ran, ran, ran, down the stairs, into fumbled boots and out into the rain, leaving his cagoule stretched across the back of a kitchen chair.

As Mrs Levi helped her mother-in-law back to bed, David ran to his bedroom and stared out of the window. A tear dripped down his cheek.

JEAN PIMP
Sorrow Upon Sorrow

Winding its way through the countryside like a cold lava trail, filled with a gangrenous soup of stinking mire, the trench was the only shelter for a pathetic band of ragged skeleton creatures who were once recognisable as soldiers, smart and proud, their pride reflecting in the shine on their buttons and boots. Now their boots were unseen, lost in the grasping, glutinous glue that gyrated all beneath them. Huddling under makeshift shelters the days were bombarding Hell, the nights black and fearful, the young, soft-skinned boys to whom razors were alien cried for their mothers in the velvet blackness, their sobs rising above the gurgling morass they were rooted in. Beady eyes watched from seeping holes, the black rats grew fat on mislaid bodies, floating excrement and the putrefying flesh of the injured. Old soldiers despaired at the useless slaughter, the pious cried out to a God deaf to their pleas. The young had no hope and just went mad.

His mother had lovingly called him Brian, breast fed him on her knee, heard his first prayers, watched him suddenly grow up and wept when he was called for his country. Now he sat on a log, soaking his feet in a vile brew of diluted human waste. A rusted enamel mug in one hand, a long-awaited letter in the other. The sergeant said, "Drink your tea and read your letter", patting the boy on the shoulder. The youth was at a low ebb, the man knew that, he could read the signs. That haunted look in the eyes, tight-lipped reluctance to speak, he had seen it all before.

Crumpled and torn the scrawled on paper fell and floated like a leaf on a pond, the boy watched it and dreamed of home. The farmhouse, when on baking day his mother, elbow-deep in dough for the bread, would sit him by the fire with a hot crust heavy with butter. He felt a terrible longing to be there in that warm kitchen with his dear mother. That could not be, his mama was dead. It was there in the letter. Dry sobs racked his body, gasping and heaving uncontrollably, his hope gone now. He snatched up the rifle that leaned by his side, lifting it high to his shoulder he fired in the air screaming incoherently, the bullets whizzed and ricocheted round the trench. A young soldier close by was hit square in the stomach, blood oozing through his fingers as he clutched his body, a strange astonishment on his face. Brian, the beloved son of a dead mother had killed only once in this bloody war.

The blood was hot and spurting, washing the caked mud from the boy's fingers, slowly spreading like a large red poppy growing from his chest. He had no understanding of his injury, the warm moisture felt comforting, he had no pain, just a faint feeling of surprise. Brian had been his friend, he had watched his violent outburst, now he felt his comrade's arms about him, felt his hot tears wash warm against his cheek. Was this war really a game where each took his turn and then returned home? He hoped so, he felt very tired, perhaps they would take him home and let him rest, if it was his time to go.

DAVID PIPER
An Ordinary Gunner Under Combat Stress

I always considered my father to be just an ordinary mortal, a quiet and gentle person, considerate and good natured. He had been in the Royal Artillery for eighteen years and spent six years in India during the 1930s. In 1940 he was posted to Malta with thousands of other servicemen to help defend that tiny, vulnerable island, and remained there during the worst of the bombing and the siege until 1945.

When I was a youngster I was full of questions about the war and he sometimes talked about the heavy bombing, some of the incidents that happened, the mates he lost, or how badly wounded some of them were. He also mentioned the three bi-planes that were Malta's air defence when he arrived, the legendary Faith, Hope and Charity. I always had a general impression of how things were but it was not until recent years and some studying of the Malta conflict that I came to realise just how bad the situation had been and how people had really suffered. I distinctly remember his comment, they could set their watches by the timing of the air raids during those terrible days of the siege.

My father's convoy arrived near Malta in early 1940 to be greeted by enemy bombers and the raids persisted for six hours before they could enter Valletta Harbour. During this time the convoy formed a protective circle and the troops were shut down below decks. He recalls that everyone on board during this time was sea sick, the only time he had ever been sick at sea in all his travels. He always praised the courage of the marines and sailors on board those ships and said they treated the troops they were carrying like "kings".

Besides the Maltese forces on the Island there were a number of infantry battalions, several light anti-aircraft regiments, a number of heavy anti-aircraft regiments, Field artillery regiments and Royal Navy and Air Force personnel. Everyone not flying or manning guns or searchlights helped to keep the runways clear, fill in bomb craters, unload ships, clear wreckage and rubble, build defences and the myriad of unpleasant jobs that this war torn island had to do.

My father had to help unload and clean up the ships that limped into Valletta Harbour after running the gauntlet of U-boats and air raids in the Mediterranean. Many enemy aircraft were shot down over the island and many aircrew were killed. Someone had to clear the wreckage and dispose of the bodies.

The bombing of Malta continued through 1940, 1941 and 1942 with air raids averaging 100 – 150 per month, first by the Italians and then more intensely by the Germans. Then the strategy changed and the Germans decided that they needed Malta in order to control the Mediterranean and protect their supply routes to North Africa, Greece, Italy and the Far East. At this stage they went all out to annihilate this tiny island and the siege began in earnest. Air raids during 1942 were intensified to average 250 per month reaching a climax of 285 in one month. Each raid was said to be the equivalent of the blitz on Coventry and this pressure was kept up for months on end. On some days the raids lasted all day and right through the night and many islanders virtually lived in the air raid shelters.

During this time the island was fighting back with the few Spitfires and Hurricanes that were able to reach the island in one piece. Bombing raids were planned from Malta on enemy shipping in the Mediterranean to hit the enemy where it hurt and preventing supplies reaching the Axis forces in North Africa. Anti-aircraft cover was cleverly arranged on the island so that the bombers had to fly through barrages of steel – when there was enough ammunition to use.

The problem was that the supply convoys trying to get through the Mediterranean to deliver their precious cargoes were being ravaged by U-boats and continuous air strikes, so food, clothes, ammunition, fuel etc. were in very short supply and running out rapidly. At one point at the height of the siege, the islanders had just enough food to last for a further six days, and these were very meagre rations. The island's saviour was the convoy of August 1942 which included the "Ohio" and the Maltese still celebrate its arrival to this day calling it the "Convoy of Santa Maria". It was hit with everything that Germany could throw at it and most of the ships were lost but the survivors were able to limp into Valletta Harbour. In the War Museum in Valetta there is a picture of the "Ohio" limping into the Grand Harbour being supported on either side by destroyers.

The people of Malta and the servicemen there had to endure over 3,300 air raids during those fateful years and the island was awarded the George Cross to reflect the bravery during the Second World War and the nature of these people is such that they have long since forgiven their tormentors for assaulting their homeland.

After demob from the army my father settled down with his family in the village of Shrewton on Salisbury Plain close to Larkhill, where he worked, and Boscombe Down. For some time after the war if an aircraft was heard overhead my father would not settle until he had checked that is was friendly. There was no counselling in those days. My Father died in 1978 and I knew that he had suffered some deprivation during the war but I had not appreciated how much he had suffered along with those islanders during the nightmare of that siege, and what a quiet courage he possessed.

JOHN POARCH
Lest We Forget

Staff meeting was almost over when the phone rang. The vicar picked up the receiver and said, "Hullo! St Michael's Vicarage."

Tim Smith watched his boss listen carefully and tried to work out what the conversation was about from the disjointed bits he heard.

"Oh! I'm sorry...when did...I'm not surprised, of course...Yes...Yes...No ...Yes, that should be all right but can I confirm that in about half an hour? Thank you!"

Tim raised an eyebrow in interrogation.

"Alice Bridgewater has died," said the vicar. "I don't suppose you had an opportunity to get to know her."

Tim scanned his memory. The name rang a bell. He had taken a Harvest Festival service in the lounge at Restholme and there had been a tiny old lady, her head sunk on her chest, propped up in a high-backed armchair and the warden had roared in her ear, "Alice! This is the new curate," and Alice had raised her head with an effort and smiled and then drooped forward again. "Alice Bridgewater", the warden had whispered by way of explanation. "Poor dear!" She must have been getting on for a hundred.

"Yes," said Tim, "I remember her. It won't be a big funeral, I suppose."

"Oh yes it will!" said the vicar. "Not that there will be a lot of people there. So many of her friends have died and there's no family to speak of. But the Legion will be represented. Alice used to run the Women's Section and organised the Poppy Day Appeal from her tiny flat – you couldn't move for poppies! – until she moved to Restholme. So the Legion will be there. And I'll be surprised if the mayor doesn't come – I must make sure he knows. Anyway, not a large congregation. But I'm expecting a packed church."

Tim wondered how the vicar was going to solve that conundrum and his bewilderment must had shown because he saw the vicar smile and he waited for the explanation. There was clearly more to Alice Bridgewater than he would have guessed.

The vicar was in reflective mood and there was a long pause before he started to speak again. "I've known Alice for nearly thirty years," he said, "ever since I first came to the parish. She wasn't much given to talking about herself and a lot of what I know I've pieced together from things others have told me. But I remember, when I had known her for some little time, asking her why she had never married. And I don't suppose her answer could have been more simple or more revealing. She said, 'I lost my man in the First War'".

The vicar was silent again and Tim had a sense of being on holy ground.

"She was seventeen at the time," the vicar went on. "She wasn't engaged, but there was an understanding. Luke was his name. He was in the Royal Engineers and he was killed on 18th October 1918 – easy to remember because it happens to be St Luke's Day. When the news came through Alice was at the aircraft factory where she worked – she used to sew canvas on the wings of planes – and they sent her home. But the next day," and the vicar shook his head in disbelief, "she was back at her bench again."

Tim saw in his mind's eye the tiny bent figure in the high armchair.

"Not that she was hard, Tim. Far from it. Or even bitter. What we saw in Alice was divine compassion. Luke had a younger brother who survived the war by thirty years. I say survived! Most of those years were spent in hospital. But those times when he was able to face the world, Alice looked after him. In fact, years before 'counselling' was discovered, Alice was ministering to life's wounded. There was no fuss. No drama. I used to enlist her help. She had a knack of sharing people's pain."

There was another pause.

"She seems to have been a remarkable lady," said Tim.

"I expect The Advertiser will dust down their files," the vicar continued, "and reprint the story they dug up for her ninetieth birthday – Party for Local Heroine, I think they called it – this was the Second War, of course, and it was during the last big raid they had here. A bomb destroyed a house but didn't explode, and there was a young boy trapped in the cellar, and she crawled through to be with him until they could clear the debris for the medical team."

"She got a medal for that, I expect."

"No," said the vicar. "And she wouldn't have wanted one –

never saw herself in the heroic mould. Though I've never seen such quiet heroism in all my life – and I'm not thinking now about the bomb incident."

"When do they want the funeral?" asked Tim.

"Next Wednesday, November 11th, in the morning."

"Won't that be difficult with the other things going on?" His boss was a dry old stick, reflected Tim, but there were some things he felt strongly about, and observing Armistice Day happened to be one of them.

"Actually it might work together rather well. And, when you think of it, there could hardly be a more suitable day."

Tim was beginning to sense that he knew the answer to the vicar's conundrum, but he thought he would prompt him anyway. "So, you're expecting a packed church for Alice Bridgewater!" he said.

"That's right, Tim. A mighty host. And, if we listen very carefully, we may hear the trumpets sounding for her.

IVOR PETER POWELL
My War

It seems rather strange at this distance, but war for young boys like myself could sometimes be quite exciting and often was a great adventure. I am not trying to pretend we were not often terrified. Especially during the blitz when we were taken from our beds to shelter under the stairs or in our neighbour's Anderson shelter when things were too bad to stay indoors.

War had always been part of my life even before then. My Dad had fought in the First World War and had been wounded during the second Battle of the Somme. My uncle, too, a Company Sergeant Major, had won the Distinguished Conduct Medal for gallantry in the trenches. Quite frequently we children were treated to these old soldiers telling of their reminiscences.

The Second World War saw the enlistment of two of my brothers as well as numerous cousins, all of whom joined the Royal Air Force. I was therefore very familiar with service life and its consequences.

To return to ourselves as little boys, we committed ourselves to learning as much as we could about the war as we confidently expected that one day we too would take our places in the Services. It became a kind of quest, or competition, to see who could outdo the other.

We challenged each other with aircraft recognition and anyone who could not instantly recognise aircraft of our own and the German Air Force did not have much prestige in the gang. I can still tell the difference between an ME109E and an ME109F! I could easily recognise the outline of a Dornier 17 or an FW190.

In common with my school mates I collected shrapnel, or indeed any souvenirs from the hostilities. Once they brought to our town a complete enemy aircraft which had been shot down and was almost intact. It was put on show and we all turned up to see it. We also came prepared with a series of screwdrivers and hacksaws hidden under our jackets. At the end of the week it was quite amusing to see the aircraft had been practically stripped and there remained just the bare airframe! Everything of value had been taken by the souvenir hunters!

After each air raid the next morning our first task was to search the streets for pieces of shrapnel or cartridge cases to add to our collection. Sometimes we were envious when someone found the fins of an incendiary bomb which had burned out the previous night. Once at school someone brought in a large portion of a German parachute which had been used attached to a flare which the German bombers used to drop to illuminate their target areas.

These flares were awesome things. I can well remember seeing them descend a certain November night in 1940 when the first big blitz on Bristol took place. We emerged from our home at the height of the raid to seek shelter in the Anderson shelter next door. The whole sky was ablaze with flares descending and the fiery tracer bullets of the anti-aircraft defences streaking upward toward the German aircraft. It was like hell on earth and at that time we did not think it so much of an adventure.

Once, after a heavy air raid, we were exploring the next morning for souvenirs and we went to one of our favourite haunts which was a local quarry, partially filled with water. We often went there to catch newts. On this occasion I was delighted to find two complete incendiary bombs lying in the water. I could not wait to retrieve them and show my friends. My prestige was bound to go sky high with these! We took them home and tried to see if we could ignite them. These were the type which ignited on impact and we threw them into the air hoping for them to provide a super fireworks display when they landed. It was not long before the nervous neighbours had sent for the air raid wardens and they turned up at our house asking for these bombs to be surrendered. I always remember their saying to me, "You can have the fins back – after the war!".

My collection grew and along the mantelpiece in my bedroom was lined a series of bullets and cannon shells, with pride of place going to a 0.5 inch cannon shell from an American plane! My Mum was not too pleased but I convinced her they were all safe.

At school we heard how one of our classmates had found a practice firing range at the local RAF station and had come back from there with a number of 20 mm cannon shells. Everyone in the school was interested and gathered around eagerly to see the haul.

A few days later I was sitting in a particularly boring history lesson at school. It was a bright, sunny, autumnal day and the groundsman was cutting the grass on the sportsfield outside. One of my friends, sitting right next to me, was preoccupied with something in his lap. All of a sudden there was a tremendous explosion and from that instant the reality of war was changed forever for me. Never again would I look at it in the same way.

The carnage of that classroom brought home to us all the dread seriousness of war and what it could do. I had known that boy since birth. We had lived next door to each other and I had grown up with him. In an instant he was blown to pieces and we, as young children, were called upon to witness this terrible situation.

No more was war an adventure. It was months before I could sleep properly and today – more than fifty years afterwards – that picture is as vivid as it was then. My collection of souvenirs disappeared instantly. I do not know to this day what became of them but I suspect my mother had a hand in it. I did not mind. I had had enough.

DAVID PRATT
Christmas 1914

You've heard the story before. How the guns fell silent on Christmas Eve, the men on both sides sang carols and then came out of the trenches and fraternised in No Man's Land. And it's true. I saw it. I was there.

I was a private in the 7th Cheshire Light Infantry. First day of the war I'd volunteered with my brother Tom, he nineteen and I seventeen and lying about my age. Tom had been killed at Mons, twenty feet from where I stood. I hadn't let myself think about it much.

It was nearly midnight when we heard them singing "Silent Night". We were manning a Forward Observation Post, eighty yards from their front line. Wilf Toogood took out his mouth organ and began playing. We heard shouts of "Merry Christmas, Englanders!"

I was watching through a periscope, there was a new moon and I saw a white flag come up over their parapet. "They're coming out," I said. Men jumped to the fire step. "No," I said, "there's a flag". Wilf took the periscope and looked through it. Then he started tying a handkerchief to his bayonet.

"Don't do it, Wilf," I said. "You'll be shot".

"We're all going to get bloody shot, anyway," Wilf said, and began to wave the flag above the parapet. Then he climbed the ladder. We waited for his body to fall back, but there was no firing. Other men peered through machine-gun slits. Suddenly men were climbing out of their trenches all along the line. And there they were, walking toward us in their grey uniforms, the men we'd been trying to kill for three months.

We met in the fifty yards between the wire. Hardly anyone spoke the other side's language. There were handshakes, "Merry Christmas", cigarettes exchanged. I saw something flying over and ducked. It was a soccer ball, and a game started right off.

I put myself at outside left, and found myself tangling with their right half, a serious-looking bloke who played hard and ran fast. He took a pass and when I intercepted him we collided, cannoning into the muddy ground. When we got up, we let the game go on without us . He took out a cigarette case and offered me a smoke. He had fair hair cut short and features that reminded me of one of the statues outside the Liverpool Museum.

"My name is Wolfgang," he said.

"Albert," I said, suddenly formal. No one ever called me anything but Bert.

"You play football good," he said.

"How do you know English?" I asked.

"In university," he said.

That was how it began. I've often tried to recapture our conversation of the next three hours, but I can recall only a few fragments. He showed me photos of his parents. He had another picture in his wallet, of a girl with long braids. "Your girl?" I asked.

"She is my girl when I leave Germany," he said. "But I do not hear now for one month. Perhaps her letters are delayed."

I didn't have a girl, but I had pictures of my Mum and Dad and Tom together at Blackpool. "I study one year to be an architect," he said. He took out a notebook and showed me sketches he'd done, of the Front, and of villages in France.

Once he said, "This is the best time since I join up. The only good time."

We didn't talk about the war, except once when I said, "They told us this would be over by Christmas".

His face clouded. "It will not be over by next Christmas," he said. "In our rear we have trenches five metres deep, solid concrete. You will never break through. And if we could break your lines, we would have done so already."

We didn't take much notice of the flares at first, but then an officer's voice came through a megaphone. "Return to your positions at once." Some of the men began to move. Then a machine gun opened up two hundred yards away. It was getting dangerous. "It's over," I said.

"Wait," Wolfgang said. He took out his notebook, and glancing at me once or twice, sketched my portrait, scribbled "Wolfgang" at the bottom, tore it out and gave it to me. In haste, I tried to think what I could give him. I ripped a button off my tunic. I didn't have time to cut it off, and in any case it's two days field punishment for damaging your uniform. I waited for him to move, but he just stood there. The shooting was coming down the line. "Go back," I called as I started to run.

I rolled into our trench and fell the eight feet to the bottom. A fat major was ordering men to the machine gun posts. The moon had set but flares were going off everywhere. I grabbed a periscope and looked out over No Man's Land. Wolfgang was still there! He hadn't moved. He was just where I had left him, standing easy. "Go back," I screamed "No!" at the top of my voice, but I don't remember.

I stayed in France for four years. Right until the eleventh hour of the eleventh day of the eleventh month in 1918 when the guns stopped at last. After the war I joined the Post Office and retired as post master. I never married, never fathered a child. I've never attended a parade on Armistice Day. I've never worn my medals. People congratulate me on surviving. But did I survive?

E J RAE
Remembrance

I can never honestly claim that I joined the army with any grand notion of doing my duty for King and country although I was proud to do so. My main objective had more to do with avoiding the wrath of my father when he discovered that his only son was about to be arrested for attempting to break into a neighbour's home. I was not intent on robbing the house, only hopeful of a few moments of passion with my girl, Elsie, away from the gimlet sharp eyes of her mother. Unfortunately for me, Elsie had been sent to stay with her grandmother the very night I chose to climb the tree outside her bedroom window. I shinned all the way up only to see the horrified face of her mother as she closed the blinds.

I knew that any attempt to explain the real reason for my visit would only cause more trouble, so, after writing letters of apology to all concerned, I dashed to the nearest recruitment office and signed on the dotted line.

The year was 1917 and I was 18 years old. I confess to feeling quite noble at the thought of saving a young girl's reputation and this feeling buoyed my up until the moment I found myself on board a troop-ship bound for France. Reality hit home very forcefully as I began to realise that this was no romantic sacrifice, I was going to war and there was a distinct possibility that I might never return. I thought of my poor parents and sweet little Elsie left at home and was overwhelmed with sadness and guilt for the shabbiness of my behaviour. There could be no going back and I vowed there and then to one day make them all proud of me again.

My first night in France brought me into contact with "Mad" Eddie Wango, a giant hulk of a man with a great booming voice and the most delightful laugh it has ever been my pleasure to hear. He sauntered over to my bunk and showed me how to run a candle over the seams of my clothes to burn the lice eggs that had appeared from nowhere when we arrived.

"Mad" Eddie, a veteran of almost two years in the trenches, was a Liverpudlian with a sense of humour that matched his size. I listened open-mouthed as he confided his master plan for thwarting the enemy, he said that very soon his secret device, designed to capture all the lice that plagued the British Army, would be in operation and once it was, he intended to slip behind enemy lines and deliver his live cargo to the Germans, he was confident that within two days our enemies would have all scratched themselves to death and we could all go home!

My astonishment lasted some moments after Eddie stopped speaking and it was only when I became aware of the peals of laughter all around me that I twigged to the fact that I was the latest in a long line of new recruits to fall under the spell of "Mad" Eddie Wango's story-telling skills. From that moment on we became firm friends.

Eddie was a natural choice for any operation that required speed or stealth, time and time again he slipped behind enemy lines, never failing to emerge with some form of booty for his mates back in the trenches. I recall one rainy, wind-swept dawn Eddie appeared, grinning like a fool and laden with all kinds of fresh food, we broke our fast royally that morning on new-baked bread and sausages washed down with genuine coffee.

By 1918 we had fought our way to the German's main defence line at Hindenburg and I was well acquainted with the pitiful sights and sounds of man and beast as they breathed their last amidst the carnage of the battle.

Eddie and I often volunteered for the scout patrol in No Man's Land, watching carefully for surprise attacks.

One terrible evening we were sent out on patrol as usual, I was feeling very battle-weary and not a little sad having received news from home that my lovely Elsie had married a sailor and gone to live in Aberdeen with his parents. Perhaps it was the sorrow of my loss that caused me to react with such horror when a sniper forced us to dive for cover and I found myself flat in the mud gazing into the sightless eyes of a young British soldier, he had died holding a blood-stained photograph of a pretty young woman. I sobbed with anguish as the full tragedy of war hit me and I swore that somehow I would return the photograph to its subject and let her know that he had died with her image before his eyes.

I reached out to take to take the picture only to be dragged flat again by Eddie as another burst of sniper fire sprayed above our heads, we burrowed deeper into the mud and waited for the sniper to lose interest and move on. Eddie was now nearer to the corpse than I and after a while he indicated that he could reach the photograph simply by reaching out a little way. I saw Eddie's arm raised a few inches from his body then my whole world exploded and I fought to burrow deeper as the combined flesh and bones of my best friend and the booby-trapped soldier rained down on me.

Eddie Wango, my friend and saviour, the man who taught me the true value of living had sacrificed his life for mine and a blood-spattered photograph.

I remember and honour you always. God bless you, we shall meet again.

JOHN RAVENSCROFT
A Long Shot

I'm expecting to dream about the bullet again tonight. It comes in phases, my bullet-dream, whenever life gets especially difficult, so tonight it's got to be on the cards. This morning, you see, we buried my father.

It's always the same, every time. March 1918. The Second Battle of the Somme. I'm a tiny impossible figure, sitting astride a bullet that has just left the barrel of a German MP18 submachine gun. I cling on grimly as we fly across the shell-pocked waste of No Man's Land. Damp, early morning air unzips behind us and the world around me is silent, unreal.

We're heading directly towards a solitary British soldier, our point of impact the dead centre of his skull. I can never make out his face at first, he's too far away, but it doesn't matter. I know who he is and that we have blood and bone in common. The solitary British soldier is my grandfather.

We cover the ground at over a thousand feet per second, yet I find that somehow I have plenty of time to look around me, to weigh up my situation. I know what's going to happen when this bullet strikes home and the consequences that will follow from my grandfather's sudden, messy death. I have to try to stop it.

Leaning forward I wrap my arms around the bullet's nose, then jerk my body hard, fist to the left, then to the right, but it's no good. Nothing I do brings about the slightest change in our trajectory and my grandfather's skull gets ever closer.

I don't want to see this. I turn my head and look behind me, back along our flight path towards the twisted entanglements of barbed wire that marked the German outpost line. They're rapidly receding into the distance, as is the kneeling figure of the German sniper, still squinting down the barrel of his MP18. He's getting smaller and smaller as we get further and further apart but however great the distance between us I can see his eye, clear, sharp, focused through and beyond me to his bullet's ultimate destination.

I don't know his name, this kneeling German soldier, but I feel that I should. It doesn't seem right that the man who fired this shot, a shot that has travelled on and on through three generations of my family and is still in flight, should remain anonymous. I've often wondered about him. Did he, like my grandfather, have a wife and children? Did he survive his war? And if he did, did he too sometimes dream of this moment, of the soft explosion to come?

I shake my head and look forward again, back towards the British trenches. I can see Grandfather quite clearly now. He's staring right at me, his right hand raised to shield his eyes from the glare of the rising sun. It's almost as though he's saluting me. His mouth is half-open in a silent call; his breath, a puff vapour, seems to hang frozen from his lower lip.

I've seen this face so often in my mother's photograph albums. Our family pictures go all the way back to the turn of the century and as a child I loved to flick through them, laughing at the old-fashioned cars, the Edwardian ladies, the bowler-hatted men. So I recognise my grandfather when I see him, even though I never got the chance to meet him in life.

We share similar features, my grandfather and me: same nose, same chin. I think how strange it is that I am now older than him. My hair is thinning and going grey at the temples: he is not and never will be.

The bullet moves forward, closing the gap. Grandfather's time is short now. Very short.

There is a picture of him sitting in a rose garden somewhere. My grandmother, heavily pregnant with my father, sits by his side. They both look very young, sitting amongst the roses, smiling for the camera. At their feet crouches a dog, apparently about to leap into my grandmother's lap. I still remember the thrill that ran through me when I turned over the photograph and saw she had noted down names and a date: Me, Sam & Nipper – July 1913. Her copperplate handwriting was faded but still beautiful to see.

Mere yards away from his forehead I stare into my grandfather's face. Four years of mud and fighting and death have changed him, of course. He has a sickly pallor and the eyes of a soldier who has seen too much. But he's still the same man who sat smiling in the rose garden that day. He's still my father's father.

Just before the impact I wonder what would have happened if the sniper's aim hadn't been quite so perfect. If this bullet had only wounded my grandfather, or even missed its mark altogether, how different might all of our lives have been?

My grandmother would not have told my father, while he was still too young to understand, that her own life stopped on the day she learned of her husband's death. I doubt that she would have spent the next forty years periodically disappearing into depression, virtually unaware of the needs of her son.

And if that were so, my father, a good but troubled man, might not have found himself fighting his own war, a sad, lonely war of liver against bottle, a war that finally did for him just last week.

And what of me? As the bullet shatters my grandfather's skull I invariably jerk awake and lie in the darkness wondering how much of my personality was set in that one awful moment so very long ago.

"It was a long shot," my grandfather's best friend wrote in a letter posted to my grandmother shortly after Armistice Day.

And he was right, of course. It was a very long shot.

RICHARD REEVE
Dismissed

They rode into camp hot, dusty and wounded. The last five horses carried corpses over their saddles. Major Tindler watched them from his office window. His concern was that the corpses wore red coats, that was to be expected, but one of the corpses was that of the Lieutenant in charge of the patrol.

The Major went to the door, "Sergeant Pollard, I want a report now." He left the office door open and returned to his desk and sat down.

The Sergeant entered, hooking up the collar of his dusty tunic, "Yes, sir?"

"Is that Lieutenant Plummer out there over his horse?"

"Yes, sir, dead, sir, lost five men."

"How was the Lieutenant killed?" The Major tapped a pencil on his desk.

"We was ambushed, sir, usual place, Khyber. Lieutenant caught it straight away," the Sergeant stuck out his chest, "and I took charge, sir."

"And you extricated yourselves immediately?" The Major raised an eyebrow quizzically.

"It was 'ard, sir, but we gave a good account of ourselves before we withdrew," the Sergeant stuck his chest out even more.

"But you lost five men, Sergeant. Right, get off and get a meal."

When the Sergeant had gone the Major felt uneasy about the affair and decided that he would investigate.

When he had finished his duty the Major strolled towards the Mess. Captain Attwell caught up and joined him. They walked together, "Hear Lieutenant Plummer was killed out there today."

The Major nodded, "Lost five men in that damn Khyber, Plummer was one of them, led the troop."

"He wasn't popular with the men, you know," the Captain said.

The Major frowned, "He was young and a little too full of himself. Minor aristocrat, I understand."

"Lord Inglemoor's youngest, I believe, did think a lot of himself, not one of us really," Attwell lowered his voice, "bit of a fool is the word. Still mustn't speak ill of the dead, what."

The Major slept uneasily, something lurked close to his consciousness but never breached it. After he had taken the parade he walked across to the charnel house.

The attending Corporal saluted, "Can I help you, sir?"

The Major looked at the five bodies laid out on the slabs, each covered in a grey sheet. Against the wall stood three plain coffins.

The Corporal saw the Major's glance, "The carpenter's just finishing the last two coffins, sir. The burial's at noon."

The Major nodded, "Which of them is Lieutenant Plummer, I'd like to see the body?"

"They've all been cleaned up proper, sir. The MO signed them off all right," the Corporal didn't look at him.

"Which one, Corporal?"

The Corporal hesitated then crossed to one of the bodies and lifted the edge of the grey sheet. The Major walked across, took the sheet edge and pulled it fully back. The Lieutenant had a look of surprise on his face at his fate and so did the Major. The body was unmarked. The Major rolled the body over, the wound that he was looking for was dark blue in the neck, at the base of the skull.

The Major looked at the Corporal, "Is this why you were so reluctant to show me?"

The Corporal fidgeted awkwardly, "Eh, I don't know, sir."

"Then I want the Medical Officer here, I'll wait here."

"Yes, sir," the Corporal marched out, glad to be away from the Major.

The Major rolled the body of the Lieutenant over. The boy was young, too young to have had the artificial authority over older, more experienced men. Any Army authority is an unearned authority sometimes. A boy used to privilege finding himself in the sometimes hard and rude condition of Army life had been known to commit suicide but this wasn't suicide, he had been executed.

Back in the office he called for his orderly and ordered that Sergeant Pollard be brought before him.

He waited ten minutes, then the Sergeant and the orderly stood to attention before him. He dismissed the orderly.

He looked steadily at the Sergeant for a long moment, "All right, Sergeant Pollard, tell me exactly what happened out there on patrol, particularly concerning the shooting of Lieutenant Plummer."

"Yes, sir. There was fifteen of us, Lieutenant Plummer was in charge. We was ridin' easy, we didn't expect anything to start before we got into the pass. We left Hashia so we was, well, relaxed." He looked at the Major, to try to ascertain whether he was believing him, "We was just going to enter it when they opened up on us." The Sergeant fidgeted.

"Attention, Sergeant," the Major said, quietly.

The Sergeant came to attention again.

"Then, what happened? Did you dismount to return fire?"

"The Lieutenant ordered us to charge," the Sergeant looked unhappy.

"And you did?"

"No, sir, the Lieutenant went down under his horse and he was yelling for help. Privates Saddler and Philey went down bloody. There must have been twenty of them shooting at us. We was returning their fire 'ard. I was down behind the rocks shooting anything that moved."

"Was the Lieutenant still calling for help at that point, Sergeant?"

"Eh, I think so, sir, it was all confused, you don't see things singly."

"Then?" Then Major stared, a steady stare. The Sergeant seemed to give up all evasion, "I saw Private O'Brian crawling out to the Lieutenant, sir. I thought 'e was going out to 'elp 'im to get the dead 'orse orf 'im."

"And?"

"'E didn't, sir, 'e shot 'im and the Lieutenant stopped crying out." The Sergeant shuffled but the Major ignored it.

"Then you should have arrested O'Brian then and there, or as soon as possible," the Major said, harshly.

"It wasn't possible, sir, so I shot 'im dead."

The Major did not answer at once, then, "I didn't hear that, Sergeant and I'm sure that you imagined it. You're dismissed."

The Sergeant spun on his heels and marched out.

The Major closed the file.

EDITH SANDERS
The Time Machine

What is memory? To me it is a unique part of the time machine that is my body. Throughout my life, sights, sounds and emotions have been keyed into the computer in my brain. This sophisticated system has recorded events and filed them away, to be brought back again when duly stimulated.

My earliest recollections seem to be when I was four years old. I remember a bedroom darkened by blackout curtains, lit only by a tiny round candle called a night light. The flame was almost as small as the first spark from a match. It cast flickering shadows on the walls and left the rest of the room in darkness.

I was afraid of the demons who danced wildly about the walls. My granny slept in the same room, and I was always re-assured when she came to bed.

One night we were awakened by my Mother, who told us to get up and get dressed. I knew that something was wrong, but I did not know what it was. My Mother lifted me upon her knee and gave me a biscuit from a round blue tin. I was shaking, and my teeth were chattering so much, that I could not eat.

I could hear a terrible wailing sound, which turned out to be the siren, warning us of an air raid. We quickly joined our neighbours in the cellars under our building. My father, who was on ARP duty, arrived later.

We sat in the darkness with only the glow of a candle to comfort us. We listened to the dull drone of aircraft, and the thumps and bumps of destruction, till at last, the all clear sounded. I have never forgotten that night. I still have the blue biscuit tin. It is a bit battered and sorry looking, but I could never throw it out. I keep my acrylic paints in it now.

Strange how colour can press the recall button to the past. I recently bought a birthday present for a friend. I could not believe the range of toiletries in the shop. It was the soap, in all the colours of the rainbow, that sent my thoughts backwards.

During the last war, economy was a dire necessity. In our house, we kept a large jar full of pieces of soap which were too small to use, but too large to throw out. I was fascinated by the kaleidoscope of colour shining through the glass jar. It reminded me of a stained glass window in church.

I often watched as my granny emptied the pieces of soap into a pan and boiled them. They congealed, and when the mixture was cold, it was cut up and used again. Another colourful picture flits into my mind. The red, white and blue of the Union Jack fluttering from every window when the war ended.

Last year I visited many of the war cemeteries in Normandy. When I saw the rows of neatly tended graves all around me, I wept for the men who lay there. I went to Arromanches and stood for a short time looking down at the beach. I could almost smell the fear, and see the carnage.

Two little boys, eating ice-cream cones, sat on the wall beside me. I saw them as symbols of peace and hope for the future, but I wondered if they were being taught to remember the past. Remembrance is many things to many people. It is the power to forage in the canyons of our mind and reclaim the past. It is a top class camera clicking away and developing snapshots of our daily timetable.

Sometimes we deliberately seek to remember. We press the video of our life and switch on the tape. We take the back off the clock and look into the workings. We open our reporter's notebook and translate the jottings.

On other occasions, something automatically triggers the cerebral index. It could be a face in the crowd, a certain voice, food, music, perfume, almost anything. Unpleasant episodes are always in our mind. We cannot forget them, we must never, ever, forget the men and women who fought and died in the last war. They died for us.

Survivors of war often find it hard to come to terms with their experiences. This can result in depression and mental breakdown. An accident or senile dementia can also cause the mind to malfunction and delete information. Think how awful it must be to cope with a daily jigsaw of thoughts where the pieces never fit.

Mental illness is one of the most heart breaking things that can happen to a person, both for them and their loved ones. Memory is a very precious gift. It is the personal history of a life, without it, how do we know who we are?

JACK SHARP
The Effects Of War

The story of War is interesting and its effect on mankind fascinating.

War is intentional violence and therefore might be considered criminal but it is also a process used for resolving conflict and has often led to negotiation and reconciliation.

It can occur as the result of abnormal social or political situations of civil anarchy (like Sadam Hussein's Iraq); or inter-group relationships strained by differing ethical view points about religion (as in Bosnia); or socio/political/cultural/ attitudes (as in many parts of Africa). However, recent Wars of significance have been between Nation States, or groups of Nation States, of differing political ideologies attempting to impose their points of view upon others, who fight to resist them (as World War 2).

From these various causes of war there have inevitably arisen contrasting effects upon human existence. Although such naturally occurring events as famine and pestilence have had terrible effects, because of the more effective control of such events, war has been even more catastrophic (economically, socially and politically). But it has also been an important factor in spreading civilisation around the world.

The religious wars of the 16th/17th Centuries (like the "Thirty Years War" in Europe), were largely orgies of wanton destruction and violent crime carried out by foraging parties of mercenaries who, by their ravaging and victimisation of the civil population, caused pestilence, famine and abject poverty such that even cannibalism was practised.

These were followed by relatively limited wars of the 18th Century when armies, loyal to their sovereign, became more permanent standing forces. Pikes gave way to muskets with bayonets and a more specialised tactical system came into being. These armies were still relatively small due to economic considerations and their effects tended to be more localised.

By the 19th Century, wars had become less frequent. They were dominated by the Napoleonic Wars in Europe, which introduced compulsory service and made use of artillery with rapid marches of troops. Also, the American Civil War, which was one of the first industrial wars; having machine industry producing more effective rifles (increasing range from 100 to 600 yards), railways and steamships making the supply of large armies easier and the more rapid deployment of troops. The effects of these were increasingly devastating over more extensive geographical areas. In spite of this the effects upon industry and the unifying of the United States of America into a single political entity were soon to be seen.

However, it must be the World Wars of more recent history that have had the most profound effect upon mankind.

World War 1 saw the two largest field armies ever assembled, each of nearly 2 million men. Using neo-Napoleonic tactics of advance they became bogged down facing each other across Europe. Guns, shells and aircraft could not solve the stalemate. The effect was estimated at 10 million dead soldiers; an equal number of civilians; 10 million wounded and maimed with another 20 million around the world affected by war-spread epidemics and famines. The economic costs were enormous.

A more hopeful effect was that people everywhere agreed that such results should not be repeated. A political attempt to limit war was made by the founding of the League of Nations. Unfortunately, the crippling sanctions on Germany didn't help and 21 years later war broke out again.

World War 2 introduced the combined air-tank-infantry attack on land (the Blitzkrieg tactics): new devices for amphibious landings: submarines and strategic bombing, culminating in the dropping of the atomic bomb: landmines, anti-tank guns, rockets, sonar and radar detection, jet planes and atom bombs were used, resulting in even greater world-wide casualties and exorbitant economic costs.

Today, science, industry and propaganda are major instruments of war, having produced the hydrogen bomb, inter-continental ballistic missiles and earth satellites. War has become too destructive (even to the victor) for it to be a useful part of policy. Yet political, economic and social ingenuity has been unable to construct either an equilibrium of power or world institutions, such as the United Nations, to control us. Thus, relatively small wars still occur (as in Korea, Vietnam, Lebanon and other parts of the Middle East and Africa and Bosnia) all of which have the same devastating effects on their peoples. Despite this, mankind seems unable to draw back from them.

This story of war and its multifarious effects covers a long period of time. The effects ranging from those immediate, of devastation, tragic loss of life, together with economic, social and cultural costs, to the longer term resolution of conflictual circumstances by negotiation and settlement of differences. There is, however, an effect of war which may prove more significant to mankind than all others. Historically it has consistently increased the capacity of man to destroy and kill. This capability has dramatically increased in recent years.

Over these years it has been said that, "There will always be wars and talk of wars". History suggests this to be true (indeed, the writing of this story proves the point).

We can but hope that the longer term effects of war will prevail and mankind will find a better way to resolve its disagreements, before indulging in the final holocaust leading to its own extinction.

LOUISE SHAW
Final Liberation

I don't know why, so many years after those terrible days that I should remember, but I do. For fifty years I have hidden behind my new life, the one that God gave to me. In my head I think of that other life as B-B and am thankful for the time given to me aB-B, after Bergen-Belsen.

Perhaps it is the fears of an old woman that need to be laid to rest? Perhaps it is the time I live in; a time of false memories and disputed abuse. Perhaps a fear that should I voice the terror of those days, somehow I would bring them back to life. And there is nothing on this earth or in the heavens above that could force me to do such a thing. "The past is past, Anna." Mrs Rosenthal used to chide me, "You must put all that behind you now and find yourself a husband."

I took her advice and found myself one solid and dependable, Daniel Jones, a man of few words and little emotion. Much like a watchful Alsatian, he lived alongside me in our poky terrace in the east end. Our quiet home, where money was short and treats few. Where together and in mutual silence we raised three beautiful sons, all with golden curls and eyes of liquid acacia honey. The house we will drive past this morning in the hearse with his body.

In later years as our lot improved and Daniel's quietness assumed a luminosity amongst his men, we moved into a semi, with full fronted bays and piped gas. It is in this house I grew to harness the power of silence. As more treats arrived and dinners grew larger, I knew to ask nothing, just to accept. It was something that came easily to me after my childhood of watching and scavenging and surviving in that place I dare not even name.

I check my watch, it is a plain gold fronted affair, a "ladies" watch. I slip the safety chain off and remove it from my bony wrist. Carefully I turn it over, To my Annie. No words of love or endearment, merely ownership. I slip it back on and turn to face myself in the mirror at the end of the long bed. The bed that heaved with Daniel's carnal pleasures and my sorrows.

The face that looks back at me is not the one I own, it is the face of a fine boned old lady, framed by wisps of autumn curls and mapped with deep rivulets of skin. The sort of lady that frequents department stores and regal coffee shops. It is not my face. I preserve my face in deep purple parchment in a space between memory and death. I guard my ten year old face, the child with wide eyes and bangs, who laughs a lot and demands answers to impossible questions. The face I cling to and will resurrect on my own death bed.

At the camp we had no mirrors or cause for them, occasionally I would catch one of the older girls peering at the bottom of a heavy pan in a vain bid to find herself there. But really there was no cause for such things; you were there until you weren't. There was no point in claiming anything as your own, not even your face. The guards would sometimes grab for one of us, pinch our already too-pinched cheeks and shout some obscenity to their friends. One time, they caught and held me down, rubbed themselves into my lips, barged their strength into my tender body until I wished for no face at all. After that day I thought myself invisible; my nose became flat, my eyes still, my eyes void.

But I lived to tell no tales. An empty wasted story, recreated so many times in the dance-halls and the tea-shops, a story the young Nazis still deny, a story so sad that my words cannot convey it. So why now, Anna? Why now?

It is the lipstick. While searching for Daniel's cufflinks I find the lipstick. The waxy slither of scarlet that followed the British Red Cross Society into Bergen-Belsen on April 15th 1945. The child-woman toy that returned my identity, that bridged two worlds and made me feel for my face.

They gave one to all the women in the camp. Some of the women would have taken it to their grave, wasted the little colour they had in their lives, only I would not let them. When they died and fell, I trawled for this bounty amongst their colourless limbs and marked their kissing, cursing, drying lips with scarlet.

Once my job was done I would find a place to sit and cradle my token, then with trembling fingers, I would delicately trace the cupid bow of my own lips. Slowly and quietly like a silver screen siren.

I reach into the drawer and take out the lipstick. With two hands I bring the mottled gold canister towards my face and hold it to my nostrils; it has a magical smell, one that transcends all others. So many memories are contained within this tiny scrap of colour.

I remember my life with Daniel; the marriage that should have brought me freedom. I ease the lid and twist, anticipating the breath of its release. I ease my survivor's face towards the fractured mirror, purse my lips and resolutely draw the final line of liberation.

JOHN SHAWCROSS
Marcel's "Guest"

Marcel cursed the rain as he opened the barn doors in the pre-dawn gloom. Inside, he could just see the silhouette of the old tractor. He climbed into the driving seat with the ease of years of familiarity and started the engine. As he waited for it to warm up, he saw his wife leave the house and start towards him, hurrying across the rain-lashed yard, into the shelter of the barn.

"Your lunch," she said, without expression. Marcel took the proffered bag, then without looking at her, asked.

"Is there extra?"

"As always," she replied.

Marcel looked at the bag.

"Am I mad?"

"It affects us all." She smiled. "Some more than others. Now go to work."

Marcel drove through the quiet lanes to his fields. He chain smoked as he waited for the gloom to lift. As soon as it was light enough he would begin ploughing. It would be the worst kind of day, he thought. Heavy rain followed by sunshine. The worst kind of day. If it had rained all day he could have remained hunched in his oilskins. Not looking back. If it had been fine, the ground would have been harder. The ploughshares would not bite so deep.

The Eastern horizon began to pale and brighten, as the sun appeared, and the rainclouds moved on. Marcel started his ploughing.

He had completed three furrows before he heard the first ominous "clunk" of metal on metal. He stopped the tractor and went to see.

The metal object could only be one thing. A British shell. Marcel rolled it to the edge of the field and placed it on its base by the side of the road. From his pocket he pulled out an aerosol of yellow paint and sprayed the unexploded shell. Later that week the army would come along and remove it, as they did with the hundreds of other lethal objects ploughed up by the farmers.

Marcel thought again about selling up. The truth of the matter depressed him. No-one would buy a Somme farm. They were deadly. Year after year people were hurt or killed by the "Iron Harvest". The wartime munitions dragged up by the ploughs. Usually the farms passed down through the generations. From father to son. His own son had been wiser than his years. Marcel did not blame him for leaving.

As the sun rose higher, Marcel made several more visits to the edge of the field, piling the unexploded munitions carefully. He was aware that he was sweating in the May sunshine. Grimly he took off his oilskins, annoyed at the clear day. "No guests yet," he muttered and resumed his ploughing.

"One more hour perhaps, to finish the field." He pondered. Then shrugged. His body clock told him it was lunchtime. He was a Frenchman and lunch was sacred. Stopping the tractor he sat down in its shade and took out his meal. Bread, cheese, paté, some wine and a bottle of cold coffee. A simple meal but then Marcel was a simple man not given to extravagant tastes.

He thought it was going well. That he could enjoy his meal in peace. Then he saw it. Something sticking out of the ground disturbed by the plough. Wearily he got to his feet and strode over to investigate that which had caught his eye.

From the furrow a skeletal arm reached upwards, fingers pointing accusingly at the sky. The brown shreds of uniform told Marcel that this was an English soldier. Marcel did not grimace as he dragged the rest of the body to the surface. He had seen this sight many times before.

"Will you join me for some lunch, Tommy? I insist! Perhaps we will have a little talk, eh?" He muttered quietly as he pulled the skeletal remains behind the tractor, out of sight of the road. It would not do to be seen by passers-by.

He arranged the corpse into a sitting position and leant it against the tractor wheel. From his bag he pulled the "extra" that his wife had packed. Marcel carefully placed the food and drink before the soldier.

"A little bread and cheese, perhaps some wine, Tommy. Eh?" Marcel cursed his lot to farm the Somme charnel house where the English had their great battles. Thousands upon thousands of them had fallen here - not all of them had been found...

...Marcel was finding them. He recalled one memorable year when he had five "guests" for lunch. Horrified, he watched them surface behind his plough and felt as though his land had been strewn with Hydra's teeth - the skeletal warriors emerging.

"Enjoy your lunch, Tommy." He instructed his guest. "Tell me, Tommy, is it good to feel the sunlight on your face again?"

The empty eye sockets stared straight ahead.

"Ah, I thought so - smoke?"

Marcel lit a cigarette and balanced it on the soldier's lower jaw.

"You see, Tommy - you give me a little problem." Marcel shifted uncomfortably and explained.

"The shells I can put by the side of the road for collection. You, I cannot - it would upset the tourists, yes?" Marcel chuckled at the thought, then continued. "The authorities give me a number to call if you or your friends drop by. However, they do not understand farming. First a Gendarme will visit to verify the call. Then a few days later, some Englishmen will collect the body and take it away. Those few days make all the difference to a farmer, my friend. We cannot interrupt the ploughing for you. It is - how you say - life must go on, yes? Enjoy your lunch, Tommy. Then, I am sorry but you must go back down again."

Later that afternoon Marcel surveyed the finished field with pride. He noticed the arrow-straight furrows that were ready for seeding. He thought about his "guests" that he had ploughed back under the soil.

"Sleep on, mes braves," he said quietly.

DOUGLAS SMITHSON
A Flight To Captivity

Monday the 18th Sept 1944. The Horsa Glider was loaded with a jeep, 6 pounder anti-tank gun and ammunition etc. accompanied by three Anti-tank Gunners, Spinner (S/Sgt. Arthur Newton from Stockport) was 1st Pilot and myself (Sgt. Douglas Smithson from Huddersfield) 2nd Pilot.

We got away well from Fairford, our airfield, and flew across country towards the North Sea. Conditions were good, so when we crossed the coast, I took over and flew over the North Sea. Our tug, a Stirling, was above us and we were in the low tow position. Our height was 1100 ft. and we could see some of our fighters above us and an Air Sea Rescue launch below.

An island in the Scheldt came up so Spinner took over. Except for the noise of the air flow it was peaceful. Suddenly peace was shattered. The Rear Gunner of our tug was heard shouting to his Pilot to go to starboard and up along with various expletives and at the same time yelling that a Dakota was heading towards them. I immediately looked to my left and saw a Dakota, pulling a Waco glider, sliding towards us.

I told Spinner to go right and up. We had no time to think. I watched as the Dakota came nearer. The Pilot could not have seen us. He carried on steadily and I watched our tow rope just miss his wing. That was the last I saw of the Dakota. We climbed and so lifted our tug's tail and caused it to head downwards.

As we were only 1100ft. up at the start of the bother and his plane heading for the ground at 160 m.p.h, the Pilot did not like the situation one bit. He pulled back on his control column to make his nose go up and his tail go down. As a result of our nose going up and his tail going down the tow rope snapped and we were in free flight. The sea beneath us. We quickly decided to come down on the island instead of trying to go out to sea and hope to be picked up.

The Horsa could only last an hour before sinking. Spinner brought the glider into line with the poles and wire that had been put up by Germans to prevent airborne landings, and made a good landing. Landing wheels could be ditched at sea but we left them fixed as we did on "D" Day because we thought they would break any wire and help to stop the Horsa quickly, which they do. No damage was done. Spinner was a good pilot.

Out of the glider fast! The gunners prepared the gun for destruction, Spinner unloaded our own kit and I talked with some Dutchmen who had seen us land. One of them told me that a local Quisling had informed the Germans where we were and that they were already coming towards us. Once the gun and the glider were blown up we went towards a dyke (about 15ft. high.) away from where we expected the Germans to come.

We climbed over the dyke and there was the sea. I posted a Gunner on top of the nearby dyke to keep a look out. Two young Dutchmen then came to us and clearly tried to help but boats or a place to hide were not on. They said the Germans were very near and after showing us where we were on our escape map, they left us. The Gunner on guard signalled to me to go to him.

There on top of the dyke 30 yds. further along, was a German soldier looking out to sea. He had not seen us. We slid down the dyke and ran to join the others. We all moved to a small hollow between two connecting dykes hoping to be out of sight of the German looking for us. As he had his hand to his brow and only looked seawards I was sure he would not see us and I remember that, at the time, I thought he was only making sure that his Officer would see him and know that he was only doing his duty, I even thought it funny.

However we had no sooner moved to our new place, when our hopes were dashed, I looked across the field at another dyke parallel to where we were. There, on top, at about a distance of 100 yds. was a German soldier, prone behind a machine gun which was pointing straight at us. More soldiers were with him. It was the moment of truth! I asked if anyone had a white handkerchief to wave.

The Germans came across to us and we gathered together in a corner of a field. We started talking together as if at a Sunday School Treat. I had that day's *Daily Express* with me which I showed the Officer. The front page of which was full of arrows showing the advancing Allied Forces. He shrugged. We knew the war was over for us.

As I was standing on my own a few yards away, a soldier came near me and tapped his shoulder a few times and said what I understood to be "Nix Deutch". I looked at his shoulder badge and read the word Armenia and realised he was telling me that he was not a German. I gathered that he thought I could do something for him and that he was not really fighting for the Germans. What he thought I could do, I couldn't imagine.

After waiting about for some time a Ford Pilot (a pre-war V-8 Ford) arrived and we five prisoners got in along with the Officer, Sgt/Maj, and two German soldiers. How we all squeezed in, I don't know, but we did and to crown everything, two more stood on each running board. We drove to the nearby Police Station and were now proper Prisoners of War. We never did get to Arnhem.

LEN STEPHENSON
Help And Understanding

1943. North Africa. Jack Burns had joined the army as a Territorial in 1938. Now, after chasing Rommel's army from El Alamein to Benghazi, his battalion the 4th Essex Regiment, was resting. As infantry they formed part of the 4th Indian Division.

Jack had taken part in many desert battles and been promoted to Corporal, all this with only one week's leave in Cairo. His wife had not seen him for three years. Now he was reading a letter from her to say that their marriage was over. She had just borne another man's child.

Luckily for Burns he did not have time for this to sink in, for the Division had to make a sudden move to take up its position in the battle line-up at a place called the Mareth Line. It was there that he was riding in a truck when it was suddenly dive-bombed by a lone German Stuka, and Corporal Burns found himself trapped under an upturned truck. When he was rescued he was unharmed, except for some bruises and shock.

His battalion was too busy fighting, for him to receive treatment, so he then had to rejoin them in the thick of things. By this time Jack's nerves were beginning to get frayed, but he tried his hardest not to show it. He was able to lead his section successfully, until the 4th Indian Division made a forced march to join up with the First Army.

He had been mentioned in despatches, and his name had gone forward for a Military Medal. During the final attack on Tunis, and the defeat of Rommel, Corporal Jack Burns and his section were taking cover behind a burnt out tank, when it received a direct hit. All the section were killed except Jack, who lay in shock with his left arm blown off.

After weeks in military hospitals, he was eventually sent home to England. There he received his discharge from the Army; with a small pension and a suit of civilian clothes.

While he had been abroad, his mother had been bombed out of her home, after losing her husband in another air-raid. She now lived in a small flat in Ilford, Essex. Jack had no alternative but to join her, for he and his wife had lived in two rooms before the war; now they were ruins and she had gone.

Jack felt totally disorientated. All his friends had been called up in the forces, and only youngsters seemed to be left behind at home. He started having very bad dreams of war, usually ending as he woke up, just as a shell or bomb was about to burst on him.

He had to get used to being without an arm, and attended a military hospital which dealt in rehabilitation of armed forces casualties. His nerves were slowly becoming very frayed. One day when he was returning from shopping for his mother, there was a sudden enormous explosion from the direction of his home. In sudden panic he raced to the corner of his road, where his flat had been, there was now a pile of smoking ruins.

This was the final straw. Jack Burns became a gibbering wreck, as he clawed his way through the ruins to the remains of his dead mother. The ambulance took him to hospital, where with understanding treatment, he slowly recovered. During his time there he was attended by an attractive nurse. She had auburn hair and a pretty face with soft brown eyes and was of a small stature. Jack fell in love with her, and she seemed to like him a lot.

When he finally left hospital they kept in touch with each other, and occasionally went out together. This gave Jack back his self-confidence again, and a reason for living. He wrote for several jobs that were advertised in the newspapers, but with no luck. Then suddenly his luck changed.

He opened a letter and found that an interview had been granted him, for a position as manager of a garden centre, about five miles out of town. He had told them in his CV that he had no experience of garden plants etc, but was willing to learn, so he felt fairly confident. About that time, the tremendous news broke, that Germany had surrendered, and the war in Europe was ended.

At last the day of the interview arrived. Jack found that he was one of only five people who had been granted interviews. When his turn came he felt that he did quite well, especially when he was told to wait in the next office. Another candidate for the job joined him there, followed by the interviewer.

With a smile he said, "Well it's going to be one of you two, but the managing director will make the final decision. You will be first to see him, Mr Johnson. As soon as you hear this bell ring, I want you to go to the MD's office opposite."

Turning to Jack, he told him to follow suit when the bell rang again: with that he left them waiting and wondering. Almost immediately the bell rang, and Johnson, taking a deep breath, left the room.

After what seemed like an eternity, but in fact was only a few minutes, the bell rang again and Jack found himself knocking on the MD's door. "Enter!" called a firm voice, so Jack turned the handle and went inside.

"Well, well, so it really is Jack Burns, Essex Regiment. How old are you son?" asked the man at the desk. It was Jack's old platoon sergeant. After the war he had gone back to his parents' garden centre, taken it over, and turned it into a flourishing business.

Of course Jack got the job, and was sent on a two weeks training course. It was just the therapy that he needed, and he took to it like a duck to water. Once he had finished the course, and had been doing the job successfully for a month, he made a big decision.

He rang Julie, his ex-nurse, and asked her out to dinner that night. She agreed, and after an enjoyable meal, Jack proposed to her. Much to his surprise and delight, Julie accepted at once.

As he gently placed the ring on her finger, he whispered, "I love you very much, my sweetheart. You have shown me that the effects of war can turn out wonderful, as well as pitiful. Without your help and understanding I would never have found that out. God bless you!".

PW STOCK
Smithy

When I joined the Training Battalion at Shornecliffe my Sergeant was Les Smith. There were thirty of us in "Smithy's" platoon. Most were teenagers reluctantly doing their National Service. There were also half a dozen "regulars" who'd signed on for "five and seven", I was one of them.

Smithy, for all his forty years was lean, tanned and athletic. He'd got another six months to do before he completed his "22" and got his pension.

When he took us for "weapon training" he would hold the rifle, a 303 Lee-Enfield gently, caressingly.

"This is the best friend you'll ever have." He spoke softly. "Look after it, never let it out of your sight. Love it like a woman. Sleep with it and above all else." He paused, looking round, "eyeballing" us one by one. "Keep it clean. One day your life could depend on it."

Among the campaign ribbons on Smith's battledress were the Africa and Burma Stars but he was rarely given to reminiscence and then only briefly. During one training session he took the bolt out of his rifle and held it between a stained thumb and forefinger.

"If you let this get dirty or gritty you might find your rifle won't work - just when you need it." He told us how in Burma he kept the bolt of his rifle in a chamois leather pouch in his pocket. "I kept that bolt like I keep my prick - clean, bright and lightly oiled...it never let me down."

Someone laughed. Smithy didn't even smile. The look on his creased, young, "lived-in" face as he fondled the six inches of bright steel made the hairs on my neck bristle.

For the first few weeks we concentrated on getting physically fit. Some found this hard. To Gavelliga, a fat, erstwhile ice-cream seller, always referred to as "The Wop" it came very hard - as did all matters military.

To Euan Evans and his twin brother Gavin, both ex-miners it was a "doddle".

"Dead cushy here, boyo! Ever worked in a pit?" I like the Euan brothers - soft spoken, helpful but the real "hard men" in the platoon. Smithy made no victims and had no favourites but he quietly respected the Welshmen.

He had explained his simple philosophy on our first day. "No-one fails in this platoon. I've got a record." He paused, scowled. "And I'm going to keep it. I don't want no prima donnas." He relished the words. "They get people killed. You're all going to pass and do your bit in operational battalions - none of my recruits gets a cushy posting to the Depot!"

There was a shuffling of boots. It was Music Hall stuff but nobody even smiled.

Among the more dramatic episodes in the training programme was firing a "Bazooka". The British Army Bazooka at the time was a fearsome device which launched a bomb shaped projectile designed to knock out a tank at a range of about eighty yards.

My turn came and the bomb didn't go off. Smithy swore - he would have to go and blow it up by detonating a slab of guncotton alongside it. The bombs were sensitive and a number of instructors had been injured carrying out this drill.

Back in the firing trench after the bang I noticed his fingers trembling as he lit up his Woodbine. He saw I was watching, gave me a quick grin. "Still get a touch of the shakes sometimes...the old malaria...never quite goes..."

Throwing live hand grenades was a bit like the bazooka experience only more "intimate". We practised with dummies and once the instructor was satisfied we went out onto the Throwing Range for the real thing.

The grenades were derivatives of the old "No 5's" - green banded, Amatol filled Mills bombs. After pulling out the safety pin and releasing the striker lever you had about a five second delay while the powder fuse burned before the grenade exploded.

On range day Smithy was in charge. One by one each of us went out from the safety of the viewing bunker to throw our bombs. The drill is simple and safe and holding a live bomb concentrates the mind.

"No problem." I muttered as I gripped my first bomb in my sweaty palm, pulled out the pin, kept a tight grasp on the handle, swung back my arm, lobbed the bomb, watched(!) where it landed and ducked below the parapet. Just like the cinema.

Except for Gavelliga who swung back his arm and dropped his bomb just behind Smithy who had been talking him quietly through the drill.

Smithy moved like a lean, brown snake. He picked up the grenade, its little smoke trail just visible - and it exploded in his hand.

He was buried with full honours in a small churchyard in Sandgate, just outside the camp.

Our "Pass-Out" parade was held a couple of weeks later on a wet day in June. No bands, no generals. A tired looking colonel - a war weary garrison commander - took the salute and presented the best recruit, Euan Evans with his prize - a chromium plated .303 rifle bolt.

Among the few anxious relatives who turned up were Gavelliga's elderly Italian parents. They embarrassed us all by weeping copiously and wanting to shake hands with their son's friends. Gavelliga had been only slightly injured - he still proudly sported a bandage round his head. For his own "safety" since the accident he had been sleeping in the guardroom.

We had all subscribed to pay for Smithy's headstone - he had no relatives. We thought a good, solid piece of granite was appropriate.

It was nearly fifty years later when I went back to the area and found the grave. It was overgrown and mossy but the inscription was still legible. Propped against the headstone was a big bunch of white lilies. The small card had a green fleur-de-lis in one corner. On it were five words - "Clean, Bright and Lightly Oiled."

SAMEER KAK SUKHDEV
The Obsolescence Of War

Dateline : 2020
Planet : Mars
What caused the end of war, I wonder. Anyway, that's the assignment I have been given for the midsummer vacation.

The year is 2020 and the topic seems a rather academic one here in Cydonia Station with daytime temperatures around 20 degrees Celsius and just the hint of the polar cap in the far horizon.

Not much research material is available either: just some CD's of "Star Trek" and my personal copy of "A Short History of the World" by H G Wells.

There is a point of view that war is a form of mass insecurity; after all, such aberrant behaviour does not manifest itself in other mammals such as elephants, whales, bears or even dogs. Why does it, or why should it occur in human beings? Though it must be admitted that in certain species of mice, if they are deprived of food or space, certain analogous traits are seen to surface. Under normal circumstances it is very rare for a member of a biological species to try to kill another member of the same biological species. The norm among mammals is co-operation; indeed the advent and spread of mammalian species is often ascribed to this factor. Thus, in most, if not all civilised societies war is proscribed as a means of advancement of state policy, as no rational justification can be found for it. Most societies justify the existence of the armed forces on the grounds of self-defence. This probably explains why most civilised nations came together to place their armed forces under the centralised command of the United Nations as per the Helsinki Treaty of 2012, effectively putting a close to a sorry chapter in human civilisation.

On planet Mars war seems to be such a far distant thing both in terms of time and space, as to seem an anachronism best confined to the Museum of Man on planet Earth. About the only effect of the two wars fought in the last century has been to instil in the collective human consciousness the need to avoid a third war at all costs. It also energised the common man to raise his voice in demand for peace, a voice that in earlier times may have been masked by appeals to community, state or nation. Thus, it can be inferred that the two wars of the previous century contained in them the seeds of the end of war itself!

Another effect of the two wars was to fuel the technology race. As men of science, schooled in the pacifist traditions of Bertrand Russell and Einstein, tend to gravitate towards the most civilised nations of the Earth, the natural corollary was to give a critical advantage to the most law-abiding nations of the Earth, thus opening a vast technological gap between these nations and others less observant of human rights and fundamental freedom.

It also gave a fillip to the moral movements represented by Mahatma Gandhi and the Dalai Lama in the East and by Martin Luther King in the West, moral movements that were to reshape the way we think; moral movements that were to reshape the very force of destiny itself!

It is often said that Man has his own best interest at heart; there was a migration of both people and (perhaps more significantly) capital to those nations that were seen to be stable, pacifist, democratic and observant of human rights. The accumulation of capital in the law-abiding societies both of the east and the west was accompanied by the flight of capital from those nations viewed as "closed" societies.

Another of the effects of war was to make the national governments aware of the need to preserve their national heritage in the form of the environment and to prevent the degradation of the same. These gave birth to the "green" movements that sought to bring to the fore the environment as an area of concern; and to forcefully project their views to the people and to the governments of the day.

Perhaps, on a more psychological plane, the two wars led to the sublimation of our aggressive instinct towards more productive channels such as the achievement of annual targets in the private sector, or at least towards less violent outlets such as rugby and football. It led to the birth of a counter-culture based on identification with the football club, often witnessing scenes of mass frenzy; identified in an earlier era with war.

It also lead to the birth of new trends in music, as the common people sought other outlets for their pent-up energies; outlets that were not so hurtful to other human beings nor harmful to points of view other than their own. These "pop" groups, like football clubs and the multinational corporations all had one point in common: the loyalties of their members transcended the national boundaries of earlier times, thus undermining the very basis of nation-state based conflicts. Their members came from different national, racial and community backgrounds; working together and bonding together across class lines to form a "citizen of the planet Earth", a citizen whose identification with the events of the day was supranational, transcending the artificial boundaries of earlier times.

Perhaps another of the effects of the technological revolution ushered in by war was to make the waging of it prohibitively expensive, so expensive in fact as almost to guarantee that there would not be any winners in a future war, if one were to be waged. If one could be excused for using the term, war could no longer be regarded as a cost-effective measure for the pursuance of state policy, effectively ensuring its own obsolescence!

The convergence of these trends was to lead to the emergence of modern man, a creature as different from Homo Sapiens as Homo Sapiens is from Neanderthal man; perhaps a further stage in the evolution of mankind earlier alluded to by that great student of human nature, Bernard Shaw. It is as a member of this species of modern man that I came to Mars and that I have taken time off to write this article.

FREDERICK PHILIP SYLVESTER
Able Four Has Casualties

The action described in the following story took place on the 26th October 1944, in the area of the Netherlands now known as WEST MAAS EN WAAL. To find St Andrius Sluis on the map, scale 1:200,00, from s'Hertzogenbosch, follow the main road to Salbommel, then just east to find Rossum and Kerkdriel. St Andries lies between these two places, where the rivers Maas and Waal almost meet.

On the 24th October 1944 a foot patrol from "A" Squadron 43rd Reconnaissance Regiment were assisted by a Dutch civilian to sink a barge across an inlet on the edge of the River Maas to prevent the small craft, which were harboured therein, from being used by the Germans who were based in a nearby 19th Century fort.

When, two days later, this same civilian came to "A" Squadron HQ with news that the fort had been evacuated by the enemy and suggested that he could lead a patrol to the fort by a route which would be hidden from the view of other German troops in the area, he was accepted by the Squadron Leader as being genuine.

A patrol of about 18 men, under the command of a sergeant, because no officer was available, set out from Dreumel, with the object of setting booby-traps inside the fort in case the Germans returned. Passing through Heerewaarden they were protected by the houses of the village. At Zevenhuisen there were fewer houses but a scattering of trees and shrubs provided cover. After Zevenhuisen however, the ground was open and the only cover was provided by raised paths and undulations.

As they approached a nearby brickworks a shot rang out and the men dived for cover. The Dutchman volunteered to investigate the shot and returned with the news that it had come from the other side of the River Waal, so the patrol continued towards the fort.

The sluice was now in sight and appeared as a single tower but the fort was masked by two derelict buildings which had had their doors and windows removed. The sergeant decided to have a look at the sluice before entering the fort area. He chose a party of four which included a Dutch interpreter who had been given the honorary rank of Lieutenant and was wearing battledress with appropriate badges of rank. A Bren team of two were sent up onto the Waal dike in case the enemy approached from behind the fort, the remainder were instructed to take cover behind the raised paths and cover the sluice party.

The sluice, which consisted of a pair of towers, between which the sluice gate operated, proved to be unattended so the party of four rejoined the covering party.

With the Bren team on the dike, the sergeant chose some of his men to enter the fort area from the left, while the remainder approached the fort from the right. The sergeant decided to cross the moat at a point which had been dammed and where the water was shallow. The other party approached along what turned out to be the main route into the fort.

The sergeant's party were crossing the flat area between the moat and the fort itself when suddenly machine guns opened up from the apertures in the fort walls. Two of the men on the approach road were killed immediately and the others took what cover they could find, some of them found themselves in a trench but were unable to see the enemy without raising their heads above the parapet. Realising that they had been led into a trap the Sergeant decided to return the way they had come but as they re-crossed the moat they came under fire from machine guns firing on fixed lines. The party scattered and crawled through a tobacco field and marshy ground to reach whatever cover was available.

The sergeant was unable to contact the others who were pinned down. One of his party attempted to see what the enemy were doing and was shot in the head. Someone shouted to the Bren Team that it was an ambush and to get out, the two left the Waal dyke, one, George, took the easy route along the dike road but was shot in the ankle, he was helped to cover by a friendly Dutchman and was later picked up by the Padre. The other dived down the embankment and over a hedge where he was met by the friendly Dutchman who had helped George and who pushed his bicycle into the soldier's hands and urged him to pedal towards Heerewaarden.

With one part of the patrol pinned down, the others tried to get away but were attacked by enemy troops who had been hiding in adjacent buildings. The Dutch interpreter was severely wounded while two brothers were slightly wounded, with a fourth man believed killed. This was Trooper Knight whose name is not recorded on the Regiment's Roll of Honour and is therefore presumed to be still alive.

The Troop Sergeant went to the brickworks to fetch a barrow or something on which to transport Tommy, the Dutch interpreter but while he was away the Germans captured the remaining men of the patrol.

After capture, Tommy successfully pretended to be a British Officer and was treated as such until he was released from a hospital just before the war ended. The captives were moved from the fort to Calumborg, via Waardenburg, where one of the severely wounded died of his wounds and was buried at the road-side. Those with minor injuries were treated at Culemborg then transported by rail to prison camp Stalag XIB in Fallingbostel, Germany.

The severely wounded were taken to Utrecht where they were treated in Soestbergen Hospital and where another of the party, Trooper Rowland Merritt, died of his wounds on 29 October. He is buried in a civilian cemetery in Soestbergen.

It was not until 1947 that the grave of Trooper Walker was found in Waardenburg by the Padre of the 43rd Reece. The Reverend Gethyn-Jones arranged for Trooper Walker's remains to be re-buried by the War Graves Commission, his grave is in Bergen op Zoom War Cemetery.

The two who were killed at the fort were seen by the prisoners as they were being taken away but it was not known where or by whom they were buried and they were consequently recorded on the memorial wall of the Canadian War Cemetery at Groesbeek, near Nijmegen, as having no known grave.

In 1983 Frank Thompson , one of those incarcerated in Stalag XIB, tried to find the Dutch interpreter who he only knew as Tommy. Through a Dutch radio programme and with help from other Dutch people, Tommy Zwollo, of Deventer, was eventually found. A reunion was arranged by the radio people who also had a video made of the meeting of Frank and Tommy at the site of the fort.

A search by the Dutch Army produced reasonable evidence that the bodies of Trooper Raymond Hadwin and Trooper Reginald Stopher lay beneath the rubble of the fort, which had been demolished by the Germans a day or two after the ambush.

It was not feasible to recover those bodies for re-burial so recently Frank Thompson set up a small committee to raise sufficient money with which to have a memorial erected near the fort site. This fund has raised just over £1500 and is presently negotiating with the Dutch authorities for a suitable memorial to be erected on or near the site of the fort.

RICHARD THATCHER
War Correspondents

STALEMATE! France, 1915. Horns locked, the ebb and flow of fortune dictating position, advancing, retreating, then beaten. Appallingly depleted the armies paused, resting briefly, licking wounds. Kitchener, pointing his accusing finger sternly from street corner posters demanded, "YOUR COUNTRY NEEDS YOU". War advertised like powder. Bands played, bugles blared. Young men, over a million, hurried to the flag for glory and excitement, seeking escape from drab, dreary downtrodden lives. Trained in warfare, in two weeks they were deemed fit to fight the Hun.

*

France
23rd April 1915
Dear Mum, im sorry I did not see you before I left and did not rite before. I was afraid i'd get sent back. I could not because im a man now and don't like to see how Bert treats you anymore. I know I needed your sayso, but they took me anyway becos I lied so please forgive me. im in France but have not yet seen any dirty huns. We spend our days marching they say to the front wherever that is. we hear big guns. They're far away but some get jittery. Sarge was shot last night they thought he was a Hun. im well just tired from not sleeping proper with gard and false alarms and all. must stop now. Please write soon, from your loving son.
Billy
PS I'M ALLRIGHT!!! XXXXXXX

*

"Look Dora! A letter came. From Billy thank God. The scamp went and joined up. If he goes and gets hisself killed, I don't know what I'll do to him when he gets back."

"Don't be silly Winnie, if he's kilt you'll just bury him. Don't you worry duck. He's a good boy."

"Ta Dora. Must go in now and answer the letter. See you."

*

London,
14th May 1915
Dear son,

Got your letter today thank God. Why'd you do it? Plenty of others could go. I don't know what I'd do without you, it's been tough since your Dad died, and you not getting on with Bert doesn't help. He's not your Dad but he's a good man and we needed a man in the house. The cat's gone since you went. Don't know where. Please try not to write bad things about Bert. It would be nice to show him the letter then.

He might like you better he sees you write regular. Hope this finds you well.

your loving mum XXXXXXX

*

France,
6th June 1915.

Dear mum, Got yours today. Letters take so long to come. I'M WELL, don't fret. Saw my first dead Hun Saturday. Young like me. Staring up in the sky peaceful like but no smile. Praps he also fibbed about his age. I hope someone tells his mum gentle like. Seen no close up live ones yet cept far off running or coming. They look wicked B's. Big guns noisy. Sometimes ours, sometimes theirs. We can tell which. Ours go BOOM, theirs go wheeeee CARUMP! The wheeeee says they're coming so we duck Attacks are stupid. One hour of big guns carumping, duck safe in the trench covered in mud and muck. We know he's coming and we're ready. Stupid I calls it. Why the warning? Us also. Stupid. Must stop writing. Guns stopped. They're coming. Bye now, your loving son
Billy. XXXXXX Write soon.

*

"Ere Bert. From Billy."

"Yeah! What's 'e up to?"

"The Army. In France."

"Do 'im good. Make 'im a man. Stop 'is troublemaking."

"Oh Bert! S'that all you can say? I'll write straightaway. Letters take so long."

*

London.
15th June 1915.

Dear Son, Got your letter today. Glad you're still well. The guns sound bad, but glad you're safe. Them trenches sound bad so wrap up well. Don't get a chill. Not much news. Oh yes I nearly forgot. The cat's just walked in. No by your leave. Never mind where I've been. Food is getting short these days. They say it's the war effort so I hope they're feeding you well. I'm sending some socks I made. Keep warm. by the way Bert sends his love. God keep you safe son and bring you back.

Your loving mum.XXXXXX

*

30th June 1915 Kitchener decides to end the stalemate. He simply orders, "End It. We'll have a BIG PUSH". So Brigade commanders order, "Push". And Battalion commanders order, "Push". Company commanders order and men push. They're pushed back with obscene losses on both sides.

*

4th July 1915. The War Office telegram said, using regretful but terribly bland words, that her son Billy was "Regretfully killed in action".

30th July 1915. A Parcel came. The contents were sparse; his cap badge; her photograph; his penknife and two envelopes, one typewritten, the other in Billy's handwriting. She tremblingly opened it. Was Billy alive? With a sense of unreality she began reading, half hoping the telegram was a mistake. The letter was short.

France,
30th June 1915,
Dear mum, going over the top tomorrow. Too busy to finish this now. Too much to do. I have writ a envelope for this and will finish when we're back. im nervis but not scared becos we're going to knock seven bells out of him this time. I love you Mum. That's silly. You already know that. ill finish this tomorrer when we're back. Till later.

Eyes misted, she picked up the other envelope.
"A" Company HQ,
Loyal Berkshire Regiment,
France
19th July 1915
Dear Mrs. Wilson,
It is my painful duty to express my sympathy for the death of your son Private William John Wilson on 1st July 1915. He was

killed on duty during our attack. I assure you he did not suffer, but died a hero's death supporting his comrades in arms. Those of his last effects we have been able to gather and an incomplete letter to you, are enclosed.

I am,

Your obedient servant,

J.R.Rodgers. Lt. Col. Commanding.

Winnie closed her eyes, and with a million other mothers on both sides wondered, "What made my son fit to be 'killed by his country'. Why him?".

F THOMPSON
Ollie's Dad

Ollie was my best friend in the Junior School and I always used to stop off at his house on my way home. His mum was ready with a piece of cake for us and then we would run down the garden to call on his dad.

There was a wooden shed at the end of the path, warmed by an old stove in winter. Inside was a desk: it smelled of wood shavings mixed with glue and varnish. A large man, wearing a blue apron, sat at a work top, huge hands deftly manipulating strips of cane. He turned to greet us, his eyes hidden behind dark glasses.

Ollie's dad always put out his right hand and as I took it he would say, "Now then, young Tom, have you had a good day?" He had a deep rumbling voice though at times he suffered from fits of coughing.

We would sit and listen as he told us of The War. He had a fund of stories, starting with the day he had volunteered to join the Grenadier Guards. We learned of the strict discipline, the drill sergeants who bawled for hours on the parade ground and their hawk-eyes for detail. We were told of spit and polish on boots that had to shine like glass, of the rifle ranges and the mad minute when each soldier had to fire ten rounds rapid.

The battalion went to France and soon went up the line into the trenches opposite the Germans. There was the mud; the monotonous diet of bully beef, biscuits and Tickler's plum and apple jam; "stand to" at daybreak; and the joy of receiving letters from home. The battalion suffered heavy casualties and Ollie's dad was promoted to Lance-Sergeant.

One day the Germans launched a gas attack. Yellow clouds of mustard gas filled the trenches and soon long lines of blind soldiers, coughing and retching, were stumbling back to the regimental aid post, each man with a hand on the shoulder of the man in front, all being led by one who was still partially sighted.

Ollie's dad was blind from that day onwards. He was sent for training at St. Dunstan's and he returned home skilled in making baskets and cane bottomed chairs.

We used to talk to him about school and about our nature

walks, describing the dog roses, the birds and all those things in the countryside that he could no longer see.

One day he said, "Here you are boys, a little present for you." They were beautifully fashioned models of a kris, the wavy curved knife of the Malays, carved from hard wood. The curves were faultless and all the work had been done with a spoke-shave.

Every year there was a service in church on Remembrance Sunday. I was in the choir then and the church would be full. The Roll of Honour was read: even in my small village the number who had died was large enough to mean that almost everyone had lost either a relative or neighbour. My aunts had boy friends who had gone to war and never returned. Like so many more, my aunts were spinsters for the rest of their lives.

After the service, when the Last Post had been sounded, there was a parade to the war memorial. Ollie's dad was always at the front, stepping out boldly, white stick like a pace stick under his arm, while his free hand was linked with another old comrade. There were legless men in wheelchairs; the one legged, hobbling bravely with the rest; the armless with sleeves pinned across chests where the medals gleamed. The unscathed were there too but all had aged before their time and few would make old bones.

So I grew up always conscious of the effects of war. Despite the anguish, the slaughter and the loss of a whole generation of young men, Ollie and I went to war, in our turn, as Britain again faced up to Germany. The winter of 1941 claimed Ollie's dad, for his lungs were too weak to withstand the bitter cold of that year.

It was probably for the best because Ollie was shot down over the Ruhr in 1943. I survived: but the killing and the maiming goes on. The effects of war are there for all to see but so few take notice of them.

HAYLEY B C THOMPSON
Remembrance

I waved enthusiastically to my brother as he boarded the plane, I remember it as clearly as if it were yesterday. It's a scene I've replayed in my mind a thousand times over. It was the last time I saw my brother alive. He was eighteen years old.

I suppose that when you're young you take your family for granted, not purposely, but simply because at the age of seven you don't look to the future; for me the future was the next five minutes, so thinking about what you would do if somebody close to you suddenly wasn't there anymore isn't really something which would enter into your thoughts is it?

Ever since I could remember, all my brother Luke had ever wanted was to join the armed forces. It was all he talked about. When I was five or so he used to tell me what he imagined the army to be like. He'd go on about all the different and exciting places he'd get to see and the interesting people he'd meet. The determination in his voice was easily detected.

Luke had only been in the army for a few months when the troubles in the Falklands began to develop. So no-one was really that surprised when he got called up to fight over there. The day he left I remember how excited he was. I'd never seen him as happy as he was that day. My father was so proud of him, he saw it as a chance for the family to gain a bit of respect. For my mother however it was her worst nightmare. Her little boy was going away to war with the terrifying prospect that he might not return. All I remember thinking was that I'd have no-one there to play games with or to read me stories when I was too scared to sleep.

It was 2.45 am when I first heard the words that Luke was dead. I watched from the staircase as my father opened the door on an army officer. I listened to what was being said. I resisted the urge to run down the stairs when my mother collapsed in a heap on the floor, sobbing uncontrollably and I didn't move as I silently watched my father smash up the full length mirror that took pride of place in our hallway, screaming that it should have been him.

It took my parents nearly six hours the next day to tell me that

Luke was dead. DEAD. I'd spent the whole of the night trying to comprehend the word but at that age I'd never really thought about it before. It took me a long time to come to terms with the fact that Luke wasn't coming home. EVER.

Sometimes I would just sit in Luke's room for hours, just sitting trying to feel him, hoping that he would walk through the door as if nothing had happened and it had all been a bad dream.

My mum turned Luke's room into a shrine after the funeral. She put everything that belonged to him in there. All of his school photos and sports medals were now placed about his bedroom. Tidying his room became an obsession for my mum, she had to keep it tidy just in case the army had somehow made a mistake and that Luke hadn't been shot in action. It didn't matter to her that she'd seen the body herself.

Talking about Luke was hard after the funeral, my dad refused to discuss him. As far as dad was concerned Luke had never existed. Dad had wiped out every memory of him. I didn't understand then that it was his way of coping. He thought that by trying to forget his son, he would somehow forget the pain he felt, the pain that was slowly eating him up inside. I tried to be like that, tried to forget but it was no good, the more I tried to forget the more I seemed to remember. That was the trouble with being young, your mind craves information and it's incapable of determining what to let in and what to block out, so it lets everything in; the pain, the memories, but most of all the questions. Questions which no-one seemed to want to answer.

It was a little while after that that my dad moved out. I was sitting in Luke's room listening to my parents blame each other for Luke's death. Mum blamed dad saying that it never would have happened if he hadn't filled Luke's head with those "Stupid bloody ideas about glory" and the idea of being a "war hero"; while dad said that if my mum hadn't mollycoddled him when he was at home, Luke wouldn't have been so quick to join up. Neither of them were to blame and it upset me that they were fighting with each other. What I remember most about that night was that it was the first time I'd cried since Luke had died and it dawned on me that I no longer had Luke there to comfort me when I got upset. It was that moment that I realised I missed Luke more than I ever had before. Or since.

It's been almost ten years now since Luke died and it's still hard to accept. People are wrong when they say that the pain goes away, because it doesn't. It's always there inside you. It's just that you learn how to tolerate it; to get on with life. In some ways it's good to feel the pain because the feeling of pain comes from the love there was and still is. I don't mind the pain because at least it's something. The alternative is emptiness. Out of pain and emptiness I'll have pain any day. Besides, I've still got my memories and that's the most important thing.

BRIAN C TOTHILL
The Pledge

The descending sun cast shafts of light across the swollen unharvested folds of Kentish countryside.

Two young boys, hugging their knees, sat together. Both unaware of the lengthening shadows. Both oblivious to the subtle change as summer skylarks begrudgingly gave precedence to the sombre evensong of rooks.

That glorious summer of 1929 passed with the ponderous inevitability of swans in flight. A seemingly endless vacation reached conclusion. The boys, divided by race and culture, were united through friendship. They had yet to feel the remorse of final parting.

Carl, a tall willowy fourteen year old, was from pure Teutonic stock. He wore pride in a natural manner and excelled at individual competitive pursuits. His prowess with the rapier was already noted in high places.

The German youth spoke guttural English, thanking his friend for a wonderful holiday. He made a promise to write often and vowed his friendship would be forever. Above his ice-blue eyes the flaxen hair fluttered momentarily from a slight shift of the sweet scented breeze.

Harry was a few months younger and still in his thirteenth year. Unlike Carl he was short and stocky. He played team games under duress and was thought of as an honest plodder by those who judged him.

His frank countenance and slow to arouse temper were legacies from his Anglo-Saxon lineage.

Harry responded to Carl's declaration adding his own vow of friendship, one that would last until death.

Both boys spat on their palms and awkwardly shook hands, binding the pledge in solemn ceremony.

Summers rotated with winter over a decade. Every day crammed with the relentless process of turning young boys into men. The quickening pace of events in Europe - soon to culminate in the hostilities of another World War - influenced by the doctrines of family and academy across the continent.

The bond of friendship pledged during those earlier days,

remained with them. They wrote often, comparing their separate and diverging lives.

Carl passed through the rigid disciplines of Germanic upbringing. Absorbing the doctrines of Nazi Germany. Proudly he responded to the promises of his Fuhrer. He emerged from his training to become a revered commander of a Luftwaffe fighter squadron.

The path that Harry followed during these formative years, meandered through rural England tranquility. Country folk waged battle only with natural farming adversaries. Indulgent in the apparent security of Great Britain in the late thirties, most paid little heed to the gathering European storm.

During 1941, Harry was selected, trained and commissioned for air-crew with the Royal Air Force. Stoically performing his duties as a fighter pilot, he soon became leader of a flight of Hurricanes. His squadron was based at Manston, an operational airfield buried deep within the bosom of his beloved Kentish Weald.

Four sinister grey shadows skimmed across the flattened tops of billowy white cloud. Seemingly, each raced ahead of the Messerschmidt poised a hundred feet above them.

Evening raids, deep into southern England were routine for Carl at this stage of the conflict. For the Flight Commander this strategy provided the excitement he sought. His flight plan from his airfield in north-west France was to fly low across the English Channel. Crossing the coast he would quickly seek the safety of altitude. He knew his intrusion would be detected by ground observers ready to raise the alarm.

"Nineteen Squadron. Blue Flight. Scramble - Scramble."

A frenzied call over the tannoy was complemented by the frantic alarm, beaten from the suspended steel triangle.

The pilots who had been sitting or sprawling in the late afternoon sun were pitched into action. The sudden alarm was not unwelcome. Waiting to do battle was a perilous period. Nerves were stretched to the limit and pilots "died" a thousand times before ever leaving the ground.

Following well practised procedures by the ground crews, Harry soon led his flight formation towards the cloud base at 8,000 feet. Somewhere behind this screen lurked the marauding killers.

Harry, scanning a starboard vector, detected the progress of four alien specks moving north-west at five miles range.

"Blue Leader! Four bandits. Green. Two o'clock. Angels nine-oh."

Harry's calm message was conveyed simultaneously to each compatriot.

Within five seconds he wheeled the echelon onto an interception course.

"Attack as you see, tally-ho," commanded Blue Leader.

The echoing click of his R/T switch signified his delegation of command from himself, to each of the young pilots. Harry, with the sun low behind his aircraft, selected the most starboard of the invading quartet and closed quickly on his unsuspecting victim.

Some sixth sense caused Carl to feel the presence of danger. His rear view mirror reflected a minuscule white spark below and behind his companions. The tell-tale flash of reflected sunlight off a perspex canopy was no stranger to him.

"Break formation, scatter and re-group above zone five-four."

Carl delivered the command crisply, concisely and once only. He pulled back hard on the stick and commenced a climb and roll that would take him to safety. The downward swoop of the manoeuvre had started when Carl became aware of the looming calamity.

Harry's thumb stabbed the cannon firing button. The enemy, clear now in every detail, was suspended like a trapped fly within the web of the gunsight.

A short burst was sufficient to hurl a score of cannon shells into the victim.

Black, oily smoke, a flash of orange flame.

The German flyer, with his plane, disintegrated. Harry, with a feeling of elation, kicked the rudder bar over, hauled the stick to the pit of his stomach and commenced his climb.

The two planes collided head on. Each pilot for a brief instant aware of imminent tragedy. The two machines, locked by the force of the impact became inseparable.

The wreckage fluttered silently towards the welcoming embrace of lush Kentish pastures.

The song of the summer skylarks and the call of the competing rooks, were briefly silenced - then resumed.

J H TRYTHALL
Not A Soldier

Peter White was not a soldier. Never could be, never would be. Gentle, kind, frail, he'd been my friend since the age of twelve.

In our last year at school, in 1943, we paraded once a week. always on a Thursday with the school cadet force, and then one evening a week we went on training sessions with the Home Guard. It was generally accepted that when we left school after the Higher Certificate examination, we'd go straight into the army. I would, I knew. I didn't think Peter would. He never played games. He was what my mother called a sickly child.

Our call up papers came when we were at home that Summer of 1943, when just hopefully the War was beginning to turn in Britain's favour. We went together to an army depot just outside London. There we stripped to our underpants, and were checked out by a series of medical orderlies and doctors. To my surprise we BOTH passed.

'I can't believe you've passed,' I told Peter. I didn't mean it rudely. We'd talked about our call up on many an occasion. In fact it was the general topic of conversation among all our age group. Peter's mother felt confident he would fail.

Peter just smiled. He was very accepting of life, in contrast to myself. I was always fighting battles, restless and unsatisfied. It's why we got on so well I suppose. I was the ideas man. He followed my enthusiasms uncomplainingly. At the age of twelve, when I first got to know Peter, I devised a system of semaphore with home made flags. He'd stand patiently one end of a meadow while I signalled to him frantically from the other. I've never forgotten that meadow. It was full of butterflies and tiny flying insects and wild flowers of every variety. It was something you don't see nowadays, sadly, with the current use of pesticides. My happiest memory of Peter is associated with that meadow. I can picture him still, standing tall and smiling amid the long grass.

'Oh Peter,' I would cry in anguish long after the War had ended, even today, 'I wish you were still with me'.

Peter went into the Ordnance Corp, the R.A.O.C. it was called. I went straight into an officer training camp, thanks to all the preparation that I'd had with the cadet force at school. We met together a few weeks after 'D' Day. It must have been about August, 1944. It was a nightmare, that time, like nothing else that I had come across before, or since. Constant tiredness and dirt, our ears assaulted by the noise of gunfire, our minds dulled by the rumble of tanks, we fought our way up the coast until halted by German resistance at Caen, where I was wounded in the shoulder. It's a time I've never like to talk about, even to my wife or my children, a time best forgotten. Fear was the strongest element, but there was also a camaraderie of men, something I marvelled at.

I was driven by ambulance back to that inventive structure, the Mulberry harbour, made out of ships filled with concrete and sunk in the form of a crescent to make a harbour wall. There standing on the beach was Peter, still tall and gawky, but even thinner, his uniform hanging from him as if on a coat hanger. He looked tired and drawn. He was supervising the unloading of stores, clipboard in his hands. I went over to him slowly, my left shoulder heavily bandaged, my arm in a sling, exhausted by what I'd been through.

'Peter,' I called.

He turned and looked at me, that lovely, inane grin spreading over his face in welcome.

We forgot all about rules of military behaviour, a lieutenant embracing a corporal, who neglected to salute.

'God, it's good to see you,' I exclaimed. 'Are you OK?'

He shrugged indifferently, lost for words. He was never one to say much.

'I'm off back to England for a spot of leave,' I told him, indicating to my shoulder.

'I'm sorry,' was all he managed to say. Affection was in his face, delight at seeing me.

Then out of the clouds above burst a lone Messerschmidt, strafing the beach with bullets. We both flattened ourselves, the jolt of falling so hurting my shoulder that I cried out in pain.

Almost as quickly as it had arrived, the German plane zoomed up into the clouds, and disappeared, the noise of its engine receding. I got up slowly, tucking my legs beneath me balancing with just one arm. Alongside me, Peter lay still. I bent down and touched him. There was no response. I saw a gaping hole in his back. Blood came pumping out. I screamed for help but there was nothing anyone could do.

This quiet, gentle man, left a poem among his things, written on a piece of yellow army order paper:

'A soldier not, completely wrong,
I wish I were like other men,
In deed and word and body strong.
Alas I'll never be like them.

Meadow I dream, with flowers wild,
Some butterflies in colour bright,
In play with friend so strong yet mild,
To laugh again in world made right.

T S TURNBULL
Border Control

The wind gusted sheets of fine rain across the deserted and remote country road leading to the border. Corporal Branson was not a happy man, marooned here and on his own, chilled and deserted by his mate who had taken off in the jeep for HQ, summoned by a supposedly urgent message. He pulled his greatcoat tightly around him. What a place for a checkpoint, he thought. On both sides of the road hills climbed toward woods. An ideal place for snipers. Apprehensively he wondered why they had not had a go before.

In the distance the noise of a car. Coming towards the checkpoint fast. In the middle of the road with his rifle at the ready he was a standing duck. The car slowed and stopped just short of him. Relieved, he stepped to the driver's window. Then a bullet smashed into the road a few feet away. Instinctively he swung round and in that moment a gun was jammed into his back.

"Don't turn round, soldier; just drop your gun and get your arms up. Any funny stuff and you're dead. I'd like a chance to put a bullet or two into you, you murdering scum."

With his back to the car Cpl Branson scanned the hill facing him and saw a lone figure standing, a rifle in his hand. Meanwhile another man had emerged from the car who handcuffed him and shoved a hood over his head. Then into the car and off.

The car whizzed along for some time then slowed and bumped its way along some winding country lane. Eventually it stopped. Cpl Branson was hauled out, thrust into a room that smelt of decay and neglect and forced onto a hard chair. His feet were then tied together and he was left hooded and handcuffed.

They're going to murder me, he thought, but why here? Why not back at the checkpoint? He soon had the answer. He was to be a bargaining tool; his life for that of some republican VIP captured recently.

"You must be crazy," he mumbled through his hood. "They'll not agree to that. You might as well shoot me now. You're going to anyway."

"Now don't ye be sayin' that," someone replied. "They're a bag of shit but sure they'll not murder one of their own." But Cpl

Branson knew that the powers-that-be would never do a deal with the IRA. Especially not for someone like him. He was as good as dead.

He tried to be calm. He had to die sometime and maybe the hour had chimed for him. Funny old thing life. He had always imagined getting married to Deidre, having kids, maybe moved to other combat zones, seeing the world a bit, living to a ripe old age. All this cut short! It was a frightening thought, as if Death had slipped him a visiting card. He didn't want to die, not now, most certainly not now anyhow. He'd no strong religious feelings, hadn't thought much about heaven or hell, didn't know if there was an afterlife or not. If not he wouldn't see Deidre again or his Mum or his sister. He couldn't stop the wrenching sob.

Silence for some time with only the noise of his captor humming and munching something, probably an apple.

Then, "Well we can't just sit here, me starin' at ye an' ye sweatin' away there full of all the horrors of Hell. Tell us somethin' about yerself. Are ye married? Have ye a girl?"

"Go to Hell," Cpl Branson replied.

"Well I hope not, in the name of all that's holy. I'm a good Catholic."

Cpl Branson did not answer. But he couldn't go on just thinking or he'd go mad. He might as well make the most of his time talking.

"I come from near Bristol. Joined up when I left school. I've a girl called Deirdre. Funny that; she comes from Ireland. Came over when she was twelve and still has an Irish accent. We're going to get married when I get back. If I get back."

The reminder of his danger stabbed him but he continued. "She's just an average girl. Goes to work in a factory. Pretty too and good figure. You'd like her. She's full of stories about her Irish childhood. I love to hear them over and over. Makes Ireland sound kind of magical. I miss her like Hell. Write her long letters and phone her when I can."

Cpl Branson choked back a rush of feelings. There was another long silence.

"If yer so fond of yer Irish tart and her stories what are ye doin' here fighting us and terrorisin' our women and kids I'd like to know?"

"For Chrissake you should know the answer! You're supposed

to be a soldier too. You go where you're sent and do what you're told. I've nothing against you personally or your country, just about how you go about things."

How they went about things was beyond his captor's control. He himself was just doing his job. Deep down he could sympathise with Cpl Branson. He was just doing his job too; it could have been the other way round. He seemed a decent bloke, the sort of bloke he might have gone for a drink with. Perhaps he could do with a drink too and a ciggy.

The door opened and there were a few whispered words.

"...no exchange...shoot...dump body...phone papers."

A pause. More whispering. Then protests: "No, I can't...not his fault." A cold voice, distinct and impersonal: "OK, if you haven't the guts I'll do it for you."

These were the last sounds that Cpl Branson ever heard. Apart from the explosion of a gun.

NICK K WARDLE
Back Home

I sat back in my father's armchair and puffed out a blow of contentment. My face beamed as I stretched my feet out to rest on a footstool.

My tranquillity was interrupted by my mother approaching with a tray rattling away as she moved close.

"There you go boy, get that warm tea down ya gullet," she insisted. She placed the tray on the table next to me. "I've made you some of your favourite cake too. You look like you could do with putting some weight on. Didn't they feed you in the army?"

I smiled at my mother and studied her face. The war had lasted four long years and it seemed to have aged her rapidly. The thick dark hair had turned to a slightly wispy grey and deep wrinkles were rutted all over her once smooth face. Even those sparking green eyes, which my father had said were the reason he fell in love with her, had now dimmed.

"Hurry up with that tea now son," she urged, pointing at the mug as she spoke. "We have a party to go to at seven. The whole village is proud of you and want to tell ya so."

I watched my mother move away, making a fuss of adjusting pictures and checking for dust. I was looking forward to the party. It would be great to see everyone again.

I finished my tea and then got ready for the party. I was running late, so I told my mother and father to go on without me and that I'd catch up with them. Mother wasn't happy as I think she wanted to arrive with the village "hero".

While adjusting my tie, my thoughts centred around Doris Mills. I remembered the scent of her perfume and her innocent smile. It was one of the things which kept me going during the war. I'd spent many nights shivering with cold and had only my rifle to huddle up to but then memories of giving her a lift home from work on my bike somehow made me warm. Sometimes I would hold conversations with her in my head, silly really. I always thought that we would get married once we'd grown up. Well, now I was grown up. I'd been to war for heaven's sake. Surely that proved that I was a man?

I wasn't usually a vain person but I felt that I should make the effort to look good seeing as everyone would be turning out to see me. With this in mind it took me several attempts to get my centre parting just right. It was nice to be able to wear "civvy" clothes. My black suit was a little large but wasn't a bad fit.

When I was happy with my appearance, I opened the front door and then shut it behind me. I stood on my doorstep, shut my eyes and breathed in deeply through my nostrils. The air of the English countryside felt pure.

A bang shattered my serenity. My eyes flew open and saw the sky awash with colour. I think I saw green and blue but mostly flame orange. A horrible screeching sound made my body freeze with terror. Another bang followed and I sensed sweat pouring down my forehead. I could feel the colour drain from my face and I felt weak. My mouth was dry and had a horrible taste. I wanted to run but my limbs wouldn't respond. My eyes glazed over and my legs appeared to be crumpling beneath me.

"Come on Private!" I urged myself. "Get a grip of yourself!" I regained enough strength to be able to clench my fists. "They are only fireworks." My teeth gritted together and I repeated, "it's over", time and time again until my sight cleared and I felt colour return to my face.

My shirt had stuck to my body because of the sweat. I pulled it away and was surprised to feel how soaked it was. I felt cold. I needed a whisky and a warm fire so I went back inside and tended my needs.

A sense of shame soon washed over me as I sat in my father's armchair, sipping my whisky. How could I let a few stupid fireworks turn me into a gibbering wreck? Shells, grenades and machine guns hadn't bothered me while in the field. Perhaps I'd spent the war living purely on instinct? What if I'd been drugged in order to become a ruthless, blood-thirsty killer? I'd heard a rumour about something called "Shell Shock" but was told that this was an excuse for cowards to get out of the front line.

I mulled over many questions that evening but couldn't find any answers. Worse still, I didn't know where to turn for the answers. I was no longer part of a battalion and didn't have a C.O. to command my thoughts or direction.

I'd forgotten all about the party and Doris Mills.

JANE WENHAM-JONES
Coventry

Ruby's Mum and Dad take her under the stairs when the bombs come. Johnny's go down beneath the garden. But Eva has to stay in bed. To show the Germans she isn't scared.

"We're not running like rabbits," says Mother with her fierce face, mouth a line, hair pulled back in a tight bun.

"You sleep now," she says, as she closes the black curtains.

Mustn't let any light in or the Germans will know where we are.

Christine sleeps. Christine always sleeps. Fair hair spread on the pillow, thumb in her mouth.

But Eva is older. She knows what the Germans can do and she is afraid. She lies very stiff and still,. hoping they won't come tonight.

She can hear Mother in the kitchen. Clattering saucepans, running water. Mother's always busy. There's so much to do. Mother works all day but her work is never done.

She hears her speaking to Daddy, then Daddy has gone; the door shuts behind him. Mother's steps come down the passageway and into the bedroom. Eva keeps her eyes shut. Mother will be angry if she is still awake.

Eva is in the garden, playing with Ruby. They have a big doll but they've got to hide it or it will be taken away to have its arms and legs pulled off. Eva is carrying it, her arms wrapped around it to keep it safe, trying to creep towards the house before she's caught, but there is someone behind the bush watching them and Ruby starts to scream....

Eva's awake. The bed is hot and she hears the first high whistle whining outside in the darkness. She can't see but she can feel Christine's body warm against hers. Eva jumps at the explosion but Christine does not move.

Then the familiar noise begins again before the thwack of another explosion somewhere outside. That one was louder. She lies tight-still, her hands pressed into balls. She will never get used to this noise, her heart always thumps and thuds.

Please, please God, don't let one of those come straight through our roof and crash on my bed. Don't let our house be knocked down like the one in Green Street. I promise I will be good and go to sleep when I'm told to and I'll drink all my milk up every day if you don't let the Germans get me...

And then she feels it. The pricking in her legs. And she knows they are under the bed. Her breath comes out of her in a big rush and then she lies very, very still, knowing that she mustn't breathe at all. She can feel the sharp pointy tips of their swords - they are pushing them up through the mattress. There must be three or four of them, the pricking is faster now, all up and down the backs of her legs and bottom as she lies straight and stiff like a dead person.

She doesn't know if they are doing it to Christine; her sister is still pressed against her, she is breathing so loudly the Germans must be able to hear, but she doesn't wake up.

Eva wants to scream. She wants to shriek and shout so that Daddy will come but she can't open her mouth and if the Germans hear her they will take her away.

Outside the bombs are falling over and over, so loudly her head is rattling inside. Crash, crash, into the road, like the sky is raining bombs, so many they will surely hit her house soon. She doesn't know where Mother is. Mother never goes to bed when bombs come. Eva heard her telling Mrs Harding she never gets undressed so she's ready just in case.

Eva wants her Mother now even though Mother won't like it if she calls out. Eva's chest is all wet underneath her nightie and they are still under the bed, still pushing their swords up through the mattress.

She will have hundreds of little red spots all up her legs where they have jabbed at her. And then the whining sound is right over her head, making her ears tingle and there is a huge bang and the smashing, tinkling of glass and the windows are cracking, glass falling into the room, across the bed in sharp showers and now Eva is screaming, screaming, screaming, till her throat hurts and she cannot stop.

At last Daddy is here, scooping her up, taking the sheets and blankets in his arms too, saying:

"It's all right darling, all right, I've got you."

He doesn't know about the Germans under the bed. Christine has woken up, she is crying too. Eva tries to tell him about them and their swords and how they have been pricking her but he says "shush, shush"

and takes her into the kitchen.

Mother's got her pinny on. She wipes Eva's face with a flannel and gives her a piece of bread. She's got to finish the sandwiches for the ARP's outside. Those men are hungry. They've been pulling out bodies all night. Daddy brings Christine in. She's still crying.

Mother gives her bread too.

"Enough now," she says. Daddy has to go out. Back to the digging.

Eva and Christine chew. Sat on chairs in their nighties. Eyes all wide open but stretched tight like they are when you've got up but it's still night.

Except it is getting light now. The air is grey. Mother cuts the sandwiches. Across and across again.

"Get dressed now," she says. "I'll just take these outside."

Outside there is a hole in the road. Stretching right across to the other houses. The bomb is still in it and Eva and Christine cannot go beyond the gateposts today.

There are stones and bits of concrete everywhere, piled up in heaps against the walls. The milk cart stops up the road and the milkman picks his way carefully along the edge of the hole, leaving the horse the other side, snuffling in its nosebag..

"No school, eh," he says. Mother bustles out.

"Got my work cut out today," she says, shooing Eva and Christine away. The Milkman looks at the shattered windows and shakes his head. But Mother walks past him. She has a carrot in her pocket for the horse.

"Look at him," she says, looking across the crater at the animal patiently waiting. It is a strange voice. Eva turns back to see.

Years later it is what she will remember most clearly. The broken street and Mother's face in the early morning light.

For a moment - as she looked at that horse - it was soft with love.

RICHARD WHITTLE
Tag Lady

"What's that you've got, Andrew? Take it out of your mouth...it's a dog tag. Where did you find it?"

"In the car. I didn't take it from a dog, Daddy, honest! Perhaps it's the lady's?"

"Where's you Mum...? Jackie...! Andrew's got a military dog tag...says he found it in the car...says it might be the lady's. What lady...?

"A bag lady," Mum called from the garden. "I gave her a lift as far as the nursery."

"God! Have you any idea what those people carry?"

"Carrier bags, Daddy. Lots and lots and lots."

"She was tired," Mum called. "I couldn't..."

"You could! They're alive with lice," Dad said as he buttoned his police sergeant's tunic, "and I'll take this," he added, as he strode from the room, "it's found property."

"Daddy didn't kiss you goodbye," Andrew said when Mum came in.

"He was cross. Better not tell him that you gave that old lady your sandwiches."

"Or my apple."

"Or your apple."

On the whole it hadn't been a bad day for Annie and at this rate she'd be at the Sally by Friday. The car trip had helped of course, as had the supermarket trolley she'd found - though she'd cut her hand fixing it. She settled under an old oak set back from the road and arranged her bags around her. From a pocket in her coat she took a now-grubby apple core, nibbled it quickly, then put it back.

The cut on her hand was a bugger actually, but nothing a quick dab of iodine wouldn't cure. She selected her green Harrod's bag, rummaged through it and took out a small brown glass bottle. She pulled at the pink rubber stopper but it crumbled and broke - just her bloody luck - last week her glasses, today her dog tag, now the bloody iodine. She settled back against the tree-trunk, pulled her coat up around her neck and waited for night.

At dusk came the drizzle, drifting in waves over the surrounding fields and carrying with it a faint whiff of smoke from a bonfire. It also brought fragments of bark down the tree-trunk and then down her neck. She went to scratch herself but stopped suddenly, remembering that was how she'd lost her first dog tag.

A plane flew low overhead, scurrying south before nightfall and before distant thunder brought heavier rain from the west. She hated planes - that sort of plane - the kind with propellers that buzzed. And she hated thunder because it reminded her of heavy guns - the guns that never stopped.

When darkness came she drifted in and out of sleep and vivid memories. She was driving now, driving her ambulance, first along a beach and then to the ramp of a landing craft, tank. She was ill that night, she remembered...seasick. It was her birthday; she was nineteen, just two years out of grammar school. And it was a Thursday...D plus 9, they'd called it.

She'd driven off the beach easily at the other end, she recalled, and things might have gone well if she'd seen the direction sign at the junction - and if the MP had stopped her going the wrong way. It wasn't her fault that she got a flat tyre and couldn't slacken the wheel-nuts; it wasn't her fault that she had to leave the damn ambulance, nor that she wandered for days until the Americans found her.

"I slept under trees, actually," she told them politely. "And I seem to have lost my dog tag..."

They weren't in the least bit worried about the ambulance, or the tag. They told her she'd walked over fifty miles and gave her a shower...hot water, she remembered. When she told them she was a nurse they said there was no way they'd let her go back and they sent her to a forward dressing station where she worked with their medics. They treated her like a princess and they made her a new dog tag, one like theirs.

It was weeks before they tried to trace her unit. They worried that she'd be posted as missing but she didn't have any relatives, she told them - not now - not since the blitz. And anyway, she said, she'd sort that out later when she reported losing her ambulance. Their officer told her there was no way anyone would worry about that, no way. He said that about everything. That's how they were, the Americans.

"That trolley's got the supermarket's name on it," the police sergeant said, as he strode across the grass to the shambling figure under the oak. "It'll have to go back."

Annie stopped loading her carrier bags and stared at him.

"It was broke. I fixed it. You police?"

"You know I'm police."

"Car's not black."

"Police cars have been white for years, love. It says 'POLICE' on the side in bloody great letters. You really can't see that...? Your eyes are that bad?"

"Glasses broke."

"So where are you going?"

"Sally Ann."

"That's thirty miles! Better ask them for some glasses."

"They're broke."

"Then ask them for some that aren't broke."

"They got iodine?" She fumbled in her pocket and held out an empty brown bottle. The sergeant took it and held it gingerly between finger and thumb. She grabbed it back.

"Iodine?" he asked.

"Cut meself."

"Iodine went out with the ark, love. So do you want a lift, or what...? get in the back...okay?"

"Nursing Sister Ann Robertson," the sergeant said to the woman at the hostel. "Blind as a bat...broke her glasses."

He turned to Annie and held out a shiny brass disk.

"This yours?" he asked. "Ask for a lace so you can hang it round your neck. You know it's an offence to lose it?"

Annie nodded and gave a brief toothless smile as she took the tag and clenched it tightly. There was no way she'd ever lose it again...no way.

JOHN U WILHELMY
Saturday, September 2nd, 1939

Puffing into Southend's station
from the capital of the nation.
The Train.
Disgorging thousands, bright and early,
eager for the hurly burly.
Hurrying, scurrying, keen to reach,
the pier, the sea, the mud, the beach.
On that day.

Settling down in family clusters,
Ma's in charge and quickly musters.
Her tribe.
Running, jumping sons and daughters
rush towards the sparkling waters,
Leaving Dad in "Sunday best",
in a deckchair needing rest.
On that day.

Glowing sun's heat raises blisters,
on the tender skins of sisters.
Feeling sore.
With calamine Ma gently rubs, while
Dad goes off to search the pubs
for neighbours living in his street
who now he wants to greet and treat.
On that day.

Hunger striking little bellies,
Ma unpacks pork-pies and jellies.
From a bag.
Then fruit and ham and chocolate slices,
with pop and sweeties she entices,
hoping all her care suffices.
But not until they've had their ices!
On that day.
Dad, unsteady from his drinking,

Stumbles back, too little thinking,
Of his kids.
Who say they want to play at cricket
and order him to build a wicket,
of coats and towels and spades and pails.
With driftwood slivvers for the bails.
On that day.

Sinking sun and chilly breeze,
Makes Ma's paddling ankles freeze,
In the sea.
Daughter screams as sunburned rashes,
Sting from brother's crafty splashes,
so he runs away in fear
from Father's promise of clipped ear.
On that day.

Day's soon done and dusk is falling.
Ma collects them all by calling,
Them to come.
To the Kursall off they troop,
A tired, still hungry, grumbling group.
But brightened by the lights and noise,
the fish and chips and saveloys.
On that day.

Towards the station soon they wend,
money gone, no more to spend.
From empty pockets.
Quieter now they drag along,
when Ma suggests a jolly song,
to help ignore the soaking rain.
Just before they catch the train.
On that day.

Crowded in a rattling carriage,
Ma surveys the fruits of marriage.
And is content.
Sees the kids around her sleeping.
Winks at Dad her thanks for keeping,

them and her fed, clothed, – if poor;
his strength and love that makes life sure.
On all the days.

At the door Dad's fingers fumble,
for the key that lets them, tumble.
Into their home.
The kids, asleep, dream of their capers
while drowsy Dad, re-reads the papers,
to learn of jackboots marching steady
and asks himself, "will I be ready?"
For the War.

1998 ENTRANTS

J E ABBOTT *Daddy Was Killed In The War*
JULIE ACHILLES *Hilda*
EVELYN ALLEN *They Also Serve*
JULIE ACHILLES *The Blind Soldier*
J ADAMS-VOGT *Growing Up*
J ADAMS-VOGT *A Letter Found In My Grandmother's Bible*
CHRISTOPHER ALLAN *George In The Jungle*
D N ALLAN *Remembrance – 1995: May – 1940*
M G ALLGOOD *My War*
STELLA ALISON *My War Helping To Keep In Touch*
PETER J ALLEN *The Effects of War*
SONIA ALLEN *Remembrance*
JOYCE ANDERSON *Brown Sugar*
JOYCE ANDERSON *Don't Look Back*
JOYCE ANDERSON *The Mine Dance*
JOYCE ANDERSON *The Green Lady*
JOYCE ANDERSON
Seahorses In The Garden
JOYCE ANDERSON *The Ice Box*
JOYCE ANDERSON *The Man In The Lavender Suit*
JOYCE ANDERSON *Lady In Red*
JOYCE ANDERSON *Pukka*
JOYCE ANDERSON *Deep Freeze*
JOYCE ANDERSON *The Last Bullet*
JOYCE ANDERSON
Shadows In The Playground
JOYCE ANDERSON *Last Man Standing*
JOYCE ANDERSON *Run Rabbit*
JOYCE ANDERSON *Game Over*
JOYCE ANDERSON *Stone Dead*
JOYCE ANDERSON *The Window*
JOYCE ANDERSON *Pipers In The Sand*
JOYCE ANDERSON *Day Tripper*
JOYCE ANDERSON *The 11th Hole*
JOYCE ANDERSON *The Mine Dance*
DADO ARREST *My War*
B J ATKIN *For Whom The Drum Rolls*
MARY ATKIN *Remembrance*
SUE ATKINSON *Tea*
KEN BALDWIN *Christmas Conscience*
STANLEY SIMM BALDWIN
Awkward Squaddy
ALICE BARNETT *Long Memories*

M J BARON
Shellshock – The Effects Of War
BRIAN BARRATT
The Day Jerry Saved Grandad's Life
BRIAN BARRATT *The Black Liquid*
A BEAUMONT *April Visit*
MICHAEL BIRT *Just Like A Hun*
SYNDEE BLAKE *Little Vimy*
K BLAKELEY *My War*
DAVID BLAXILL
Somebody Ought To Remember George
BARBARA BOSTOCK
Jim – Brylcream Boy
P B BOSTON *Midnight Encounter*
SUZANNE BOSWORTH *A Bit Of Peace*
BILL BOUGHTFLOWER
My War Or They Did It Without Me
VIVIENNE BOYES *Remembrance*
JANE BRACEWELL
Bernadette's Bereavement
GILLIAN BRAMMAN *The Gift*
L J BREAKWELL *The Effects Of War*
G E BRIEN
With A Label Tied Around My Neck
G E BRIEN *Recollections of War*
GORDON BROOKS *Traumatic Stress*
MATTHEW BROUGH
Pearson's Promotion
J C BROWN *Hide And Seek*
CHRIS BUCKLE *The Cigar Box*
GORDON BUNCE *A Young Man's War*
PRISCILLA A BURTON *Paper Warrior*
PRISCILLA A BURTON *Devil Machines*
JULIA BURROWS *Headmaster*
DENNIS CARROLL *My War*
P CARROLL *Captain Letts' War*
MERLE CARTWRIGHT
A Bit Of Country
FRANCES CARVILLE *Counting Down*
KEN CHAPMAN
Love Affair With A Great Lady
V CHARLES *Only The Voltures*
V CHARLES *An Englishman, An Irishman and A Scotsman*
IAN CHICK *The Effects Of War*
M CHILLINGWORTH
My Man Of Mystery
S J CLARK *Remembrance*
S J CLARK *When Bugles Call*
V CLARK *Sentimental Journey*

V CLARK *The Effects Of War*
W CLIMIE *I Was There*
TIM P COLLINS *Together Again*
RON COLLINS
A Very, Very, Close Thing
CATHERINE COOPER *My War*
GORDON COOPER *Sleep At Last*
SGT MICHAEL L COPLEN
The Long Walk
JOHN COPLEY
Carmen Miranda In Kapok
MARTIN COX *The Summer Of 41*
JULIAN COX *Saving Grace*
JULIAN COX *Something Sharp*
MARIAN CRADDOCK *Remembrance*
D CRANE *Kent 1994*
J CREE *Remembrance – Another Day Of Reckoning*
JOHN CREE *The Effects Of War On The Children*
JOHN CREE *The Money Lender*
M J CRITCHLEY *My War-Islington 1944*
M CUNLIFFE *Lightning Strikes Twice*
K M DANIELS *My War*
DIANA DAVIES *Reunion*
DIANA DAVIES *The Children Of God*
E DAVIES *Mutiny*
MILDRED DAVIDSON *Aftermath*
K S DEARSLEY *On A Foreign Field*
SANDRA V DELEMARE *Bert's Flowers*
B E DERBYSHIRE
From The Maypole To Tesco
ELADU DERF *Proof Of Passage*
SARAH DEWEY *Remember, Remember*
BRIAN DIXON *I Can Tell You*
C DOEL *My War*
K DONKIN *A Bit Of A Blow*
K DONKIN *The Raft*
WALTER DOWNS
Should Auld Acquaintance…
SARAH J DOWNING *Extracts From The Journal By Richard Sebastian*
OWEN DUFFY *Gulf War Memoirs*
GUS EGE *The Cycle*
E EDWARDS *The Blackbird*
L R EDWARDS *The Island*
JOHN F EGAN *First Trip*
JOHN F EGAN *Side Effects*
JUNE ELFORD *How Love Fled*
C R ELLIOTT *Ramrods Silver Wings*
JOHN ELLIOTT *Bodies In The River*
RONALD ELY *You Have Nothing To Fear, But Fear Itself*

D ENTICOTT *Weep For Reggie*
MARY EVANS *The Hidden Cost*
ROY FALLOWFIELD *The Aftermath*
ROY FALLOWFIELD
The Cruelties of War
MAGARET FARRAND *My War*
SALLY FAWCETT *Walsh's War*
JULIAN FIDLER
The Unsuspecting Refugee
WILLIAM FINDLAY *Uncle Jackie's War*
MERTON FINK *Remembrance*
ELAINE H FISHER *Will*
DAVID FLETCHER
Messages From Mons Graupius
KAREN FLETCHER
As One Door Closes…
NORMAN FORD *Marching Orders*
NORMAN FORD *Laugh? I Nearly Died*
M G FORM *My War As It Was*
PAMELA FRASER *September Saturday*
MAUREEN FRAZER *Love Survives*
MAUREEN FRAZER *For Valour*
COLIN GADEN *Memories of 1944*
GAZ GALLAGHER *The Queen's Shilling And Beyond*
BERNARD GALVIN *My War, 30 March 1943-22 September 1947*
SUSAN GAMBLE *Remembrance*
MURRAY GARDNER
Birds And Birdmen
FIONA GASKIN *Agnes Armstrong*
PETER GASKELL *Dawn Cauldron*
KEVIN GAVIN *Why?*
PAUL GENNOE *Home Comforts*
JEAN E GENTRY *My War*
H S GIBB *A Waste Of Good Life*
ERIC GILDER *Two Faced*
REBECCA GILES *Tough Times*
D E GLAZE *Remembrance*
PENNY GLENN
Passion, Anger And Pain
ARNOLD GODSIFF
War And Remembrance
JAMES GOFF *A Return To Normality*
DENNIS GORDON *Unknown Soldiers*
JOHN GRAHAM *My War*
WILLIAM GREALISH
Remembering Danny Boy
J T GREEN *Not Forgotten*
DAVID GRIFFITHS *The Cornflower*
SUSAN GRIFFITHS *Remembrance*
ANN GUILDER *Alone*

CHRISTINE HAIGH
The Scrapper And The Nut
GORDON HALL *An Introduction To The Life Of A National Serviceman*
H R HALL *The Human Price Of Victory*
TOM HALLGARTH *Moonlight Sonata*
JUDITH HAMILTON *Dada*
OMAR HANIF *Remembrance*
MARY JANE HANSCOMB *My War*
JULIE HAYMAN *Muckers*
C F HAYNES
It's More Fun To Be An Innocent
M HAVEY *Somewhere In France*
K HEEKS *Remembrance*
IAN HENDERSON
Their Eyes On The North Star
JILLIAN P HENDERSON
A Prayer For The Living
PETER HEWISON
The Subaltern Was Afraid
BERNIE HEWITT *Suit Yourself*
ROBBIE HIFT *The Anniversary Of Sharpeville Riots*
SANDRA HILL *The Wall*
J HINDE *Time To Go Home*
J HINDE *The Letters*
J HINDE *The Coming*
J HINDE *Mikado*
J HINDE *Pardon Still Outstanding*
J HINDE *Of King, And Country*
J HINDE *The Rumour*
J HINDE *O Brightest Star*
J HINDE *The Voyagers*
J HINDE *The Home Coming*
J HINDE *Origin Of The Sun*
J HINDE *Old Soldiers Never Die! They Join The LDV*
J HINDE *Margin Of Error*
HELEN HINES *Rock*
ROBERT HOGG
Memorable Motorcycling
ROBERT HOGG *The Home Coming*
ROBERT HOGG *The Born Soldier?*
ROBERT HOGG *A War Baby*
ROBERT HOGG *Egypt Invaded 1940*
ROBERT HOGG *The Sahara*
ROBERT HOGG *Tobruk Remembered*
ROBERT HOGG *The Dream*
L HOGGETT *The Executive Monkey*
K S HOLMES *Part Of My War*
CONSTANCE L HOLLAND
Waiting For The Band To Play
R A HOPPER *A Decent Sort of Coward*

BRENDA HORNESS *My War*
TREVOR HOWELL *An Old Soldier*
TREVOR HOWELL
When The Drums Begin To Roll
BERYL HUGHES *The Guinea Pig*
BERYL HUGHES *Welcome Home*
BARBARA HUMAN *Expecting Me To Answer When I'm Dead*
EDWARD HUNTER *Shellshock*
EDWARD HUNTER *Forgotten Hero*
EDWARD HUNTER *Yours Sincerely*
MARION HUSBAND
Remembering Ginger
JOHN HYGATE
Conduct To The Prejudice
SHEILA JACKSON *Remembrance*
CARL JACKSON *War's A Bastard*
D JANSEN *A Soldier's Song*
R E JEFFRIES *Not A Grand Finale*
JOHN ALAN JONES *The Hunt*
CHRISTINE JONES *The Evacuee*
PHYL JONES
England's Defences Breached
RON JONES *Lack Of Moral Fibre*
MICHELLE KENNEY *Winging The Long Cold Sleep*
RORY KILALEA *Forces Sweetheart*
RORY KILALEA *George*
RORY KILALEA *Temba Went Penga*
HAROLD HENRY KING
In The Beginning
HAROLD HENRY KING
Success And Incident
HAROLD HENRY KING
The Time, The Place, The Action
JEAN KING *Plenty Of Apple Pie*
B J KINSELLA *Wars End*
STEVIE KNIGHT *Message Of Love*
GEORGE KNOX
The Day The Soldiers Came
GRETA KRYPCZYK-ODDY *Mogambo*
CLIFFORD LACKEY *Blood From A Stone... An Effect Of War*
CLIFFORD LACKEY *Tis An Ill Wind*
JAMES LANCASTER *My War*
JOHN LANDELLS *Alamein And The Desert-Memories And Thoughts*
JOHN LATHAM *Mr Butter*
JOHN D LAW *We That Are Left*
LINDA LAWRIE *Message Received*
LINDA LAWRIE *Future Ghosts*
GEORGE LEE *Soldiers Don't Cry*

LETITIA LINTON
Time After Time, Forever
GRAHAM LEWIS *1994*
GRAHAM LEWIS *Renaissance*
JOHN V LEWIS *The Collar Sergeant*
STEPHEN LEWIS *The Day That*
Changed My Life
WILLIAM LEWIS *The Seige Of Tobruk*
CHRISTINE LLOYD *Lost At Sea*
JACK LOVELAND
Time Is Not Always A Healer
JOHN LUNN *Autumn In France*
LESLIE BRIAN LUX *The White Cat*
LESLIE BRIAN LUX *Sandcastles*
REVEREND CANON D B MACKAY
Paradise Regained
PATRICK LAURANCE
The Lighter Side Of War
JOHN V LEWIS *Unwanted Intruders*
M C MAIR
The Effects Of War-Blue Sandals
DOREEN MALLETT *My War*
T F MARLAND *From Pegasus A Poppy*
MARJORIE MATTHEW *The*
Unfortunate Escort
I M MCCALLUM *Ron's War*
ROBIN MCDERMOT *The Trigger*
CHARLES MCGREGOR
A Transient Delusion
L A MCINTOSH *My War*
ELIZABETH MCKAY
A Day To Remember
JAMES MCKINTY *Sheila*
L MCMAHON *My War*
A A MCNALLY *Tommy*
ROSE MCNAMARA *The Angels Of*
Mons, A Ghostly Tale Of World War 1
C MEADE *Shadows Of The Evening*
PATRICK MEAD
Forr-Yoo The Warr Iss'Over
T S MELDRUM *White's Hill*
SUSAN MELVILLE *War Baby*
JANET MERCER *On The Steps*
K MERCHANT
A Christmas Eve Ghost Story
ARTHUR MOORE *My War*
R D MOORWOOD *The Brass Coin*
DARRELL MORFETT
Peace In Whose Time?
MIKE MORGAN *The Last Great War*
Soldier – A.D. 2013
MIKE MORGAN *Alamein Angel*
S J MORGAN *Settling Down*

DAVID MORRIS *While He Was Dancing*
JOAN MORRIS *Remembrance*
ARNOLD MORTON
Loss And Rediscovery
KEVIN W MUIR *Volunteer For Nothing*
MAUREEN MULHOLLAND *The Effects*
Of War On My Father
MARIA MURPHY *Go*
JACKLIN MURRAY *Generation Bridge*
MICHAEL NELSON *The Silence*
WILLIAM R NEWRICK *Making History*
WILLIAM R NEWRICK *Defensive Sex*
WILLIAM R NEWRICK *Suspicion*
WILLIAM R NEWRICK *The Glasshouse*
WILLIAM R NEWRICK *The Effects*
WILLIAM R NEWRICK
The Nelson Dilemma
WILLIAM R NEWRICK *Extra Rations*
WILLIAM R NEWRICK *War's Victims*
WILLIAM R NEWRICK *Friendly Fire*
WILLIAM R NEWRICK
Sheltered Existence
WILLIAM R NEWRICK
The Warriors 01
WILLIAM R NEWRICK
The Warriors 02
WILLIAM R NEWRICK
The Warriors 03
WILLIAM R NEWRICK
The Warriors 04
WILLIAM R NEWRICK
Class Distinction
WILLIAM R NEWRICK *What Did You*
Do In The War Grandad?
WILLIAM R NEWRICK
Displaced Person
WILLIAM R NEWRICK
Symbol Of Unity
WILLIAM R NEWRICK *A Long Walk*
TONY NICHOLS *The Omen*
ERIC NICHOLSON *Remembrance*
GWENDOLINE NYSS-SANFORD
Remembrance
TOMMY F O'CONNOR
Cherokee Prodigal
LEONARD GEORGE OLIPHANT *It*
Was A Long Time For Some Dates
HARRY OWEN *The Khamsin*
ROGER PAINE *Marks Of Respect*
BRUCE PALMER-SMITH
Decision Time
BRUCE PALMER-SMITH
Sad Memories

BRUCE PALMER-SMITH *Torture*
BRUCE PALMER-SMITH *The Cafe*
P A PARKIN *The Effects Of War*
ALAN PARKES *The Nobody Man*
MARK PARGETER
Major Green Will Look After Me
S PASS *The Effects Of War*
COLIN PEARCE *One April Day*
LES PEATE *Going Home*
PETER PEEL *My War 1*
PETER PEEL *My War 2*
JOHN PEMBERTON *The Meeting*
A PENNY My War
JEFF PHELPS *Empty Sands*
ANDY PHIPPS
To The End, They Remain
ANDY PHIPPS *Echoes*
KAREN PHILLIPS *Jack's War*
JEAN PIMP *Sorrow Upon Sorrow*
DAVID PIPERS *An Ordinary Gunner*
Under Combat Stress
MOYRA PLATTS *Old Soldiers Never*
Die......But Young Ones Do
JOHN POARCH *Lest We Forget*
JEAN POLLARD *Effects Of War*
A E POWELL *Corporal Joe S B S*
DOLORES E POWELL
A Grandmother's Remembrance
IVOR P POWELL *My War*
DAVID PRATT *Christmas 1914*
E J PRIOR *The Legacy Of War*
STEPHEN PROUT *Peter's War*
E J RAE *Remembrance*
JOHN RAVENSCROFT *A Long Shot*
DAVID RAYMENT *The Builder*
DEREK READ *Combat Stress*
ANGELA READMAN *Glad Rags*
RICHARD REEVE *Dismissed*
JACK REUBEN *Memories Everlasting*
DOROTHY RICKETS *Two Of A Kind*
DOROTHY RICKETS *Love Is Blind*
DOROTHY RICKETS
The Great Commander
DOROTHY RICKETS *A New Life*
MARK RICKMAN *The Film About The*
Actress And The Hotel Porter
PAUL RIGBY *Shattered*
J D ROBB *Combat Stress*
GEORGE C ROBERTSON *John And*
Fred And Mary And Marcia
LINDA ROBINSON *Remembrance*
JULIA ROWLES *The Twilight Zone*

JOHN RUSSELL
My Personal War Experience
A J RUSTIDGE *Bridge*
SUZANNE RUTHVEN
A Little Known Engagement
LES RYAN *Some Mother's Son*
EILEEN RYDER *We Got There First*
T SANDELANDS *The Portrait*
EDITH A SANDERS *A Silent Malady*
EDITH A SANDERS *The Time Machine*
PAULINE SCAMMELL *They Also Serve*
JACK SHARP *The Effects Of War*
LOUISE SHAW *Final Liberation*
JOHN SHAWCROSS *Marcel's "Guest"*
J R SHAWLER *The Sergeant*
HELEN M SHAY *The Shining*
R A SHEPHERD
Lamb Chops Under The Waves
FRED SKULL *A Fey-full Wife*
GEORGINA SKUSE *My War*
S A SLOAN *The White Beret*
G E SLOPER *Luigi Never Came*
AMELIA SMITH *Father Dear Father*
M SMITH *No Escape*
DOUGLAS SMITHSON
A Flight To Captivity
M J SOAR *My War*
ELIZABETH SOMERVILLE
Remembrance
ROSINA D SPEED *The Bridge*
ROSINA D SPEED *Memories*
MR B P SPERRIN
More Than One Victim
DONALD B SPROUL *Beneath Suilven*
HARRY STANDEN *Virtual Reality*
A STANDLEY *My Remembrance*
L STEPHENSON
Help And Understanding
R STEPHENSON *Memoirs Of My First*
Years In The Army
ALAN STEWART *Remembrance Sunday*
P W STOCK *Warden*
P W STOCK *Smithy*
P W STOCK *A Day To Remember*
P W STOCK *Dave Winters*
P W STOCK *Yesterday's Hero*
P W STOCK *The Polish Canteen*
P W STOCK *Bloody Amateur*
P W STOCK *Farmer's Boy*
SARAH STOKELY *Love After Death*
SILVANA STRATFORD *My Joe*
JENNIFER STUART *My War*

ARCHIE STURN
The War – 1939/1948 "My War"
SAMEER KAK SUKHDEV
The Obsolescence Of War
V R SUMNER *Stress Will Out*
KATHLEEN SURTESS
Working Class Hero
DAVID SUTCH *Remembrance*
H O SWAIN
Wartime Memories Of A Child
F P SYLVESTER
Able Four Has Casualties
LINDA TAPSELL
Out From Under The Sand
G N TAYLOR *Waterloo Lane*
FELICITY TESSARO
The Curse Of The Spear
P TETLOW *Somebody's Son*
RICHARD THATCHER
War Correspondents
H B THOMAS *The Wolf*
F THOMPSON *Ollie's Dad*
GEORGE THOMPSON *Engagement*
Near Beauzeville, Normandy, 25th August
1944
H B C THOMPSON *Remembrance*
R J TOOTELL *The Effects Of War*
BRIAN C TOTHILL *War Games*
BRIAN C TOTHILL *The Pledge*
CHRISTINA TOTHILL *We'll Meet Again*
JOHN TRYTHALL
The Effects Of War – Hatred
JOHN TRYTHALL *A Face Of Stress*
JOHN TRYTHALL *Meringues*
JOHN TRYTHALL *Not A Soldier*
MARTIN TULEY
Remembrance Day Standards
T S TURNBULL *Border Control*
HAYES TURNER *Under Pressure*
HAYES TURNER
Where Do Poppies Grow
DOROTHY VINCENT
A Shot In The Dark
ALAN WALKDEN *Sting In The Tail*

D R WALKER *The Sentry*
J H WALKER *Remembrance*
NICK WARDLE *Back Home*
JULIA WAREING *My War*
R C WARNE *Combat Stress*
MAUREEN WARNER
Tomorrow, Just You Wait and See
MICHAEL WATSON
Homage To Macedonia
N WATSON *Two Stick Charlie*
N WATSON
An Air Sea Rescue Christmas
SARAH WAY *A Hard-Won Peace*
ALLAN WELLS *Own Goal*
ALLAN WELLS *Jelly Cream*
ALLAN WELLS *Van Gogh*
HOWARD WELSBY *Poor Bob*
JANE WENHAM-JONES *Coventry*
BILL WESTALL
The Man Who Came Back
TERRY WESTERN *The Mouse*
HAROLD WHIELDON *A Lucky Escape*
E A WHITEHEAD *Memories*
RICHARD WHITTLE *Tag Lady*
A G WIGLEY *Charioteers*
A G WIGLEY *The Waiting Game*
ALMA WILLIAMS *Big Black Boots*
HEULWEN P WILLIAMS
The Experience Of An Evacuee
JOHN U WILHELMY *Johnny Scribe*
JOHN U WILHELMY *His First Suit*
JOHN U WILHELM
 Saturday September 2nd. 1939
JOHN U WILHELMY *We Were Close*
JOHN U WILHELMY
The Saints Were Kind
JOHN U WILHELMY *Early Delivery*
JAN WOOD *In Loving Remembrance*
MAUREEN E WOODS *Beating The*
Enemy
JOY WOOLATT *Holy Moses*
JOHN WRIGHT *Beaky And The Geneal*
BETTY YOUNG *My War*
J D YOUNG *Zero-Six-Four-Five*

THE EX-SERVICES MENTAL WELFARE SOCIETY

The Ex-Services Mental Welfare Society *(Combat Stress)* was established in 1919, following the return of ex-servicemen from the trenches of the First World War. It is the only organisation which helps and treats ex-servicemen and women who suffer from the mental trauma of battle.

Today, the Society has responsibility for nearly 5,000 casualties of the Second World War, and all the campaigns undertaken by our armed forces since 1945, including the Gulf War and the NATO Intervention Force in the former Yugoslavia. For many of those who suffer profoundly and depend upon the Society, three or four weeks of treatment and respite at one of its three national nursing homes make it possible for them and their families to cope.

We would like to acknowledge the support of our two sponsors in helping to defray the costs of running the Competition:
The Royal Armouries is the national museum of arms and armour. It was opened in Leeds by HM The Queen in 1997 and is one of the most popular visitor attractions in the UK.

Raised in 1685, The King's Regiment today draws its infantrymen largely from the cities of Manchester and Liverpool and numbers the war poet Wilfred Owen amongst its famous sons.

For further information on the Society, please contact:
Colin Crawford, Ex-Services Mental Welfare Society,
Broadway House, The Broadway, Wimbledon, London SW19 1RL
Telephone: 0181 543 6333 or Fax: 0181 542 7082
Cheques or postal orders may be made payable to:
'Ex-Services Mental Welfare Society'

&PEACE
&WAR
1999

ROYAL ARMOURIES

The King's Regiment

THE EX-SERVICES MENTAL WELFARE SOCIETY
1999 SHORT STORY & POETRY COMPETITION

1999 SHORT STORY & POETRY COMPETITION

THEMES

Support the Ex-Services Mental Welfare Society in 1999 by writing a poem or a short story on the theme of *'A Century of War'*, *'The Pity of War'*, and *'Humour in Uniform'*.

PRIZES

Overall Winning Entry: £500
Best Poem: £250
Best Short Story: £250
In addition, there will be 40 Runners-up prizes worth £25 each.

COMPETITION RULES

CLOSING DATE FOR ENTRIES: 11am, Thursday 11th November 1999.

RULES

Short story entries must be no longer than 1000 words.

Poetry entries should be no longer than 750 words.

Entries should be double-spaced and typed, but legible hand written entries will be accepted.

Entrants requiring the return of a manuscript, or a copy of the winning entries, should enclose a stamped, self-addressed envelope.

Winning entries will be advertised on 24th December 1999. Competition judges have yet to be announced.

A minimum donation of £5 to the Charity, plus a £1 competition administration fee, to be submitted per entry is requested.

All donations will be used to further the Society's aims in support of ex-servicemen and women suffering from the mental trauma of warfare.

ENTRY FORM REGISTRATION

NAME:

ADDRESS:

POSTCODE:

CONTACT TELEPHONE *(in case of queries)*:

BRIEF BIOGRAPHICAL AND BACKGROUND NOTES
(eg. personal history, reason for writing, current or last occupation etc)

PLEASE FIND ENCLOSED MY ENTRY FOR THE 1999:

☐ POETRY COMPETITION   ☐ SHORT STORY COMPETITION

MY ENTRY TITLE IS:

I enclose a cheque made payable to *Ex-Services Mental Welfare Society* for the sum of £

(a minimum of £5 plus £1 administration per entry is requested)

Please return your entry with a cheque by 11th November 1999 to:

The Competition Secretary

Ex-Services Mental Welfare Society

Broadway House

The Broadway

Wimbledon

London SW19 1RL

Telephone: 0181 543 6333